Praise for *The ~~Paris~~*

'Gripping, dramatic and packed with fascinating detail ... an
involving read about love, trust and heart-stopping bravery'
Jill Mansell

'A tense and thrilling tale ... You won't be able
to turn the pages fast enough'
Natasha Lester

'*The Paris Deception* immerses readers in the oppressive
atmosphere of occupied Paris ... Bryn Turnbull is a
natural storyteller and her prose sparkles with all the
fizz of vintage champagne. A tour de force!'
Gill Paul

'*The Paris Deception* deceives, intrigues and enthrals!'
Kate Quinn

'Unforgettable ... a powerful, page-turning tale of two
extraordinary heroines ... a stunning read!'
Chanel Cleeton

'Turnbull effectively combines fascinating background with
plenty of wartime suspense ... This will be a page-turning delight
for anyone who loves tales of women in the resistance,
especially Kristin Hannah's *The Nightingale*'
Booklist

'Anyone who likes historical fiction with a
hint of danger will enjoy this'
★★★★★ Real reader review

Also by Bryn Turnbull

The Last Grand Duchess
The Woman Before Wallis

About the Author

Bryn Turnbull is the bestselling author of *The Woman Before Wallis*. Equipped with a master's of letters in creative writing from the University of St. Andrews, a master's of professional communication from Ryerson University and a bachelor's degree in English literature from McGill University, Bryn focuses on finding stories of women lost within the cracks of the historical record. She lives in Toronto.

Published by arrangement with Mira Books,
An Imprint of Harlequin and HarperCollins Publishers.
First published in the USA in 2023

First published in 2023 by Headline Review
An imprint of HEADLINE PUBLISHING GROUP

First published in paperback in 2023 by Headline Review
An imprint of HEADLINE PUBLISHING GROUP

1

Cataloguing in Publication Data is available from the British Library

Paperback ISBN 978 1 0354 0631 9

Offset in 11.27/14.08 pt Bembo Std by Jouve (UK), Milton Keynes

Printed and bound in Great Britain by Clays Ltd, Elcograf S.p.A.

HEADLINE PUBLISHING GROUP
An Hachette UK Company
Carmelite House
50 Victoria Embankment
London EC4Y 0DZ

www.headline.co.uk
www.hachette.co.uk

To Alec...and Pierce Brosnan

The
PARIS
DECEPTION
BRYN TURNBULL

REVIEW

Article 46: Family honour and rights, the lives of persons, and private property, as well as religious convictions and practice, must be respected. Private property cannot be confiscated.

—Extract from "Laws and Customs of War on Land," from the Hague Convention, October 18, 1907

PROLOGUE

March 1939
Berlin

It took only seconds for the paintings to catch alight but hours for the flames to die into ash.

Oil, after all, had a tendency to burn: it smoked and blistered like skin, layers of paint peeling back upon itself as the pigments—yellow ocher and cadmium red, vermilion and chartreuse and burnt sienna—blackened into char. Works that had once been beautiful were reduced to their basest parts; lit by the flames, they were nothing more than composite pieces of destruction, chemicals and flax and wood, each burning into nothingness as the flames licked ever higher.

From her place in the shadows of the moonless night, Sophie watched a book sail through the air, its cover opening like the wings of a bird. It hung, suspended, above the smoke before arcing into the conflagration, its leaves curling as flames kissed the spine. She looked at the man who had thrown it: he stared, stone-faced, into the bonfire before bending over the wheelbarrow to pick up another accelerant, his fireman's badge glinting as he fed the flames. Had he been alone, Sophie would have run up, pulled the wheelbarrow from his grasp, saved what she could—but this was state-sanctioned destruction, and twenty other firefighters were feeding the bonfire too, a fifty-foot monster fueled by a generation's worth of art. Did it bother him, she wondered, watching his sweaty face transform into gargoyle features by the flickering light, to be fueling a fire instead of putting it out? His professional solicitousness suggested that it did not; if he were revolted by the work he was doing, he didn't let it show.

The stench of burning paint reached Sophie's throat, and though she retched at the acrid taste, she did not turn away. Like everyone else watching from behind the line of soldiers' rifles, she wasn't there out of morbid fascination but for posterity, committing the frightening scene to memory. Thousands of works of art—millions of dollars—destroyed. Complex Cubist paintings, passionate Expressionist works, belligerent Surrealist pastiches and baffling Dadaist collages—all gone in the space of a night. Like so many others watching—curators and connoisseurs and restorers, the artists and authors who'd not yet gone underground—Sophie had been summoned by a whisper network of sympathetic specialists still operating within Germany. Despite her vow to never step foot within the Reich again, she had come to bear witness to Hitler's destruction of Germany's cultural heritage.

The last time Sophie had seen the paintings had been in Munich, two years ago, at the opening of the *Entartete Kunst* exhibition. She'd attended out of professional curiosity, quelling her fears about traveling to Germany in order to see the odious concept in action. *Entartete Kunst*—Degenerate Art—

had been as horrible as she'd anticipated, a master collection of modern art displayed in cruel chaos, jingoistic propaganda condemning the pieces as the work of sick minds, Jewish conspiracies and homosexual perversion. Pulled from public galleries across Germany, each work of art was introduced in deliberately obtuse terms by a prim tour guide, who wrinkled his nose in a moue of distaste as he recited scandalous stories about the artists on display. She should have known then what was in store for each and every work of modern art in Germany's museums and libraries. She had it on good authority that many of the pieces had been sold to new-world collectors willing to turn a blind eye to the fact that their purchases would swell the coffers of the Nazi regime, but she'd never dreamed the Nazis would destroy what they couldn't sell—that anything which didn't reflect Hitler's twisted ideas about the Reich and its people would be consigned to the flames. The very notion went against the core of Sophie's being.

The sun had begun to rise, pale in a gray sky, by the time the firemen turned away from the ashes, but Sophie stayed rooted where she was. She turned to the man beside her: his cheeks were streaked with ash, but for a runnel in the grime where tears had fallen. Sophie guessed she was similarly marked, and though she didn't know him, she walked over and threaded her hand through his. He looked down, surprised by the intrusion—but then, slack-faced, met her gaze. Was he an artist, she wondered, watching his work go up in flames? A gallerist, or a fine-arts restorer like her? Not that it mattered: he was there to witness tragic history in the making.

Sophie squeezed his hand and then released it. She walked away, shoulders rounded against the sudden chill of the morning.

PART ONE

1

June 1940

Sophie Brandt bent over her desk, working a small awl beneath the rusty nail wedged into the frame of a painting. She lifted the nail, carefully pulling back the canvas from the shattered edge of the stretcher. The painting—one of Gauguin's earlier pieces—had been left mercifully undamaged in the fall that had broken the stretcher, remnants of which she'd swept up off the marble floor of the gallery, inspecting the debris for any flakes of pigment that might have been rattled loose by the careless rumble of German tanks down the Rue de Rivoli.

She lifted the canvas and set it aside, clearing away the broken stretcher before pulling out a new one she'd made based on the old frame's measurements. To Sophie, this was the most intimate part of the restoration process: the canvas, devoid of the musculature provided by the frame or supports, holding only a suggestion of its former shape. She worked quickly, tacking the linen to the stretcher midway down the painting before pulling it tight over its new bones. The painting seemed to breathe as she worked, responding to her touch with a relieved groan as she hammered the stretcher keys in place.

She turned the painting over, satisfied at its taut appearance. Paul would be proud. Sophie had been a restorer at the Jeu de Paume museum in Paris for nearly two years now, and while she'd made friends in the French art community, there was no one, perhaps, she was as close to as Paul Rosenberg. Until recently, he had been one of Paris's most preeminent art dealers, specializing in the modern art which Sophie loved best. He'd become Sophie's first true friend in Paris—and, she suspected, had put in a friendly word with Monsieur Girard at the Jeu de Paume that had resulted in her job offer.

Paul had escaped France at the first rumblings of war, his beautiful gallery shuttered before the mass exodus of Parisians made it difficult to leave the city. But for the paintings he'd deposited at the Jeu de Paume for safekeeping, it was as if Paul Rosenberg had never lived in Paris.

Sophie recalled her last visit to his quiet gallery. They had lingered in front of Picasso's portrait of Paul's wife and daughter. It was a good likeness, thought Sophie, one that captured the quiet, steady presence of Madame Rosenberg, and the wonderfully disgruntled expression on the baby's cherubic face.

"They'll be here soon," Paul had said, his thin moustache set over stern lips. He turned away from the painting. "Your countrymen. Come to claim their due."

"Not my countrymen," she'd replied. "They've not been my countrymen for a long time."

Paul lit a cigarette. "Brave words," he'd told her, snapping the brass lid of his lighter shut. "But once the Germans arrive, will you be so quick to disassociate yourself?"

Holed away in her laboratory, Sophie listened for the sound of jackboots outside the open casement windows, the faint snarl of German echoing through tinny loudspeakers from the Arc de Triomphe.

She walked over to the window and pulled it closed, fastening the latch before returning her attention to the painting. She thought once more on Paul's question.

Now that the Germans were here, she didn't know the answer.

2

One week earlier

The sky over Paris was dark, the sun a pale coin in the sky that flickered in and out of focus behind billows of soot-blackened clouds. In her attic apartment, Fabienne wrenched open the window, wedging the stump of a paintbrush in the frame to keep it open as she eased herself onto the sill.

Though the fires were burning in the city's petroleum reserves on the outskirts of town, the smoke had made its way into the Left Bank's narrow streets, choking the crowded cobblestones with its acrid stench. Fabienne could see the logic behind the city's decision to burn what they could rather than leave behind spoils of war for the enemy, but the move had sparked panic among the fleeing population. In the streets below, she watched a man and woman argue beside an idling Peugeot, its roof rack laden with suitcases. A child, wailing, as his father swept him into an overflowing handcart.

"You're too late, you know!" Fabienne called down. Tucked six floors up in the eaves of her building's mansard roof, Fabienne knew the couple couldn't hear her, but it felt good to shout all the same. "They'll be here by this evening!" She reached back into the kitchen to pull out a half-drunk bottle of red wine. "What's the point, when they've already won?"

And the Germans had won—that much was clear. They'd won without having to fire a gun within the city limits; they'd won without having dropped a single incendiary bomb. The thought that Paris had given up without a fight rankled Fabienne. Surely someone, somewhere, shared her sense of injustice? Paris was the city of *la Révolution*: the city of barricades in the streets, its citizens fighting and fucking and acting out their passions with the conviction of players in a penny dreadful. Surely Paris could muster some semblance of resistance before rolling onto its back for the German army?

She tapped her cigarette against the windowsill and the ember floated down, past the modest fourth- and fifth-floor apartments, where she could hear Madame de Frontenac pleading with her balding husband through the open window; past the elegant second-story apartment with its gracious wrought iron balcony. Had the apartment's residents, the Lowensteins, left Paris? Fabienne pictured Madame Lowenstein, with her cream-colored Chanel suits and iron curls; Monsieur Lowenstein, his beloved black-and-white toy poodle tucked beneath his arm. She hoped they'd been able to get out—she hoped most of the city's Jewish residents had been able to flee, before the long line of refugees choked the railroads and motorways to a standstill.

In a few short days, everything Fabienne knew would change: it was inevitable, once Paris became a conquered city. What would remain of the France she'd known her whole life? What would remain of herself? Her talent, her courage, her convictions—all the parts of herself that Dietrich had once loved. What would remain, at the end of the war?

She watched the long line of vehicles snake its way along the Boulevard Saint-Germain and turned back into the gloom of her empty apartment, wishing she could feel some appreciation for the gravity of the moment: fear, panic, worry. Anger at the thought of her beloved city left unguarded; despair at the notion that she'd been left behind to survive in a city circling the drain of war.

She glanced back at the half-finished painting on her easel, the canvas she'd not been able to finish in over two years; swirls of color, black on blue. Desiccated paintbrushes lay on the crossbar, the dried oil on the bristles matching the exact shade of her husband's eyes.

There was nothing to be frightened of because the worst had already happened. There was nothing more the Germans could take from her.

3

September 1940

Sophie walked down the shallow front steps to the Jeu de Paume's main entrance, surprised at having received a summons from the volunteer curator, Rose Valland. Two weeks ago, the museum's director, Monsieur Girard, had assembled all of the staff in the great hall and let them go en masse. Sophie had taken the news with stoic acceptance—what call was there for art restoration during a war?—but she'd dragged her heels on finding another position. She'd come to Paris to work for France's National Gallery, the greatest art collection in Europe. Without that job to sustain her, she had little else to offer the City of Lights.

She walked through the door, jarred by the emptiness within. Long and narrow, the museum had been home to the National Gallery's modern works of art, its fifteen small galleries spread across two floors connected by a grand marble staircase; now, the museum's walls were blank, empty frames and chalked-on words noting where masterpieces by Picasso and Dalí had once hung. Sophie had been part of the clandestine removal of the paintings months earlier: the spiriting away of France's public collection under cover of darkness, a monumental feat accomplished in three long nights thanks to the impeccable planning of Jacques Jaujard, director of the Musée du Louvre. The Jeu de Paume's collection had been part of the operation too: anything that could be safely transported had been boxed up and sent away to countryside *chateaux*, carried off by a vast assembly of museum staff, art students and volunteers sent by trustworthy patrons.

She crossed to the back of the Jeu de Paume's empty galleries and down the staff staircase into the museum's cavernous basement. While the gallery space was relatively modest, the basement was a rabbit warren of rooms that had once housed the extensive permanent collection when it wasn't on display. It also held the administrative offices. With the exception of Sophie's small restoration lab on the second floor, the Jeu de Paume had little in the way of wasted space.

She wandered past the empty display racks and easels, wondering at Rose Valland's presence: along with the rest of the staff, the volunteer curator had been dismissed weeks ago. She knocked before opening the door to Rose's office: inside, she was packing up her desk, file boxes and stacks of paper strewn across the heavy oak tabletop.

Rose looked up. "Sophie," she said, gesturing to the seat opposite hers. "Thank you for coming in."

Sophie sat, balancing her handbag in her lap. Despite being a volunteer, Rose Valland was, Sophie believed, the hardest-working member of staff at the museum. Tall and plain, with round glasses and graying hair escaping in wisps from a hastily drawn bun, Sophie doubted Rose ever left the museum;

she couldn't picture her going home to a husband or family. More than once, caught up in the restoration of some work or other, Sophie would leave the museum thinking she was the last of the day staff still there, only to hear the gentle hammering of a typewriter echoing from Rose's office.

Rose smoothed her broad hands across the top of her desk. "I've been asked to reopen the Jeu de Paume," she said, without preamble, "and I'd like you to join me."

Sophie raised her eyebrows. "Really? I'm—"

"Surprised?"

Sophie smiled. "Well, yes," she replied. "Why? And how?"

Rose knitted her fingers together in a businesslike gesture. "The Germans," she said, putting a delicate stress on the word, "have taken a special interest in our facility. Have you heard of the *Einsatzstab Reichsleiter Rosenberg*?"

Sophie nodded. The ERR was a group of German curators, art historians and connoisseurs who'd taken up residence in Paris, ostensibly to oversee the protection of France's national art collection for the duration of the war. But she wondered at exactly what form the ERR's so-called protection took: at the moment, it seemed that the ERR's activities involved seizing works of art from those unlucky galleries that hadn't been part of Jacques Jaujard's midnight evacuation.

"It seems that the ERR has outgrown its current headquarters at the German embassy," Rose continued. "I've been asked whether our museum would consent to house their expanding collection."

Sophie frowned. Beneath Rose's mild words, she could hear an undercurrent of something electric. "I see," she said carefully. "And how does this expansion involve me?"

Rose sat back in her chair. "I've agreed to serve as the overseer of the Jeu de Paume," she replied. "And I've been given permission to bring a few select staff members back on board.

The ERR will be transferring a specialized team to work out of the museum—the *Sonderstab Bildende Kunst*. We'll be working with them on a day-to-day basis, cataloging the contents of the new collection and safeguarding them while this terrible war continues." Rose looked pleased. "Think of it. The museum filled with art once more."

"And the provenance of this art?" Sophie frowned. "France's national collection has already gone to ground, and Monsieur Jaujard doesn't seem inclined to collaborate. What's left for them to take?"

Rose lifted a piece of paper from her desk. "Perhaps you've not heard. Beyond the protection of public collections, the ERR has been given orders to safeguard all cultural property declared *stateless* under the terms of a direct decree from Herr Hitler." She passed an official-looking document across the table. "As part of my staff, you will be helping the ERR assess, catalog and repair any works that need intervention." Rose smiled. "I've seen your work. I would trust no one else with this task."

Sophie read the decree. In her mind's eye, she was back home in Stuttgart, watching young men in brown shirts stroll past the university's front steps.

"I had Herr Rosenberg translate it for me—I have very little German," Rose commented, watching Sophie's eyes slide across the page.

"Stateless," she said aloud. "What does that mean?"

Rose hesitated. "They mean private collections. So many people left Paris in the early days of the occupation...often with only the clothes on their backs."

Sophie lingered over the page a moment longer, her attention catching on a single phrase: *the safeguarding of Jewish property*. She set the paper back on Rose's desk, her heart hammering as she stood. "I'm sorry, Mademoiselle Valland, but I must decline." Though Sophie longed to return to her work at the museum, the thought of working with Germans—working *for* Germans—was more than she could bear. "Confiscating private collections—I can't—"

Rose, too, stood. "Sophie, please. I know I'm asking something very difficult of you," she said. "But this is an opportunity. Can't you see that?" She looked around her tiny office. "Fifteen years I've worked here, and this is the best they've done for me. A volunteer position. When I ask for anything more, they tell me that it's beyond their means to offer me anything other than pride in working for the national collection." She shook her head, her gray eyes hard. "I've dedicated my life, my education, to art, and they still can't afford to pay me a proper salary. This is an opportunity to be recognized for my work. I want that opportunity for you too." She looked at Sophie. "War makes strange bedfellows, I admit. But think about the opportunity it creates for us."

Sophie edged back into the room. "And you're comfortable, are you, with what they're doing?" she asked. "Taking art from people who've fled in fear?"

Rose's expression tightened. "It's art," she said. "Someone has to take care of it. At least if it's here, we can ensure that it's properly accounted for."

Sophie let out a breath. Though still appalled, she had to admit she saw reason in Rose's argument.

"Can I take a day to think about it?"

Rose pulled a large box out from beside her desk. "Of course," she said. "I'm moving into Monsieur Girard's old office. When you've made your decision, you can find me there."

Sophie left the museum, her hands shaking as she unlocked her bicycle from the fence. She lifted one foot to the pedal and kicked the ground, relishing the moment of release as she pedaled down the easy slope into the Jardin des Tuileries.

With its manicured lawns and wide avenues, the Jardin des Tuileries had always been Sophie's favorite place in Paris. Its sense of history appealed to her, and while the flowers were in constant flux, the park itself never seemed to change. The statues and skyline transported Sophie back in time—perhaps not to a simpler time but to a more picturesque one, a world where the beloved paintings she restored in her laboratory were freshly finished.

To Sophie, the Jardin exuded permanence, but it too was already showing scars from the growing conflict. Now, Sophie cycled past German soldiers knee-deep in soil, digging up the pristine lawns for vegetable plots. The sight broke Sophie's heart. She'd moved to Paris for the beauty of it all, the dreaminess of its winding cobbled streets and fairy-tale neighborhoods, the endearing devotion of the residents to the mythology that made it the City of Lights. But reality had already begun to seep through the cracks of Sophie's world. Now, with the arrival of Hitler's army, the doors she'd locked shut had blown wide open.

The notion of working for the Germans sickened Sophie— the thought of smiling at men spewing pious pseudoscience, justifying their blind allegiance to a madman. She'd grown up in Stuttgart during the early days of Hitler's rise to power. She'd seen the poverty and desperation that had led to the successes of his National Socialist party; the relief in the faces of men and women when he gave them someone to blame for their despair. She thought back to her last year at comprehensive school, to the pointed comments from teachers whose faces creased with derision at her academic ambitions, questioning whether her talents weren't better spent in the service of a husband. She recalled the riots caused in the wake of brownshirt rallies: the Führer's high voice amplified by the crack of a loudspeaker, giving young men an unearned sense of authority, permission to prey on the weak.

Five years ago, she'd shifted her allegiance to a new homeland. Under cover of darkness, she and her brother had crossed the border into Strasbourg and spent their meagre savings on forged papers that listed their place of birth as Lausanne, Switzerland. Few knew of Sophie's past: with the exception of Paul Rosenberg, who'd written her a letter of introduction to the Louvre, no one in her professional circle knew she'd been born in Stuttgart.

She got off her bicycle to pass beneath the Arc de Triomphe du Carrousel, steering it by the handlebars as she purchased a sandwich from a seller near the Musée du Louvre. Sophie had come to Paris in the hopes of working in that hallowed sanctuary and had been pleased, though a little disappointed, to receive an offer from the modernist Jeu de Paume instead. Rose's gravelly voice echoed, persistent, in her mind: *I've dedicated my life, my education, to art, and they still can't afford to pay me a proper salary.*

Sophie unwrapped the sandwich, and the tangy smell of mustard wafted up from the wax paper.

Rose's voice echoed again in her ears. *War makes strange bedfellows.* A similar opportunity would never have arisen in peacetime, Sophie was sure of it. But was that reason enough to turn her back on her principles? How had it been reason enough for Rose to turn on hers?

She leaned her bike against a lamppost, watching a newspaper-seller hawk the latest headline: nighttime bombings had begun in London, the Germans flying in under cover of darkness to pummel the city into submission. Thankfully, the Germans had spared Paris a similar fate in exchange for its surrender. For now, the Germans had won. What else could Sophie do but try to get on with her life?

But the idea wasn't without risk. Though her forged passport had been exchanged for legitimate identity papers at the start of the occupation, there was still a risk that the ERR might go digging into her past. However polite the Germans might be toward the conquered French, she knew they wouldn't take kindly to someone who'd rejected the Reich.

Sophie sighed, wishing that Dietrich was sitting on the bench next to her, his blue eyes crinkling into a smile. *Cheer up, Sophette,* he would have said. *All you need to do is look at it from a new perspective.*

She bit into her sandwich, thinking of Dietrich and his no-nonsense approach to decision-making. He would have given her the advice she sought by cutting to the heart of the matter, surveying her options with a clear-eyed distinction between practicality and principles. He would have told her that principles were what mattered, in the end; that principles, above all else, were more important than ever in times of war. After all, they were what wars were fought for.

Sophie closed her eyes. And what had principle gotten Dietrich in the end?

A wife who'd indulged his recklessness and encouraged him to become the face of an antifascist movement, with no regard for his safety.

A slow death in the back of a Parisian alley, an early grave.

She opened her eyes, driving away the thought of her doomed brother and his bohemian wife. Had Fabienne ever truly loved Dietrich, or had she only ever cared about the principles he fought for?

She stood and brushed sandwich crumbs from her skirt before returning to her bicycle, then pedaled back to the Jeu de Paume to give Rose her answer.

4

September 1940

Fabienne leaned back into the thick velvet padding of the banquette at Café Voisin, tucking a dark wisp of cropped hair behind her ear as she watched the young man she'd been speaking to walk up to the bar, his calfskin boots gleaming. He raised a hand to signal to the bartender, and Fabienne caught a glimpse of a perfectly starched shirtsleeve. His uniform was so crisp, so new, that she doubted that he'd ever seen any real action before being posted to Paris. She cast a glance at the soldiers that filled the room like mold: boys, every last one of them. They'd walked through the front door of an unlocked house, yet here they were, acting for all the world as though they'd fought heroically for the privilege of dining in one of the world's most beautiful cities.

She downed the last of her Burgundy, knowing she was drinking too quickly, too recklessly, and looked across the room to where Lotte, vibrant in a backless yellow dress, was charming an officer in a gray suit. With her blond hair and voluptuous figure, Lotte—Fabienne's lodger—was the embodiment of the American phrase *blonde bombshell*. Fabienne, with her rail-thin figure and heavy-lidded eyes, didn't begrudge Lotte her good looks: these days, beauty was a currency more valuable than the franc, and Paris was filled with Germans more than willing to pay for the pleasure of a beautiful woman's company. Between the two of them, these evenings out were enough to give them the money they needed to heat their little garret, now that jobs were scarce and food was scarcer.

The officer sitting next to Lotte snaked his hand around her waist, and she batted it away, laughing. Subtly, she threw a glance over her shoulder to meet Fabienne's eye. With a barely perceptible nod, Lotte turned her attention back to the officer, and Fabienne relaxed. Most of the German soldiers who'd been stationed in Paris seemed so anxious to prove that they weren't an invading horde—smiling as they hammered their German signage to French street corners and handed out cans of Scho-Ka-Kola to children who didn't know better than to accept. But the others—officers Fabienne had met in the lobby of the Majestique or Le Meurice—those were the ones to be wary of. They'd smile and charm, but they were cold beneath the shine, their manners born of steel rather than courtesy.

Her stomach rumbled, and she thought of her larder. She'd tried to brazen her way through the early days of the occupation, presenting two-fingered salutes to bucket-helmeted foot soldiers and drinking her way through the long evening curfews. But hunger, it seemed, was a force more powerful than principle, particularly when her options for obtaining legitimate work were limited.

She clasped her hands on the tabletop, remembering the

days when oil paint had permeated her skin so completely it felt as though she'd gotten it tattooed along her smooth palms; when Dietrich, slinking into her studio after his shift had ended, wrested the paintbrush from her hand to wrap her in his strong embrace. They'd lived as best they could back then, spending their money on canvases and India ink, bottles of wine and loaves of bread; colorful fabrics for Fabienne to turn into spectacular robes and trousers for them to wear at parties that lasted until dawn. Between her burgeoning career as an artist and his shifts at the Citroën factory, they'd accumulated a decent nest egg.

Who would have guessed that, with the devaluing of the franc, the Germans would have obliterated the foundations of their comfortable life so completely?

Fabienne could feel despair tugging at the edges of her mind, and she looked up to catch the bartender frowning at her. She could scoff at his hypocrisy—as though feeding the Germans was no less collaborationist than bedding them. Fabienne, at least, knew the two were equally transactional.

The soldier made his way back to the table, a fresh bottle of Burgundy in his hand. Fabienne pasted a smile on her face and reached for her glass, letting her fingers drift to touch his as though by accident.

He was little more than a boy, really, and she let him stammer along in broken French. All these Germans wanted the same thing: to tell their friends back home they'd fucked a Frenchwoman. Was that a substitute for having done so little to conquer the city? Fabienne lifted the bottle, watching him stumble over the punch line of a joke he'd already told. Given how much he'd had to drink already, he'd be lucky to make it up to his hotel room under his own steam. Fabienne would support him under the shoulder, take his boots and shirt off for him once he collapsed in the bed, wait around until morning for him to ask, sheepishly, if they'd done what he'd promised to pay for. With the night ahead of her and a half-torn brassiere beneath her green dress, Fabienne would relish the time she'd take to set up a convincing tableau.

Fabienne looked at the soldier through her heavy eyelashes. "Tell me more," she said, filling his glass to the top.

5

October 1940

Sophie breathed in the still air of the Jeu de Paume's restoration lab, watching dust motes dance in the yellow glow of the electric lights. She'd arrived at the museum as early as curfew allowed, and the sun hadn't fully risen over the city's rooftops: through the laboratory's arched windows, Sophie could see only herself, reflected against the slowly brightening sky.

She crossed to the lab's two wide worktables, positioned to catch the sunlight that would soon pour through the south window. Long bookcases lined the walls, filled with many of the tools of Sophie's trade: solvents and scalpels, mulberry paper and rabbit-glue adhesives in half-filled jars; tubes of oils and boar's hair paintbrushes of varying sizes. At the back of the room, several easels held paintings partway through restoration: a Miró awaiting a final coat of varnish; a Klee, partway through the relining process.

As the only art restorer left on staff, Sophie had grown used to working alone. Most days, she barely spoke to anyone, unless Rose came up from the basement to inquire after some painting or another. But though the ERR had formally requisitioned the Jeu de Paume, they'd not sent over any paintings: for now, Sophie did what she could to keep busy, helping Rose catalog the few works remaining in the basement, and working slowly on the handful of paintings that required intervention.

Loath as she was to take credit for her work, Sophie knew she was a talented restorer. Her work was artistry of the subtlest kind, breathing new life into a painting by repairing worn canvas or chipped paint; by renewing a work's true colors, lost under decades or centuries of discolored varnish. More than once, she'd put her skills to use by rectifying past mistakes of her own profession—she'd even removed an anachronistic fig leaf or two, censoriously painted over mythical figures by overly conscientious Victorians. In short, Sophie considered herself at her best when she was invisible: through the removal of old varnish or the addition of new overpaint, she could reveal the original intention of the artist, her own work made masterful by its very absence.

She turned on the wireless, then took her most recent acquisition from its easel—a Pissarro she'd begun cleaning the day before, its pastel composition currently darkened by tobacco grime trapped on the layer of varnish.

She tied back her auburn hair and put on her glasses and gloves, then unscrewed the lid on a solvent solution she'd made the day before. A chemical pang hit her nose as she wrapped a small length of cotton batting around a thin dowel, then dipped the stick into the solvent. She set the cotton softly, delicately, on the painting, barely breathing as she twisted the dowel. The grime adhered to the cotton, and satisfied that she'd lifted the varnish without damaging the paint, Sophie continued onward, working in patches down the length of the canvas.

As happened so often when she was working alone, the echo of her father's voice whispered in her mind: *Gently, now, Sophie.* An art restorer himself, Papa had taught Sophie everything she knew: how to mix solvents and reline canvases; how to build new stretchers for paintings when the old one was worn out or damaged. Unlike her sociable brother, who'd spent his hours after class in tearooms and dance halls with his friends, Sophie preferred to spend her free time in Papa's laboratory, bounding up the steps of Stuttgart's Academy of Fine Arts to the room where her heavy frame and blunt manners didn't seem to matter, where what mattered was the steadiness of her hands, the sharpness of her eyes.

She closed her eyes, picturing sunlight streaming through her father's laboratory window, refracted by jars of solvent and linseed oil; the photograph of the great Otto Röhm, Papa's hero, whose work on acrylic resins had formed the basis of her father's own research.

Sophie smiled, thinking back to his experimentations. He was determined to develop a line of petroleum-based paint specifically for art restoration.

"Imagine, Sophie," he used to say, his eyes shining as he mixed acrylic resins with pigments on glass plates. "Paint that looks and feels like oil, but which can be identified and even removed by future generations of restorers without damaging the artist's original work. Röhm saw the potential in acrylic paint for industrial purposes, but I see it as the future of our profession."

The sun had fully risen when the doorknob rattled. Sophie looked up, pushing her spectacles up the bridge of her nose as a man in a dark suit walked in, carrying a large briefcase.

"Sorry," he said. With her glasses on, the man was a blur, and Sophie watched the pale circle of his bearded face. "I'm so sorry to interrupt. I was under the impression the lab was empty."

"Who told you that?" said Sophie. She removed her glasses, and the man came into focus. He was of medium height, with broad shoulders, graying hair and a handsome, guileless face.

He came forward, favoring his right leg as he hefted his suitcase onto the table opposite Sophie's. "I had rather hoped to settle in quietly, but I'm disturbing you at your work." He spoke softly, his French rounded by a German accent. "Gerhardt Hausler. Formerly of the Gemäldegalerie Alte Meister."

Sophie removed her gloves and took his outstretched hand. "And what brings you so far from Dresden, Herr Hausler?"

Hausler's hazel eyes crinkled as he smiled. "I was seconded by the ERR," he replied. "I suppose that means you and I will be working together, Mademoiselle...?"

"Brandt." She'd known that the ERR would one day arrive at the Jeu de Paume, stacking their *stateless* paintings in the galleries, but naïvely, she'd hoped that they would leave her laboratory alone. "You're a restorer, then?"

Hausler opened his briefcase to reveal jars of solvents, brushes and pigments. "Yes," he said, running a hand across his trimmed beard. "I'd rather thought I'd been denounced when I was approached by the *Wehrmacht*...or worse, that they'd decided to put me back in the infantry, though I did question what use I'd be with just the one leg. Imagine my surprise when they told me art restoration was considered an essential military skill set." He pulled the jars out one by one and set them along the table. "I won't pretend this isn't preferable to being on the Western Front. I had enough of that sort of thing at the Somme."

Sophie watched him unpack. "I suppose there are more of you downstairs."

"You suppose correctly. My colleagues are downstairs, but they won't make themselves as obtrusive as me, I think."

"I see." Sophie watched Hausler a moment longer, thinking back to the day she'd submitted her application to the University of Stuttgart, alongside a letter of recommendation from her father.

It hadn't taken long for the university to respond with a politely worded rejection, citing the German government's new policy which sharply restricted the number of female students permitted in institutions of higher education.

"Will you excuse me, Herr Hausler?"

She unbuttoned her overcoat and walked out of the lab, leaving Hausler to unpack in peace.

Sophie walked down the staff staircase, wiping dust from her hands with a kerchief she'd stowed away in her pocket.

She shouldn't have been surprised, but she was amazed that Rose hadn't given her advance warning that the Germans would be arriving today. As she stepped into the back gallery, two soldiers wearing *Luftwaffe* gray hurried past her, carrying a tall canvas shrouded by a white sheet. She crossed through to the grand gallery that served as the museum's entrance hall. Out the open front door, she could see a line of flatbed trucks being relieved of their contents. Soldiers carried immense crates in teams of two and four, cigarettes fitted into the corners of their mouths, as men in civilian clothes—ERR staff, Sophie presumed—directed them into different galleries.

Rose Valland stood in the middle of the grand gallery, clipboard in hand as she conversed with a tall gentleman in a serge uniform. As he turned, Sophie could see a glint of red and black pinned to his velvet lapel, and her stomach turned: it had been years since she'd seen a swastika up close.

Rose smiled. "Colonel Bohn, might I introduce Sophie Brandt?" She rested a hand on Sophie's arm. "Sophie is our talented young restorer here at the Jeu de Paume. She kindly consented to remain on staff."

Tall and stern, with deep-set eyes and salt-and-pepper hair beneath the glossed brim of his cap, Bohn gave Sophie a thin-lipped smile. "Delighted to meet you, Mademoiselle Brandt. Mademoiselle Valland tells me you're quite indispensable to her work."

"She's too kind," Sophie replied.

Bohn's polite smile warmed. "Your humility does you credit," he said. "In the Reich, we recognize talent and strive to cultivate it, where we can."

She smiled, knowing full well the value that Bohn and his associates placed on women workers. Were she to close her eyes, she would feel the ghostly weight of twin plaits down her back; a kerchief around her neck, twisting tight.

"Of course," she replied, swallowing back bile.

"Brandt," Bohn mused. "Might you have German ancestry, *mademoiselle*?"

"Sophie is from Switzerland," Rose interjected smoothly.

Bohn frowned. *"Sprechen Sie Deutsch?"*

Sophie looked from Rose to Bohn and back again. Barely, imperceptibly, Rose shook her head—Sophie glanced back, but Rose was staring at the museum's doors. Had it been her imagination?

"I don't," she replied, the lie falling easily from her lips. "But I can learn, if you like."

Bohn's expression eased. "That won't be necessary," he said, and Sophie felt as though she'd passed some test. "So long as you respect your homeland's policy of neutrality in all matters."

"Colonel Bohn is the director of the *Einsatzstab Reichsleiter Rosenberg*," Rose continued. "He will be working out of the Jeu de Paume with his team of specialists."

"Of course," said Sophie. "That's what I came to talk to you about, Mademoiselle Valland—"

Bohn let out a bark of laughter. "Oh dear. Hausler isn't making trouble already, is he? Don't worry, *mademoiselle*. There will be enough work for you both, I assure you." He sighed, watching the soldiers pile the crates against the walls. "So many of the works under our jurisdiction come to us in various states of disrepair. I'm afraid their former owners didn't always give these masterpieces the respect they deserved."

Behind Bohn, a man in civilian clothing followed the last of the soldiers into the gallery. The soldiers carried another tall canvas shrouded beneath a trailing white sheet, and the civilian shouted a warning as the sheet snaked around one of the soldiers' ankles. He darted forward to pull the sheet from the painting, and Sophie nearly gasped: Paul's portrait of Madame Rosenberg stared serenely back at Sophie from the canvas, her disgruntled child in her arms.

Sophie turned her attention back to Bohn, a sickening feeling settling in her stomach as the Picasso slid from view.

Bohn sighed. "What else could one expect? Jews can't appreciate the intrinsic value of art. They only see it in monetary terms. It's a disgrace, really. Here, we will give these masterworks their due."

Sophie could feel Rose's eyes burning into the back of her neck. "I am at your disposal, sir."

Though Sophie hadn't meant her words as a personal compliment, it was clear that Bohn had taken them as such. "The Führer has been most insistent that we protect Paris and its treasures from harm, but I'm afraid we cannot count on our English adversaries to be quite so conscientious."

Looking past Bohn once more, Sophie watched as the soldiers uncovered other pieces: a van Gogh from Paul's gallery; a Vermeer that Sophie knew had been part of the Rothschilds' private collection. Blood began to pulse in her ears, insistent and loud.

"I'm sure it goes without saying, *mademoiselle*, that the work we're doing here is of the utmost importance." Bohn stepped closer to Sophie, and she could smell his cologne, heavy and overbearing. "As such, I will require the utmost discretion from all who work within these walls."

Sophie stepped back. "And you will have it."

Bohn smiled. "Very good," he replied. "Please excuse me, ladies. I require a word with Dr. Gurlitt."

Sophie turned to address Rose, but she'd already walked off, her stout heels tapping on the marble as she strode toward a far-off exhibition hall.

6

October 1940

Fabienne walked through the double doors into the courtyard of her apartment building, her string bag laden with turnips and ersatz coffee. As exhausted as she was, Fabienne was glad she'd had the foresight to bring her ration book to dinner last night: this morning, she'd been first in line at the butcher's shop, and she'd had her pick of the minuscule portions of stewing beef her ration ticket allowed. Still, she longed for her bed. She pulled her feather boa over her shoulders, wishing she could scrub away the feel of the German foot soldier she'd been trapped with after curfew. He'd been young and overeager, with no head for wine but a wallet well worth emptying.

Closed away from the prying eyes of German soldiers, the courtyard had become something of a hub for Fabienne and the other residents of her building. In one corner, Monsieur Minci and his son were repairing the frame of the small hutch they'd built, each hammer blow terrorizing the family of rabbits that lived within. Across the way, Madame de Frontenac shot Fabienne a scowl before tending to her small garden of carrots.

She crossed into the stairwell and vaulted up the marble steps, feeling Madame de Frontenac's fiery gaze fade. Much as she loathed being a topic of conversation among the neighborhood gossips, Fabienne knew she wasn't the only one making a living off the Germans. Was it fair of them to judge Fabienne for doing what she had to in order to survive?

On the second story, Madame Lowenstein stepped out of her apartment, a pillbox hat nestled in her gray curls. Fabienne caught a glimpse of the generously apportioned rooms within before she snapped the door shut, and her heart sank: she'd hoped the Lowensteins would have left Paris by now.

"Another late night for you and your lodger." Madame Lowenstein rummaged through her handbag to pull out a cigarette and a lighter. "Is the curfew really so hard to abide by?"

Fabienne drew her boa tight around her neck. Madame Lowenstein's husband was a jeweler, well respected by Paris's couturiers. Consequently, Madame Lowenstein was always impeccably dressed, more daring in her sense of style than other women in their late sixties. If anyone was to notice that the hem peeking out from beneath Fabienne's coat belonged to an evening dress, it would be Madame Lowenstein.

"I know things have been difficult for you since your husband's passing," she continued in an undertone, "but you needn't resort to this. My husband's in need of workers, and you've an artistic eye." She pulled a cream-colored bangle from her wrist and held it out. "Bakelite," Madame Lowenstein explained, a spark of pride shading her words. "A manufactured product. Lev says it's the future of fashion."

Fabienne took the bangle, swallowing down the sudden

urge to cry. She'd heard that the Germans had assured the new Vichy government that Paris's fashion industry would endure—but then, she'd also heard in horrific detail about the events of *Kristallnacht*. Now that the Germans had arrived, it was only a matter of time before similar reprisals would happen here. As a Jewish businessman, how long would Monsieur Lowenstein be allowed to continue operating his atelier?

"You should have left," Fabienne said gently, handing the bangle back to Madame Lowenstein. "When you had the chance. Why didn't you go?"

Madame Lowenstein slipped the bracelet back over her wrist. "We had many long conversations about that very question," she said, straightening her glove. "Lev signed over the business to his partner—he's Protestant, so the atelier should be safe with him. We had even booked tickets to New York before we heard about what happened to the passengers on board the *SS St. Louis*. But in the end, we don't want them thinking we're afraid…thinking that we've some reason to be ashamed of who we are. Paris is our home. It's been our home for generations." She smiled. "Come to the atelier and talk to Lev. You deserve better than this."

Fabienne sat on a bench outside 21 Rue La Boétie, staring up at the filigreed façade of the building that had once housed Paul Rosenberg's gallery. She'd been here many times as a patron and once as an artist. If she closed her eyes she could be back at her own gallery opening, staring up at her creations, Dietrich squeezing her hand as they met her adoring admirers. She'd sold four paintings that night, and Dietrich had beamed with pride as Paul extolled the virtues of Fabienne's work: her subtle touch, her bold use of color and form.

That night had been the high point of her life, earning money as an artist, her love by her side.

But then, that's the trouble with a high point.

She looked up at the windows of Paul's gallery, at the crisp new banner that hung over the gallery's heavy oak doors. *L'Institut d'étude des Questions Juives.* Black-suited Germans circled in and out of the building, nodding at uniformed guards standing where Fabienne and Dietrich had once waited for their taxicab.

It's inevitably followed by a low.

Fabienne got to her feet and walked on, recalling the lightness of that long-ago evening; Dietrich's blue eyes. She'd painted him a thousand times, but even still it felt as though her husband was fading from her memory. Now every painting she attempted seemed to wither. She'd been an artist then—was she an artist still? Now that every canvas crumbled before her eyes, now that she made a living as a German plaything?

Collaboration horizontale. It had all seemed so simple, when Lotte had suggested it: they were both widows, after all, looking to make a living. *You can't eat paint*, she'd told Fabienne, arching a perfectly shaped eyebrow.

What would Dietrich say, if he knew she'd reduced herself to this to survive?

"Mademoiselle!"

Fabienne looked up. Without realizing it, she'd walked all the way to the Place de la Concorde. Across the square, scarlet and black banners fluttered from the Hôtel de la Marine. A German soldier jogged toward her, his rifle hiked up over his shoulder.

"Papers, *mademoiselle*."

"Of course." Fabienne sorted through her handbag. She'd been issued a new identity card at the beginning of the occupation, had stood in line for hours at the prefecture as they recorded every possible detail about her: height, eye color, nationality. The police officer had smiled when he took her photograph, the registrar behind him stamping the card with the lazy haste of a bureaucrat. *If you have nothing to hide, you have nothing to fear,* he'd said calmly. But she'd watched the family ahead of her receive their identity papers, turning them over to examine the heavy red stamp that marred the top of their pages: *Juif.*

The soldier's eyes flickered from the card to Fabienne's décolletage. "You photograph well, *mademoiselle,*" he said. "Is there somewhere I might escort you? To a café, perhaps?"

Fabienne jerked her head in the direction of the Concorde metro station. "I'm going home," she replied. "All the way across the city. It would be a wasted journey for you."

The soldier's charming expression congealed. "I was only doing my job."

"And *such* a good job of it too," Fabienne retorted before walking away. She worried, for a moment, that the soldier might follow her—but then she stopped short.

A woman emerged from the metro, carrying a large briefcase. Though her plump figure was concealed beneath a shapeless tweed jacket and calf-length skirt, she was instantly recognizable to Fabienne: her full cheeks and blue eyes; her auburn curls which hung limply beneath her hat, as though she'd not pinned them properly the night before.

Fabienne hadn't seen Sophie since the day of Dietrich's funeral. She did her best to avoid the places she knew Sophie tended to haunt: the Louvre and the Jeu de Paume, the Latin Quarter. Places that had once meant so much to her—places she'd cut out of her heart, just as Sophie had cut her from her life.

Sophie stepped onto the sidewalk and caught sight of Fabienne. "You're still here." She held her briefcase awkwardly, as if wishing she could hide behind it. "I wasn't sure. I thought perhaps you'd left."

Fabienne had dreaded this moment; Sophie, it seemed, had dreaded it too. She blinked, knowing that Sophie was also thinking of that final, fateful night. Dietrich's lifeless body, laid out across the cobbles while German voices retreated into the night. Political pamphlets, falling like snow in the light of a streetlamp.

Just as it had back then, Fabienne's stomach dropped with the certainty that it had been her encouragement, her actions, which had led to that terrible moment.

"Well," Sophie said finally, glancing at the Jeu de Paume. "I don't want to be late."

Fabienne looked over Sophie's shoulder. Though the museum was hidden behind a heavy stone wall that separated the Jardin des Tuileries from the Place de la Concorde, she could see the looming columns and arched glass of the museum's north façade. Two soldiers walked through a gap in the wall, chatting easily in German. "I thought the Jeu de Paume had closed," she said, as a red flush rose in Sophie's face. "Unless—"

"It's none of your concern," Sophie started, but Fabienne pushed past her, following in the soldiers' footsteps, blood rushing in her ears. *It couldn't be*, she thought to herself. *She can't possibly—*

She stopped, staring at the soldiers flanking the museum's entrances.

"You're working for them?" Fabienne felt as if the ground had given way beneath her. "After everything that happened?"

"It's not what it looks like." Sophie grabbed Fabienne's arm, but Fabienne jerked out of her grasp.

"Reverted to form, have you?" Fabienne snarled. Somewhere, deep in the back of her mind, she could hear her own hypocrisy, but she didn't care. Anger burned through her immediately, furiously bright. "After everything we went through—everything *you* went through! Dietrich would be spinning in his grave."

Sophie flinched. "He wouldn't be in his grave if it weren't for you," she spat back.

She spun on her heel and strode toward the museum, leaving Fabienne feeling as though she'd been slapped.

7

Sophie passed her *Ausweis* to the museum's guard with a trembling hand. She resisted the urge to look around. Was Fabienne still standing at the steps to the metro station? She bristled as Fabienne's taunt echoed in her mind: *Reverted to form, have you?* And what of the thousands of other Parisians who'd had to find work in their newly occupied city? What of everyone else who'd had to find ways to muddle through?

The guard handed Sophie back her *Ausweis*, and she passed through the doors, lifting her chin. Given that Fabienne had all but pushed Dietrich into the spotlight that had made him a target for Hitler's followers, it was she who had reason to be ashamed.

A clipboard in hand, Rose Valland was standing in the grand gallery with Bohn as he spoke to Hildebrand Gurlitt. Small and serious, with round glasses that mirrored the curve of his cheeks, Gurlitt was a frequent visitor to the museum.

By reputation, Sophie knew that he specialized in the sorts of modern works of art that the Jeu de Paume had exhibited before the occupation. Now, it seemed, he was helping the ERR in an advisory capacity: he ambled from painting to painting, occasionally leaning in to say something to Bohn.

They paused in front of a landscape by van Gogh, its bold lines and bright colors giving it the appearance of having been painted in a fever dream. Gurlitt shook his head, and with a flick of his wrist Bohn had the painting removed by a hovering soldier.

As the soldier carried the painting off, Rose caught Sophie's eye and stepped away from Bohn and Gurlitt.

"What are they doing?"

"Preparing the museum for an exhibition," Rose muttered, scribbling something on her clipboard. She looked up, adjusting her spectacles. "We've a guest arriving early next week to view the works, so it will be all hands on deck, I'm afraid. Follow me."

"An exhibition?" Sophie looked through the narrow door into the gallery behind the exhibition hall where two soldiers were unravelling a spectacular Aubusson; behind them, another followed with a potted plant hefted in his arms. "For whom?"

"I'm not sure. Someone rather high-ranking, or else they wouldn't be taking such care over the details." Rose sighed. "We've been asked to make something of an effort. Monsieur Jaujard was kind enough to send over the rugs from the Louvre."

Sophie's heart plummeted as she trailed Rose through the museum. Definitely a Nazi—and someone fairly senior. Who else would have the ERR in such a frenzy?

Rose led Sophie into the museum's smallest gallery, located opposite the staff staircase that led up to the restoration lab.

She edged into the room, bypassing a soldier teetering atop a high ladder as he screwed an iron curtain rod across the gallery's entrance. Against one wall stood a heavy-legged display table, empty but for the van Gogh that Sophie had seen carried off from the front gallery earlier.

"I'm told our upcoming guest isn't an admirer of modern art," Rose began. "Bohn has asked that we bring all modern pieces here, so that our guest might explore the rest of our collection unencumbered by degenerate artworks. I'd like you to take on the task." She pulled a leather-bound ledger from beneath her clipboard and handed it to Sophie, who recoiled from the swastika embossed in gold on its cover. "The ERR has been good enough to compile an inventory of everything in the museum. You might find it useful."

Sophie hesitated: the job would take hours. "I don't know whether my talents extend to record-keeping. I-I wouldn't know where to start."

Rose's expression tightened. "I would do it myself, but my work with Bohn precludes it, and the ERR is overstretched as it is. I know it's outside your purview, but please, Sophie." She glanced at her watch, bringing the conversation to a clear close. "I'm afraid I must carry on, so I will leave this task to you." She set the ledger on the table and retreated without waiting for Sophie's response.

Sophie opened the ledger. Within, Bohn's staff had compiled dozens of pages' worth of information, each painting in the growing collection listed by artist, medium and description. She lingered over a slender column, *Inventar*, that turned her stomach, a list of names printed in tidy, typewritten letters: *Kahnweiler, Rothschild, Weil-Picard, Rosenberg.* The names of familiar connoisseurs and collectors, Jewish families to whom the paintings rightfully belonged.

Stateless paintings; *abandoned* collections. There was noth-

ing "stateless" about the collection of Alphonse de Rothschild; there was nothing "abandoned" about Daniel-Henry
Kahnweiler's expansive gallery of modernist art. Did it make
the Germans feel better about their theft to deliberately ob-
fuscate the terms under which these collections were seized:
to pretend that they'd "saved" the possessions of those they'd
forcibly driven from France's shores?

Hundreds of works of art were listed in the book already,
with more brought in every day by Bohn's raiding teams. She
ran her finger down the ledger, noting that certain works of
art—modern pieces—had been marked with a tidy code: EK.

Entartete Kunst.

Degenerate Art.

The Nazi party had developed its theory of degenerate art
early on in its rise to power. Seeking to obliterate the avant-
garde decadence of the Weimar Republic, the Nazis had pulled
all modern art from Germany's public collections, seeing in the
canvases ideological dissonance, dangerous modes of thinking which had led to Germany's failure in the Great War.
Only ideological purity, artistic purity, could thrive under
the Nazis, art which depicted the world in classical lines and
forms, which held a mirror up to the world and reflected it as
it was, without interpretation or originality.

Numb, she picked up the ledger and walked through to the
nearest gallery to begin sorting through the paintings lined
along the walls. The work was slow, and as she passed from
canvas to canvas she couldn't help admiring each one: the play
of light on a woman's collar in a peerless van Dyck; the bold-
ness of the brushstrokes in a Cézanne pastoral. In Germany,
the Cézanne would be branded degenerate—and yet, his work
was no less masterful than van Dyck's. Why were the Nazis so
threatened by the fact that Cézanne chose to break the rules
of the medium, rather than play by them?

Because it presents a way of thinking they can't control. Hitler's goal was to create a thousand-year Reich, crystallized in amber. What need was there for innovation, when the Nazi party had already created perfection?

She continued sorting through the canvases and came across a small painting by Ernst Ludwig Kirchner. Colorful and emotive, his work depicted Germany as it had been before the war, moody and pensive, peopled with prostitutes and socialites alike. This particular canvas showed two nude women—prostitutes—in a moment of repose.

Over six hundred of Kirchner's paintings had been seized by the Nazis, twenty-five of them presented in their *Entartete Kunst* exhibition as the product of a diseased mind. Was it diseased to show the corrosive impact of war on a person's sense of self? As one of the founders of the German art movement known as *Die Brücke*, Kirchner had considered himself a titan of the Weimar Republic; and yet, with the rise of the Nazi party, he'd been expelled from the Academy of Arts in Berlin, been branded an outsider, stateless, neither German nor anything else.

The Nazis made it clear that Germany had no room for an artist like Kirchner, and he'd taken their hatred to heart: isolated and despairing, he'd shot himself in 1938, an early, silent victim of Hitler's regime.

Sophie turned the painting over to examine a stamp on the back, declaring the piece to be the property of Paul Rosenberg.

"Do you need help, *Fräulein*?"

She turned to see a *Luftwaffe* soldier standing at the door of the gallery. "These paintings, here," she said, indicating a small pile of paintings that included the Cézanne and the Kirchner. "They're to go to the, um, storeroom across from the staff staircase."

"Very well." The soldier called over to two others, and

between the three of them, they moved the paintings out of the gallery.

She watched them retreat, their shining boots heavy on the parquet floor, and Fabienne's voice echoed once more in her mind. *Reverted to form, have you?*

Sophie had first seen a swastika in 1933, shortly after Hitler's appointment as Germany's chancellor. At fifteen, Sophie had been too young to follow politics closely, but she'd listened to Papa's frustrated diatribes at the dining table, bemoaning the brownshirts for disrupting city hall meetings; she'd watched Mamma's face tighten over headlines about the newly formed *Gestapo*.

"Thugs and bullies," Papa had declared, swatting the back of Mamma's paper. "It's a wonder Hindenburg doesn't see through the whole strongman act. Dietrich." Across the table, Sophie's brother, digging into a near-empty jar of marmalade with a butter knife, looked up. "Save some for your sister."

Mamma pushed the marmalade out of Dietrich's reach. "The church supports him," she said, "and he's proven to be a formidable bulwark against the Communists. So long as Hindenburg keeps him on a short leash, he might prove an effective leader."

Papa had sighed. "Well, he's untrustworthy," he concluded, before kissing Mamma on the cheek and setting out for his restoration laboratory at the Academy of Fine Arts.

Only six months later, Papa had returned home for dinner wearing a swastika pin.

"It's business," Mamma had explained, setting down an overflowing plate of cabbage rolls. "Quite a few members of the university's board of directors are National Socialists. It makes sense for your father to want to impress them."

"National Socialists? At a university?" Dietrich looked up, incredulous, but Papa avoided his eye.

"And we've enrolled you both in Hitler Youth groups. Your uniforms are in your bedrooms, and you start tomorrow. Sophie, pass me your plate."

"Youth groups?" Dietrich's gaze swiveled to Sophie. Youth-group uniforms had become all but ubiquitous in the halls of their comprehensive school, Hitler Youth tan and *Bund Deutscher Mädel* blue around every corner. "Did you know about this?"

Sophie shrugged, thinking of the BDM girls in her classroom, with their matching uniforms and easy camaraderie. In her rough-spun skirt and hand-stitched sweaters, Sophie felt so out of place: ugly, where they were beautiful; awkward, where they were confident. "It might be nice," she offered. "We might make friends."

"It's to be expected," Mamma tried. "All of Stuttgart's finest families enrolled their children months ago."

Dietrich ignored her. "Papa, please. You said yourself that Hitler isn't to be trusted. Do you really want us to make friends with his followers?"

"Your mother and I suspect that membership will become compulsory. If you volunteer, you'll be positioning yourself for advancement." Papa looked up. "We're only thinking of your future."

"Thinking of your *career*, more like. You really want me to become one of them? Beating up Jewish people in the streets?"

"Dietrich!" Mamma said sharply. "I'll not hear talk like that, thank you very much."

"It's what they do, though, Mother! They harass old men and say the most hateful things—you want that for me? For Sophie?" He glanced at Sophie, who held her tongue. She didn't want to add fuel to the fire by either agreeing with Dietrich or siding with Mamma and Papa.

"We're not asking you to abandon your beliefs, Dietrich.

We're asking you to help your father," Mamma replied. "Think whatever you like, but go through the motions! What will change, really? You'll say a few words, wear a new shirt. Does it really matter?"

"You remember Dr. Bergmann? In the Department of Antiquities? Or how about Dr. Seidel? She came to your confirmation, Sophie," Papa added. "They spoke out against the National Socialists, and they've both been dismissed from their posts."

Sophie looked up in alarm. Following in her father's footsteps by attending the Academy of Fine Arts was her greatest ambition. What would it mean for her application if Papa was branded a dissident?

"We all know Dr. Seidel was dismissed from her post for being Jewish," Dietrich countered. "Her son, Harry, was in your class, do you remember him, Sophie? No one's seen either of them in months, and—"

"Dietrich!" Mamma snapped again, slamming her delicate fist on the table with surprising force. Dietrich fell silent, and Sophie's cheeks burned with the realization that she'd been so preoccupied with thoughts of fitting in that she'd not noticed her classmate's absence.

"You're too young to know what life was like after the war," Mamma continued bitterly as she spooned a second cabbage roll onto Dietrich's plate. "Too young to be anything other than ungrateful. You didn't have to eat sawdust mixed into your bread or watch your parents starve, your brothers killed at the Front… This country was in flames after the Great War. Say what you like about Herr Hitler—he's bringing Germany back up to standard."

"A standard built on hatred and lies," Dietrich muttered.

"A standard built on providing better for our children," Mamma shot back. "You've never wanted for a thing in your lives. You have no idea how good things are because you've never seen how bad they can be."

Dietrich pushed away his untouched plate and stormed off to his bedroom. But when Sophie came down for breakfast the next morning in her crisp new BDM blouse, Dietrich was at the table, sullenly straightening the swastika on his uniform's armband.

Sophie was examining a large Rubens when she saw Colonel Bohn make his way up the staircase, Hildebrand Gurlitt nodding at his side.

"The Vermeer, of course, will have pride of place," Gurlitt was saying; behind them, Rose Valland stopped to direct two soldiers carrying a Vasari into a different gallery. "And Goudstikker's Cranach, *Venus und Amor.* Perhaps in one of the smaller galleries, so that it might be seen more intimately."

"Of course, I leave all such decisions in your capable hands," Bohn replied.

As Gurlitt progressed into the next showroom, Bohn lingered behind. "The Vermeer and the Cranach, Mademoiselle Valland. I trust you will give them the attention they're due." He sighed, watching as the soldiers carried a dreary canvas by Isaac van Ostade up the stairs, its muddy fields reminiscent of spring rain. "I've never much appreciated art," he muttered, and Sophie caught Rose's eye. "Seems a ridiculous thing to be concerning ourselves with, when there's a war on... Still, the Führer's an artist, so I suppose there must be some merit in it."

"Well, van Ostade is better known for his winter scenes," Rose replied smoothly, her fingers tightening over her clipboard. "You must be honored that the collection holds such interest."

"So long as my superiors are happy." He rested a hand on his chest and bowed. "I'm sure that with your help, Mademoiselle Valland, the exhibition will be a resounding success. Please excuse me."

Bohn followed the van Ostade; once he was out of earshot, Sophie sidled close to Rose.

"If this museum is meant to safeguard private collections, why are we holding an exhibition? Surely there are better ways to allocate our time?"

Rose started down the staircase. "The art is to be sent to Germany," she said bluntly. "Herr Hitler intends to establish the finest museum the world has ever seen. Some of the works stored here will form the foundation of his collection."

Sophie froze. "He can't do that," she replied. "This art doesn't belong to him. It doesn't belong to *us*. The ERR is safeguarding the paintings, but they still belong to the families they were taken from."

Rose's expression was almost pitying. "Not anymore."

Sophie followed Rose down the staircase and through the galleries, where soldiers on ladders hung paintings from long chains: a Titian and a Brueghel the Elder, Dutch masters and Renaissance portraits.

Rose picked up her pace, and Sophie trailed her. Across the door to the small gallery that was to be Sophie's storeroom, someone had hung a heavy damask curtain, pushed to one side; within, the room was already starting to fill up with Sophie's selections, brought in by efficient *Luftwaffe* soldiers.

She closed her hand around Rose's arm. "How can you say that?" she asked. "The Goudstikkers are good people. Paul Rosenberg is a friend. How can you let them do this?"

Rose looked past Sophie with a frown. "I don't expect you to understand," she replied, "but these are the cards we've been dealt. We simply have to play them as best we can." She shifted out of Sophie's grasp and opened the service door to the museum, letting in a burst of brilliant sunshine. "Please,

Sophie. Don't give me reason to believe my trust in you was misplaced."

Her stomach twisting, Sophie turned and walked into the storeroom. Within, the soldiers had lined canvases three- and four-deep along the walls; soon, she would have to start hanging them in order to maintain enough space to navigate the room.

In her mind's eye, she saw beautiful girls skipping past in their blue uniforms, Dietrich sullenly affixing a swastika to his arm. Sophie's own freckled reflection in her school gymnasium's mirror, lifting her chin as a BDM troupe leader measured the span of her cheekbones, the width of her child-bearing hips.

8

November 1940

"Phenol and formaldehyde." Lev Lowenstein held out his arm, inviting Fabienne to pass behind the glass display case in his small showroom on Rue du Faubourg Saint-Denis. Beneath the glass, various pieces of jewelry lay on satin cushions, earrings and necklaces and bracelets in vibrant colors and shapes. "Combine phenol and formaldehyde in the right ratio and heat at a low, steady temperature—*et voilà!*" He chuckled, pausing to stroke Hugo, his fat little poodle, as he dozed in an overstuffed armchair. "We in haute couture wouldn't dare admit owing much to the Americans, but we do have them to thank for resinoid jewelry. The product of the future."

He opened a discreet door to the side of the showroom, and Fabienne passed through, pausing at the top of a set of stairs to admire Monsieur Lowenstein's basement workshop. The showroom, with its elegant glass cases and sumptuous furnishings, was clearly a space meant for impressing the atelier's clientele, while the workroom below was clean and utilitarian, long tables occupied by women bent over bangles and buttons, sanding down the smooth edges of a bracelet or soldering earring backs. Camphor-scented dust swirled in the air, kicked up as a tall, dark-haired woman wearing a ruby-colored kerchief over her mouth and nose buffed a ring on a belt sander: the noise was a distant hum, underlaid by the sound of a wireless.

"Of course, Dufy, my business partner, takes care of the showroom—sorting out the commissions, keeping the ledgers," Monsieur Lowenstein was saying as Fabienne continued down the staircase. "I prefer the creative side of things, working with our clients to realize their artistic visions." They reached the bottom of the staircase and made room for Hugo, suddenly alert, to dart past. "It's a nightmare whenever Chanel and Schiaparelli have it in mind to visit on the same day. Neither can bear even the hint of the other. Schiaparelli once declared she could tell Chanel had been here before her by the scent of N°5 lingering in the air."

Fabienne smirked, surveying an unoccupied table holding electric drills of varying sizes. "Surely they have such different aesthetics that there's hardly a competition between them."

Lev chuckled again. "You'd be amazed what those two can turn into a competition."

They continued toward a glass-fronted office. "Our trade used to be in gold-smithing—semiprecious stones, jewelry, clasps," he went on, "but the Depression changed our industry entirely. The major ateliers—Chanel and Schiaparelli among them—began to look for ways to bring in new clientele. Not just Paris's wealthy doyennes." He paused to wipe his shining forehead with an embroidered handkerchief. "Our challenge lay in finding a product simple, beautiful and durable enough to appeal to even the most discerning of tastes. We discussed several options, then—*voilà!*—cast resinoid jewelry. Bakelite, to the layperson." He paused next to a worktable where the woman with the red kerchief was polishing a ring on a motorized buffer. "Myriam, may I?"

"Of course." Myriam pulled the scarf she'd been using to protect herself from the dust away from her face to smile at Fabienne, meeting her gaze with honey-colored eyes. She held out the ring, a simple orb, half-black and half-white.

"Of course, the possibilities for Bakelite are endless. Telephones and poker chips, automobile parts and household products," Lev continued as Fabienne admired the ring. "Here, we focus on the possibilities it holds as an object of beauty. Buttons, brooches, bracelets, pins, hair ornaments... It can mimic the appearance of almost any natural material. Coral, jade, jet, ivory..."

Myriam offered Fabienne another bauble, a bracelet made of thin layers of color, banded and fused together. *"Sublime, n'est-ce pas?"*

Fabienne admired the bracelet's undeniable beauty. To her surprise, it was warm to the touch, with a depth to its color that made it hard to believe it was a manufactured product. The artistry, too, went beyond natural ornamentation, its pliable nature allowing Myriam to carve a striking geometric design into the multicolored bracelet. It wasn't fussy like something that Fabienne's mother would wear. Looking at it, she could see why Lev Lowenstein called Bakelite the jewelry of the future.

She slipped it on her wrist, and Lev chuckled. "Well?"

"It's art," she replied as she returned the bracelet to Myriam. "But I don't understand. Why haven't the Germans shut down the atelier?"

Lev's cheery expression faded. "They all want their wives to have the best Paris can offer," he said. "Lucien Lelong made quite a compelling argument in favor of keeping the ateliers open. We hold our noses at the thought of our new clientele…" At his feet, Hugo gave a sudden shake as though dislodging a fly from its back, and the sound of his bejeweled collar seemed to pull Lev out of his sudden melancholy. He looked at Fabienne and smiled. "But at least my workers are able to feed their families. And now that includes you. Let's find you a table."

9

The freshly washed windows of the Jeu de Paume sparkled in the autumn sunlight, the crisp breeze sending golden leaves buffeting beneath the trucks parked between the chestnut trees. Standing shoulder to shoulder with Rose Valland and Gerhardt Hausler, Sophie glanced down the short line of curators and soldiers who stood waiting along the museum's long façade. Though she could hear the sounds of Paris outside the Jardin des Tuileries's tall gates, Sophie felt as though she were a staff member in some far-flung country chateau, waiting with the rest of the household for the long-gone lord's return.

From the steps of the museum, Bohn glanced at his pocket watch. He stepped forward, as if to say something—but then two dark Mercedes chugged around the corner, crushing the chestnut leaves beneath their tires.

To Sophie's surprise, the cars were unmarked: no flags flew

from their bonnets, no military vehicles drove in their wake as they trundled up the horseshoe curve that led to the museum from the Octagonal Basin. Beside her, Rose leaned close.

"I've been asked to escort our guest through the collection. I'd appreciate it if you were to join us," she muttered.

Sophie watched as Bohn stepped toward the cars, flanked by two soldiers. "I'm behind on my work as it is," she whispered back. "Why me, particularly?"

"I'm told our guest enjoys the company of a pretty woman." Rose glanced at Sophie sidelong. "I've been called many things in my day, but never *beautiful*."

Standing on Sophie's opposite side, Hausler cleared his throat. "It's quite all right, Mademoiselle Valland cleared everything with me."

Sophie let out a breath, irritated that Rose considered Hausler her superior. "And that's my value to this exhibition, is it? My pretty face?"

Rose looked pained. "Please, Sophie," she began, but Sophie turned her attention back to the car.

She recognized the man who stepped out immediately from the front pages of newspapers back in Stuttgart; from magazines passed around her BDM troupe, touting him—with his broad shoulders and sharp cheekbones, his record as Germany's greatest ace pilot—as the Aryan ideal, the hero's hero. But whereas the Hermann Göring of Sophie's imagination looked as if he'd stepped off a plinth designed by Albert Speer, the Hermann Göring who stood before her now had lost his impressive physique: the buttons of his overcoat strained over his stomach, his eyes—two sapphires—perched above the fleshy rise of his cheeks.

He touched the brim of his fedora in a greeting to Bohn, hefting an ornately carved walking stick in his bejeweled hand.

"Reichsmarschall," said Bohn, raising his hand in a stiff-

armed salute as a tall man in a double-breasted suit emerged from the opposite door of the Mercedes. "We're honored to have you here."

Göring clapped Bohn genially on the back, and Bohn winced at the overly familiar contact. "My friend, I'm here not as a commander but as a lover of the arts." He cast an eye over the assembled staff, his gaze resting on Sophie for one jolting moment. "There are so many demands on a *Reichsmarschall*'s time, so today I am incognito, merely a curious student. It's a privilege to have this collection to myself."

Sophie raised her eyebrows. Aside from Hitler himself, *Reichsmarschall* Hermann Göring was the most recognizable man in the Nazi High Command. Did he truly expect people not to know who he was?

Bohn snapped his fingers, and his secretary hurried forward with a leather-bound book in her polished fingers. "My staff took the liberty of compiling an inventory of all the works you're going to see today. A souvenir, of sorts."

Göring beamed. "How kind…but, then, the best restaurants always provide a menu." He waved his hand, rubies glinting from his fingers, and his companion stepped forward to accept the book. "I'm sure Dr. Richter will find it most interesting." He looked up wistfully at the museum. "I must confess that being so close to a collection of such renown without seeing it is…agony. Might we go in?"

"Of course." Bohn ushered Göring toward the entrance, and Rose glanced at Sophie with a worried expression. For a moment, Sophie considered refusing Rose's request—but then she turned on her heel and followed in the *Reichsmarschall*'s cologne-scented wake.

Though Sophie had helped to arrange exhibitions at the Jeu de Paume museum before, even she could admit that the building's fifteen galleries looked immaculate, Rembrandts and van Dycks and Steens sparsely hung on the gallery's many walls. Complemented by sculptures and stained glass, easels and potted palm trees, the paintings looked as if they'd always been part of the museum's collection, displayed to their best possible advantage in the morning light.

"This floor contains pieces from the Rothschild collection," Bohn was saying, his glossy boots sinking into the carpet as he led Göring up the staircase. Rose and Sophie followed, Göring's man Richter behind them. "My men had a devil of a time rooting them out, let me tell you. These Jews have such clever hiding places... I doubt we've even found half of Rothschild's collection."

Göring reached the top of the landing, breathing heavily from the effort. "What matters is that they were found, my dear fellow." He removed his fedora, and Sophie knew that for all his odiousness, his reverence for art was genuine. "I must commend you for your industry, Bohn."

Bohn inclined his head. "The honor is entirely mine, sir," he began, but Göring interrupted him with a pat on the arm as he caught sight of a painting, set on an easel opposite the staircase.

"Is that...?"

"You have a good eye, *Reichsmarschall*." Bohn stepped toward the easel, and Richter looked up from his ledger. "Vermeer's *The Astronomer*. The jewel in Edouard de Rothschild's collection."

Along with the rest of the entourage, Sophie held her breath as the *Reichsmarschall* approached the painting slowly, as though it were a holy relic—which, as one of only a handful of precious canvases painted by the Dutch master Johannes Vermeer, it practically was. It portrayed a man studying a celestial globe, one hand gently curled over the table's edge as he leaned into a beam of light spilling through a many-paned window. Though small, it seemed to glow, the richness of the pigment inviting the viewer into the astronomer's private moment of enlightenment.

"Extraordinary," Göring breathed, and it felt to Sophie as if she'd stumbled upon an intimate moment, the *Reichsmarschall* caught in something private, obscene. "Simply extraordinary." He looked up. "Richter, my dear fellow, come closer."

Dr. Richter stepped forward, tucking the ledger beneath his arm. Tall and long-faced, he looked intelligent—a handsome reminder, perhaps, of the virile young man Göring himself had once been.

"Masterful," Richter murmured. "You see how he captures the light? And how the tapestry falls just so…" He straightened. "I presume we shall mark this down for Carinhall, *Reichsmarschall*?"

Göring sighed. "Regrettably, the Führer has made his preference for a Vermeer well-known," he replied. "Perhaps we will send it to him as a Christmas present. A gift, for the Linz museum."

Rose cleared her throat.

"I must protest," she said, quietly but firmly. "As the only representative of the French people, our government will object in the strongest possible terms to a Vermeer leaving French soil."

Göring leaned toward Bohn, switching from French to German. "I thought you had this museum entirely under your control," he murmured, and though he was smiling, the glint in his eyes had turned quite brittle. "Why have you retained the services of outsiders?"

"We felt that our own experts were better employed with the raiding teams," Bohn muttered back. "The soldiers you've put at our disposal require some oversight from professionals who understand the value of what they find. Rest assured, the women are of little consequence."

Göring inclined his head. "See that they remain that way." He turned to Rose and switched back to French with a smile. "My dear *Madame*...your name?"

"It's *Mademoiselle* Rose Valland. Assistant curator. And my colleague, Sophie Brandt."

His smile broadened further. "*Madame* Valland. I know how terribly complicated this must all appear, but you must understand that this work would be leaving France to serve a higher purpose." He moved toward the Vermeer, grazing his fingers along the frame. "As part of a private collection, this masterpiece was cloistered away, seen only by a handful of people. Locked away, forgotten. Overlooked, even, by those for whom its beauty had become commonplace." His features darkened for a second, and Sophie knew he was thinking horrible things about the Rothschilds. "Of course, art should—it must!—be in the possession of those who truly appreciate its merits. People like yourself, my dear *madame*. But is it not better for such a work to belong to the *people*, rather than to a person? To be appreciated and admired by the world, rather than by a single family?"

Göring spoke in a honeyed voice, with the patronizing charm of a man used to getting what he wanted. Whatever he said, Sophie knew that Göring's ultimate goal for Vermeer's *The Astronomer* was hardly altruistic. He saw its value as a stepping stone, a pawn to be traded for more: more art, more influence, more luxury.

Göring leaned on his walking stick and nodded in a paternalistic way. Behind him, Bohn stared at Rose, his expression thunderous. "That is what our Führer aims to do, my dear. He wants to share this work with all the people of the Reich."

"Even so," Rose responded, and though her voice was

steady, Sophie could see her fingers trembling. "The French will not allow such a work to leave the country."

Göring smiled. "Borders, restrictions…what does it matter, when we are all part of the same thousand-year Reich?" He patted Rose on the arm. "I appreciate your passion, my dear, but in this instance, it is misplaced. We have a glorious purpose to fulfill, all of us together."

He turned back to Bohn, and they started into the next gallery, Richter trailing behind them.

By the time Göring had finished touring the museum, the shadows of the chestnut trees were stretching long in the Jardin des Tuileries. All told, Göring had selected twenty-seven paintings for himself, along with five stained glass windows, four tapestries, three sculptures and an antique sofa. Rothschild's Vermeer, of course, was destined for Hitler's museum in Linz, along with dozens of other masterworks.

"I'll return tomorrow. I've not yet had a chance to look at what's in the basement," Göring said as he descended the staircase. In the gallery below, a pianist played an elegant Brahms melody while *Luftwaffe* soldiers stood with flutes of champagne on silver trays. "Gurlitt has let slip that one of the Brueghels would look particularly fetching in my dining room."

Sophie lingered at the top of the staircase. Watching Göring and his companions parse through the Rothschilds' belongings had been among the most disheartening experiences of her life. They spoke of the Rothschilds as if they'd abandoned their stunning collection of art in rain-soaked *chateaux* before fleeing for their lives to America, when in fact, the collection had been safeguarded in some of France's most secure bank vaults.

How would the Rothschilds ever gain back what they'd lost here today?

"You look tired, *mademoiselle*." Sophie looked up. Richter, Göring's right-hand man, stood next to her. "I'm afraid we've overstayed our welcome. But the *Reichsmarschall* is so passionate. I daresay he was more excited today than when he conquered Poland."

Sophie didn't return Richter's smile. "The *Reichsmarschall* has excellent taste."

Richter craned his neck over the banister, watching Göring's fedora-topped head below. "He's got good taste. I rather think he leans a little too heavily toward Dutch masters, but what collector doesn't have his preferences?" He smiled once more and held out his hand. "Konrad Richter. I'm sorry I didn't get a chance to introduce myself earlier."

"Sophie Brandt." She took his hand. "I work in the restoration laboratory."

"Ah…a good woman to know." Unbidden, he pressed his hand to the small of Sophie's back and guided her down the stairs. "Can I interest you in a glass of champagne?"

"I really shouldn't, not while I'm at work…"

Richter plucked a flute from a nearby tray, a film of bubbles rising to the top of the glass. "Come, now, it's been a good day. We have plenty of reason to celebrate."

Knowing that it was easier to relent, Sophie accepted the glass. "You might want to tell that to the pianist. His selections are a little slow."

Richter chuckled. "When French musicians play for a German audience, they think all we want to hear is Wagner, Brahms and Beethoven. According to them, we lost our good taste in the 1880s."

Didn't we? Sophie sipped her champagne, hoping that a suitable excuse for ending the conversation might come to hand.

"But I suppose it's not unexpected. These people want to feel superior about *something*." Richter lifted his glass to his lips. "Of course, I tend to keep such opinions to myself in polite company, but you're an outsider as well, aren't you?"

"I'm from Switzerland," Sophie replied, and Richter grinned.

"I know. I must confess, I asked Mademoiselle Valland about you. I hope you don't mind."

"Is it my place to mind?" She drained the rest of her champagne, hoping to deter Richter from his line of questioning by obstreperousness alone.

"*Mademoiselle*, I'm afraid I've offended you." He stepped closer. "I hope you and I can be friends, in time. I wouldn't want to think we're not on the same side."

Though Richter's tone was perfectly cordial, something about the way he spoke turned Sophie's blood to ice. He stepped closer and pulled a silver cigarette case from his waistcoat. "I noticed in Bohn's inventory that there was very little mentioned in the way of modern works," he continued, offering Sophie a cigarette.

Sophie declined, and Richter leaned closer still as he fitted a cigarette in the corner of his mouth. She could tell this was pageantry, a deliberate attempt to manufacture a sense of collusion that wasn't truly there. "We were told that the *Reichsmarschall* doesn't enjoy degenerate artwork, so we kept it out of the exhibition," she replied. "They're—they've been moved elsewhere in the museum."

"Of course the *Reichsmarschall* can't admit to his love of modern art. Who could, when the Führer has gone to such lengths to condemn it?" He pulled the cigarette from his mouth with a rakish grin. "But he and I do share a certain admiration for Impressionist works. I understand that you're personally involved in cataloging the degenerate collection. Might you show it to me? Discreetly, of course."

Sophie didn't respond immediately. How could she refuse Göring's right-hand man access to what he wanted?

"Discreetly, then," she replied.

"Discreetly," he repeated. "Really, *mademoiselle*, there's no need to be nervous. We're colleagues, you and I."

10

November 1940

Fabienne hurried home along Boulevard Saint-Germain, her mind on the warmth of her attic apartment. When she'd left for the atelier that morning, the day had been temperate enough; now, late in the afternoon, a chilly rain had begun to fall, and Fabienne cursed her lack of foresight. She pinched the collar of her coat tight, knowing that she would find some relief from the cold in her little garret—*hot air rises*, she recalled Maman saying in years past—but a poster pasted to the side of a Morris column caught her eye and she stopped, all thoughts of comfort driven from her mind.

The poster advertised an ongoing exhibition at the Palais Berlitz, a picture house that Fabienne recalled visiting in happier times to watch overwrought actors locked in passionate, fictional embraces. Now, it seemed the theatre was peddling fiction of a darker kind: she tore her gaze away from the hateful image it depicted to read the title.

Le Juif et la France.

The Jews and France.

Trembling, she tore the poster from the column and let the ragged strip of paper float into the puddle at her feet, pressing it down into the water with the toe of her shoe for good measure.

In the kitchenette, Lotte was tending to a nearly screaming kettle over a kerosene flame, her hair still in rollers, the unzipped back of her evening dress showing the cream V of a silk slip. "Hello," she said, glancing over her shoulder as Fabienne tossed her keys onto the divan. "Did you have fun spending another day pressing your nose to the grindstone?"

"At least the grindstone's warm," Fabienne retorted, picturing the curing oven used to set the atelier's resinoid jewelry solid. "Lev says we can't afford to let our fingers stiffen, not when we're doing such fine work."

"You know, there are other ways to keep warm." Lotte poured hot water into a *cafetière*, lips upturned in a smirk.

Fabienne set down her handbag. "Is that…?"

"Real coffee?" Lotte replied as the intoxicating scent bloomed in the air. "As I keep telling you, friendship with the Germans has its advantages." She tilted the *cafetière*, letting a dark stream pour into two cups.

"The atelier has advantages of its own," Fabienne replied, and to her surprise she found that she meant it. She thought of her oil paints, which she'd scarcely touched since Dietrich's death. If she couldn't bring herself to paint, at least her work at the atelier opened the possibility of art in another form, which set her mind ablaze with the possibilities of three-dimensional creation. "It's really quite amazing what this plastic can do."

"You've told me—*phenol formaldehyde.*" Lotte crossed to the mirror and began pulling curlers from her hair. "I don't need a science lesson every time you come home. Isn't formaldehyde embalming fluid? Is it really safe to have dangerous chemicals in the hands of someone like Lev Lowenstein?"

Fabienne watched Lotte through the snaking steam of her coffee. "How do you mean?"

"Well…" Lotte shrugged, plucking her curls loose so they settled near her shoulders like sea-foam. "Can we really trust his allegiances? Someone with his *affiliations*—"

"He's Jewish, you mean." Fabienne set down her cup, her mind flickering once more to the poster she'd ripped from the Morris column. "You're sounding an awful lot like those German friends of yours."

Lotte turned, the shrewdness dissipating from her gaze. "Of course I don't mean anything like that."

"Then, don't say such things," she snapped. Lotte turned, but not before Fabienne saw the hurt in her expression. "I've had a long day, and I'm sure you don't want to keep your officer waiting…"

"Of course." Lotte turned her attention back to the mirror, looking as relieved as Fabienne felt at avoiding a confrontation. She bent to apply her lipstick, the pose exaggerating the curves of her hourglass figure. "Enjoy your coffee. Why not take out those paints of yours?" Her reflection met Fabienne's gaze. "You could do a picture of Hans and me, dancing at La Rotonde. That's where he's taking me tonight."

"Not with your dress like that, he isn't," sighed Fabienne, coming forward to help Lotte with the zip. Not for the first time, she wished she'd found someone a little more worldly to be her lodger than Lotte, with her wide eyes and her callousness, her throwaway prejudices. How many Lottes were there in Paris, content to let the Germans' propaganda spread unchallenged through the city?

Still, she thought as the zipper snagged at Lotte's waist, *naïveté can cover all manner of sins*. How could it be that everyone in Paris was losing weight as a result of rationing, yet Lotte had managed to gain five pounds?

She stepped away, leaving the zipper half-mast. "You're pregnant," she said. "How far along are you?"

"You can tell?" Fabienne took the zipper in hand once more, bringing it over the stubborn portion of Lotte's waist to draw it up completely. She turned, her cheeks flushed. "I'd hoped to be able to hide it a little longer."

Fabienne closed her eyes, feeling, for a split second, Dietrich's hands on her belly—then she pushed the sensation away. "How far along are you?"

"Four months."

"Whose is it?"

Lotte bit her lip. "Does it matter?"

"If he plans on doing the decent thing, yes." Fabienne took another breath to calm herself down. How could Lotte have been so stupid?

Lotte sat on the divan to fasten her shoes, letting a curtain of curls fall over her face. "*The decent thing…* If he'd done the decent thing, he'd be back in Stuttgart with his wife and children."

Fabienne lowered herself into an armchair. "*Merde*, Lotte. If our neighbors find out you've got a Nazi bastard—"

"Don't use that word," Lotte shot back. "Hans isn't a true Nazi, not really. He's a bookkeeper. And he's going to get a divorce. He told me so."

Fabienne could see her newly settled life slipping away from her. She'd have to kick Lotte out of the flat, and then what? And Lev Lowenstein would be well within his rights to give her notice at the atelier, given her poor judgment in tenants. It was a miracle Lotte had escaped the notice of sharp-eyed Madame de Frontenac as it was. "How could you not have taken proper precautions?"

"We did, but you know how these things can be. And Hans really is different from the others." Lotte laid a hand on her stomach, fingers rounded over empty air as if imagining the bump that would be there in a few weeks' time. "We want this baby. Truly, Fabienne."

Fabienne had wanted her own baby too. Nearly a year ago, she'd been counting down to her own due date until the shock of Dietrich's death had cut the baby loose, unmoored by her grief, perhaps, or simply the result of a tragic fate in the making. She'd only been about three months along, not far enough to feel the tug of a child quickening in her belly like a fish on a line, a kite on a string. She'd concluded the miscarriage had been a curse: her last connection to Dietrich, severed like a cauterized artery. But given that the war had begun only a few months later, perhaps the loss of her child had been a blessing in disguise.

"We'll just have to wait," she muttered. Perhaps Lotte would share in Fabienne's blessed curse and miscarry before she could bring a child into the world during a war. "We'll wait and see what happens."

11

"How was it?"

Sophie hung up her overcoat and turned to find Gerhardt Hausler taking advantage of the early morning sunlight to add a layer of overpaint to a work by Breitner. "Yesterday's tour."

Sophie exhaled as she crossed to her worktable. "It was fine," she replied, inspecting her work in progress. She'd repaired a tear in the corner of a middling Giordano—a puncture wound made by one of Bohn's men as they pulled the canvas from the Weil–Picard collection. She'd patched the tear, knitting together the fibers from the new canvas and the old as best she could. Today, she'd begin the painstaking process of filling in the missing paint.

She unscrewed the lid on one of her jars, and Hausler looked up.

"Good gracious, that is pungent." He set down his scalpel and circled to Sophie's bench, then picked up the jar for a closer look.

"Do you mind?"

"What is the binding medium in that? Gasoline?" Hausler watched as Sophie stirred the mixture with a wooden dowel. "I've never smelled anything like that in all my days."

"Petroleum." Sophie smeared a dab of the mixture on a glass plate and began mixing it with a touch of pigment. "It's an acrylic resin mixed with mineral spirit—petroleum—and pigment. It dries quickly, but it can be removed from the canvas without damaging the original oil paint."

Hausler leaned against the table, watching with interest. "A paint that allows one to remove the restorer's handiwork as opposed to the artist's... That's rather ingenious. Is it your own formula?"

"I read about it in the papers of Dr. Martin Dix," she replied.

"I don't believe I've heard of him. Where's he based?"

Sophie paused, picturing her father's smile. "Stuttgart."

Out of the corner of her eye, she saw Hausler shift. "Would you be willing to show me his methods?"

"If you like."

She almost missed Hausler's amused tone as he made his way back to his easel. "Not much of a conversationalist, are you?"

"Not when there's work to be done, Dr. Hausler."

Several hours later a knock at the door pulled her from her work. She looked up, her back protesting at the sudden change in posture, to find Konrad Richter standing in the doorframe.

He held up a small cloth-bound book. "My dissertation on the work of Jacob Philipp Hackert, Mademoiselle Brandt. I thought you might find it of interest."

She set down her paintbrush and stepped forward, wiping

her hands on her overcoat before accepting the book. "How thoughtful."

"Please excuse the intrusion. I wanted to express my gratitude for last night," he said, and though Sophie knew he was referring to her tour of the degenerate collection, she couldn't help blushing at the insinuation beneath his words.

"Ah, of course. Dr. Richter, may I introduce Dr. Gerhardt Hausler?"

"We met in Berlin. In '37," Hausler interjected, stepping forward to offer his hand.

"Of course," Richter replied, and though he smiled, he didn't take Hausler's hand. "This is only a quick stop, I'm afraid. I simply wanted to thank you, *mademoiselle*. I hope to see you again soon."

"Of course," Sophie replied as Richter retreated down the staff staircase. She glanced at Hausler—his short exchange with Richter was yet another reminder of his privileged position in Nazi art circles, and yet the mood between the two men had seemed decidedly chilly.

"Quite a formidable fellow," Hausler murmured, turning his attention back to his easel.

Sophie thought back to the night before: Richter, holding up the curtain covering the door to the storeroom like it was opening night at the opera; Sophie, sliding beneath his tall figure. "I suppose so."

"Did *he* enjoy his visit?"

Sophie let the tinny noise of the wireless come between them. Last night, she'd led Richter through to the back of the museum, the sound of the piano fading with every step. Uncomfortably, she thought of what others might think if they were to see her slipping into the museum's darkened corners with Dr. Richter. Did she have reason to question his intentions? No. Like Göring, Richter was too blinded by the promise of personal gain to let something so base as physical urges deter him.

Sophie turned her attention back to the laboratory. "Herr Hausler, were you involved in the *Entartete Kunst* exhibition?"

Hausler straightened and set down his palette, shifting the weight off his false leg. "Weren't we all? It caused quite the stir." He removed his glasses, his usually pleasant face grave. "I can't pretend that I agree with the party's stance on modern art, but what was I to do? What was my institution to do, when we were asked to hand over our collection?"

Sophie didn't respond. In her mind's eye, she watched black smoke billowing from the bonfire in front of the Reichstag, paint blistering on charred canvas.

Hausler wiped his glasses with the hem of his shirt. "You heard, I'm sure, of what happened to the collection when the exhibition was over. The thought of such destruction… They were martyrs. Every artist; every canvas. Martyrs to the ideology of the Reich."

Though Sophie had been asked to treat the small gallery downstairs as a storeroom, she hadn't been able to help herself in giving the modern collection some semblance of order. She'd displayed what she could on the walls, the canvases hung as tightly as if they were stamps in a scrapbook: Harlequins and prostitutes were wedged next to mothers and daughters, cityscapes and wine bottles. Whereas the rest of the museum—with its negative space, its judicious selection of treasures—showcased the best in classical composition, the works here shattered the human form, expanded subjects beyond the constrictions of two dimensions, took the laws that governed Beaux Arts academies and broke them, reshuffled them, built them anew. Beyond doubt, Sophie knew that this room now contained the most significant collection of modern artwork in Europe. Even at its height as a public institution, the Jeu de Paume would never have displayed them all in a single space: Picasso, Braque, Matisse, Modigliani. Dalí and Degas, Cézanne, Toulouse-Lautrec and Mondrian, Kandinsky and Kirchner. Along the picture rail in the middle of the room, Sophie had placed dozens of smaller canvases, one atop the other in treasure-trove excess, each one waiting to be admired.

Like Sophie herself, Richter had seemed overwhelmed by the offerings in the storeroom. He'd taken one step, and then another, toward the paintings on display.

"Mein Gott," he breathed. "And Bohn's made no provisions for any of this?"

"Not to my knowledge, no," Sophie replied. "But there's nothing to be done with them, is there? Not when they're at odds with the aesthetics of the Reich."

"What a waste," Richter had murmured. He bent to examine Dalí's *Swans Reflecting Elephants*. Unframed, it sat on the rail next to the small Kirchner showing two prostitutes in repose. Slowly, gently, he ran his fingers along the Kirchner frame. "But I suppose we must all make sacrifices."

She looked up at Hausler, her blood running cold in her veins as the echo of Richter's voice faded from her mind. "Martyrs," she repeated automatically.

Rose Valland had separated the modern artworks from the rest of the collection, concealing them from Göring's prying eyes and grasping fingers, hoping that Göring's greed would blind him to the presence of sedition in his midst. She had hidden away the works too dangerous for those from whom the Nazi party demanded blind loyalty, blind faith, unquestioning devotion—paintings that questioned stasis, demanded change. Art that challenged established norms, took aim at dogma and skewered it at its heart.

Rose had trusted Sophie to help safeguard those works of

art, knowing that they represented a new way of thinking, one which the conquering Germans had already burned out from the core of their own country.

And Sophie had led a lion directly into the heart of the sanctuary.

12

The windows of the garret were fogged with cold, obscuring the view of the street below. Pulling the woolen cuff of her outermost sweater over her fist, Fabienne rubbed the condensation away to watch errant snowflakes dance in the amber glow of the streetlamp. Below, a group of young German soldiers tripped along the cobbles, drunkenly singing carols.

She backed away from the window as the belted strains of "O Tannenbaum" drifted off. Christmas was still days away, and despite the Germans' efforts to make it a holiday like every other by hoisting fir trees in squares across Paris, Fabienne knew that she would remember the Christmas season of 1940 for one reason: it was the first she would spend entirely alone.

She poured red wine into a glass and sank into the divan, picturing the apartment as it had been two Decembers ago. Dietrich had decorated with tinsel, strewing it over every available surface—where he'd found such a bewildering supply had been anyone's guess, and Fabienne hadn't bothered to ask. She simply helped, draping the tinsel over the icebox and the wardrobe, making the apartment feel like the set of some Surrealist production of *The Nutcracker.*

Back then, during the eerily quiet days when the governments of the world were trying to keep Hitler quiet by giving him scraps of territory on the outskirts of Germany, nothing had yet happened: no invasions, no bombs lighting up the night sky; no quotas restricting Jewish children from attending school, or their parents from earning a livelihood. But Dietrich and Fabienne had known what was coming. Dietrich was well into his career as a political agitator, speaking to Communist and Socialist groups about the threat Nazi Germany posed to the world, and the possibility of war settled like fog over their every thought. But that one night, that one Christmas, they'd allowed themselves to forget the coming storm.

They'd made love that night, quietly, whispering beneath the sheets in an attempt not to wake Sophie, who had come for dinner and passed out drunk on the divan. But she wouldn't have woken even if the sound of gunfire had erupted from the building next door, and the next morning the fog descended again as Dietrich set out to raise the alarm.

The guns had come, albeit briefly, but by then, Dietrich was already gone.

The door to the second bedroom opened with a creak, and Lotte emerged, stone-faced. Behind her, Hans stepped through the door, carrying the two valises that Lotte had moved in with.

"Well, that's the last of my things," she said, a brittle current beneath her matter-of-fact tone. She snugged a white mink coat over her shoulders. "I've left the last week's rent on the mattress."

Fabienne rose from the divan. "And the key?"

Lotte opened her mouth but then seemed to think twice about what she'd planned to say. Instead, she rummaged through her pocketbook, a red flush rising in her creamy cheeks. "You know, I'm disappointed in you," she said. "I thought you'd be more understanding. I really did."

Fabienne sighed, unwilling to engage in an argument they'd had countless times in the past few weeks. In her head, she could hear the echo of Lotte's pleading the night before. *Can't you see that there's an advantage in my condition? When the war's over, you'll be begging for a German child of your own.*

"You must see that there's no way around this," Fabienne offered. Of course, Hans would take care of Lotte, just as he would the child: he would, no doubt, find them some elegantly appointed flat that had once belonged to one of Paris's wealthy denizens, an apartment where the former occupants had once held Shabbat dinners. She pictured Lotte's white coat stained red, her good fortunes soaked in the blood of Germany's victims—but Lotte, of course, would only see the shine, the sparkle of a world to which she had no claim.

Lotte dropped her key on the table, then tossed back her blond curls. "Think whatever you want about me, but I know that I'm choosing love," she declared.

Fabienne turned to the window. "Good luck, Lotte. I mean it."

She could hear Lotte's huff of indignation, the scrape of the valises as Hans picked them up off the floor. "You'll need it more than I will," Lotte shot back, shutting the door with a firm click.

Fabienne exhaled heavily, then collapsed onto the divan. It was done—it *had* to be done. But despite her conviction, Fabienne couldn't help regretting the loss of someone she'd once considered a friend—her only friend, in recent months.

She lifted her glass to her lips, her fingers twitching around the stem as they so often did when she was upset, seeking a paintbrush with which to work out her frustrations. Hans would ensure Lotte's welfare, but what of Fabienne's? She'd run the numbers time and again, and even with her job at the atelier she could scarcely afford her flat without Lotte's rent. How would she manage to keep herself afloat?

She lifted her wine glass once more, surveying the distorted living room through the base of the empty glass. Last Christmas, Lotte had served as a distraction from her grief, opening bottle after bottle of wine and letting Fabienne indulge in her own recklessness—perhaps that was the reason Fabienne had been so blind to her true nature. But was Fabienne really so different? Sure, she'd seen the error of her ways, but she'd willingly turned a blind eye to Lotte's continued conduct because it had allowed her to live a comfortable life. She winced at the grubby realization. She would *still* be ignoring Lotte's conduct if Lotte hadn't been so very brazen about it. But hadn't that always been her way—to avoid unpleasant truths, to evade the consequences of her actions? Still, the result of Fabienne's belated show of principle would be the very thing she'd tried to avoid: the loss of the flat she'd shared with Dietrich, the only place she'd ever truly felt at home.

Perhaps this was her penance.

She turned, the room spinning slightly, at a short, sharp knock at the door. Lotte, no doubt, come to have the last word. Much as she didn't relish another argument, Fabienne hated the thought that Lotte might try to cause a scene. She pictured her neighbors opening their doors, craning their heads up the stairwell to catch the show.

She unlocked the door and opened it, ready for one final confrontation—and bit back her opening salvo at the sight of the woman on the landing.

Sophie's overcoat was sodden at the shoulders, the ridge of snowflakes that she'd carried in from the cobblestones forming two damp epaulettes on the threadbare serge. Beneath the brim of her cloche hat, Sophie's cheeks were rosy, bitten by the cold—and by the effort, no doubt, of climbing up six flights of stairs with a battered briefcase.

Sophie shouldered past her, and Fabienne, bewildered and off balance, stumbled into the doorframe to avoid bumping into her estranged sister-in-law.

Without preamble, Sophie set the briefcase down on the kitchen table. Fabienne glanced down at the puddle forming at Sophie's feet as she pinched the clasps. The case sprang open, and Fabienne stepped forward.

A painting rested atop Sophie's bottles of solvent, a small canvas, wrapped in linen. Sophie twitched aside the linen to reveal two naked women, one hunched over and one leaning back, their faces painted in broad swathes of blue and green.

Even in her wearied state, Fabienne recognized the canvas for what it was. *Kirchner*, she thought, feeling oddly and unwarrantedly triumphant.

"Fabienne." Sophie looked up, light glinting off her fogging spectacles. "I need your help."

PART TWO

13

June 1936

The long, vaulted galleries of the Louvre amplified every whisper, each footfall audible as crowds of hundreds circulated amid masterpieces, but to Fabienne, twisting her brush in paint as if turning a dial on a wireless, all noise dimmed when she applied color to canvas.

"She's been at it for hours, now," she heard someone whisper, and out of the corner of her eye she saw she'd gathered something of an audience. It was to be expected. The Louvre was a public space, after all, and the novelty of creation was as fascinating to the museum's visitors as the finished works themselves. It was a practice encouraged by her instructors at the Académie des Beaux-Arts: to pack up her battered box of paints and plant herself in front of a canvas, attempting to learn the mastery of the artist by reproducing the painting as closely as she could. She didn't mind people watching while she painted, nor even when they commented about her work—at least, not until some man inevitably interrupted with some inane attempt at flirtation. Didn't they realize she was working?

She mixed cadmium yellow and viridian with zinc white, adding the barest whisper of cerulean on her palette knife in an attempt to approximate the pale shade of green that van Gogh had used to paint an olive tree in a copse of billowing wheat, ruing, for a moment, the texture of her cheap pigments. She would have preferred to buy better quality paints—Old Holland or Mussini, custom-mixed oils from Sennelier on the Left Bank. As antiquated as the practice was, she even dreamed of mixing her own paints, purchasing ground pigments—bright powders made of minerals and plant matter, their vibrancy pulled from the earth in all its forms—and mixing them with oils of her choosing: linseed and walnut and poppy, each with its own drying properties that lent the pigments their unique look and feel. But Fabienne was still a student, with a student's pocketbook. She couldn't afford to be so choosy in her materials.

She daubed the paint on her canvas, then pulled her focus back from the olive tree to survey the composition as a whole, satisfied with her work. Van Gogh's *Wheat Field with Cypresses* was a study in the art of movement, above all else, and she felt she'd captured that, at least in some small part: the unpredictability of the wind as it caressed periwinkle clouds and ran through a sea of golden wheat. But her colors were off, just slightly, on the cypress grove. She pursed her lips, comparing her flat reproduction to the three-dimensional effect van Gogh had achieved in the original.

She loaded her paintbrush once more and added lighter touches of yellow and green to the grove. *There*, she thought, satisfied, as the trees seemed to round beneath her brush, her paints thick and gleaming. She turned her attention back to the olive tree, adding dashes of darkness on its twisting trunk.

"Beautiful work," she heard from over her shoulder, and though Fabienne was used to ignoring the occasional compliment, something about the delivery—quiet and kindly, with a hint of an accent—made her look up.

Though he wasn't the most handsome man Fabienne had ever seen, his was a face she immediately longed to paint: young, with deep blue eyes and a freckle-dusted nose that, she suspected, had been broken at least once. His suit sat too large on his thin frame, and Fabienne might have mistaken him for a youth but for the creases that scored deeply down his cheeks and in the corners of his eyes.

He smiled, and Fabienne couldn't help feeling the corners of her own mouth lift in response. "Thank you," she replied, dabbing excess paint onto the edge of her palette. She waited for him to continue. The men who spoke to her always did, adding some predictable line: *But the art's not nearly as beautiful as the artist!* "My sister tells me that you're the most accomplished of the academy students who paint here. I hope you don't mind, I had to see for myself."

"And was she right?" Fabienne asked.

He stepped close to examine her easel, then looked up at the van Gogh. "She was."

Fabienne chuckled. "From what I understand, sisters usually are," she said. "Though, not being one myself, I can't say for certain."

He inclined his head and made as if to turn away, and to Fabienne's own surprise, she called after him. "I have to ask, what gives your sister such authority on the offerings of the academy students?"

He grinned. "She's a student at the École du Louvre," he replied and stepped closer once more. "Art history, though she plans to be a restorer. She's here most evenings, like yourself, to study the greats."

Fabienne flipped open her paint box: half-squeezed tubes and dozens of brushes, rags and jars of spirit. She plunged her brush in a jar of turpentine, turning the clean spirit muddy. "So you've seen me here before, have you?"

"I join her here when I can. She likes to tell me about what she's learned," he explained as Fabienne wiped and stowed away the brush. "I feel as though I've attended her classes myself, with all she's taught me."

"Two students for the price of one," Fabienne offered. "Perhaps you ought to enroll yourself."

"One's all we can afford at the moment, so we make do," he said, and Fabienne paused as she closed her paint box. Had she caused offence?

He chuckled. "I was never one for books, anyways. That was Sophie's specialty. But she tells me what she's learned, and it seems to stick, somehow, better than anything I ever learned in a classroom. Dietrich Brandt," he said, circling around the easel to offer his hand. "I'm pleased to meet you."

Fabienne hastily cleaned remnants of paint from her fingers. "Fabienne," she replied. Out of the corner of her eye it seemed that van Gogh's wheat field swayed as if in a sudden gust, caught in the updraft created as they clasped hands.

14

December 1940

Fabienne stared down at the open briefcase, her reeling mind suddenly still. The painting seemed to stare back at her, the two girls depicted on the canvas leaning toward each other, as if laughing conspiratorially at Fabienne's bewilderment. From the street, she heard the punctuated laugh of a soldier, staggering with his compatriots across the cobbles.

"Is this a…?"

"Kirchner. Yes." Sophie leaned against the sink. "You haven't got a drink going spare, have you? Only it's been a long day."

For you and me both, thought Fabienne as she crossed to the cupboard to pull out two glasses. In many ways, the painting was not nearly as shocking as the arrival of the person who'd carried it. The last time Sophie had been here, she'd made it quite clear that she'd never return, much less with a priceless painting in tow. *A Kirchner*, Fabienne thought again as she poured two glasses of Burgundy. How had Sophie managed to get her hands on that?

Sophie took the proffered glass of wine but didn't return Fabienne's perfunctory toast. Clearly, she was as rattled as Fabienne felt. She'd been a frequent visitor once, alongside Fabienne's artist friends and Dietrich's political colleagues, discussing the merits of Picasso's and Braque's experimentations with form. She'd been here the night that Fabienne had invited André Breton, who'd nodded approvingly at Fabienne's paintings before Dietrich had said something to drive him away.

"What are you doing here?" Fabienne asked. "You told me the last time you left—"

"That I would never return. I remember." Sophie crossed her arms, resting her tumbler of wine in the crook of her elbow. "But I'm not here to dredge up the past." She fixed Fabienne with a hard stare, her expression hardened further by the single bare bulb hanging over the kitchenette table. "This painting. Can you reproduce it?"

Whatever Fabienne had been expecting to hear, this surely wasn't it. "Can I *what*?"

"Reproduce it." Sophie tapped her glass impatiently. "Don't play innocent. You know what I'm asking. Don't make me say it out loud."

Fabienne bent over the suitcase, and Sophie stepped out of the light as she lifted the painting to study it closer. Two figures, painted with vibrant pigments and loose brushstrokes—well, that was characteristic of Kirchner, she supposed. The two girls stared out at the viewer, one with a half smirk on her face, both backlit by the sun streaming in from the window behind them, their limbs captured as swoops of green and pink and yellow, exaggerated and angular. Like most of Kirchner's paintings, the canvas was more about feeling than form, capturing the indefinable essence of a moment, rather than the moment itself.

"I suppose it's possible," she murmured, but it was the very simplicity of the piece that made it challenging. How could she reproduce a feeling?

"You *suppose*?" Fabienne looked up to see Sophie square her shoulders beneath her damp overcoat. Belatedly, she realized she should have offered to hang it up. "I need better than that."

Fabienne had forgotten Sophie's direct manner: it was a quality she'd once admired, back when they were close. "I don't know what you want me to tell you, Sophie. You show up here after all this time, and you want me to...to what, to forge this painting? I'm surprised it even bears saying, but it's illegal, and you know as well as I do that it's impossible to sell an exact replica." She tilted the painting, the better to study the angle of the brushstrokes. "I could paint a...a study, for this piece, one of the girls, perhaps, but what do you want with it? Do you plan to sell it on the black market?"

"It's not for the black market. What do you take me for?" Sophie shrugged out of her damp jacket, and Fabienne caught a glimpse of its ragged lining. *Perhaps she* ought *to be selling on the black market*, she thought, and the idea suddenly didn't sound quite so bad: flooding the market with counterfeit Rembrandts and Vermeers for greedy German officers, taking advantage of their deep pocketbooks and devaluing their acquisitions in one. "Those days, back at the Louvre. You were the best at what you did, the best at reproducing artwork—"

"They were good enough, Sophie, but I never tried to pass them off as anything but studies."

Sophie's lip curled. "There it is—that little glimmer of moral fiber."

"As I recall, you were the one who barged in here and asked

for my help." She stared at Sophie for a long moment, expecting her to storm out, but then Sophie sighed.

"You're right," she said, "and I'm sorry for that. Truth be told, I wish I had another option. I wish I could tell you more, but if I give you my word that what I'm doing isn't underhanded—"

Fabienne snorted at the blatant falsehood. "Once, your word might have been enough for me," she said, though she was already thinking about how she would approach the challenge of reproducing the painting. *That shade of red might be tricky, but with the right blend of pigments...* "Is it illegal?"

Out of the corner of her eye, she saw Sophie shift. "One might argue that legality is something of a fluid concept in times of war."

"One might." Fabienne set down the painting. "Is it dangerous?"

"For me more than for you," Sophie replied. "Very few of the people I interact with these days know of our... connection, and I intend to keep it that way."

The people I interact with... Fabienne's mind flashed to when she'd seen Sophie outside the Jeu de Paume: German guards, surrounding the building. "Legality might be a fluid concept at present, Sophie, but it won't stay that way—not for long, God willing. Can you promise me that our actions will fall on the right side of history, when all is said and done?"

Sophie let out a deeply held breath. Perched on the kitchen counter, with one foot curled beneath her and the other touching the floor for balance, a glass of wine in her hand, she looked, incongruously, like a cowboy in some American picture: a gunslinger in a saloon, waiting for trouble to walk through the door. "You have my word on this. If *he* were here—if Dietrich were still alive—he would approve of what I've asked you to do."

Fabienne hadn't said his name aloud, not since the funeral. For one split second, it had almost felt like the old days, Fabienne and Sophie sharing confidences over a bottle of wine, but with the mention of Dietrich, reality had come flooding back. It was a low blow, and it was clear that Sophie knew it too. She avoided Fabienne's eyes, staring instead at the painting as she waited for Fabienne's answer.

"Well," Fabienne said bitterly, "in that case, how can I refuse?" She planted her hands on the table and stared down at the painting, Dietrich's memory suddenly, unbearably present, as though he, too, were looking at the canvas from over her shoulder. "I will need to keep the original while I work."

Sophie straightened. "Of course. You have until next Monday. No later than Monday, do you understand? I'll pick it up in the morning, once curfew lifts."

Fabienne walked Sophie to the door, as eager for her to leave as Sophie seemed to be to go. Between her unexpected arrival and Lotte's difficult departure, Fabienne was reeling—she longed to be left alone in her apartment, for however long it remained to her.

Her apartment.

"One final thing," she said suddenly. "I'll expect compensation. When you come to pick it up. The risk I'm taking, let alone the work involved… I'll need to be paid for what I'm doing."

Sophie turned on the threshold. For a moment, she looked crestfallen, but then she nodded. "Of course."

Her sodden shoulders nearly dry, Sophie started down the stairs, but despite herself, Fabienne couldn't help asking one final question.

"Why me?"

Sophie paused.

"You know other artists, surely," Fabienne continued. "You're talented yourself. Why does it have to be me?"

Sophie turned. "I trust you," she said finally. "Despite everything that's happened between us, I still trust you."

15

Sophie descended the staircase, moving as quickly as she could manage. Though it had been years since she'd been here, she could still recall where the ancient stone steps were overworn, where the rounded banister's iron nails wore through the wood. She crossed through the small courtyard, and it felt to Sophie as if muscle memory was propelling her forward beneath the swaying laundry on wire lines and through the oak door that opened onto Boulevard Saint-Germain.

She'd lost her mind: that much was clear, Sophie knew, as she charged onto the sidewalk.

What else could explain her hopeless request? She pictured the look of shock on Fabienne's sallow face, knowing that even as she'd asked that she was demanding the impossible. No one could recreate an oil painting in little more than a week. And that was assuming that Sophie could return the forgery to the museum before anyone noticed the original was gone. What had she been thinking?

Sophie crossed the empty street, stepping into brown slush before reaching the opposite sidewalk. No, she hadn't been thinking of the consequences as she'd carried the Kirchner out of the storeroom and up to the restoration lab. She'd not thought about the risk as she folded the canvas carefully in linen and set it in her briefcase, grateful for Gerhardt Hausler's brief absence as she clasped the case shut. No, she'd been thinking of the flames outside the Reichstag all those years ago, the heat on her cheeks as they consumed Germany's cultural heritage.

For that was the final fate awaiting the Kirchner, along with all the other works in the storeroom—the Room of Martyrs, as she'd come to think of it: destruction, once the collection became too unwieldy to manage, to prove the supremacy of the Nazis' ideology on race, on culture, on thought itself. The rest of the works in the museum—those that Göring and his cronies were singling out and sending into the Reich—those could be recovered, once this terrible war was won and the Nazis were held to account for their crimes. But modern art? Degenerate art? It would all be consigned to the flames if Hitler had his way.

She walked east, eyeing the brasseries along Rue Monge as waiters hoisted chairs onto empty tables. She glanced at her wristwatch in the spilled light of a café: only twenty minutes until the curfew went into effect, and Sophie knew better than to dawdle. Her luck had held far longer than she'd hoped already.

There would indeed be consequences for Sophie if her theft was discovered. And what right had she to pull Fabienne into her ill-conceived plan? She flinched at the recollection of what she'd said in the flat, how Fabienne had shut down entirely at the mention of Dietrich. Perhaps it had been unfair of her to throw his name in her face, but Sophie knew that he would have approved of her actions—approved and lent his support, in some form or another.

She reached her apartment block and slipped through to the crumbling courtyard, then sped up the staircase before unlocking her door with trembling hands. She consulted her watch once more—only five minutes to curfew—and she strode to the window, not stopping to turn on a light. She knew her small apartment by memory, knew to sway her hip so as not to bump into the squashy love seat while passing the kitchen table. She knew every print on the wall, reproductions of paintings that had hung in the Jeu de Paume before the war.

She knew, too, the view outside her third-story window: the boulangerie on the street corner opposite, with the bench where homeless people had slept, before the war had pushed them all south. She looked over the rooftops at the shadowed dome of the *église* two blocks over. Even in the pale glow of the half-moon, she would have known the curlicued balconies of the building opposite, the narrow windows of apartments abandoned since last May's mass exodus.

What would she do, if she were to open the window and find the unmarked vans that idled in front of the Jeu de Paume waiting below to take her away? She shuddered, picturing Bohn and his men kicking down her door and dragging her out into the night, the van continuing on down the Boulevard Saint-Germain, soldiers pouring out in front of Fabienne's apartment block.

Could she live with Fabienne's death on her conscience, if it came to it?

But then, if Fabienne's role in the forgery were discovered, Sophie doubted that she herself would be in a position to regret anything at all.

16

Fabienne and Dietrich strolled through the Jardin des Tuileries in the deepening twilight, Fabienne's painting case swinging loosely from Dietrich's arm. She glanced back at the lighted windows of the Louvre, amazed at Dietrich's patience. Though she'd continued working at her van Gogh until the museum's closing hour, Dietrich had been standing outside the entrance, waiting with an offer to walk her home.

The night was fragrant with the scent of cut grass and lilac as couples and children, their features barely visible in the dusk, sauntered past.

"So you're an artist," Dietrich remarked as they passed by the Grand Bassin, the fountain's waterworks splashing merrily in the dark.

"That's stating the obvious," she retorted lightly, "given

that the only reason I'm not holding your hand is for fear of getting turpentine on that jacket of yours."

Without looking down, Dietrich threaded his fingers through hers, slowing his loping stride to match her pace. "And is that what you want to do with your life? Paint?"

Fabienne had been asked that same question more frequently than she'd cared to admit, almost always accompanied by an undercurrent of derision—*Painting? Really?*—but Dietrich had spoken without any hint of judgment.

"My parents would be horrified to hear me admit it, but it is," she replied.

"Why would they object?"

She shrugged, shying away from a door she'd rather keep closed. "They're farmers. They just don't see the point of it," she replied.

Dietrich squeezed her hand. "It's not always easy for parents to understand their children," he said. "Do they live in Paris?"

"No," she replied, intending to leave her answer at that—but then she surprised herself by elaborating. "I come from a small town east of the city...a village, really. Wine-making, you know. I was engaged to be married, but a few days before the wedding, I just...packed a bag and left. Came to Paris with ten francs in my pocket and a box of paints."

"I'm sorry," Dietrich replied softly. "What happened?"

She sighed, picturing the wedding dress she'd left hanging in her bedroom, illuminated by a moonlight glow as she slipped out into the darkness. "I grew up. I suppose that sounds heartless," she continued, lifting her chin in an attempt at nonchalance. "He's a good man, and he'll make a good husband. But I knew that I was meant to be here, in Paris."

Dietrich nodded. "You wanted a different life, and you chose to pursue it," he said slowly. "How could such a thing be heartless, when to stay together would have caused pain to you both? It takes courage to know your path and stay true to it, when the world is telling you to do otherwise."

Fabienne could feel something loosen in her chest: a tightness she hadn't known was there. "You think so?" She fell silent, thinking of her handsome young fiancé, his dark hair and crooked smile. "I suppose it's all in the past, now. He's probably married with ten children, and I'm here selling my studies to pay for schooling...and painting my originals when I have the time."

"You're pursuing your dream," Dietrich replied, and Fabienne looked at him askance. Had anyone ever understood her so immediately, so completely? "What do your originals look like?"

Fabienne lifted her gaze, contemplating the question. Though the Jardin was too heavily lit up for the night sky to be properly visible, she could make out a handful of stars overhead, faintly dotting the blue. "They look...modern," she concluded, thinking of the loops and swirls that made up her work, her palette, dabs of blues and greens, which gave her subjects an almost aquatic glow. "I've not shown them, not properly. Just to friends."

"Perhaps you might show them to me, one day," Dietrich said, but then he shook his head. "Forgive me, I don't mean to presume."

"It's all right." In fact, Fabienne was pleased at the thought of becoming close enough to Dietrich to show him her work. "Perhaps I will."

They continued on, the silence between them companionable as they passed beneath the rustling leaves of the chestnut trees. From somewhere nearby, they heard the sound of hooves on packed earth, the trotting of a horse and rider.

"And what about you? What do you do to keep yourself busy through the days?"

"I'm a mechanic," he replied. "I work on municipal vehicles. Buses, trams. I always fancied myself a councilman, but perhaps that's something for the future. I'm a union representative at the Citroën factory."

"A union man?" Fabienne asked. "You're interested in politics, then?"

"All my life," he replied without elaboration.

"Me too," Fabienne offered. "I'm part of the Socialist students' organization at the academy."

"Socialism." Dietrich's tone brightened. "Do you have strong views on this?"

"Strong enough to believe in the rights of workers. Strong enough to know it's the best alternative to what the right has to offer." Fabienne knew that Socialism was less than palatable to many people, but she'd long ago stopped tempering her opinions to suit other people's sensibilities, particularly in the wake of last month's elections which had swept a coalition of left-wing parties into power. "We've got a Socialist prime minister, now—and look at all he's accomplished already. Strengthening the unions, standing up to the far right..." Her heart swelled at the bright possibilities, and she echoed the new government's slogan. *"Tout est possible!"*

"An artist, a Socialist and an optimist," Dietrich concluded. "Is there anything beyond your reach?"

She smiled, stepping over a loose cobble on the path. "I don't know that I'd call myself an optimist. A realist, perhaps. I see what's happening elsewhere in Europe—Germany, Spain—and I think that banding together is the only way to keep our country moving forward." She glanced at Dietrich. "But perhaps you'd have a more informed view on the matter than I do."

"Because of my accent?" He let out a breath, tilting his head in a sort of acknowledgment. "My sister tells me to be more discreet, but I'm afraid that discretion is something I've always struggled with. We left Germany a year ago. I didn't see a future in it. I still don't, not with Hitler in power. He's leading the country down a dark path."

"And that's why you came to France?"

He looked up, squinting, into a gaslit streetlamp. "We could have gone anywhere. My sister chose France for the museums, but I have come to appreciate so much more about this city. I've been able to build a life for myself here. Sophie has gained an education." He slowed, circling to face Fabienne head-on. "I hope you can appreciate that I don't share this information with you lightly. We tend to tell people we're Swiss, to avoid uncomfortable conversations."

For Dietrich to trust her with this part of him sent a thousand questions spinning through Fabienne's mind, but for now, she rested a finger over her lips. "Your secret is safe with me."

They resumed their stroll, Dietrich's hand a warm and comforting weight in hers. She longed to know more: how he'd left Germany, whether he had family still living there. Even now, so many years after the Great War, Germany's actions cast a long shadow in France, and Hitler's recent activities as chancellor—bulking up Germany's army, making belligerent claims about foreign policy and Germany's Jewish population—had set its shadow growing once again. She didn't blame Dietrich's sister for concealing the truth of their origins.

He let out a wistful sigh, and as he met Fabienne's gaze all thoughts of the past fled from her mind. "I couldn't see a future in Germany. But in Paris, I dream of what my life will hold."

They had reached the far end of the Jardin des Tuileries; on either side of them, two paths rose in a gentle horseshoe curve toward the Musée de l'Orangerie and the Musée Jeu de Paume. Beyond the Jardin's open gates, motorcars circled the Place de la Concorde, swirling around the Luxor Obelisk like leaves caught in a draft.

Fabienne allowed herself to slow. There was something different about Dietrich: his steady manner; his slow-to-ripen smile. Another woman might grow impatient at his lack of pretension, his careful silences, but Fabienne led him out into the square, already picturing the quiet corner of a nearby brasserie where they could continue their conversation.

She wanted to know everything about Dietrich Brandt, and they had all the time in the world.

17

December 1940

Frost laced heavily on the paned windows of the atelier, but the workroom was warm, heated by a curing oven and a dozen workers deep in concentration. Fabienne scraped her broom across the floor, sending particles of resin swirling in the air. Though she longed for the opportunity to try her hand at a set of earrings, she knew better than to ask for a more complicated task than what she'd been given. Her mind was far too fixed on the question of forging the Kirchner for her to be of any use beyond work she'd done a thousand times before.

She swept the dust into a pile, thinking about the technical aspects of finishing a painting within a week. After Sophie's departure, Fabienne had stared at the Kirchner for hours, and while she was confident that she could replicate his practiced strokes, she knew that the true test of a forgery lay not in the top layer of paint but in the countless brushstrokes beneath: the slowly built-up layers of impasto that gave a painting its depth.

She swept her broom across the dust pile, obliterating the tidy mound. Though the dust now lay flat across the floor, individual particles lay one atop the other, creating a small rise on the tiled floor. *Oil paint takes months to dry*, she thought to herself, *even when painted thinly.* The Kirchner had been painted over twenty years ago: even if Fabienne were to create a perfect reproduction, the paint would remain wet for weeks, months. Anyone with a cotton swab, rubbing alcohol and the barest modicum of common sense would uncover the illusion with ease. If someone were to perform even a cursory examination of the painting, they would know within seconds that it was a forgery.

She sighed, thinking of the equipment in her flat she'd used to test different compositions of paint: her ground-up pigments and tubes of commercially prepared oil paint; her small jars of oils, linseed and lilac, walnut and lavender. Certain oils had the ability to dry faster than others, but even if she were to mix the fastest-drying of her oils with pigments, she still had no hope that the painting would be dry within a week. Even if she had a month, it would be wet to the touch.

"*Pardon.*" Myriam brushed past her with a tray of buttons. Fabienne fell into step beside her. "May I see?"

Myriam paused and held out the tray so that Fabienne could admire its contents. It contained dozens of Bakelite buttons topped with rhinestones, the plastic smooth and cream-colored. "How beautiful."

"*Merci,*" Myriam replied. "They're for a Rochas commission. I'm about to set the resin so that the rhinestones hold solid. Would you mind?"

"Of course," Fabienne replied, hurrying forward to open the curing oven's door.

"The heat must be low and steady," Myriam offered as she slid the tray in, "or else the liquid resin might become brittle. I'd be happy to show you how to work with it, if you like."

Though she'd been at the atelier for a month now, Fabienne still found it astonishing that Paris's couture industry continued to operate in the midst of war. Even with the reduction in the number of fashion houses—and the introduction of haute couture ration cards, which set stringent new limits on the kinds of clothing available for purchase—Paris's fashion still endured. But the war would doubtless bring further changes to the industry. Only last week, Lev's partner Dufy had mentioned that couturiers were relying on their supplies of prewar textiles to put out their 1941 collections. Next year's collections would have to be ersatz, created from manufactured products with names that lay unfamiliar upon everyone's lips: rayon and fibranne, created from wood pulp and flaxseed.

Short and round, with prematurely white hair and an even disposition, Dufy was usually a cheering presence at the atelier, but his heavy brows had creased with worry at the thought of their jewelry being used on substandard materials. "It will be a dark day, indeed, when we have to put our buttons on a rayon blouse," Dufy had said ominously.

She watched as Myriam returned to her workbench, knowing that fibranne was the least of their concerns. If rayon and fibranne kept their atelier in business, Fabienne would wear such materials without complaint.

She circled to the dustbin, staring at the resin on Myriam's workstation, thinking of her mixed paints. If she were to mix her pigments with resin and somehow induce the paint to harden...

She shook her head, sheer practicality stopping her in her tracks. Even if she were to spirit liquid resin from the atelier and mix it into her pigments, how would she set the mixture solid?

Fabienne was pulled from her thoughts by the sound of shouting from upstairs. Moments later, the door swung open, and a gendarme stormed down, followed closely on his heels by Dufy, taking the steps two at a time.

"I must protest, in the strongest possible terms!" Dufy raged as the gendarme reached the workroom floor. Behind Fabienne, Myriam let out a small noise, little more than a squeak. "On whose authority—?"

Ignoring Dufy's continued protestations, the gendarme tucked his brimmed cap beneath his arm and addressed Fabienne and her bewildered coworkers. "Good afternoon, ladies. As many of you are no doubt aware, the Vichy government signed several new laws into being, regarding the status of Jews in France." He paused. At the top of the stairs, Lev Lowenstein watched, stone-faced. "One such law concerns alien residents of the Jewish race. Papers, please."

Dufy stepped forward, the chain on his pocket watch swinging above his belly. "Sir, I will not allow you to harass our staff in this way—"

"If you do not let me go about my business, I will arrest you for perverting the course of justice," the gendarme snapped, and Dufy, shocked, fell silent. "I ask again. Papers, everyone. The sooner you comply, the sooner I can let you return to your work."

Along with the rest of the staff, Fabienne circled to retrieve her handbag, her heart pounding as she stood in line before the gendarme. *Alien residents...* She'd never heard people referred to in such stark terms.

The gendarme took his time examining Fabienne's identity papers.

"I was born in Épernay," she said, and though she knew

that the gendarme had no reason to single her out, she couldn't help the frisson of fear that crept up her spine.

He handed back her identity book with a nod. *"Merci, madame."*

Fabienne stepped aside, relieved, as the gendarme turned to Myriam. She looked up at Lev, still standing at the top of the staircase. His papers, no doubt, had already been examined. The look of anguish on his face had to do with his staff below. He'd been so proud to bring Fabienne into his small circle of workers—Myriam and Beatrice and Lea, workers he and Dufy had been able to keep employed through the uncertainty of the occupation.

Madame Lowenstein's words echoed in Fabienne's mind, from a long-ago conversation. *Paris is our home. It's been our home for generations.* Lev wasn't the target of the gendarme's inquiries—not yet. But if the French police were questioning Jewish people of foreign descent, how soon before their gaze turned to those who'd been born in France?

The gendarme cleared his throat. *"Madame*, you'll have to come with me."

"I-I don't understand." Myriam's voice trembled as she looked around the workroom, her brown eyes wide. "I was born in Algiers, under the terms of the Crémieux Decree, I'm a French citizen."

The gendarme clasped his hand around her upper arm. "Not anymore, you're not."

In a shot, Lev bounded down to bar the bottom of the staircase, Hugo yipping fiercely at his heels. "How *dare* you manhandle one of my workers!"

"The Crémieux Decree was abolished at the beginning of October. As an Algerian Jew, this woman is no longer a French citizen, and she is no longer protected under French law," the gendarme shot back, roughly elbowing past Lev with Myriam in his grasp. Behind him, Dufy shouted in protest, following closely on the gendarme's heels. "I'm required to bring her in for questioning at the prefecture—"

"*Monsieur*, I've lived here my whole life. Please!"

"Myriam, we'll send a lawyer," Lev shouted as they reached the top of the stairs. "We won't stand for this!"

"Please, *monsieur*, I'm sure there must be some way—"

"Let her go!"

"I will be writing to Marshal Pétain personally to express my outrage," Dufy blustered. "Surely the Lion of Verdun will rectify this gross abuse of power!"

The gendarme's expression was almost pitying as he looked back at Dufy. "Marshal Pétain signed the order personally." He tightened his grip on Myriam's arm and pulled her through the door, leaving the atelier in an uproar.

18

Sophie stepped out of the museum and wrapped her overlarge coat as tightly as she could around her middle. She could hear Dietrich's voice in her head, amused and exasperated as he chided her for her lack of style—*You might as well be wearing a tablecloth*—but she was thankful for the excess tweed as the chilly afternoon air hit her cheeks. She walked into the Jardin des Tuileries, unwrapping the hunk of cheese she'd brought for lunch, wishing she had a piece of ham—or, better still, a pillowy baguette—to accompany it, but the vendor who'd once sold such treats in the park was long gone, either driven off by deprivation or arrested.

She wandered down the steps behind the museum, wishing she had time to linger beneath the trees—but Hildebrand Gurlitt had turned up at the museum with a list of several damaged works of art he wanted repaired in time for another visit from Hermann Göring. Whereas the last show had displayed pieces from Edouard de Rothschild's private collection, Gurlitt had asked for several pieces from Alphonse Kann's gallery to be put on show—including one work by Greuze which had been damaged during Bohn's latest raid. It would require quick work on Sophie's part to restore it in time for Göring's arrival... Her mind was so fixed on how she might repair a tear in the canvas that she almost walked past the woman standing beneath the shade of a mulberry tree, the wide brim of her burgundy hat pulled low over her eyes.

"Burgundy?" Sophie hissed as Fabienne fell into step beside her. "I thought you had more sense than to turn up here looking like a...a..."

"A what?" Dressed in a matching jacket and high heels, Fabienne stood out like a beacon: she flicked the butt of her cigarette to the ground and adjusted the fit of her calfskin gloves. "First rule of deception, Sophie. If one has something to hide, they might as well do it in plain sight."

"I thought we'd agreed to keep any signs of our...affiliation...to a minimum," Sophie whispered through gritted teeth. She resisted the urge to look around, terrified of drawing the attention of the soldiers who strolled through the gardens. "What are you doing here?"

Fabienne strode ahead. "It's about your commission. I'm afraid I can't manage it."

Sophie nearly stopped in her tracks. "What do you mean, you can't manage it? You told me it could be done!"

"I know," Fabienne replied, urging Sophie on with a sweep of her handbag-laden arm. "But the deadline you've set, it's impossible. An oil painting, in the span of a week?" She looked down, rearranging the set of her glove. "You must admit, it was an unreasonable request."

"I'm not asking you for a–a forensic recreation," Sophie sputtered. "I only want something that can fool the eye."

"The eyes of some of the most renowned art dealers left in the city." Fabienne spun delicately to face the museum, nodding at the façade with a jerk of her chin. "I've been watching the comings and goings all morning. Hildebrand Gurlitt won't be easily fooled."

Sophie exhaled, feeling as though a thousand sets of eyes were watching from the nearby windows of the German-occupied Le Meurice hotel. "I can give you more time. You told me it could be done."

"Be reasonable." Fabienne leaned closer. "You know why my reproductions are good? It's because they have *life* to them. They have the sort of depth that only comes from layers and layers of paint. And you know as well as I do that those layers take time to dry. Months. Years, depending on how thick the impasto is." She crossed her arms and stepped back with a shrug. "I'm sorry, but it can't be done. The moment anyone takes a closer look at the painting—if they tried to rub it with an alcohol swab—"

"They'll know." Sophie pictured Gurlitt studying the painting, its glossed swirls reflected in the round panes of his glasses, or Richter, running his elegant hands over the frame.

She glanced back at the Jeu de Paume. "I may have a solution," she said. "It may not be perfect, but it might just work. I need to get back to the museum. Can you meet me at Les Deux Magots? Six o'clock?"

19

Though the Boulevard Saint-Germain was devoid of automobiles, Les Deux Magots was packed, men and women sitting cheek by jowl beneath the serene gaze of the two plaster alchemists set high on the café's central pillar. Though the days of the café's famous *chocolat chaud* were long gone, Fabienne twitched her fingers around a glass of Sancerre, watching the waiters as they threaded between tables.

Fabienne let out a breath as Sophie's tweed figure appeared outside the paned glass window. She approached the door, the weight of a modest suitcase throwing her off balance as she came into the café. She tucked a lock of hair behind her ear with varnish-chipped fingers, and Fabienne recalled the gesture from years past. There had always been something disheveled, distracted about Sophie. In years past, Dietrich used to tease her that even if she were to arrive at an event in an evening gown, she'd still have paint smudges on the hem.

Did she have friends these days, a sweetheart? Without Dietrich to bring her out of her shell, Fabienne suspected not. She recalled a young woman from the Sorbonne's Student Union of Socialists who'd always seemed to set Sophie's cheeks aflame whenever she attended one of Dietrich's rallies…

But in the wake of Dietrich's murder, perhaps Sophie, like Fabienne, had cut all ties to her former life.

When Fabienne lost her husband, Sophie had lost her brother. In all the long, dark days following Dietrich's death, it was the thing that Fabienne tended to forget.

She lifted her hand, signaling for a waiter to bring a second glass of wine as Sophie made her way to the table.

"Going away for the weekend?" Fabienne said as Sophie wedged herself into the chair opposite.

She grimaced, pushing the suitcase beneath the table. "Your supplies—your paints," she muttered, nodding hastily as a waiter set down a minuscule glass of white wine. "Perhaps we would have been better to do this somewhere else. The Bois de Boulogne—"

"You were the one who chose this location, not me," Fabienne retorted, holding out her glass. "Plain sight, remember?"

"Since when did you have any experience in subterfuge?"

Fabienne raised an eyebrow. "If I did, I'd hardly tell you about it, would I?" She could tell that she was getting under Sophie's skin but couldn't quite help herself: taking a pithy approach seemed easier, somehow, than adopting Sophie's rigid fear. "Now. What makes these paints better suited to our task at hand than my oils?"

Sophie tapped her glass against Fabienne's. "I've mixed the pigments in a solution of acrylic resin and petroleum. It will look and feel similar to oil paint, but its drying time is much quicker." She sighed, drumming her fingers against the glass. "It won't be perfect, but you'll be able to paint multiple layers in a matter of hours. It ought to withstand some basic scrutiny."

Fabienne frowned. "Can I mix the pigments together?"

"Yes. You'll have to work quickly, though. When I say they dry fast…" Sophie glanced around the room, shoulders hunched. "I would recommend opening a window while you work. These paints have a…strong odor."

Fabienne took another sip of her wine, her heart thrumming at the thought of working with Sophie's paints. "Interesting. Petroleum and…?"

"Acrylic resin," Sophie replied. "The general method has been in use for some years as a cheaper alternative for industrial paints, but there are some artists in South America who have adapted it for artistic purposes. My father studied how it might be used to develop a line of restoration-specific paints…" Sophie screwed her eyes shut as she rubbed her brow. "It's all very technical, I know."

"No," Fabienne said. Beneath the table, she pulled the briefcase closer to her legs, longing to examine the jars within, study the texture of the paint, see how it felt on her brush. She thought of the liquid resin used to create Atelier Dufy's beautiful jewelry. How did Sophie's acrylic resin dry without the use of a curing oven? "It's clever."

"It's more than clever." Sophie fixed Fabienne with an even stare. "It's revolutionary."

She couldn't help admiring Sophie's passion. "I stand corrected," she replied. "How much have you given me?"

"Enough to get you started."

Fabienne nodded. "I'll see what I can do." She stood, smiling apologetically to the woman sitting at the next table over as she edged out of the banquette. Sophie scattered a few francs across the tablecloth and followed.

The sun had ducked behind the *église* opposite the café,

and Fabienne pinched the lapels of her burgundy jacket tight against the growing chill.

"Well," said Sophie. She fiddled with her gloves, as if wishing she still carried the suitcase that Fabienne had set down on the sidewalk. "I suppose I'd better let you get on…"

"Just a moment longer. Earlier, we'd touched on the matter of payment." Fabienne lowered her voice. "There's a couple that lives in my building, and they need papers."

Sophie's gaze darted up the street. "You can't be serious."

Fabienne huffed. Did they really have to go through this whole charade? "You've been living off of false papers for years. I know you can get them."

"From a-a contact in Strasbourg, maybe, but I can't just hop on a train. I'll pay you in money, ration tickets—"

Fabienne clasped her handbag, letting Sophie bluster for a moment longer. She glanced at the lit windows of the café. Who was to say that they weren't being watched by someone at a corner table?

"This is how it works," she said finally. "You want my help. This is what I want in return." She picked up the suitcase, hearing the clink of glass jars within as she touched the brim of her hat. "After all, it's not as if I'm doing this to build my own reputation. You're procuring the services of a professional artist, *chérie*. I expect to get paid for my work."

20

The train sped through the honeycombed tunnels of Paris's metro, and Sophie closed her eyes, the swaying movement lulling her into a doze before the compartment lurched around a corner. She jolted awake, reaching in a sudden panic for a handle, but not before tripping over the feet of the person next to her. Looking up, her heart dropped as she met the eyes of a German officer.

"Are you all right, *mademoiselle*?" He rested a steadying hand on her waist while the subway car straightened along its track, and Sophie felt her cheeks redden.

"I'm fine," she mumbled, stepping away as the train rolled into its stop.

The crush of people around her shifted in the current created by the compartment's open door, and the officer tipped his cap before swirling out along with a couple in heavy tan overcoats and a woman with a cane.

Sophie dropped into the seat the woman had vacated with a sigh. She'd not expected such a crowd on the metro, not on a Sunday morning. Since the occupation, Paris's residents seemed more inclined to attend weekly church services, whether out of a newfound sense of faith or a need for comfort, Sophie wasn't sure. She didn't share in their routines. She'd learned far too long ago not to put her trust in any authority higher than herself.

At the next station, she stepped out into the overcast morning and walked along Boulevard Edgar Quinet, following the browned vines of ivy-clad walls to the limestone entrance of the Montparnasse Cemetery. Like in the Jardin des Tuileries, the sounds of the city seemed to fall away within the cemetery's brick walls, but whereas the Jardin's expansive acres were green and lush, this space was crowded and gray, limestone plots set side by side in mismatched proximity. Sophie felt a brief satisfaction at the permanence that death afforded it. Unlike Paris's parks and gardens, its administrative buildings and evacuated homes all transformed by the occupation, the city's cemeteries were immune to the harsh changes imposed by German soldiers.

She turned down a pebbled lane between ancient mausoleums, wending toward a quiet corner by the graveyard's westernmost wall. Ahead, a short man with the physique of a boxer stood before a modest tombstone, holding a bouquet of hellebore wrapped in newspaper.

He looked up as Sophie approached and removed his pageboy cap, revealing a close-shaven half-moon of stubble above his ears. "Been a while since I paid my respects," he said. He held out the flowers with something of a shrug and placed them at the base of the headstone, their purple blooms stark against the brightness of the new stone. "Pulled them from a garden in the Sixteenth; I'm amazed they survived the frost." He stepped back and jammed the cap on his head. "The house had been taken over by some Kraut. Better they're here than gracing some Nazi *Hausfrau*'s table. I think he'd have approved."

Sophie looked down at the tombstone's modest lettering: DIETRICH DIX. "He would have." She could feel the weight of tears threatening behind her eyes and looked away, wishing for some sign—a bird flying overhead, the sudden break of sunlight through the clouds—that her brother was listening. "I didn't notice at the time... Fabienne chose a good spot for him."

"Here among the artists and dreamers." He jerked a mittened thumb over his shoulder. "Baudelaire's not too far away. He'd have liked that."

"La plus belle des ruses du diable est de vous persuader qu'il n'existe pas," Sophie mumbled, thinking of Göring's smiling elegance.

"And we're living in a city of devils now." He held out his hand, and Sophie took it. "It's good to see you, Sophie."

"And you, Louis." Together, they stood, hands clasped, in front of Dietrich's grave.

"How are the children?"

Louis chuckled. "Loud." They'd walked nearly the entire length of the cemetery; ahead, a rook had landed atop a narrow mausoleum and was watching them through glassy eyes. "Toinou is nearly six now, and Madeline can't stand when he tries to trail after her. You'd think two years' difference wouldn't mean much, but tell that to an eight-year-old." He smiled fondly. "She's the spitting image of her mother, and thank God for that. Toinou won't be so lucky. I'm afraid he's inherited my nose."

"There's nothing wrong with your nose," Sophie replied. Though she'd not seen Louis in nearly a year, it surprised her—pleased her—how quickly they'd fallen back into the rhythm of friendship, how the same well-worn jokes and stories sustained the pace of conversation. "Give my regards to Eline."

Louis paused to light a cigarette. "You could give them yourself over dinner, if you like," he said. "She's missed you. We all have."

Sophie watched the rook open its wings and take flight, swooping over the empress trees. "I appreciate that," she said finally, "but I doubt I would be very good company."

Louis let out a huff.

"You think we don't all miss him? He was the best of us, Sophie." He tapped his cigarette, letting ash fall on a nearby headstone before scuffing it off with the toe of his boot. "I still remember that first day Fabienne brought him to one of our meetings. He'd seemed so quiet... It took ages before he opened up about living in Germany, but when he finally started talking, I thought he'd never shut up. Before he came along, we were all separate movements with our own agendas—Communists, Socialists, anarchists. We were so busy fighting among ourselves that we'd grown blind to the need for real change." He looked up, his smile softening. "Students and idealists and philosophers. But Dietrich made us put aside our differences. That first night he spoke publicly... He put a face to the threat that fascism posed. Made us realize that our differences could wait."

Sophie cleared her throat, thinking of Dietrich, standing on a makeshift soapbox in front of the Sorbonne's student union, his audience falling grimly silent as he recounted the stark realities of life under Chancellor Hitler. "And you've—you've carried on, have you?"

Louis shook his head. "Dietrich spoke for all of us, but our solidarity dissolved the moment we started arguing about what to do to the men who'd killed him. The anarchists were the first to break away. The Communists followed soon after." He dropped the butt of his cigarette. "We might have been able to pull together if you'd stayed with us. If you'd picked up Dietrich's torch."

She walked on. "Dietrich was always the persuasive one."

Louis sighed. "Things got worse after the student protest at the Champs-Élysées this past November. Most of the other agitators have been deported to Germany. We're scattered to the four winds, now, I'm afraid." He fell silent, gravel crunching dully beneath his boots. "Sophie, it's nice to see you, but what's this all about?"

Sophie took a breath; in the distance, a couple walked between mausoleums, their dark figures disappearing behind the wings of a stone angel.

"I've a favor to ask you, Louis," she said. "I need papers."

Louis didn't break his stride. "Identity papers?"

"Two sets."

"Papers are difficult to find these days. What makes you think I know where to go?"

She lowered her voice. "You know Dietrich and I got our papers in Strasbourg, but I can't travel all that way, not these days. You know everyone there is to know in Paris."

Louis stopped to light another cigarette. "Well, I can't say I'm not flattered you thought of me. But I meant what I said, Sophie. The movement is finished. These days I keep my head down, try to do my best for my family."

"I can't believe it," Sophie retorted. "You and Dietrich were as close as brothers, you worked as hard as he did to make sure that fascism never took root in Paris."

"Maybe so, but we lost, Sophie. Now that the Germans are here, there's nothing left to fight for. Stalin's sided with Hitler, and the English have fled back across the channel. It's only a matter of time before the rest of Europe falls—"

"I don't believe it. I can't believe you would abandon your convictions so completely." She pictured Louis back when she'd known him as a student at the Sorbonne, the fiery young Socialist and barroom brawler who'd become Dietrich's right-hand man. "All that you've worked for—all that you fought for—and you've just given up?"

She could feel Louis's stare harden. "That seems a little rich coming from you."

They walked on in silence, and though Sophie stung at his rebuke, she knew that Louis had reason for saying it. After Dietrich's death, she'd retreated into her work and her grief, letting go of the friends—Dietrich's friends, *her* friends—who had become all-too-painful reminders of the life she'd once had.

Had Fabienne done the same? She must have, otherwise she would have thought to ask Louis for help herself.

"Well, I'm back now. And I don't intend to give up again." She rested her hand on Louis's arm. "These people need papers, Louis. If you can help me, then please, help me. If not, let's part as friends."

Louis was silent for a long moment, his lips pressed in a thin line. "*If* I knew of someone who might be able to help—and that's a big *if*, mind—where might I find you?"

She felt a surge of triumph. "I'll come to you. I can pay," she added quickly.

"Let's call it a favor between friends. I'll be in touch." Louis turned to leave, the sun breaking through the cloud cover as he looked back over his shoulder. "You really think Dietrich was the persuasive one, don't you? Believe me," he grinned, repositioning the brim of his cap, "you're better at it than you think."

21

Fabienne dashed up the lamp-lined staircase that joined Rue Muller to the basilica above, following the sound of laughter toward La Savoyarde, a wood-paneled brasserie which boasted views of Paris that nearly rivaled Sacré-Coeur itself. Stepping onto the patio, she threaded between tables to reach the front door and opened it, releasing a billowing cloud of cigar smoke into the sunset sky.

Within, the brasserie was packed, the tables and banquettes occupied by diners and drinkers basking in the end of another long workday. Through the windowpanes, the sunset's brilliant orange rays suffused the bar, reflecting off glasses and cheap jewelry, gilding the edges of rough-spun wool coats and dusty homburgs with a golden glow.

She pressed farther into the establishment, passing the marble-topped bar to search the second, smaller dining room.

She'd meant to arrive nearly an hour ago, but the antifascist rally at the Sorbonne had run long; as one of the representatives from the Académie des Beaux-Arts's Socialist Students group, she'd considered it her duty to linger until the end.

She thought back to the rally's dismal turnout. Though they'd invited student groups from each of Paris's major universities, only a handful of people had turned up, lured by the promise of free food and drink rather than by the lively discussion Fabienne had hoped for. Though the country was still governed by the left-wing coalition known as the Popular Front, recent stumbles—including the ousting of Prime Minister Blum—had drained the movement's early momentum. It felt to Fabienne as though the real reason for the coalition's existence had been forgotten amid the day-to-day considerations of running the government. The Socialists argued with the Communists and the Communists with the Social Radicals, sniping about unionization and holiday hours and wage inflation. Petty problems, compared to what was really at stake. It was up to the students to remind the government— and France's people—of the all-too-present danger posed by fascist strongmen taking up office across Europe.

If only they could stop fighting among themselves. She pressed her lips together, picturing the room where they'd set up a soapbox for Louis's speech. Though Louis—a friend and ardent Communist—had nominated himself as the rally's spokesperson, Fabienne knew that his lack of experience as a public speaker hadn't helped their cause: he'd rambled on, more concerned with the minutiae of political difference than with generating interest from prospective new members.

A passing waiter paused to let Fabienne slide by, glancing meaningfully at her paint-stained hands, and she hid them impatiently in the folds of her overcoat. With Montmartre and its *plein air* artists only steps away, Fabienne knew she wasn't the first person to step over La Savoyarde's threshold reeking of turpentine.

At the far end of the room, Dietrich stepped out from a paneled banquette, waving to catch Fabienne's attention. She reached the table, and Dietrich pulled her close to brush his lips against her cheek.

"You made it," he said, running his hand down the curve of her back.

"Barely," Fabienne replied. "I'm so sorry to be late. I'm afraid my friend can get quite caught up in the sound of his own voice. I was at a rally," she said by way of explanation to the woman at Dietrich's side. "Art and politics are perfect bedfellows, I'm afraid. You must be Sophie."

She smiled. "And you're Fabienne. Dietrich's not stopped talking about you."

Fabienne nudged Dietrich. "Is that so?"

"She exaggerates," he said, flushing red. "Fabienne, a drink?"

"Anything but champagne. And Dietrich?" She handed him her overcoat and slid into the banquette. "My friends have been saying the same about you."

She watched him hang her coat on a nearby peg and make his way toward the crowded bar before turning her attention to Sophie. She was short and pretty, with full cheeks and the sort of ruddy complexion that spoke to a childhood spent out of doors, but her drab outfit and rounded shoulders implied that she'd long since left such a childhood behind.

"It's nice to finally meet you," she said. "Dietrich has told me so much about your studies. He tells me you're up for a position at the Jeu de Paume."

She took a sip of sherry. "Only once I've finished my studies. But I doubt I'll be doing much more than cleaning portraits."

Whereas Dietrich was charming and exuberant, Sophie was self-conscious, her French the result of careful years' tailoring to trim away any hints of her German roots. "But it would be a respectable first posting."

"Not according to your brother. To hear him talk, you're well on your way to a directorship at the Louvre. He's so proud of your accomplishments."

Sophie smiled, straightening in her seat. "They're his accomplishments too. He's been putting me through university, you know. Evening shifts, overtime... It means a lot to him, to see me graduate."

"That sounds like Dietrich." Fabienne glanced across the room. At the bar, Dietrich had struck up a conversation with a short, slender man with receding ink-black hair; he turned, and she realized with a jolt that it was the gallerist, Paul Rosenberg.

"Paul!" Sophie stood, her polite expression breaking into unguarded happiness as Rosenberg and Dietrich, carrying a precariously tilted bottle of wine and four empty glasses, walked back to the table.

Fabienne slid down the banquette to make space for Dietrich, speechless as Sophie greeted Rosenberg with kisses on either cheek. How did Dietrich and his sister know Paris's most eminent art dealer?

Rosenberg sank into the seat opposite Fabienne as Dietrich began to pour wine. "Fabienne, I'd like to introduce Paul Rosenberg. Paul—"

"Needs no introduction." She held out a hand, praying that he wouldn't notice the shaking. "Your work with Picasso—"

"Pablo is the one who does the work. I merely display it," Paul replied, waving away Fabienne's compliment with a graceful sweep of his hand. "It was a fortunate twist of fate that brought the two of us together."

Fabienne bit her lip, astounded to hear the man who had

discovered not only Picasso but many of Europe's most important working artists ascribe his success to a mere *fortunate twist*. "I practically dragged Dietrich to see *Guernica*."

"Isn't it something? The one that got away." Rosenberg smiled, and though his reputation still left Fabienne awestruck, his gracious manner put her somewhat at ease. "I would have loved to have added it to my collection, but Pablo is quite right to be using it to raise awareness for the Spanish relief fund. It's going to be displayed in Oslo in the new year."

Fabienne nodded, thinking of the bombing campaign that had inspired the painting's creation: innocent villagers, bombed by German forces on behalf of General Franco in the ongoing Spanish Civil War. "A tragedy," she said, her mind turning once more to the anemic rally.

Dietrich finished pouring a glass of wine for Sophie, his expression grim. "It's more than a tragedy, it's an outrage," he said. "Did you know it was German planes that bombed Guernica? Junkers, outfitted with as many incendiaries as they could carry."

"I'm afraid Herr Hitler has made it quite clear he doesn't intend to let something like sovereign borders hamper the spread of his twisted ideology," Rosenberg said, lifting his glass to his lips. "He sees advantage in lending his support to Franco's cause."

"That's why we need to be on guard against fascism here," Fabienne replied. She could hear Louis's speech from hours earlier echoing in her head, his solid figure balancing atop a wine barrel as he strove to make himself heard. "Join forces, not allow it to take root."

"You're passionate. I like that," Rosenberg declared.

"She's an original thinker." Dietrich draped an arm over Fabienne's shoulder, snugging her close. "An original thinker, and an original artist. You should take a look at her work, Paul, if you're searching for the next Picasso."

Fabienne blushed, meeting Sophie's eye. Sophie shot her a glance and an apologetic shrug, her expression one of sisterly understanding: *You know what he's like.* "Monsieur Rosenberg, I would never presume to compare myself to Picasso—"

"I would." Dietrich beamed, squeezing her closer as Fabienne, mortified, tried to sink beneath the table. "She's magnificent."

"It's true. I've seen her painting at the Louvre," Sophie offered. "Not her originals, not yet, but her technical capabilities are second to none."

Rosenberg surveyed Fabienne with renewed interest. "Well, I'd be happy to take a look at your work."

"Not if you don't want to," she replied quickly.

Rosenberg laughed. "My dear, I don't waste my time, and I certainly wouldn't waste yours. If it's not to my taste, I'll tell you. But I have faith enough in Mademoiselle Brandt's judgment to be intrigued." He took a sip of his wine, amusement playing at the corner of his lips. "Would you permit me to offer a word of advice? Don't be too quick with humility, my dear. It doesn't tend to be a common trait among successful artists."

Later that evening, Fabienne and Dietrich wandered down the steep staircase, having left Sophie and Rosenberg discussing the merits of Paul Klee. Reaching a concrete landing, Fabienne took the opportunity to wallop Dietrich with her handbag.

"I can't believe you," she said, grinning despite herself. "Telling Paul Rosenberg about my art? I could have died!"

"Well, you weren't going to do it," Dietrich protested. "And can't I be proud of my girl? You're a remarkable artist. It's long past time you shared your work with the world."

Fabienne allowed him to pull her into an embrace, breathing in the woody scent of his cologne. "Who says I'm your girl?"

"I do." Dietrich kissed her. "But I hope I might count on your agreement in the matter."

Mollified, Fabienne shook her head as they resumed their descent to Rue Muller. "Paul Rosenberg," she muttered. "How on earth do you know him?"

"Sophie met him when we first moved to Paris," Dietrich replied. Outside the three cafés at the intersection of the road, patrons sat at chairs and tables, enjoying the crisp autumn evening. "He's been good to her—him and Madame Rosenberg, both. I know how much she misses our parents, Father especially."

Fabienne pictured Sophie's measured smile. *They're Dietrich's accomplishments too.* Dietrich had told Fabienne that their father was an art restorer with the University of Stuttgart. Did he know she'd decided to follow in his footsteps?

She turned her attention to the street. Beneath the red-striped awning of one of the brasseries, an elderly man sat smoking a pipe, running his gnarled fingers over the pieces of a chess set. From what she could tell, the man appeared to be playing both sides of the board: he reached across to the far side and removed an ivory bishop to replace it with a black knight.

"What happened to your parents? They're still in Germany, aren't they?"

Dietrich didn't respond immediately. "They are."

Fabienne fell silent, her stomach twisting as she thought again of *Guernica*: German planes, sowing destruction among a peaceful village. "Do they...do they support—?"

"You want to know whether they're Nazis." He paused, staring up at the lit windows of the tenement buildings that surrounded them, once-grand apartments divided over the centuries to make room for families and individuals and lovers. Behind the billowing curtain of a third-story window, Fabienne caught a glimpse of a flaking plaster ceiling medallion, its once-pristine edges dingy with age. "They joined in 1934. Father felt it was the only way he would be able to make anything of himself at the university."

Fabienne's stomach lurched once more. She'd had her suspicions, and she'd deliberately avoided asking questions about Dietrich's past. But the question had become unavoidable; the answer, in some ways, inevitable.

"They made us join up too," Dietrich continued when Fabienne's silence had stretched too long. "Me and Sophie, the Hitler Youth, the BDM. *All the best families have their children in the Hitler Youth*," he continued harshly, raising his voice in a mockery that no doubt was meant to be his mother. "Membership became compulsory shortly after."

"Oh, Dietrich," said Fabienne as he reached into his jacket pocket and pulled out a cigarette to light with trembling hands. She longed to draw him into her arms, but the image of him with a swastika on his armband was so abhorrent, so shocking, she couldn't bring herself to do it. "You were children. What choice did you have?"

"I was old enough to know that every word out of their mouths was a lie," Dietrich retorted. "The things they made us say...the things they made us do. The younger boys, they just took it all for granted. Every awful accusation, every ridiculous notion about why we'd lost the last war. They wanted to turn us into machines, unthinking, uncritical automatons they could aim at whichever enemy took their fancy." He looked up. "I was old enough to see it all for what it was. Or aware enough, perhaps. Far too many people much older than me refused to see Hitler for what he was."

They continued onward, Fabienne's voice echoing in her head with each and every footfall. *Fascist, fascist.*

"It's the kids younger than me that I worry most about. They're made to join up as toddlers, now. They start feeding them this—this *hate* from the time they can talk. I can remember a world before Hitler, but for them, fascism is all they've ever known."

"What made you leave?"

Dietrich looked up, squinting, into a streetlamp. "The autumn after I'd grown too old for the Hitler Youth, they conscripted me into the *Wehrmacht*. I'd resigned myself to being cannon fodder... Better dead than in service to the Führer. After basic training we were sent to Nuremberg, to attend one of Hitler's rallies... Sophie was there too, with the BDM. The older girls were sent to the rallies like they were heading to summer camp." He drifted off, his expression darkening, and Fabienne knew, beyond a shadow of a doubt, not to pry further.

"Do you know what the Nazi curriculum teaches girls?" Dietrich asked suddenly. "Needlepoint. They removed mathematics from the syllabus and replaced it with needlepoint. Why would a woman need mathematics when her role is to produce children for the Reich?" He shook his head, disgusted. "My sister was—she *is*—brilliant. She always was. But Nazi educators never saw the point of an academic woman." He took another drag of his cigarette, the ember lighting the hollows of his face. "The way I see it, I was meant to die in the *Wehrmacht*. I could live with that. But I would never have rested easy knowing that Sophie was living a life she was never meant to. I couldn't allow her to become some—some Nazi *Hausfrau*, married to an ideological brute. I just couldn't."

"And your parents?"

Dietrich tapped his cigarette to let the ember fall between the cobbles. "You want me to tell you that they changed their minds," he said. "You want me to say that our departure made them see Hitler for what he is, or that they stayed behind to help turn Germany back toward a democratic future. The truth is, Fabienne, they simply see what the party wants them to see. And why would they not? It's easier to submit than to fight. Any revolutionary will tell you that."

Fabienne carried on walking, Dietrich's revelation still ringing in her mind. *Fascist, fascist.*

"Fabienne, say something. Please." She looked up, meeting Dietrich's uneasy expression. He looked younger, more vulnerable than she'd ever seen him. The child he'd once been, a gangly teenager taught to hate.

Every child in Germany was forced to attend Nazi youth groups, twisting their minds and teaching them to accept, without question, the voice of authority. How many of them had managed, like Sophie and Dietrich, to break free of Hitler's teachings? How many were wise enough to see the truth behind the lies?

"You have to tell people," she said finally. "What it's like to live under a fascist government, what it's like to have your mind turned against you."

Dietrich shook his head. "I'm a deserter, Fabienne. If the *Wehrmacht* knew where I was…"

"Sophie, then." She took Dietrich by the hands, her conviction strengthening with every word. "Here in France, we don't know what it is to live under a fascist regime—we can't know, not really. Not like you do."

"That's the trouble, Fabienne. You *don't* know," Dietrich replied, wrenching his hands from Fabienne's grasp. "If you did, you wouldn't ask me to put myself at risk—to put my sister at risk—"

"The far right is mobilizing in France, just as it is in countries all across Europe," Fabienne countered, picturing the

afternoon's pathetic rally. "Do you want to see us become another Spain? Another Germany? We think we're a world away
from such troubles, but Spain is only a border away. Germany's
a border away." She stepped closer, willing him to understand.
"Surely you see the danger."

"Of course I see it," Dietrich shot back, "but I don't think
you realize what you're asking. We would be putting ourselves
at risk, Sophie and me. Terrible risk."

Ice ran through Fabienne's veins at the look in Dietrich's
eyes, but she pressed on. "If there's danger, we'll face it together," she said. "I can't tell you how to live your life. But
you once told me that you want to make a difference. Create
a better world. This is your moment, Dietrich. This is how you
make that change." She pressed her hands against his chest,
knowing, beyond a shadow of doubt, that this was right, that
the softening in Dietrich's shoulders was a sign that he was
coming around—that he could draw strength from the unshak-
able ground of her own conviction.

"I would have to talk to Sophie," he said finally, and Fabienne took him by the lapels, pressed a triumphant kiss to his
lips.

"Just come to a meeting," she replied, certain that if he were
to attend, he wouldn't stay silent for long. "Come and meet
Louis, talk to the other organizers. If you don't want to say a
word, you don't have to." She pulled Dietrich into the shadow
of a nearby alley, the darkness a suitable cover for her sudden
surge of desire. "Come to a meeting and hear what we've got to
say. Then tell me you don't want to help us change the world."

22

Fabienne stood before her easel, a palette knife dancing in her hand. She'd moved the easel into the kitchen and had propped the Kirchner near the window, the better to catch the morning sunlight. Though she'd studied the canvas for hours, something still stopped her from putting her brush to paint.

She rolled up the heavy sleeve of Dietrich's crimson smoking jacket, the weight of the palette knife in her hand familiar and foreign all at once. *Focus*, she told herself sternly, breathing in the fading scent of Dietrich's cologne from the velvet collar. Originally bought as a wedding present, the smoking jacket had become Fabienne's favorite piece of clothing in recent months, as comfortable as an embrace. Even now, it felt as though Dietrich was behind her, whispering encouragement as she surveyed the blank canvas.

She stepped forward to study the Kirchner again—but what

more was there to see? She'd examined every square inch of the canvas, had identified the colors that he had used for his base layers, had looked at every brushstroke, every pigment, the thickness of the impasto. There was nothing more for her to do but paint.

So why was her palette knife bare?

Focus, she told herself again, but this time it was Dietrich's voice that echoed within her head. She closed her eyes, listening for the tread of his footfall behind her, the feel of his hand on her shoulder.

She looked down at the jars of paint Sophie had given her, dozens of pigments labeled in Sophie's tidy script: *cadmium red*; *ultramarine*; *titanium white*. She opened the first jar, and the oily stench of petroleum was enough to make her feel lightheaded; she set down her knife and opened the window, then wrapped a worn paisley scarf around her mouth and nose. Irresistibly, she thought of Myriam and her ruby-red kerchief, camphor dust floating around her willowy figure.

She could feel self-doubt tugging at the edge of her mind as she opened the rest of the jars. Why was this the part of the process that she loved and loathed in equal measure? She pictured the painting, already complete, each planned brushstroke flawlessly executed; however, intention was no sure indicator of success.

Had her skill ever meant more than it did today, employed in the salvation of a masterpiece?

No less than it had for the child she'd been, painting the peeling wallpaper of her bedroom to escape the dull poverty of her life; no less than it had for the young woman she'd been, who'd traded in the certainty of a quiet country marriage for the chance at artistic greatness.

She pulled the scarf from her nose and crossed into her bedroom, opening the bedside table to pull out a bottle of scent, the last of Dietrich's cologne, barely a puddle left in the glass. She sprayed it onto the paisley fabric and knotted it around her mouth once more, and it was Dietrich who banished the sickly-sweet stench of petroleum from her study, Dietrich who steadied her hand.

Focus.

She smeared Sophie's paint on her board, impressed by the richness of the texture. Sophie had mixed them well, she noted with grudging admiration.

She ladled more paint onto the board and began to mix her palette, working quickly, briskly, before applying brush to canvas.

Sophie arrived at the flat the next morning, so early that Fabienne had initially mistaken the knock on her door as part of a brightly colored dream. She started, surprised to find herself curled up in an armchair. With a moment's regret, she noticed that a splotch of paint had fallen from the paintbrush lodged in her hair onto the chair's back.

"You've been busy," Sophie remarked as Fabienne opened the door. She stepped aside to make room for Sophie and her briefcase, feeling as though she was still pulling herself out of a dream.

"Coffee?" She shuffled past the easel into the kitchenette, rummaging in her cupboard for the kettle. "Or whatever passes for it these days…"

"Fabienne."

"Just chicory, I'm afraid, but I suppose that's all any of us can get—"

"Fabienne!"

She looked up, teacups clinking in her hands. "Hm?"

Sophie was staring at the easel with an inscrutable expression on her face, and Fabienne redoubled her efforts to lurch out of her creative fog. It had been years since she'd been so possessed, years since she'd spent hours on end at her work, unaware of the world around her. Even now, she wasn't sure whether the plate of browning apples and cheese at her side was the same one she'd put out when she'd started the underpainting, or whether Dietrich had silently replenished it in the night. She could smell his cologne. Had he stepped out to pick up breakfast? But then she remembered.

"I ran out of ultramarine so I couldn't quite match the shade of red," she said. "Although as the paintings won't be viewed side by side, I hope no one will notice the discrepancy."

"It's remarkable," Sophie breathed. She reached forward and touched the glistening canvas, lightly, in the corner. "Truly, Fabienne, it's…amazing."

Fabienne nodded, running her fingers along the heavy weave of the smoking jacket. "I'm pleased with how it turned out."

"And the paints?"

"They worked wonderfully. Dried quickly, spread easily." She rubbed her eyes, wishing she could dispel the feeling of sandpaper beneath her lids. "The one question that remains—"

"Will it stand up to scrutiny?" Sophie pulled a jar from her briefcase, along with a cotton-wrapped dowel. She opened the jar, and the scent of rubbing alcohol bloomed in the room. "If the paints have worked as they're supposed to, this painting should be completely dry," she said, dipping the dowel in the alcohol. "This is the method by which most art connoisseurs test for forgery. If the rubbing alcohol lifts any color, it indicates that the paint isn't yet dry. But if the cotton comes away clean…"

Fabienne held her breath as Sophie ran the dowel along the corner of the painting. *Careful*, she thought, watching the dowel twirl beneath Sophie's practiced fingers.

Sophie held up the clean dowel, and Fabienne let out a choked peal of laughter.

"Honestly, Fabienne, it's a marvel. I think we have a real chance. A real chance at...at saving this painting."

Fabienne nodded, pouring hot water into the *cafetière*. "How are you going to get it back into the museum?"

"With a lot of luck." Sophie set her briefcase on the table and unlatched it, pulling out jars and brushes and scalpels, rabbit glue and rice paper. Once it was empty, she ran her hands along the briefcase's empty hollow, then wedged a fingernail beneath the leather to reveal a false bottom. "I wasn't sure this would work," she murmured, gently wrapping the painting in linen before placing it in the hollow. "But necessity is the mother of invention..." She set wooden spacers in the corners of the hollow to keep the false bottom from touching the canvas. "About your...payment. I've spoken to a friend who might be able to help. You'll need to get photographs of the... subjects, but I might—*might*—be able to get it done."

Fabienne could feel her shoulders slump, relief coursing through her. She could help the Lowensteins: though she couldn't protect them outright, she could give them an additional layer of safety in Paris. "I'll get the photographs," she said. "How did you find someone so quickly?"

"Best not to know the particulars, wouldn't you agree?" With the false bottom restored, Sophie packed the suitcase once more.

Fabienne handed her a jar of glue. "What do you plan to do with the Kirchner?"

"I'm not sure yet. I'll leave it here for the moment, if you don't mind. I can come collect it later this week." She shut the suitcase, fastening the clasps before propping it upright. "After that... I'll take it to my apartment. See if I can find somewhere to hide it."

"That's a terrible idea." Fabienne rubbed at the paint that had collected in the ridges of her fingers. "You work at the Jeu de Paume. You'll be one of the first people they'd suspect, if they ever found out it had been stolen."

"It's not stealing—"

"If it's already stolen. I know." Fabienne hesitated. "I might be able to take it to a safe location outside the city."

"Would you be able to get out of Paris undetected? The trains are crawling with Germans as it is."

"Do you doubt me? I told you before, and I'll tell you again. The best place to hide is in plain sight."

Sophie stared at Fabienne a long moment. "Fine," she said finally. "I'll send word to you after…after this is all over, to retrieve it." With business concluded, Sophie turned to the door. "I suppose my thanks are in order."

"It was nothing," Fabienne replied, and despite her ambivalence toward Sophie, she didn't quite want to see her go. Impulsively, Fabienne pulled her into a hug, kissing her swiftly on both cheeks. "Just get me those papers, will you?"

23

Sophie stepped out of the metro, squinting into the bright morning as she made her way toward the Jeu de Paume. She ducked into the side entrance to the Jardin des Tuileries, and though her briefcase seemed to grow heavier with each step, she didn't dare stop: it would be too easy, too instinctual, to turn away. Rather than sneaking into the museum as early as curfew would allow, Sophie had decided to let the chaos of an upcoming visit from Göring provide a suitable distraction while she returned to the museum with the forged Kirchner.

Within, the museum's galleries were in the process of being turned over, ERR curators directing soldiers as they hung new paintings for Göring's perusal in a few weeks' time. Briefcase bumping against her leg, she made her way up the main staircase, breathing in the scent of lemon polish on the banister. At the top, Konrad Richter watched as a trim man in a pinstriped suit adjusted a newly hung Titian on the wall.

"Mademoiselle Brandt," said Richter. "Might I have a moment of your time?"

Damn. "I'm afraid I can't stop to talk, Doctor. Metro blackout on my way in to work this morning, and it's put me far behind schedule today. I'm sure you understand."

Richter grinned, falling into step as Sophie crossed into the next gallery. "I'm afraid I don't," he replied. "I've a motorcar to get me from here to there, but I prefer walking in any case. The fresh air reminds me of my days in the Storm Troopers." He lifted his arm to throw an imaginary javelin, his long limbs and exaggerated pose putting Sophie in mind of a statue by Arno Breker. "Won gold in the pentathlon, you know."

"Quite the achievement, Doctor." Sophie recalled her own days spent in state-sponsored athletics, sweat pouring down her face as she trailed her BDM compatriots around the track in the blistering sun. "What can I help you with?"

He stuffed his hands in his pockets. "I don't know whether you've met Gustav Rochlitz—that was him in the other room, with the spectacular Titian. It belongs to his gallery, but we're hoping to come to some sort of arrangement. I know the *Reichsmarschall* has had his eye on it for some time." He leaned closer as they passed into the next gallery, letting his hand stray, as if by accident, to Sophie's back. "You recall our conversation about the degenerate works in the Jeu de Paume's collection? I'd like to take him to see them. You compiled an inventory of the works recently, did you not? Could you join us? With the ledger?"

Her stomach lurched, but she knew better than to refuse. "Of course. Let me just settle in first." She quickened her pace, blood pounding in her ears with each step. To the best of her knowledge, no one had been in the Room of Martyrs since she removed the Kirchner—and she could hardly return the forgery with Richter and Rochlitz waiting below. It would be safe, concealed in her briefcase, until she returned, but would Richter notice its absence?

After dropping off her overcoat in the restoration lab, Sophie descended into the Room of Martyrs by the staff staircase, carrying the leather-bound ledger containing details of all the paintings kept there. Through the closed curtain, she could hear the sound of voices, Richter and Rochlitz, conversing in German.

She twitched aside the curtain and slid into the room.

"Thank you again for the loan of the Titian for the *Reichsmarschall*'s visit. He's such an admirer."

Rochlitz, bent over a small Degas propped on a table with an unlit pipe in his hand, straightened. "The *Reichsmarschall*, and so many others," he replied. "I'm pleased to know that the painting will be enjoyed in such an illustrious setting."

Richter smiled. "My dear fellow, I won't beat about the bush. I've been authorized by the *Reichsmarschall* to acquire the Titian for his personal collection—if, of course, you're open to some sort of arrangement."

Rochlitz packed the bowl of his pipe, tamping down the tobacco with a blunt thumb. "Every work of art has its price, of course...but I must tell you, I won't part with it for less than it's worth."

"I wouldn't dream of it," Richter replied, reaching into his pocket to offer Rochlitz the use of his lighter. "However, in these times of war, the *Reichsmarschall* is most concerned with supporting the German army and people however he can. He's putting his considerable skills, intelligence and resources toward the glory of the German people." He paused. "I'm sure you can appreciate that spending *money* on a masterwork might send the wrong message." He paused again, then gestured at the Degas. "Magnificent, isn't it? *Madame Camus at the Piano*, painted in 1869. It's masterful."

"It is," Rochlitz murmured softly.

Richter turned to a nearby Matisse. *"Still Life: Flowers and Pineapples,"* he continued, his fingers resting momentarily on the frame before pointing up at a Picasso hung on the wall. *"Women at the Races.* You know as well as I do that a fortune lies within these walls, Rochlitz. Were any of these pieces to catch your eye, the *Reichsmarschall* would be quite willing to negotiate...in exchange for the Titian. And the hunting scene you have by Jan Weenix."

Though Sophie fought to keep a sudden wave of fury from crossing her features, she couldn't help looking up. A barter, then: the prospect was deeply unwelcome. She'd known that Fabienne's forged Kirchner would have to withstand the scrutiny of the ERR's curators. Would it have to pass muster for one of Paris's top art dealers too?

"An exchange with Göring..." Rochlitz rubbed his jaw. "Forgive me, but aren't these paintings the property of the ERR? Does the *Reichsmarschall* have the authority to make such an exchange?"

Richter smirked. "It's best not to concern yourself with the particulars. Rest assured, it's all quite aboveboard. Mademoiselle Brandt," he continued, switching momentarily to French. "Herr Rochlitz and I require the inventory of the paintings in this collection. Swiss," he explained, reverting to German as Sophie passed him the ledger. "Not a word of German, but she passes muster as a secretary when the need arises."

"Would that all women were so amenable," Rochlitz chuckled, but Sophie barely heard him past the racing of her own mind. Here, at the museum, Sophie could keep careful track of each and every painting, but if Rochlitz were to acquire anything from the Room of Martyrs and then sell it on to his clients, there was little guarantee that Sophie would ever know where they might end up. Art sales could be concealed behind layers of brokers and dealers—particularly if those sales were made across international borders, to people who didn't know or care that the paintings had been stolen from their Jewish owners.

"It's an impressive collection," Rochlitz conceded as he and Richter bent over the ledger, "but you can't possibly deny that it's lost its value. What call do my clients have for degenerate art these days?" He stroked his beard, and Sophie wasn't sure whether he was truly hedging his bets or simply enjoying the petty pageantry of negotiation. "No respectable home would display art such as this, not within the Reich."

Richter smirked. "But you and I both know, Rochlitz, that your clientele extends far beyond the Reich," he replied. "Our country's leadership may not appreciate the value of modern art, but you and I are connoisseurs, my friend. We both know that a Picasso or a Dalí will one day be as priceless as a Titian."

"That's as may be, but I do have a reputation to uphold. Why doesn't Göring simply name his price and have done with it? I would prefer an outright sale to an exchange."

"The *Reichsmarschall* is quite set on an exchange," Richter replied smoothly. "And for that matter, you ought to be too. The Reich may not appreciate modern masters, but what of Switzerland? Spain? Don't tell me you've lost all your contacts in America, Gustav, not when private collectors on any shore can find reasons to overlook their scruples."

Rochlitz hesitated, but Sophie could tell that he was wavering. He glanced up at a Renoir depicting a woman in a summer dress, the colors bright and inviting as he wedged the pipe between his lips. "And these paintings would be properly valued, would they, before we agree to any exchange?"

Richter smiled. "My dear fellow, you'll be getting the better end of the bargain. Göring and Bohn want them gone, one way or another—better they end up with you, surely, than on a bonfire like their cousins in Germany? You'd be doing us a favor, really." He leaned closer, his tone deliberately casual. "Besides, my good man, does it really seem like a good idea to refuse Hermann Göring?"

Rochlitz paled. He took off his spectacles and cleaned the glass with a handkerchief, taking more time over the task than strictly necessary. "Ten works of art, Richter, no fewer," he said finally.

Richter's smile broadened. "How about we make it eleven?"

24

February 1941

Pigeons fluttered between the wrought iron trusses of the Gare de l'Est, alighting on freshly painted signs in German that directed passengers through the station. At its many platforms, trains hissed steam as German officers helped their fur-clad wives down from first-class carriages, pink and beaming at the prospect of a Parisian holiday.

Fabienne handed her papers to a waiting soldier, watching a fog of condensation from a waiting steam engine creep toward her. Although the train she'd bought a ticket for was bound for conquered Belgium, she would be traveling to the French countryside—so long as she was permitted to board.

The soldier studied Fabienne's ticket and looked up, his gaze shifting meaningfully to the unframed painting in Fabienne's arms.

She shot him a dazzling smile and held out the Kirchner.

"Isn't it awful? My brother fancies himself an artist, but I think he's better suited to his job as a plasterer. But my parents like to support him when they can, bless them, they're the only ones who would ever pay good money for his little pictures. Tell me, do you know much about art, Private…?"

The soldier looked up, letting a half smile flicker across his face. Not for nothing had Fabienne approached the youngest-looking of the ticket-takers. "Müller," he offered, a flush rising in his cheeks before turning his attention back to Fabienne's papers.

"*Müller.* Well, Private Müller, what I know about art could fit in a teaspoon, but I know what I like, and I just don't think there's a future in it, do you?" Her heart hammered wildly as she waited for the young soldier to finish examining her ticket. It had been a gamble, to brazen her way through the Gare de l'Est with the Kirchner on full display, but she'd counted on the average foot soldier not to know art: from what Dietrich had told her, cultural pursuits didn't rank very highly on the Hitler Youth curriculum.

For the moment, the risk paid off: Müller handed her back her papers with a nod. "Enjoy your trip, *mademoiselle.*"

She made her way onto the train, her hands shaking as she deposited the Kirchner and her carpetbag in the luggage rack of a deserted compartment. *First hurdle cleared*, she thought as she watched soldiers and civilians milling on the platform below. *Many more to go.*

Several hours later, the train pulled in at Bar-sur-Aube and Fabienne descended from the carriage, the Kirchner tucked once more beneath her arm. Despite being uneventful, the trip had done nothing to dispel her sense of unease, and as she stepped onto the platform she lingered, looking out on the endless sea of vines beyond the station.

"Can I help you, *mademoiselle*?"

She turned to find the stationmaster, looking grayer, more careworn, than when she'd last seen him.

She smiled, but it was clear he didn't recognize her. "Thank you. I'm going to Château Dolus. Might you have a bicycle you could loan me?"

The stationmaster squinted, as if trying to place her. "Borrowed bicycles rarely come home, these days."

"Hired, then." She took a step forward and reached into her pocketbook. "I won't be long. I doubt I'm even staying the night."

The stationmaster huffed. "Put your money away. A young lady traveling alone has got better things to spend it on." He turned, beckoning Fabienne to follow. "My son's bicycle is around back. Given the state of petrol these days, the only way back to Paris is by train. I'll expect you to return it when you leave."

She wheeled out of the station shortly after, her bag and the painting strapped atop the bicycle's back wheel. Though it had been years since she'd cycled through the village, she felt like she could still do it with her eyes closed. Time, it seemed, had always moved more slowly in Bar-sur-Aube than in the rest of France. The same crumbling barns and chalk houses lined the cobblestone streets, the same sparse trees stretching to the same blue sky. She wheeled past her elementary school, half-expecting to see the same cloaked nuns waiting at the door to chide her for her tardiness, but she continued on, flying past the modest entrance of the Église Saint-Pierre toward the river.

She wheeled round another corner into the village green and came to a stop, jarred to see red-and-black banners hanging from the butter-yellow windows of the *mairie*. Across the green, a pair of German soldiers strode into a boulangerie, their rifles slung loosely over their shoulders as they held the door for an elderly doyenne carrying a baguette. She scuttled past as quickly as her arthritic frame would let her.

Fabienne looked away, her fingers tightening over the handlebars. Time moved slowly in Bar-sur-Aube, but the war had caught up with the village nonetheless.

She sped up once she crossed the river, following the riverbank south toward the brown vineyards that hemmed in the village on all sides. In years past, Fabienne would have cycled past trucks and tractors laden down with grapes and barrels, bottle shipments and mash, but today the roads were empty; though she was moving too quickly to see, she knew that the orderly rows of grapevines on either side of her were dormant, awaiting the spring thaw. She carried on, her legs aching as muscle memory propelled her farther away from the village, an ancient proverb echoing in her mind: *God sends a poor harvest to herald war.* She let out a breath. War, and everything that went along with it.

She pedaled farther into the gentle hills that surrounded the village, sweat plastering her blouse to her back. She'd not realized how out of shape she'd become during her years in Paris. With everything accessible either by foot or on the metro, she'd hardly ever needed to mount a bicycle, and the lack of practice showed. She gritted her teeth and pressed onward, knowing that if she were to stop she might simply turn her wheels and coast back to the village.

She paused when she reached a gravel drive flanked by a pair of open, rusted gates that dipped into a shallow valley, the sun-bleached sign on the iron spokes faded almost to the point of illegibility: *Château Dolus.* Below, a woebegone chateau sat nestled in a run-down courtyard, its dusty windows catching the afternoon sun.

Fabienne let out a breath, gripping the handlebars tighter as she navigated around potholes. She hadn't thought it possible for Dolus to look any worse than it had six years ago, but she'd been proven wrong. Bedraggled chickens pecked at the gray ground, darting beneath the rusting bulk of farm-yard equipment. There were old tractors and grape presses, fermentation tanks dropped haphazardly in the garden, their tops sawn open to catch scummy pools of rain.

She stepped off the bicycle and retrieved her carpetbag and the Kirchner, shooing away an inquisitive rooster with her foot before climbing the sturdier-looking wing of the crumbling imperial staircase. She paused at the door, unsure whether to knock or let herself in—but then she raised a fist, knowing that she'd long ago lost the privilege of familiarity.

Fabienne rapped twice, worried that if she knocked too hard she might risk breaking the ancient door off its hinges. She glanced back at the chickens before directing her gaze upward to study the looming stone. In the past, she'd fancied that hope had kept the chateau standing, but now she suspected that it had been spite all along. What else could have kept it upright for so many generations?

From within, she could hear the echo of footsteps through the marble hallway and stepped back, dizzy at the prospect of seeing her mother again after so many years—

The door swung open to reveal a tall broad-shouldered young man, dark-haired and green-eyed, dressed in a rumpled linen shirt. Though he'd aged, with new touches of gray at his temples, Fabienne recognized him instantly, down to the look of shock, of hurt, on his stubbled face.

"Fabienne," he said, thunderstruck. "What the hell are you doing here?"

25

Spring 1935

Château Dolus—Chateau Deceit—was cursed.

Fabienne had known it for years; she'd known it from the time she was a child, looking up at the smirking figure of the Greek god above the lintel for whom the abode was named, or else listening in the darkness of her cavernous bedroom to the floor creaking beneath the weight of her four-poster bed, to the wind howling through cracks in the windowsill.

It had been cursed from the moment her great-grandfather had won it off a disgraced nobleman. Why the man had chosen to gamble with something so momentous as his family seat had been anyone's guess, and though he never knew for certain whether his opponent had cheated, the nobleman had damned Great-Grandfather all the same, departing from the grounds with a curse on his lips for the turreted roof and the marble floors, the vines and the outbuildings, before meeting his fate at the end of a Parisian guillotine.

It was clear to Fabienne that the curse had endured, for although Great-Grandfather had been handed the keys to one of the region's most successful champagne houses, it had only taken three generations for the estate to fall into disarray. Many years of mismanagement had taken their toll, and bit by bit, acre by acre, the business had been sold off, leaving Fabienne's parents with little more than scraps by the time she was born: the chateau itself, and a handful of vines that had been ravaged first by war, then by blight. As a young girl, Fabienne had watched as neighboring estates bought up the chateau's winery equipment, Papa negotiating prices for his meagre harvests with more successful champagne houses in the region; she'd watched as her parents sold off the tapestries and furniture, whispering late into the night about money, money. To Fabienne, Château Dolus was the sibling she'd never wanted, the parent she'd never asked for, the all-encompassing priority that eclipsed her in the eyes of her parents, that took their time, their attention, away from Fabienne herself: nominally, at least, her parents' only child.

She'd hated the chateau from the time she was little, when the windows leaked in the rain and candles flickered in their holders. And though other children might have seen magic in the estate's crumbling elegance, Fabienne only saw the cost of the upkeep, the loneliness of the nights as her parents dropped, exhausted, into their armchairs, too tired to do anything but sigh when she asked to be taken into the town to watch the pictures or visit art galleries. She'd hated champagne from the day she'd been handed a bucket and told she was old enough to help with the harvest, enduring the backbreaking work of picking grapes that could hardly be used for anything other than vinegar. She'd crumbled, time and again, beneath the chateau's ancient shadow, the family curse echoing in her ears as she contemplated a future predetermined as her parents' unwilling heir: a life spent within the estate's dwindling grounds, the next in a line of failed vintners, failed farmers.

It was little wonder, then, that the family had failed as well.

Salvation, to Fabienne, had been her love of art—art and, paradoxically, champagne itself, in the form of Count Robert-Jean de Vogüé, the head of the expansive Moët et Chandon estate that had long bought grapes from Papa. As the family sold off painting after painting from the chateau's collection, Fabienne had hung her own canvases to hide the bare walls in Papa's study, and when Fabienne was seventeen years old, de Vogüé had taken notice: he'd marveled at her use of color and line, and one day arrived at the house with an offer.

"Let me become a patron to your daughter," he'd said to Papa, as Fabienne listened with her ear pressed to the office's closed door. "She's a prodigy. There's simply no other word for it. I've no doubt she could be accepted to the Académie des Beaux-Arts."

Papa had declined on her behalf, using the excuse of Dolus itself: the family couldn't afford to let her go, not when she was the future of the estate and needed to learn its ways, not with her wedding to a talented young vintner, set to take place within the month. The family's money—its attention, its energies, its partners and its passions—needed to be at the disposal of the family business. There was no room for Fabienne's dreams: not when the dreams of too many before her had already been sacrificed on the altar of Château Dolus.

Fabienne had trailed de Vogüé out of the house, fists clenched in white-hot anger at her father's refusal. "You really think I can do it?" she'd asked, her heart beating wildly in her chest.

De Vogüé had paused, twirling his bowler cap in his hands. "I do," he replied. "You have a natural talent, my dear."

Fabienne had glanced at de Vogüé's idling motorcar, his

chauffeur waiting by the open door. "Natural talent won't mean a thing if I don't learn how to use it."

De Vogüé chuckled. "Spoken like a true artist," he replied. "I'll make you a deal. If you can get your parents' permission—and your husband's—within the year, I'll offer my patronage once more. It won't be much, you understand, but it will be enough for you to keep yourself comfortably in Paris." He set the bowler on his head and held out a gloved hand. "I would consider it an honor to support an artist like you in the early days of her career."

Fabienne had watched de Vogüé's car disappear down the long drive, its wheels sending clouds of dust billowing through the hot summer sky. The nobleman's curse echoed in her mind once more, and she watched as Papa trudged down the stairs, disappearing around the side of the chateau's crumbling walls.

That evening, Fabienne left the chateau by nightfall, carrying a carpetbag and a handful of francs she'd scraped together over the years, her engagement ring—a chip of a diamond set in a narrow band—placed carefully atop her vanity. She knew better than to jeopardize de Vogüé's relationship with Papa by taking him up on his generous offer; she knew better than to plead with her parents or try to explain herself to her fiancé. Even with a year's worth of argument in their ears, she knew that they would never support her, not when their dreams for Château Dolus came first.

She wheeled her bicycle around to the drive, looking back at the shadowed walls as she fastened her bag to the bicycle's pannier.

Whether it took a year or a lifetime, she would make a life for herself, a life of her own choosing, rather than one spent in service to someone else's dream.

26

Fabienne gripped the bone handle of her carpetbag, feeling as though the flagstones beneath her stout heels might give way. *Focus*, she told herself as she snugged the Kirchner in one arm closer to her side.

"Sébastien," she said, poorly concealing her surprise beneath a perfunctory smile, "what a surprise."

Sébastien's hold on the door handle looked nearly as firm as her own on her bag. He stared at her, his eyes wide: for a split second, it looked as though he might slam the door in her face, but then he cleared his throat. "I could say the same," he replied. "I suppose you want to come in?"

She smiled, attempting to channel the detached charm of a silver-screen starlet: Marlene Dietrich, winning over a prickly audience with class and bravado. "If it isn't too much trouble," she replied before casting what she hoped was a wistful look up at the chateau. "All this country air…it's such a change from the city. I'd forgotten what it was like."

Sébastien stepped aside, his lips pressed into a thin line as she crossed into the entrance hall.

Within, the chateau looked exactly as she remembered, with its heavy oak staircase and threadbare carpets, the half-moon window on the staircase's landing casting a single stream of dust-filled light. Sébastien shut the front door, plunging Fabienne into darkness: though the door was flanked by casement windows, the curtains had been drawn—to protect, Fabienne knew, the fading Victorian wallpaper.

She peeled off her gloves, preferring to meet the glassy eyes of a taxidermed owl set high on a wardrobe rather than endure Sébastien's disapproving gaze.

"Still no feather duster to be found, I see," she began playfully but stopped short as Sébastien stalked past her to the back of the building.

She grabbed her belongings and followed him, her cheeks burning as she jogged to catch up. She'd come to Château Dolus expecting a poor reception, but she'd never dreamed that Sébastien would be the one to open the door—that he'd still be here, in the home that had held such vivid memories for them both. As she trailed him toward the rear of the building, she pictured Sébastien as she'd known him: tall and wiry, his hair grown long over his suntanned forehead as he perched atop the handlebars of his ancient bicycle. Green eyes, staring up at the chateau, searching for her face in windows obscured by the long, golden glow of sunset.

Sébastien, kneeling in the shade of their chestnut tree, promising a lifetime of devotion.

Fabienne, holding out her trembling hand for a ring that never properly fit.

They reached the chateau's immense sitting room, and

Sébastien crossed it with long strides, his boots loud on the bare parquet as he threw open the double doors that led onto a once-elegant terrace. Beyond, the exterior was as it had always been: an overgrown, formal garden hemmed in by brick walls, its raised beds long ago given over to brown vegetable plots, dormant grapevines rising on the gentle slopes beyond. In the distance, she could see the sagging roofs of two old stone barns, set opposite one another across a dusty yard: the stables and the winery.

"They're in the winery," he said without stopping as he continued down the terrace's shallow steps. "Wait here."

As Sébastien carried on into the garden, Fabienne set down her things in the sitting room, her heart thrumming as she watched his slouching figure disappear past the brick walls. "Get a hold of yourself," she muttered, feeling as though she was seventeen once again—seventeen and restless, yearning for more than the crumbling estate was willing to give. She could feel the place, mournful and alert, judging the cut of her stylish suit and her cropped hairstyle, her painted lips. Its moldy curtains seemed to breathe with smug satisfaction over casement windows, casting a critical eye over the efforts she'd made to leave behind the farm girl she'd once been. *Back again, is she?*

She shivered and followed Sébastien out into the grounds.

Fabienne stepped into the darkness of the barn, breathing in an all-too-familiar scent of stale wine and dry earth, a century's worth of industry sunk deep into the building's chalk walls. Lined up on either side of the double doors were wooden crates, empty but awaiting the season's harvest, and though the hard-packed ground was dry, she thought of years past: sloshing through the barn in hip waders, juice running in rivulets from the ancient wooden grape press. She passed the press, surprised to see that someone had made some effort to repair the long-broken spoke that turned the wheel.

She could hear the sound of heated whispers from the back of the building and carried on toward the barrel racks. Too old to fetch a good price, they now sat empty, devoid of the barrels that had once been ideal for childhood games of hide and seek. Irresistibly, Fabienne thought of tiptoeing between the racks, searching for Sébastien's dark curls.

"Hello?"

Sébastien glanced up from behind the heavy silhouette of a tractor. Beside him, a thin woman in beige trousers spun round, a wrench in her hand; atop the tractor, a man with white hair and a graying beard looked up.

"Bonjour, Maman. Papa." She stepped forward, her stomach lurching at the twin expressions of shock on her parents' faces.

They've aged, she thought uncomfortably, noticing the white in Papa's beard; the gray in the wisps of hair that had fallen out of Maman's headscarf. As a child, Fabienne had teased her parents by calling them the lord and lady of the manor, and though in a very real sense they were, Maman and Papa had never really taken to aristocratic life. Maman, with her lithe figure and aquiline features, could have graced the front cover of any Parisian magazine but preferred to spend her days dressed in oversized shirts and heavy trousers, her hair tucked beneath paisley scarves as she pruned vines and drove tractors. Papa, meanwhile, was broad and ruddy, an engineer by nature who spent his days tinkering with farm machinery or second-hand motors, always looking for ways to ease the burden of farming for his small staff. Belatedly, Fabienne thought of the farmhands that usually graced the grounds. Even in the leanest of times, Papa had always hired a worker or two to help keep the estate from falling around their ears.

It didn't bode well to realize that Fabienne herself was one of only four people present.

"I thought I told you to wait on the terrace," Sébastien started, but Papa eased off the tractor, wiping his hands on an oilcloth.

"I'd hug you," he said, lifting the cloth in a sort of half gesture of welcome, "if I weren't worried about dirtying that pretty outfit of yours."

He smiled, and Fabienne fought a sudden, absurd urge to fall into his arms. Though she'd dressed with care this morning, determined to return to Château Dolus a success, she suddenly wished she'd worn something less ostentatious, less Parisian. She glanced at Maman, whose gaze slid from her two-toned heels to her broad-brimmed chapeau. Maman had never valued beauty. Why had Fabienne assumed that such a display would be met with anything other than disdain?

"Did you bring that *boche* of a husband with you?" Maman asked, and any slim hope that Fabienne might have had for a tender family reunion evaporated into the wine-scented air.

"He's dead," she replied harshly.

At least Maman had the grace to look abashed. "Well," she muttered, "I'm sorry to hear it."

"No, you're not," Fabienne shot back, and Maman wheeled around, brandishing the wrench as effectively a conductor's baton.

"Six years, Fabienne, six *years* without a visit, with barely a letter, and you waltz in here expecting the worst of me—"

"What else should I expect, when every conversation we have ends with shouting?"

Papa stepped between them, tucking his oilcloth in the sagging pocket of his coveralls. "Our daughter is home," he said mildly, and both Maman and Fabienne fell silent. Behind him, Sébastien huffed, pulling the tractor's engine cover open with a fluid movement. "Let's return to the big house for a glass of champagne. Perhaps we can drown our harsh words and begin again."

Maman's face tightened once more, and Fabienne swallowed back another burst of hopeless anger. "I'm sure our daughter remembers that the harvest waits for no one, and neither does our work," she replied. "You two start without me."

The sun stretched long over the vineyard, the soil hard beneath her bare feet as Fabienne weaved her way through the dormant vines. Here, the landscape beyond the estate's modest grounds was given over to grapevines, each long vista made up of stout lines of pinot noir and chardonnay, divided by thickets of forest that gave the entire scene a patchwork effect that Fabienne had long hated: the giving over of nature to forced growth, forced order. But there was something about the scene that Fabienne wanted to paint: the rolling hills and golden sunset, the moss-topped slates that made up the chateau's roof.

It felt strange, being up in the fields without a set of shears in hand to prune the dormant vines, to be walking in a pair of Papa's old Wellington boots with nothing but a coupe in one hand. She held it out over the vines, and Papa, walking in the next furrow over, held out a half-full bottle of champagne. She watched the bubbles dance up the glass, and though she disliked champagne as a matter of principle, it was drinkable, and drinkable was all that mattered. Below, in the grounds between the stable and the winery, she could see Maman and Sébastien hitching a lone horse to an ancient cart.

She took a sip, letting the bubbles flatten on her tongue before swallowing. "What happened to the rest of the horses?"

Papa sighed. "Requisitioned by the Germans," he replied, and Fabienne felt a pang of grief for the full stables that they'd once enjoyed. She recalled the gentle roan and the dappled gray mare, the colt with the shaky legs that she'd brought up herself and named Rembrandt. "But Lutin was too old for them to bother taking. You saw the flags in the village, I suppose."

"I didn't realize…" she replied, thinking about the soldiers who'd strolled so arrogantly down the high street. "I thought perhaps I could forget, out here in the countryside, what was going on in Paris."

"Hardly. The Germans have moved in with a vengeance. They've appointed a—we call him a *Weinführer*—who's putting the entire region to work. Given the number of bottles he's ordering every week, it seems that Göring is keeping the *Luftwaffe* hydrated with champagne alone. It's a wonder they get their airplanes off the tarmac." Papa squinted into the setting sun. "I suppose we were lucky that the horses were all they took. They concluded that the chateau was unfit for habitation, so they chose not to billet any officers with us. Can you believe it? *Unfit for habitation…*"

Though Fabienne was jarred by Papa's revelations, she was determined not to show it. "The curse of Château Dolus is finally working in your favor."

Papa nodded. "I'd once believed it to be nothing more than a story, but now… Blight, phylloxera," he said, and Fabienne recalled stories of the pests that had decimated the vines in the years before the Great War. "It feels like we only just got our vines back to form, and now another war is threatening them again. Hard not to believe in the curse, these days."

Fabienne thought back to her childhood years: growing up with the struggling vines, watching her parents worry about money, about the crumbling chateau, about survival. The constant hemming-in of the estate, as Papa sold off acre after acre; that sad day when Papa had decided to sell off the last of the wine-making equipment, transforming Dolus from a champagne house into a contract grower.

"Chateau Deceit," Fabienne said quietly as they carried on down the gentle slope. "No wonder it hasn't made any of us happy."

Papa twisted to look at Fabienne. "Who says I'm not happy? Your mother and I have everything we need. Would the curse have sent us Sébastien? He's kept us afloat."

Fabienne glanced down. "I ought to be grateful that he stayed on, after everything," she replied, and she knew it to be true. She'd hoped that her return to Château Dolus could be a simple thing: a reconciliation with her parents, a hiding place for the Kirchner. But Sébastien...

"You should talk to him," Papa said gently. "Explain your reasons for leaving."

"Explain them to him?" She looked at Papa. "Or to you?"

Papa tilted his head in acquiescence. "I know how hard it was for you, growing up here. Feeling responsible for all of this."

Fabienne shook her head. "When I thought about my life here, I just... I couldn't. The thought of taking over the vineyard, living in the same place I'd been born... It wasn't what I wanted."

"You think we didn't know that?"

"You knew?" Fabienne looked up, incredulous. "I heard you, that day, with de Vogüé. You didn't want me to leave. You knew I was miserable, and you didn't want me to go."

"It's not as simple as that," Papa replied. "When you work your whole life to build something...you want to know that it will be left in the right hands."

"It was your dream, Papa. Not mine." She took another sip of champagne, surprised at how palatable it was. Had de Vogüé dropped off a case?

"I've come to terms with that," Papa replied. "And for what it's worth, I'm sorry. I shouldn't have put those kinds of expectations on you. But what I can't understand is why you left the way you did."

Fabienne thought back to the night she snuck out of the house. She'd looked back, just once, at the crumbling stone of her family's home—she recalled the wave of terror she'd felt at the prospect of leaving it all behind for an uncertain future.

"Your mother and I…we've come to terms with it," Papa continued. "But Sébastien…"

"What's he still doing here, Papa?"

Papa sighed. "After you called off the wedding, I asked him whether he wanted to leave. We'd have given him a good reference, of course, but he chose to stay. He chose to support us, to support the vines. We didn't feel it right to dismiss him."

Fabienne thought back to Sébastien's first week on the farm. Fourteen years old and gangly, he'd taken to viticulture like a duck to water, constantly trailing around after Maman and Papa and asking them the questions Fabienne had never cared about, such as how to keep pests away from the grapes and when to turn the soil in the new year. They had admired his resolve, his determination to learn the art of grape-growing and wine-making. Why had they celebrated him for forging his own path, while refusing Fabienne that same choice?

"Of course not," she replied bitterly. "Why alter your long-laid plans?"

"That's not fair." Papa poured himself another glass of champagne. "He built his life around this vineyard—around you—from the time he was a boy. This estate is as much his home as it is yours."

"And he never felt the need to leave? Even after I'd gone?"

"Careful, now, my dear, or someone might accuse you of arrogance," Papa replied. "He's done well for himself, Fabienne. He brought our vines back from the brink. He's got ideas for the future."

"He always was a dreamer," Fabienne muttered, and Papa shook his head.

"Dreams backed up by hard work are plans, Fabienne, and he's got plans. He's long earned his place here, with us."

Fabienne stepped away, nudging a hard-packed ball of dirt with her toe. "And was he... He's never married?"

Papa shook his head. "What happened between the two of you...it gave him some perspective, I think. Maturity. He's a good man, Fabienne. Like your husband was, I hope."

Dietrich's face flickered before her, but she pushed him away, feeling that to stray further down this path of conversation risked a degree of confidence with her father that she wasn't sure she'd earned.

"You could have given him a proper good-bye, *chérie*," Papa said gently. "You owed him that much, I think."

Fabienne fell silent. At the time, she'd justified her actions by telling herself that it was the kindest thing to do, to leave without explanation—a clean wound, after all, was said to cauterize quickest. But she'd known even then that she owed Sébastien more than that, that it had been cowardice, not kindness, that had caused her to leave without a word.

"I need a place to stay," she said finally, tipping her empty glass to let the final few drops of champagne fall into the dust. "Just for the night. Maybe two. Is that all right?"

"Of course," Papa replied. "This is your home. You're always welcome here."

Fabienne looked down to the chateau. Below, Sébastien jumped up into the horse-drawn cart, giving Maman a perfunctory wave before he set the horse to trotting. She jerked her chin in the direction of the dust cloud that Sébastien had sent billowing up in the sky. "Would they agree with you on that?"

"Give them time," Papa replied gently. "That's all they need. Just a little bit of time."

That evening, Fabienne slipped out of bed, her toes cold on the wooden floor as she eased herself out of the covers. She glanced out the window into the pitch-dark night, then lit a candle, not trusting herself to remember each twist and turn of the chateau's halls in the dark. She opened her bedroom door and crept down the stairs, trying to remember which floorboards were apt to creak as she retrieved the Kirchner.

Dinner had been a tense affair, with Maman looking daggers at her across the table. Sébastien hadn't even shown up. Did he still live on site?

The kitchen was peaceful, still warm from the lingering heat of the oven as she crossed to a small wooden door that led into one of the chateau's four turrets. Within, a stone staircase led down into the cellar, and Fabienne gripped the Kirchner tight as she descended, careful not to let the hinges on the door creak.

Once upon a time, the cellars at Château Dolus had been bursting with wine, heavy iron racks filled with dark bottles nestled in every vaulted alcove of the chateau's foundation. She recalled going down there as a child, tasked with riddling the champagne bottles, turning them a quarter turn at a time in the light of a bare electric bulb. She didn't bother turning on the light as she walked: her small candle, flickering in the deep vaults, served as illumination enough.

She was surprised, the farther into the cellar she went, to find furniture in the alcoves—pieces brought down, perhaps, to safeguard them from German soldiers? Papa had said that the Germans had chosen not to requisition the building itself, but perhaps that hadn't extended to its furnishings; down here, the few antique pieces that had survived various financial purges were safe from prying eyes.

She made a final turn and reached the last alcove in the cellar; here, iron bars had been drilled into the entrance so that it could be used as a vault for the family silver. Now, the little room held a wine rack, with a dozen or so bottles of champagne, and a wardrobe, pushed against the far wall. In the middle of the space, a chaise longue sat at a haphazard angle, its damask silk glinting in the light of Fabienne's candle.

She opened the doors to the wardrobe, wondering for a moment how Sébastien and Papa had managed to get it down the narrow staircase on their own. Within, a few dresses hung on an iron rail, and Fabienne pushed them aside to lean the Kirchner, wrapped in her bedsheet, against the wardrobe's wall.

She sighed, looking at the bundle before shutting the door once more. The cellars were a marvel of engineering dug deep into the chalk ground, the humid environment ideal for champagne storage—less so for the provision of masterworks of art, but it was better than nothing. Sophie would have a fit if she knew the painting was being left in such humid conditions, but to Fabienne's mind the cellar was a temporary solution, and with her career in art restoration, Sophie could rectify any damage the Kirchner might sustain.

She took a breath, thinking about Sébastien and her parents, about Sophie, about Dietrich, then turned to make her way back up to her turreted bedroom.

27

Sophie stood in the Room of Martyrs, notebook in hand as Richter, wreathed in a cloud of cigarette smoke, perused the ledger.

"We're agreed, then, on the Braque, the Cézanne and the Degas," he said, as Rochlitz parsed through countless paintings on the trestle table. "And a Picasso—"

"*Two* Picassos," Rochlitz replied without turning. In the other galleries, ERR staff were preparing for another visit from Göring; with the *Reichsmarschall* due to arrive in the evening, they'd set up a bar in the grand gallery, champagne buckets gleaming beside small towers of glittering coupes.

Richter looked up. "Of course. Two Picassos. Mademoiselle Brandt, might you lend your expertise? There are a few paintings that might suit. UNB 327, perhaps, and LI 52."

Sophie began to sort through the paintings lined along the

room's walls, searching for the alphanumeric codes assigned by the ERR to each work of art. Over the past few weeks, her knowledge of the room had come in useful to Richter: with the collection reaching several hundred pieces, Richter had needed her help to guide him through it as they slowly parsed through paintings for his exchange with Rochlitz. But she knew that his insistence on having her present went beyond professional requirements. He liked having a woman to follow him around.

As long as that's all he expects from me, she thought bitterly. Though she resented Richter's presumption, she valued the assignment. She knew she wouldn't be able to stop the exchange of paintings, but proximity to the negotiations would, she hoped, come in useful once the war was over. As she recorded details of each exchange for Richter in her careful script, she committed each piece of information to memory. Tonight, she would write it all down again in her own growing records, in the hopes that they would be a starting point for recovering the paintings after the war.

"Thank you, Mademoiselle Brandt," Richter said as Sophie passed him the first piece he'd asked for, one of Picasso's collages. "I can't tell you how helpful you've been." He paused, holding her gaze a moment too long, but then Rochlitz came forward, and Sophie used the distraction to create distance between them as she set the second Picasso, an oil painting, on an empty easel.

"Charming," Rochlitz declared, and Sophie was inclined to agree. It was an early piece, painted before the turn of the century in a modernist style that could almost be described as derivative: it depicted several women, their hourglass figures enhanced by bustles and feather boas, outrageous hats rendered in hasty brushstrokes on cardboard that indicated Picasso had painted it *en plein air*.

"I'll take the painting," Rochlitz declared finally, "but tempted as I am by the collage, I would prefer another oil painting." He looked up at the paintings hung on the wall, his gaze settling on Picasso's portrait of Paul Rosenberg's wife and daughter. "Might we take a closer look at that piece?"

Sophie's heart sank. She'd hoped that the portrait might escape Rochlitz's notice, but Richter stepped forward to take a closer look.

"Ah, yes. We believe it to be a portrait of Picasso's mistress, Marie-Thérèse Walter, and her daughter, Maya." Richter stared up at the painting for a moment longer, and despite the peril she felt for the work of art, she couldn't help feel a twinge of satisfaction that the great Konrad Richter had erroneously identified the painting's sitters. "Mark it down for exchange, Mademoiselle Brandt."

She made a note on her clipboard. Was there any way to get the painting out of the Room of Martyrs before Rochlitz spirited it away? Not without great difficulty.

From beyond the curtained door, Sophie could hear the sound of heavy footsteps. Richter turned away from the Picasso and snapped his ledger shut, clicking his heels together as Hermann Göring swept into the room.

"Reichsmarschall," said Richter, stepping forward to clasp Göring's hand. "I wasn't expecting to see you until tonight's reception."

Göring beamed, and instinctively, Sophie took a step back as the smell of his cologne, floral and overpowering, hit her nose. Dressed in a crisp double-breasted uniform glittering with medals, Göring filled the room like an overstuffed bullfrog, his red face shining with perspiration.

"Only the briefest of visits, my dear Richter, before I carry on to my hotel," Göring said, his blue eyes darting from painting to painting. "But I caught wind on my train that a certain

Titian had made its way to the Jeu de Paume, and I simply have to see it for myself... Rochlitz, my good fellow, I'm so pleased that we seem to have come to an arrangement." He shot the art dealer a jovial grin. "Whoever said there's no room in war for diplomacy? I hope you're finding a few pieces to your liking."

Rochlitz chuckled. "More than a few, truth be told. There's a king's ransom in this room."

"A Führer's ransom, perhaps." Göring clapped Rochlitz on the shoulder. "But given that your negotiations with Richter aren't quite finished, perhaps we ought to leave it at that, eh?" He leaned in, his grip on Rochlitz's shoulder tightening. "But to the matter at hand, my good fellow. I've spent a long week in Berlin, staring at the same dull landscape in the Führer's study for hours on end. Might you indulge me in a private showing of the Titian? My attention will be pulled in so many different directions at tonight's reception, but this afternoon I want to focus entirely on *you*. Champagne? I'm sure we can prevail upon Bohn to open a bottle or two a few hours early..."

Sophie watched as Göring, chatting amiably, steered Rochlitz out the door, leaving her alone with Richter.

He opened the ledger once more. "He's like a child in a toy store, sometimes."

Sophie thought of the *Reichsmarschall*, with his expensive trinkets and his affable airs, his months-long campaign to pummel a defiant Britain into submission by bombing its capital city. "He works very hard, I'm sure," she replied carefully.

"He works hard and feels himself entitled to little luxuries as a result." Richter met Sophie's eyes. "And it's my job to provide those luxuries. I do appreciate your help in all this, Mademoiselle Brandt. Before Rochlitz returns, I'd like to have a few more pieces set out for his consideration." He glanced up at the portrait of Madame Rosenberg, his features tightening. "Shame about that Picasso. I'd had different plans for it. Still, business is business."

"Business is business," she repeated. *Plunder is plunder.*

He consulted the ledger. "Now, to our task. Let's see if we can locate NR 28—the Matisse from the Rosenberg Bordeaux inventory—and UNB 324, that lovely little Renoir."

After a quarter of an hour, Sophie and Richter had pulled out a dozen more works of art for Rochlitz to consider, most of them from Paul Rosenberg's collection. She'd heard he'd made it to New York. Had he opened a new gallery? Despite her attempts to find out, she wasn't sure.

Richter snapped his fingers, and Sophie looked up. "There ought to be a Kirchner," he said. "Not a particularly big one, a painting of two women. Of course, there's every possibility that we simply overlooked it, but according to the files, it's here somewhere."

Sophie paled. "A Kirchner."

"Yes." Richter tilted the ledger to show her the black-and-white photograph that accompanied the painting's entry, the vivid greens and pinks that Sophie knew so well, reproduced in muted grays. "Have you seen it?"

She cleared her throat. "Of course. It's in the laboratory, it had been handled improperly—manhandled—in its transfer to the museum. It needed minor repairs."

Richter frowned. "On whose authority?"

"On—on Colonel Bohn's."

"Really?" Richter looked mildly surprised. "I wouldn't have thought him sufficiently versed in art restoration to make such a decision."

"Well, even a layman knows that a broken stretcher needs replacing," she replied, her heart pounding so hard she was surprised that Richter couldn't hear it.

"But for him to take such an interest…"

Sophie smiled, hoping that an appeal to Richter's natural arrogance might assuage his suspicions. "We both know that Bohn can't tell the difference," she replied. "And who was I to say otherwise, when he was berating his own men for their carelessness?"

Richter's expression cleared. "Well, his team isn't exactly known for their subtlety," he said. "Very well, go and fetch it. But any further intervention to the degenerate collection really ought to go through me."

She took the staff staircase at almost a run, adrenaline coursing through her veins as she opened the door to the restoration lab. Hausler, mercifully, was absent, his tools neatly stacked on his workbench. Had he gone downstairs for a glimpse at the fabled Titian? She moved quickly, listening for the sound of footsteps as she pulled the false bottom from her briefcase to reveal Fabienne's forgery. Paint glistened beneath a layer of varnish, thick and gleaming. Would Richter notice a difference? Would Rochlitz?

She descended the staircase slowly, reminding herself to breathe. The painting itself was a skillful-enough forgery to withstand Richter's scrutiny, she was sure of it. It was Sophie herself that risked detection: her caginess, her fear, could give Richter reason enough for suspicion.

She thought of Fabienne in her burgundy suit, her breezy confidence, her blasé attitude. *Hide in plain sight*, Fabienne had told her. Was Sophie capable of such subterfuge?

She returned to the Room of Martyrs and pushed aside the gallery's curtained door.

"The Kirchner," she said, bringing it before Richter.

He nodded. "Where was the repair done?"

She turned the painting over. On the back of the canvas, Fabienne had affixed the original painting's label from the ERR.

She must have prized it off with a razor blade, Sophie thought with admiration. "New stretcher," she said and propped the painting on the table. "Thankfully the front of the piece had very little damage. A small amount of chipped paint, nothing more."

"Thankfully," Richter replied, taking a closer look at the painting.

Sophie mirrored his movement, barely breathing as she allowed her shoulder to graze his. It was a subtle enough gesture that she could explain it away as an accident, but out of the corner of her eye she saw Richter turn his head, just barely— enough to make her sustain the contact between them.

Richter studied the painting, his eyes darting up and down the two women painted in slashes of green and pink, their bare legs glistening on the canvas.

"Will you be attending tonight's reception?" he asked, and Sophie allowed a calculated smile to creep across her lips.

"That depends," she replied, her voice low. "Would you like me to?"

Richter looked at the painting again, but Sophie knew that he wasn't seeing the swirls of paint. He was seeing flesh and breath, the possibilities of a pleasure Sophie knew she would never give him.

"I would, Mademoiselle Brandt."

28

March 1941

"Papers."

Fabienne sighed and rummaged through her handbag. She pulled out her identity card, its cover creased from frequent use, and handed it to the German officer blocking her route to work.

"You know, there are easier ways of getting my attention," she said, flashing what she hoped was a winning smile—but the officer's stony expression hardened. Unlike his youthful counterpart at the Gare de l'Est, it was clear that this was a seasoned soldier, unlikely to find himself distracted by a pretty face.

"Fabienne Brandt," he said, putting a delicate stress on her married name. "And where are you going this morning, *mademoiselle?*"

"Madame," Fabienne corrected him. "I'm going to work. Atelier Dufy, it's just up the road. Opposite side of the street."

"Exact address?"

Fabienne gave him the street number, hoping against hope that the officer didn't decide to visit the atelier alongside her. It was the last thing Lev needed—the last thing anyone in the workroom needed—then to Fabienne's relief, he handed back her papers and stepped away.

She stowed them in her handbag and walked off without a backward glance. This was the fourth time in two days she'd been stopped for her papers, and the constant surveillance irked her. What were they hoping to find?

She crossed the street, shying away from the undeniable answer to her own question. They were hoping to find people like Myriam: Jewish residents of Paris who no longer had French citizenship to protect them from the Germans—or those who never had citizenship to begin with. She thought of the Jewish families in the countries Germany had invaded before reaching France—Poland, Denmark, Austria—and residents within Germany itself. How many had fled to France believing it to be a safer haven?

It starts silently, she thought, and the voice in her head sounded like Dietrich—Dietrich, that first night she'd taken him to one of Louis's rallies. Fabienne could still recall the heat of the room: the smell of stale beer and sweat; Louis, faltering atop two tables pushed together as Dietrich nursed a bottle of Jenlain in the back.

It had been months since Myriam had been pulled from the workroom floor, and from what Fabienne could tell, no one had heard from her since. Dufy and Lev had done their best to find her, even procuring the services of a lawyer and attempting to track down her estranged family, but Myriam, with her warm brown eyes and remarkable skills, seemed to have vanished into thin air.

It starts silently, she thought again as she reached the atelier, *to those too powerless to resist*. And who in Paris could be more powerless than a young woman without family, ostracized both because of her religion and her place of birth?

She walked into the atelier, and Dufy, standing behind the counter, looked up with a smile.

"Fabienne. How was your trip home?"

She paused. "It was…instructive," she replied. "Any news about Myriam?"

Dufy's smile dimmed. "Poor Myriam. We heard from our lawyer only this morning. It seems she was taken to Pithiviers. They've set up an internment camp there."

"An internment camp?"

He nodded solemnly, fiddling with the chain of his pocket watch. "The lawyer assures us it's only a temporary measure. Most likely, she'll face deportation, back to Algiers or somewhere else. We're not entirely sure."

Deportation. She carried on down the stairs.

She set down her handbag and crossed the workroom floor, resin dust billowing in the air as she knocked on the window that separated Lev's office from the worktables. The sound prompted a chorus of welcoming barks from Hugo, and without looking up from his work, Lev waved her in.

He was at his desk surrounded by a pile of loose-leaf papers, an open ledger and pencil shavings. Mounded on a second table pushed against the wall were jewelry molds: wooden replicas of pieces that Fabienne's coworkers would later cast in silver and gold or shape out of colorful resin.

She approached the desk, tilting her chin to better see what he had been working on as she sank into her chair. "Is that a new commission?"

He rubbed his balding forehead. "Nina Ricci is designing a gown for the Duchess of Windsor. She wants a silver brooch to accompany it." He passed the sketch to Fabienne with lead-dusted fingers. The brooch, depicted in two-dimensional graphite, would be spectacular when finished.

"Beautiful," she replied as Hugo sniffed around her feet.

Lev dipped his head, smiling. "I enjoy working with cast resin, but silver is my first love," he said. "Is there something I can help you with?"

She glanced at the office door, satisfying herself that she'd shut it properly. "Dufy told me about Myriam. How awful."

Lev sighed. As though he'd overheard the distressing news, Hugo walked around the table and jumped, uninvited, into Lev's lap. "Myriam's family left Algiers decades ago. I doubt she has any close relatives left there. If she's deported, she'll have to start from nothing...just like she did when she first arrived in Paris." He removed his spectacles to rub his eyes with the back of his hand. "I hate to think of her in that position again."

Dietrich's voice echoed once more in her mind, more persistently. *It starts silently, to those too powerless to resist.* But for Lev and Dufy, would anyone have noticed Myriam's disappearance? Would anyone be fighting to secure her release?

"I told you when you started working here that I think of my staff as family," Lev continued, "and what's family if I don't do what I can to keep my people safe?"

It was a touching sentiment, but it made what Fabienne had come to say all the more difficult to impart.

"Monsieur Lowenstein, I'm worried for Myriam—but I'm worried for you too," she said. "When the gendarmes come again, who's to say they won't be here for you and your wife?" She hesitated. "If I had a...*connection* who could secure false papers for you both, what would you say?"

To Fabienne's surprise, Lev smiled. "Thank you for your concern, my dear. Sylvie and I have discussed our options, and we both agree that we will stay in Paris."

"But why? After what happened to Myriam?"

He leaned back in his chair. "I have every hope that we will secure Myriam's release from Pithiviers before too long. But Sylvie and I are French citizens. Our rights are protected under the law."

In her mind's eye, Fabienne watched Dietrich stand up from his table at the back of the bar as Louis faltered on his makeshift stage. *It starts with silence*, he'd said, *and then it grows. Silence from those of us too unwilling to accept what's happening before our very eyes… Silence, as they chip away at the foundation of someone else's life.*

"Are they, though? Vichy is working hand in glove with the Germans. Pétain repealed the Crémieux Decree. What's to say he won't cede your rights next, in order to appease the Germans?"

Lev looked down at the sketch, his pencil hovering over the design. "We are well aware of the risks," he said quietly. "But Sylvie and I agree that our place is here. Myriam isn't the only young person who's lost her French citizenship. If we don't stay to fight for those like her, who will?" He set down the pencil and ran his hand along Hugo's curled fur. "The younger generation was right to flee. Of that, I have no doubt. But we won't abandon those among us who need their community now more than ever."

But it won't happen to me—it can't happen to me, you tell yourself, even as the sound of their tools grows louder: chip, chip, *as they repeal laws and implement newer, more brutal ones designed to divide.* The room had fallen silent as Dietrich had woven his way between the tables, his steps slow, deliberate, his eyes fixed on Louis. Chip, chip, *you hear, and you put your hands over your ears to drown out the noise, turn the newspaper over before you have to confront reality in its pages, the removal of students from your classroom, the disappearance of neighbors in the dead of the night.*

"And that's not to mention my responsibility to you, my staff." Lev looked out at the workroom, his expression softening as he caught sight of Fabienne's coworkers: Beatrice, shining buttons on a buffing wheel; Lea, fixing resin gemstones into silver casings. "You, without a husband to take care of you. Lea, who has a child to support. If I don't keep this atelier open, how will you all make a living?"

Chip, chip, you hear, and the noise becomes so commonplace it's the background to everything you do, so commonplace you forget you're hearing it at all—it's just the rhythm of life, the reality of the world around you. Chip, chip—until you look down one day and realize that the life they're chipping away is your own.

"My dear." Lev looked up, and in his smile Fabienne could see that his mind had long since been made up. "Thank you for your concern, truly, but you'd best get back to your work."

Creativity came slowly to Fabienne that evening as her conversation with Lev echoed in her ears. There was a nobility in his refusal to leave Paris, and though she was sure that Lev didn't have any illusions about what the Germans were capable of, Fabienne hated the thought that he and his wife might fall victim.

But victim to what? As Lev had pointed out, France wasn't deporting its Jewish citizens—yet. But Myriam's arrest was a clear indication that laws could be changed, that the moment Pétain needed Hitler's good graces, he wouldn't hesitate to chip away at those laws in some misguided attempt at leadership.

She thought of the Kirchner, hidden in the bowels of Château Dolus, waiting for its owner to return to Paris. What was the point of trying to save art if she couldn't save the people it belonged to?

A knock at the door, faint but persistent, interrupted Fabienne's train of thought. She went to answer it, leaving the blank canvas on the easel as a monument to her failure.

Outside, Sylvie Lowenstein stood on the landing in a sumptuous peach dressing robe, her fingers tangled in the strands of a long pearl necklace.

She smiled, but the gesture was half-hearted at best. "May I come in?"

"Oh...of course."

"I'm so sorry to come at such a late hour, and in such a state of—of undress," she said, snugging the collar of her dressing gown tight as she strode inside. "But Lev's asleep, and I couldn't get away before now."

"Not at all," Fabienne replied hastily, clearing unfolded laundry from the divan. "I can offer you a drink, Madame Lowenstein, a glass of wine perhaps, or a cup of tea—"

"Call me Sylvie, please." She glanced around the room, taking in Fabienne's apartment—her paintbrushes and easel, set up by the kitchen window, canvases, lining the walls. "I don't mean to pry, but are we quite alone?"

Fabienne sat in the chair opposite the sofa, her cheeks reddening at the implication. "We are."

"Good. I'm sorry to ask, but one can't be too careful. Lev told me about your...offer today. I wanted to thank you."

"It's nothing," Fabienne began, but Sylvie cut her off with a pointed glance.

"It's not nothing."

Fabienne played with the frayed arm of her chair. "It still amounts to nothing," she said finally. "Even if you were to take the papers, there's no guarantee they would help..."

"I disagree." Sylvie had settled into the sofa cushions. With the door closed, she looked calm, assured. "Lev still believes that we can come through these terrible times. Ever the optimist."

"He's a good man," Fabienne replied. "All that he did for me, all he's trying to do for Myriam…"

"And it's that sense of responsibility which makes him feel he needs to stay." She smiled, more genuinely than before. "You know, when Lev and I first married, he'd just started Atelier Lowenstein—*Atelier Dufy* now, I suppose. He'd gotten discharged from the army and had an extra year's apprenticeship to finish with a goldsmith, but he decided it was time to start out on his own. He'd given four years to the war, and he'd always fancied himself an entrepreneur. I used to roll my eyes when he told me of his plans—so many young men dream of setting up shops, putting their names in big letters above the door… You can always tell when it's a matter of pride." She chuckled. "Not for Lev. I remember him taking me to the atelier for the first time, before he'd hired anyone. All those tables down on the workroom floor. I remember thinking it would be a miracle if he could afford to fill them all with workers." She looked up, her gaze sharp and tender all at once. "Did you ever wonder why Lev only hires women? It's the same reason he was in such a rush to open his own shop, after the war ended. Too many women would be left widowed, he told me. Too many women left without their husbands to provide for them."

Fabienne shifted in her seat, thinking of Dietrich.

"We'd been lucky, Lev and I, to have made it through those terrible years and still have each other," Sylvie continued. "But Lev wanted to do what he could for those who weren't so fortunate. He wanted to make sure they could feed their children, that they would have a trade they could rely on, once the men came to take back their jobs at the banks and the factories."

She smiled. "Another woman might have been suspicious, but I never had cause for concern. Not once in forty years."

Fabienne cleared her throat. "Please, Madame Lowenstein. Sylvie. I don't want to sound alarmist, but I know what the Germans are capable of. I've seen it, firsthand."

"So have we," she replied gently. "We've been working with our synagogue to get young families out of the country... To help those who've been taken, like Myriam. We know what's coming. Lev believes that we owe a responsibility to the younger generation to stay and help others however we can."

She turned her attention to the pocket of her dressing gown, giving Fabienne time to compose herself. But she had no cause to cry—not when Sylvie was the one in danger.

"Lev believes that we can come through this war, and I hope he's right. Hitler will be defeated one day. I share my husband's optimism in that much, at least." She pulled two small photographs out of her pocket, herself and Lev, positioned against plain backdrops, the right size and shape for standard identity cards.

She held out the photographs, and Fabienne took them with trembling hands. "Does...does Lev know about this?"

"No, and I would prefer not to tell him." She stood, straightening the folds of her dressing gown. "But I would like to leave this option open to us."

Fabienne, too, stood. "I can't tell you how pleased I am," she said. "I'm not sure how long it will take to have the papers made, but I'll get them back to you as soon as I can."

"Thank you." Sylvie made her way to the door, then paused. "Lev's always been one to solve problems for those he considers family," she said, "but I worry that this is beyond even his capabilities."

Without thinking, Fabienne crossed the living room and pulled Sylvie into a tight hug. She was offering a sticking plaster—the smallest of solutions. Even with false papers, the Lowensteins would have to make their way across France to neutral Switzerland or even farther afield before they could count themselves truly safe, but it was a start, at least, should conditions deteriorate further in Paris.

"But that's the point of family," she said finally. "They're here to help, when a burden seems too much to carry alone."

29

The sound of German voices rang off the gallery walls of the Jeu de Paume, the language familiar and unsettling all at once. To Sophie, German had been the language in which she'd been taught to love: the language of bedtime stories and fairy tales, teasing Dietrich as they ran through the Black Forest on family holidays; Mamma, whispering comforts as she collected Sophie up in her arms after a nightmare; Papa, teaching Sophie how to study paintings in the Staatsgalerie.

It was the language, too, in which Sophie had been taught to hate—the language of her teachers, calmly explaining how genetic defects weakened those who weren't part of the German master race; of youth rallies and brownshirts shouting obscenities at elderly rabbis on the street; of oaths given to madmen whose eyes glittered in the torchlight glow of a hundred thousand fervent followers.

Tonight, Sophie listened to the ring of German voices as Göring and his fellow looters, concealed behind the curtained windows of the Jeu de Paume in a Parisian blackout, swapped stories of long-lost bravery, their words long since polished to perfection over hundreds of tellings.

"There I was," Göring said, his booming voice ringing over the sound of Ravel played by a pianist on a gleaming Steinway. "Three thousand feet above Alsace-Lorraine in an Albatros D.II, smoke billowing from the engine. What do I do?"

The pianist lifted his hands from the keys, and Göring smiled, enjoying the rapt attention of his silent audience: Bohn, his wedding ring glinting as he draped his arm over his secretary's shoulder; Konrad Richter and Hildebrand Gurlitt, watching with wide eyes.

"I use the momentum of the crash to my advantage," Göring concluded, underscoring his own brilliance by punching one hand into his glittering fist. "I continue firing as I make a controlled descent, taking out three Sopwith Camels as I go. I knew that if my time had come, I would take as many Englishmen to hell along with me as I could."

Bohn pulled a cigar from between his lips. "And now he's showing those bastards why they ought to have finished the job in '17!" he shouted, and a cheer rang up from Göring's admirers.

Göring flushed red with satisfaction. "Was awarded the Zähringer Lion soon after," he finished as the pianist resumed playing.

"Quite the tale of derring-do." Sophie turned. Behind her, Gerhardt Hausler, his hair slicked back in a dashing coif, leaned heavily on his stick. "It's a privilege, isn't it, to be regaled by *Der Eiserne* himself?"

Sophie glanced back at Göring. "I couldn't really follow,"

she said offhandedly, "though I like to think my grasp on the language is improving. Let me see, now, *Der Eiserne*…?"

"The Iron Man," Hausler translated. He leaned in, his smile sharpening to a smirk. "It's meant to refer to his steadfast will, but given all those medals he insists on wearing, he probably needs a spine of iron just to stand upright. Have you heard the one about him visiting the Vatican?"

"No," she whispered, warming to Hausler's lighthearted tone.

"He sent a telegram to Hitler once he got there: *Mission Accomplished. Pope Unfrocked. Pontifical Vestments A Perfect Fit.*"

She lifted her glass to her lips to hide her smile as she pictured Göring, parading through Rome in the papal jewels while the Pope trailed despondently behind. Given Göring's flamboyant nature and overt affability, it was easy to forget the power he wielded not only over the art in the Jeu de Paume but across occupied Europe at large.

"I heard he had Hitler make him a set of rubber medals," she whispered back, "so that he could wear them in the bath."

Hausler's smirk broadened; with a wink, he lifted his glass and drifted away.

Sophie turned her attention back to the room. The crowd around Göring had broken up, and the sounds of Ravel grew louder as people drifted through the galleries. At the bar, Richter refilled his glass of wine. Nearby, Göring wandered past with Gustav Rochlitz as Rose Valland stared up at a splendid Cranach.

The pianist changed tunes, shifting smoothly from Ravel to Gershwin's *Rhapsody in Blue*. Out of the corner of her eye, Sophie saw Göring stiffen.

He turned, surprisingly quick on his heels as he stormed toward the grand piano. Caught up in the American melody, the pianist didn't see the look of fury on Göring's red face as he planted a beefy hand on the piano's open lid and slammed it down with such force that the prop stick splintered.

The pianist looked up, his face frozen in abject terror—then, as though remembering the company he was in, Göring let out a bark of laughter.

"Come, now, no need to look so dramatic!" He clapped the pianist's thin shoulder, the tails of the man's jacket shaking with the movement. "Consider it like you would a critic's review, my good fellow, and choose more patriotic selections in the future."

Silence followed—and then Bohn's secretary laughed, her voice a thin, shrill punctuation before Bohn joined in, and then Richter. Göring turned around, shaking his head with theatrical amusement as he rejoined Rochlitz. Before long, the sound of German conversation filled the air once more, accompanied by a weak and tinkling rendition of Strauss's *The Blue Danube*.

Sophie set down her champagne coupe with trembling fingers. She needed to get out of the room, to be anywhere but here, in the company of Nazis and monsters, men who reveled in casual violence and hatred. She walked quickly out of the grand gallery, breezing past a stern-faced Rose Valland. What had she been thinking, accepting a position from men such as these?

The back gallery was nearly deserted but for a few ERR staff members Sophie knew by sight alone, and she slipped past them, feeling as though her chest might burst if she didn't find some moment of solitude. She inhaled deeply, seeking to quell the tide that threatened to overcome her. She fought to overcome the uncontrollable trembling as her body flooded with the need to rage, to flee, to fight—but what could she rage against, here in this museum? How could she flee, when

Göring's guards were posted at the door? Who could she fight, when the Germans were already victorious?

She headed for the Room of Martyrs, hoping to use the quiet space to collect herself. Although she didn't smoke as a rule, she pushed aside the curtains while reaching into her pocket for a stash of cigarettes and shook one out of crumpled packaging, searching her pockets for a lighter, a set of matches—

Standing at the picture rail, Gerhardt Hausler turned, his eyebrows raised in polite inquiry.

"I'd heard Rochlitz had made his selection," he said mildly, glancing back at the paintings that now lined the picture rail. Eleven in all, Picassos, Braques and Matisses destined to be crated up and sent to Rochlitz's gallery. "I wanted to see them for myself before they leave the museum. Eleven paintings for a Weenix and a supposed Titian. I'd say that Rochlitz got the better end of the bargain."

Sophie lingered at the door as Hausler walked slowly along the line of paintings, the heel of his cane tapping gently on the floor. "I didn't realize you were in here, Dr. Hausler. I'll leave you—"

"Please, don't go, Mademoiselle Brandt." He looked up. "Stay with me. We share a laboratory, but we never seem to get a chance to talk properly, you and I." He smiled, his tone easy and conspiratorial. "I won't tell anyone about the cigarette, if that's what's worrying you."

If only you knew. Though her earlier sense of terror had begun to dissipate, something in Hausler's tone kept her on her guard, tension prickling at the back of her neck. Was it intuition, telling her to run, or was she mistaking Hausler's genuine cordiality for danger?

She lit the cigarette, clearing a billow of smoke from the air around her.

"Good," said Hausler. "I'm glad you're staying, Sophie. May I call you Sophie?"

"Of course," she replied.

"And I'd like it if you called me Gerhardt." He snaked around the back of the table to admire a Dalí on the wall. "I don't know that many people in Paris who might call me Gerhardt. It's difficult to make friends, these days. But you know something of that, I think."

Sophie inhaled deeply, letting the tobacco calm her jangling nerves. "Something of what?"

He shrugged. "Moving to a new city. Making new friends. Remind me, Sophie, where did you grow up?"

Her heart dropped. "Lausanne," she replied, attempting to lend conviction to her tone.

"Of course." He rapped a knuckle on the frame of a nearby Matisse. "Henri was known to visit Lausanne. Pablo too."

"It's a haven for artists," she replied carefully.

"Indeed." Hausler's smile dimmed. "I wonder whether any of these pieces will find their way to Lausanne. I'm told Rochlitz has quite an extensive client list in Switzerland."

"All the more reason to enjoy them while we can," Sophie replied, and Hausler looked at her with a peculiar expression.

"I must say, I'm rather impressed with Dr. Richter. I've never thought much of him, but he's got quite the start of a lucrative business here, if he remains in Göring's good graces. After all, it's not as though Bohn knows what to do with the degenerate collection."

Sophie's neck prickled again. From down the hall, she could hear the sound of Göring's booming laughter and the faraway lilt of conversation. Were there still ERR curators in the nearby gallery, or had they returned to the party?

She chose her words carefully. "There's no room for degeneracy in the Reich."

"No room for degeneracy." Hausler sighed, then consulted a gold watch on a chain. "Well, Rochlitz has good taste, I must say—even if his eye leaves something to be desired."

Sophie looked up sharply. "How do you mean?"

He stowed the pocket watch away and jerked his chin in the direction of the picture rail. "The Titian he's so proud of is a *presumed* Titian, at best. And that Kirchner... Well, it's not exactly a Kirchner, is it?"

Sophie paled, and a look of triumph crossed Hausler's lined face.

"I thought as much," he said and stepped forward to wrap his fingers around Sophie's arm. "We're going to take a walk up to our laboratory, Mademoiselle Brandt. And then I suggest you tell me everything."

30

The train carriage rang with song and laughter, the sound of a hundred girls drowning out the clatter of the train's wheels as it sped northeast through the dawn-lit countryside. To Sophie, sitting halfway down the carriage, the rambunctious energy of her troupe-mates felt enough to propel the train without the use of coal. How could they not be excited at the prospect of attending their very first *Reichsparteitag* in Nuremberg? She watched as Ella, a brawny, golden-haired troupe leader with a black-and-silver badge pinned to her middy blouse, conducted a rousing rendition of the "Horst Wessel Song," occasionally gripping the back of the nearest seat for balance as she walked through the rocking carriage.

Seated beside her, Greta nudged Sophie's arm, sending a jolt of electricity shooting straight to Sophie's core.

"You're not really singing," Greta hissed, giving Sophie a

freckle-dusted smile, and Sophie, who had been mouthing the words silently, joined in. Greta laughed, and Sophie's heart lifted as the song reached its thrilling crescendo. As self-conscious as she was about her singing voice—about her unruly hair and blemished complexion, her awkward manners and lack of grace—she would have done anything to make Greta smile.

Ella held up her hand. "All right, all right, settle down," she said, but there was little she could do to quell the sense of excitement as the countryside began to give way to the scattered outskirts of the city. "Settle down, girls! I know we're all eager to attend the *Reichsparteitag*, but before we arrive I want you all to promise me that you'll behave yourselves. Understand? It is an honor to represent the *Bund Deutscher Mädel* in such a historic event, particularly in today's opening ceremonies, and I know that none of you will disgrace the name of Stuttgart—are you listening, Frieda?" She raised her voice playfully, and a girl at the back of the carriage let up an obliging squawk of protest. "I know that all of you will make me proud. Be good, and you might even catch the Führer's attention."

The carriage erupted into whispers.

"The Führer!" Greta squeezed Sophie's hand. "Could you imagine? What would you say, if you got to meet him?"

Sophie shook her head, savoring Greta's touch. "No," she said emphatically. "There's no way the Führer would talk to us! He's far too important."

Greta leaned over, resting her braided head on Sophie's shoulder to watch the passing countryside. "He'd listen to you. You've always got such important things to say."

Sophie barely heard Greta's compliment. How could she, when the scent of Greta's perfume was so intoxicating? "We'll only see him from a distance, I bet. Besides, I'm more excited to visit with my brother."

"Dietrich," Greta mumbled in agreement, the rocking of the train lulling her into a doze.

Dietrich. Sophie hadn't seen him since his eighteenth birthday, when he'd begun his compulsory training with the *Wehrmacht*. He'd written to her, of course, and she'd written back, but this rally, which brought together all the Führer's supporters from across the Reich, was the first opportunity she'd had to see him in six months, and judging from the bitter tone of his letters, Sophie had a lot of news to catch up on. But as excited as she was to spend time with Dietrich, she couldn't deny that part of the allure of her troupe's week-long trip to Nuremberg was this: the possibility of spending time with Greta, sharing confidences that Sophie had only ever dreamed of until now.

The train slowed as it crawled into the city, and Sophie pressed her face to the glass to catch sight of the medieval turrets of Nuremberg Castle, sienna brown against the cerulean sky. With its half-timbered buildings and round towers, the castle had once been a classic example of Gothic architecture, but the city's fresh new identity as the home of the Nazi party had led to a recent conversion. The castle had been gutted and modernized, stripped of centuries' worth of additions in an attempt to make it useful once more.

The future always takes from the past, she thought to herself ruefully, wishing she could have seen the nineteenth-century additions before they'd all been taken out. *But progress cannot be halted by something so basic as sentimentality*. That, at least, was what she'd been told by teachers and BDM troupe leaders alike, ever since her application to the Stuttgart State Academy of Fine Arts had been denied: that progress was made on the basis of individual sacrifice, made on behalf of the common good.

It still hurt to think that her dreams of becoming an art restorer were all but over. How could they not be, when the common good required her to become a wife and mother? She'd done her best to accept what fate had in store for her—but sitting here, with Greta's head on her shoulder, she couldn't help picturing a different reality.

The rest of the day passed in a blur, and Sophie swallowed her melancholy as she walked arm in arm with Greta through the swastika-lined streets of Nuremberg, its medieval buildings a quaint contrast to the magnificent modernity of Zeppelin Field. Alongside thousands of other girls from hundreds of other BDM troupes, Sophie performed a dance in glorious unison to officially open the Nuremberg rally, swirling beneath the eye of their leader as he stood atop a mighty podium, one arm outstretched in a strong salute. Here, even Sophie could concede that the good of the whole outweighed the pain of the individual. What did it matter if she was unhappy, so long as she could make her country, her Führer, proud?

That evening, Sophie sat on the floor beside a bunk bed while Greta combed her hair into two thick plaits. They'd been invited to a dance with members of the *Wehrmacht—real men*, so Ella had told them excitedly as they all got ready in their thirty-bed dorm within Luginsland Tower's heavily sloped walls.

"Our first party," Greta whispered from over Sophie's shoulder. "Who will you dance with?"

In her mind's eye, Sophie held out her hand, and Greta took it. "I don't know," she said, as she pictured herself dancing with Greta, cheek to cheek. "Whoever asks, I suppose."

Greta finished tying the plaits and patted Sophie's shoulder. "I'll dance with anyone who holds a rank of *Unteroffizier* or higher." She rummaged in her pocket, surreptitiously glancing around to make sure Ella's attention was elsewhere before pulling out a battered compact of rouge. "Go on," she whispered. "I'll make sure Ella doesn't see."

Hastily, Sophie dipped her finger in the rouge and smeared it across her cheeks, using the compact's small mirror to see an inch of her skin at a time. She knew that their troupe leader would reprimand them both if she caught sight of the rouge—for a good German girl, a healthy complexion was attained through activity and exercise rather than artifice—but perhaps if Sophie was subtle, Ella wouldn't notice the difference.

Greta pursed her lips.

"You've... You need to blend it in more, I think," she said, and cupped Sophie's face. Gently, she began to work the rouge into Sophie's cheeks with her thumb, her touch as light as a whisper.

"There," she said quietly, her fingers lingering on Sophie's cheeks a moment longer than necessary.

Reluctant as she was to let the moment pass, but all too aware that someone else—another troupe member, or Ella herself—might see, Sophie shifted out of Greta's grasp.

"The...here," she mumbled, handing back the compact.

Greta took it, her cheeks suddenly, furiously red without the help of makeup. She turned away, busying herself with the compact—something had shifted the moment Sophie had pulled away, and Sophie hated herself for it. Wasn't Greta's attention the only thing she'd ever wanted?

At the other end of the room, Ella cleared her throat. "Now, I know you're all excited for the dance," she said indulgently, and Sophie saw several of her troupe-mates wriggle gleefully in their seats, "and I expect you all to conduct yourself in accordance with the Führer's wishes."

She paused, and Sophie braced herself for a lecture she'd heard too many times before in her seventeen years in classrooms and at youth groups, in the years before she'd joined the BDM. *Behave like a lady*, she'd been told when she was thirteen, fifteen. *Men will take advantage if you let them.*

Ella smiled. "You will no doubt hear this speech many times over the course of this week, but it never hurts to hear it again. For some of you, this is your first time at Nuremberg—" Sophie and Greta exchanged glances "—and I want you to know what a privilege it is to be here. When you joined my troupe, you became part of the oldest ranks of the *Bund Deutscher Mädel*, and that means that you, my girls, are the most important people in the whole of the Reich."

Sophie reached behind her and squeezed Greta's knee.

"As you know, it is our duty—our destiny—to help the Reich grow into the strong, pure homeland that it once was and will be again," Ella continued as she walked between the bunk beds. "This rally offers an opportunity like no other for you to achieve that destiny." She swept an arm out toward the room's dormer window, where the golden glow of sunset was creeping across the floor. "This week, Germany's finest young men have gathered together to celebrate the might of our country. We're here to celebrate with them, and to help build the future of Germany.

"At tonight's dance, and at all the events that follow, you will meet some of the most racially pure men that the Reich has to offer. It is your duty—*our* duty—to take advantage of this gathering to begin building the next generation of the German *Volk*." She glanced around the room, beaming. "A racially pure *Volk*, a generation devoid of impurities. A generation of *Übermenschen*."

The sunset glow had reached Ella's face, giving her amber eyes an avaricious gleam as she surveyed the troupe. "This week, you must fulfill your destinies as mothers of the Reich. Come home with a child in your bellies for the Führer, and you will have done your glorious duty."

★ ★ ★

The *Ballhaus* was large and dimly lit, filled with handsome soldiers and troupes of girls who, like Sophie, had come dressed in the long skirts and kerchiefs of the BDM. In a wood-paneled alcove, a brass-heavy orchestra played a sedate selection of dance-hall hits, the crooning of the singer blessedly familiar amid the unfamiliarity of Sophie's first-ever dance. Already, a few couples had begun to turn on the worn parquet—the boldest men, with the bravest girls—while a cluster of soldiers wearing *Wehrmacht* gray stood by the punch table, topping up their glass teacups with slugs of liquor from battered flasks.

Still standing in the doorway, Sophie took a breath while Greta pinched more color into her cheeks.

"You buttoned your shirt wrong," she said casually, and Sophie wheeled, mortified, to face the wall as she fixed it. "Where should we start, do you think? I quite like the look of that group at the punch table...although, if you want to do a quick turn around the room to see if Dietrich is here, that would be fine too."

Of course—Dietrich. Sophie was still so stunned that she'd forgotten why she'd been excited to come to the dance in the first place. Ella had given each of them a small glass of schnapps before they left the hostel, but the liquor had done little to dull Sophie's nerves—she'd never so much as kissed a boy, nor was she entirely sure she ever wanted to. How could she perform her duty to the Reich when it involved so much more than she'd ever imagined?

"All right," said Greta with a peevish glance. "You can just stand there, but I'm going."

Sophie looked around the room for something—anything—to distract her. Dietrich: Was he here, somewhere, one of the countless soldiers with a standard-issue uniform and regulation blue eyes? Standing at the punch bowl, Troupe Leader Ella poured herself a drink, casting her glittering gaze about the room. She caught sight of Sophie, and Sophie shot out her hand to grip Greta's arm.

"Is this—does this feel entirely right to you?" she said.

Greta's answering gaze was blank. "I'm not sure what you mean, *Schnucki*," she said gently, then drifted into the crowd.

Sophie could feel someone staring and looked around. Still at the refreshment table, Ella indicated, with a rigid jerk of her neck, for Sophie to follow Greta onto the dance floor.

She took a step, and it felt to Sophie as though she were moving through quicksand. Already a few of her troupe-mates had begun to dance. Near the orchestra, Frieda was quick-stepping with a foot soldier, her uniform so childish, so juvenile, next to his crisp dress jacket. She ran a hand along his arm, laughing, and Sophie turned away, picturing Frieda's blue blouse swollen over an advanced pregnancy, smugly triumphant as she gave herself to a man she barely knew. Offering up her child, her precious *Übermensch*, to the Führer.

Sophie had reconciled herself to the thought of giving up the job of her dreams for the good of the Reich, but giving up her body? Her heart?

Her life?

A soldier stumbled up to her through the fray, and it was clear by his glassy eyes and ruddy cheeks that he'd already had a lot to drink.

"Dance with me?" he asked, holding out a hand. He was a few years older than Sophie, but a child still. With his unshaven cheeks and puppy-fat physique, it was clear that he was a new recruit. Was his state of inebriation the result of his own attempt to banish jitters?

Over his shoulder, Ella met her eyes and nodded.

"Of course," she replied and allowed him to steer her onto the dance floor.

The soldier's breath was hot on her shoulder as they danced, his fingers thick and grasping on her waist as he tried, persistently, to pull her close. She turned her head, the better to survey the room. Where was Dietrich?

A few couples over, Greta was dancing with an *Unteroffizier*, and Sophie felt a pang of regret. The look on her face was as tender, as gentle, as it had been when she'd rested her head on Sophie's shoulder on the train. She met Sophie's eye and blushed before returning her attention to her partner.

Sophie pulled free from the soldier's grasp, apologizing over her shoulder as she darted through the crowd.

"I'm so sorry. I need some air—"

Outside, the moonless night glowed in the light of yellow streetlamps, and the air was cold on her burning cheeks as she walked away from the *Ballhaus*. *Breathe*, she told herself, hoping against hope that Ella hadn't seen her abrupt departure from the dance hall. She tucked herself into a nearby alley, the outer wall of the *Ballhaus* blessedly cool as she leaned against it, pressing her forehead into the stone to let herself succumb, for just a moment, to the tears that she'd tried so hard to hide.

She could leave—pretend she'd met some dashing soldier and sneak back to the hostel, feign sleep when Greta returned to whisper details of her adventures with the *Unteroffizier*. With twenty girls under her supervision, would Ella really notice the disappearance of one? It was what she wanted, after all, for her girls to slip away into dark corners...

She pictured the route back to the hostel, only a few turns away up gentle cobbled roads. Over the rooftops, she could see the sloped walls of Luginsland Tower, illuminated by the same cold spotlights that sent up columns of white around far-off Zeppelin Field. She could be back in her bunk in twenty minutes, if she didn't dawdle. Perhaps she would see Dietrich at tomorrow's military parade, or else she would write to him once she was home in Stuttgart, to apologize for missing him.

She turned, pulling her kerchief from her neck to dry her tears.

"Why so sad, *Fräulein*?"

A group of soldiers had spilled out of the dance hall, their tunics unbuttoned as they passed around a silver flask. She wiped her cheeks once more and balled her rouge-stained kerchief in her hand, then started walking in the opposite direction.

"*Fräulein!* Hey, *Fräulein!*" One of the soldiers broke away from the group and jogged up, circling to cut off her route. He held out his hands, his handsome face guileless and alert all at once.

"I just want to make sure you're all right," he said, and over the sound of the brass band echoing out of the *Ballhaus*'s open doors, she could hear footsteps behind her.

Terror flooded through her veins, obliterating every emotion other than the primal urge to flee.

"Let me pass," she said quietly.

"Not until I know you're all right," the soldier replied, reaching into his pocket. "What sort of gentleman would I be if I didn't ensure a lady's safety? This is a big city, *Fräulein*, and we aren't the only people in it. Jews, subhumans—they would do almost anything to lay their hands on a pretty thing like you." He held out a green packet, and out of the corner of her eye she could see his friends, circling her like wolves around a deer. "Cigarette?"

"Let me pass," she repeated more forcefully, and she lunged forward, but the soldier dropped his cigarettes to catch her with both hands.

"Now, is that any way to treat one of Germany's brave defenders?" He pushed Sophie against the wall and leaned close, seeming to relish her attempts to struggle free. "And when all we want is to help you do your duty." He brought one hand to her throat to pin her in place as he fumbled with his belt buckle, and Sophie could feel his breath hot on her cheek as his friends egged him on. "A child for the Führer—"

In a flash, so quickly that Sophie only saw it as a blur, the soldier was gone, and there, breathing heavily, stood Dietrich. He glanced at Sophie, his face like thunder, before turning back to the group of soldiers. The ringleader was spread out on the cobbles, his once-perfect nose bent and streaming with blood, but his friends, momentarily scattered, had regrouped.

Dietrich held out one arm to shield Sophie behind his back, and in his free hand she could see the glint of a pocketknife.

"Get the hell out of here, Schmidt," he growled, and two members of the pack darted forward to drag away the ring-leader, his shining boots knocking against the cobbles as they retreated down the darkened road.

He turned and pulled Sophie into his arms. With a sort of detachment, she realized that he was trembling almost as much as her. "Are you hurt? Sophie, are you—"

"I-I'm all right, Dietrich," she stammered. "I'm okay."

He stepped back and looked at her as though ensuring with his own eyes that she was unharmed, breathing as though he'd run a marathon. "Where's your hostel? We need to go, pack your things."

"Pack? Dietrich, I can't—there's the parade tomorrow—"

"We're leaving," he said flatly. He took Sophie's hand and began storming up the road. "Schmidt's in my regiment, and he's a ruthless bastard, but if it's not him, it will be someone else trying their luck. If you think I'm going to let you get thrown to those monsters again... We'll get on the next train, anywhere is better than here—"

"Leave Nuremberg?" She wrenched her hand out of his. "Dietrich, we can't. Your entire regiment is here. You'd be deserting."

"All the better." He stared at Sophie, and in the light of a nearby streetlamp she could see how pale he'd become, how drawn. "You know that I've never believed in all of this. This—this insanity, this megalomaniac running our country... The things they taught us in the Hitler Youth and now in the *Wehrmacht*, it's all built to divide, Sophie, to divide and blind."

He glanced over his shoulder, and Sophie knew that their time was limited. Between her troupe leader and the soldiers that Dietrich had scared off, someone would come looking for them before too long.

"I worried about you, every single day since I was conscripted. But you seemed happy, in your letters, making friends. I didn't feel I had the right to take that away from you without reason. But what I just saw, what I just heard... What was going on in that dance hall... It's a cult, Sophie. It's a cult, and I can't bear the thought of you being one of its victims."

She took a step forward. "Where would we go?"

"Anywhere, so long as it's not here. I can't live in this nightmare anymore." He paused. "Tell me you're happy here. Tell me that this is the life you want, and I will leave you alone. But you must decide."

She thought, with a moment's regret, of Greta's soft smile, her freckled cheeks. "It's not the life I want."

Dietrich held out his hand, and together they disappeared into the shadows.

31

March 1941

Sophie's mind was racing as Gerhardt Hausler escorted her up the staff staircase and into the laboratory. She could run, of course—but how far would she get, with Göring and his underlings in the galleries? With soldiers patrolling the Jardin des Tuileries?

He pulled her into the restoration lab and locked the door.

"One moment." He thumped past her as Sophie leaned, weak-legged, against her worktable. "Don't want to be overheard," he muttered, opening the supply closet door to reveal a mess of additional tools and boxes. "Bohn and his secretary have been known to get quite adventurous in this building. We can't be too careful... Now." He positioned himself against the edge of his own workbench and faced Sophie, his fingers dancing on the head of his cane. "The Kirchner."

Think, Sophie told herself, striving to hide the depths of her panic behind a façade of calm. "What makes you think there's something wrong with it?"

"The shade of red used for the left-hand figure is off," he replied. "It's close—very close—but it isn't quite right."

"I see." Sophie gripped the edge of her table. "And you could tell from a glance, could you, that the red was off? Anything could have darkened it. Smoke damage, light exposure, oxidization…"

"I got more than a glance at it." From beyond the closed door, Sophie could hear the distant clatter of the ongoing party. "I'm quite familiar with the piece. Why did you do it?"

"Who's to say I did anything?" Sophie shot back. "I'm as surprised as you are. It came from a private collector, perhaps he'd been taken in by some criminal—"

"Paul Rosenberg would no sooner mistake a Kirchner than he would shoot off his own foot," Hausler snapped. "I examined this piece when I first arrived at the Jeu de Paume months ago, and unless your methods of conservation are vastly different than mine, the colors in that painting have changed. So I must conclude that you've replaced the original with a forgery." He crossed his arms, light sparking from a gold signet ring he wore on his smallest finger. "A good forgery, I admit, but a forgery nonetheless. I'm surprised that Richter didn't see it. In all the excitement of his work with Göring, he's losing his touch."

Hausler had outmaneuvered her, that much was clear. But perhaps she could still turn the situation to her advantage.

"You know what the Nazis did to Kirchner's other pieces," she said fiercely. "You know what they'll do to that painting if they get hold of it." Her mind turned to Rose Valland. She would be so disappointed to learn that Sophie was no more than a common thief. Would Hausler allow her to take her supplies with her when he dismissed her? Or was the prospect of dismissal more than she could hope for? "He's one of the most important artists of our time. I couldn't allow them to further destroy his legacy. I just couldn't."

"Was," Hausler replied.

Sophie looked up. "I beg your pardon?"

"He *was* one of the most important artists of our time." Hausler straightened, pulling his waistcoat taut over his slender frame. "We were friends, you know. Ernst and I. And Emil Nolde. Otto Müller. All the members of *Die Brücke*, really—back in the days of my wayward youth." His expression softened momentarily as he ran a hand through his silvering hair. "I was part of his circle—or, rather, I longed to be. They were all my heroes, creating art that sought to shape the future, rather than reflect the past." He removed his spectacles and pulled out his handkerchief to clean the lenses with brusque efficiency. "I had a…particular friend among Ernst's admirers, a young man…"

He trailed off, absorbed in the task of cleaning his glasses, and Sophie thought, irresistibly, of Greta with her freckled smile and her plaited hair shining in the summer sunlight.

Hausler cleared his throat. "*Die Brücke* drifted apart during the Great War, of course—all of us, scattered by our regiments. Ernst enlisted as a driver in a field artillery regiment, but he had an…episode in 1915 and was never quite the same after that."

Sophie had heard about Kirchner's breakdown. He'd been committed to a sanatorium and had spent much of his remaining life in and out of institutions. Had Hausler visited him, during those dark years after the Great War?

"He never really left that battlefield, you know. Neither did I, I suppose. I went off to the academy in Dresden to train as a restorer, while Ernst ended up in Davos." He smiled. "A little far to visit regularly, but we corresponded until the end of his life."

Sophie cleared her throat. "And your...your particular friend...?"

Gerhardt's smile dimmed. "We joined up together in 1915, just before Ernst was invalided out," he said. "Willi saved my life, more than once. Pulled me out of a crater after I'd been blown halfway across no-man's-land by a British bomb. He was...braver than me, by far." Silence bloomed between them, the implications of which were as tender and meaningful as if Hausler had put his feelings to words.

Finally, he cleared his throat. "Six hundred of Ernst Kirchner's works were destroyed when the Nazis took power and branded him a degenerate. Ernst never recovered from the insult of it all. *Die Brücke* was founded on the promise of creating a new art for Germany, for a new and modern world. But Hitler saw Ernst's work as degenerate."

"Along with so many others," Sophie interjected, and Hausler nodded slowly, caught, she suspected, in the mist of painful memories.

"Ernst's art was meant to shape the future... In the end he couldn't bear what the future had become." He stood, his lined face somber. "His wife, Erna, is still there, I believe, in Frauenkirche. Not many of us were able to travel there to pay our respects."

Sophie pressed a hand to her lips. She'd known the broad strokes of Kirchner's story—that his death had been declared a suicide—but to hear it from a personal friend had given vivid color to the sheer tragedy of the artist's final days. She pictured Ernst's widow, and in her mind's eye Erna shared Fabienne's sharp features, standing alone at the side of his grave, living in the house they'd once filled with art and memories.

"How can you work for them? Knowing what they did to your friend…how can you bear it?"

"You think I had a choice in the matter?" Hausler returned his spectacles to the bridge of his nose. "Willi and I were living in Berlin—a small apartment, two bedrooms for appearance's sake. But someone—a neighbor—gave us up to the authorities. The brownshirts came in the middle of the night. They took us to the police station… Willi was taken to a concentration camp, along with other…other men like us. Alongside the artists and the Jews and the Gypsies and the political dissidents…"

Hausler's signet ring glinted as he adjusted his grip on his walking stick. Had Willi worn a similar one when he'd been taken away in the night—another soul, another story, another victim?

"They kept me at that police station for days. To give me time, I suppose, to think about my options. I had talents, they said, that were of use to the Reich. I could join the party, join the ERR—or I could follow Willi into Sachsenhausen." He shut his eyes, his face twisting with anguish. "I thought I… I thought I'd be able to do more, as part of the party— that I might be able to…to save Willi. Have some measure of influence over his fate, perhaps have him…have him taken elsewhere, out of the Reich, where he might be able to…to live…" He looked up, pleading with Sophie as though she could change the outcome of what had happened so many years ago. "What would you have done, if you'd been given the choice?"

She leaned forward and gripped his trembling hands in hers. Had Greta ever found someone with whom to share the affection that had slipped through Sophie's fingers? Or had she resigned herself to the fate of an ideologue, ground down beneath blinkered ideals of Nazi womanhood?

In some ways, Sophie hoped that Greta had chosen the latter, for such a choice would at least mean life.

"The day I signed my oath of allegiance, they told me that Willi...had died there. Without me." Hausler's voice broke, tears streaming down his cheeks. "My choice should have been a simple one. I should have followed him into that camp, I should have died alongside him, but Willi died thinking I'd forsaken him—and I had."

"You didn't," Sophie replied fiercely. "The choice wasn't yours to make. What they did to you and Willi was monstrous. But it wasn't your fault, Gerhardt."

"If not mine, then whose?" Hausler smiled sadly. "I abandoned the man I loved, let him be branded a degenerate like Ernst. Like me." He took a deep, shuddering breath. "Like those paintings downstairs. If you've managed to save even one, you've been braver than I ever was."

"So we save more," Sophie whispered, clutching Hausler's hand tighter. "We get as many as we can out of the museum. For Willi and Ernst both. For Dietrich and Paul." *For Greta*, she added mentally, letting hope and pain and anguish sweep through her heart all at once. "We'll save what we can. All of it, for those that we've lost."

32

The cobbled footpath along the banks of the Seine gleamed in the afternoon sunlight, a brief but furious downpour having transformed it into a sodden, shallow lake that threatened to spill over the embankment into the churning brown of the river. Walking with her shoes in hand to protect them from the worst of the water, Fabienne looked up at the looming stone walls which buttressed the Quai Saint-Michel. While most of Paris had taken refuge in the cafés and apartments, she enjoyed the moment of solitude, feeling as though the Seine and its tumultuous waters were there for her, and her alone.

She passed beneath Pont Saint-Michel, listening to horse-drawn carriages clatter overhead. Two years ago, the bridge had been overrun with automobiles, carrying passengers onto the ancient and crowded Île de la Cité—to the serene and majestic Notre Dame, with its elegant Gothic spire, or perhaps to the Palais de Justice, if not across the river entirely to the Marais district beyond. Fabienne recalled visiting the Marais as a child, accompanying Maman on her infrequent visits to Paris to purchase necessities not available in Bar-sur-Aube— or to offer items from Château Dolus for sale in the Marais's vibrant consignment shops.

She emerged from beneath Pont Saint-Michel as the sun broke through the clouds and put on her shoes to wander up the stone steps to Quai Saint-Augustin. Along the top of the stone wall, the *bouquinistes* had begun to reopen their stalls, letting rain slick off of the green boxes that housed their used books.

She turned onto Pont Neuf, stepping back from the curb as two women on bicycles whizzed past, their split skirts billowing in the updraft. She walked on, hopscotching over Île de la Cité before landing on the Right Bank where Sophie stood waiting, hands clasped as she leaned over the limestone barricade to watch the Seine.

"You're early," she commented.

Fabienne mirrored Sophie's pose. "So are you."

Overhead, the setting sun had gilded the storm clouds, transforming the sky above Paris into a painting by Turner. "I used to come here when I first moved to Paris. I didn't know the city well enough not to get lost. But I always knew where I was if I was on the banks of the Seine." Sophie smiled thinly, her features illuminated in the brilliance of the sun's golden rays. "Who wouldn't want a moment alone with this view?" She let out a breath, dropped her head as she threaded her fingers together. "Thank you for coming, Fabienne. I appreciate it."

Fabienne nodded as Sophie turned her attention back to the river. "Is this about the papers? Are they ready?"

"I'm afraid not. Soon, I hope."

"*Merde.* These are my friends. Every day that passes—"

"You think I don't know that?" Sophie snapped. "I'm doing my best, I-I'm… These things take time."

"If this isn't to do with the papers, why did you ask to meet me?"

"It's about the painting." Sophie's attention shifted, and Fabienne turned around: a pair of gendarmes was nearing them on the bridge, billy clubs loose at their sides. "Come on," she muttered.

They skirted the metro entrance, walking slowly, deliberately, away from Pont Neuf. "You weren't discovered, were you?"

Sophie waited at the curb for a swarm of bicycle taxis to pass. "In a manner of speaking," she replied, looking up at the looming Art Nouveau façade of La Samaritaine department store. "I've come to ask you if you would be willing to expand the terms of our arrangement."

"How so?"

The street cleared, and Sophie stepped onto the cobbles. "By repeating it."

She led Fabienne toward the elegant double doors of the department store and plunged through. Within, its grand gallery stretched up five stories to a glass ceiling held up by painted iron trusses, giving the space a light and airy feel. They passed by stalls of gloves, bowler hats, hosiery, and Fabienne did a double take. Since when could anyone in Paris afford new stockings?

"Sophie," she hissed as Sophie led her past a display of hatpins. She closed her hand around Sophie's arm, and Sophie looked back at the front door as though to confirm that the gendarmes hadn't followed them.

"Sorry," Sophie said as Fabienne waved off the attentions of an overly helpful store clerk. "Can't be too careful."

The store clerk's eyes narrowed, and Fabienne tucked Sophie's hand in the crook of her arm with an overly bright smile. "Nor too obvious," she retorted in an undertone. The clerk's expression relaxed, and Fabienne steered Sophie away, hoping that they looked to anyone watching like two good friends out on a shopping excursion. "Can we start over, please?"

Irritation rippled over Sophie's features. "I need your help."

"By repeating the...terms of our arrangement," Fabienne muttered as a well-dressed woman in a fur stole sauntered past, breezily conveying instructions to her anemic-looking companion in German. "Yes, I gathered that much, but isn't it terribly risky? Wasn't it risky enough doing it the once?"

"Of course," Sophie replied. "But the risks are worth taking." She picked up a set of white gloves. "I want to reproduce as many works of art as we can. Get them all out of the museum." She turned the gloves over, running her finger along the stitching before setting them down.

Fabienne stopped short. "Sophie, have you really considered what you're asking? What we did once was lucky enough, and we only succeeded by chance. You told me yourself that Göring is in and out of the museum on a regular basis. Do you really think he would take kindly to what we're doing?"

"Some risks are worth taking," Sophie replied staunchly. "Besides, we've considered all the variables, and I think we can—"

"*We?*"

Sophie looked up. "My colleague has offered his services," she said, and Fabienne nearly felt the floor give out beneath her. "He's going to help mix the paint, get the canvases out of the museum. He's got some ideas—"

"Your *colleague*?" Little wonder Sophie had requested a meeting in public, the better to manage Fabienne's reaction.

"*Merde*, Sophie, what's to say he won't go to his superiors? He could be reporting us right now!"

"He wouldn't."

Fabienne fell silent. "I can't," she said finally, dropping her arms to her sides. "I'm sorry, but I can't. I barely even have any of that paint left—"

"I can make more paint," Sophie interjected, but Fabienne shook her head.

"Even still. It's too risky, Sophie."

Sophie let out a huff of impatience. "I thought you would understand." She stepped back, shaking her head. "I know it's dangerous, but we have a duty."

"A duty to whom?"

"To the owners of the paintings. To the artists themselves." Sophie tugged on Fabienne's arm, and they continued walking past the displays of clothing and jewelry. She lowered her voice. "The works of art in the Jeu de Paume are stolen. The Germans have been looting private collections. That's what they're doing there. Housing looted works they've stolen from Jewish families. Thousands of works of art. Tens of thousands."

Fabienne's grip on Sophie's arm weakened. "Tens...of thousands?"

Sophie nodded. "Tens of thousands," she repeated steadily. "Many are from gallerists—Paul Rosenberg. Daniel Kahnweiler. But they've stolen from private collections too. The Rothschilds had hidden their artwork in bank vaults all across France, but the Germans were able to open the vaults and take everything. The extent of what they're doing...it defies logic, Fabienne."

Fabienne remained silent, letting Sophie steer her through the store. She'd suspected that the Germans were doing something underhanded with the artwork at the Jeu de Paume, but she'd assumed it had been France's public collection they'd been after—never the possessions of individuals and families.

"Göring's stolen millions of dollars' worth of art for his private collection, and millions more for Hitler. But there's a whole room of artwork separate from the rest—Impressionist, Cubist, Fauvist, Expressionist—anything that doesn't reflect the values of the Nazi party. *Degenerate*, they call it." She stopped dead. "You're an artist. Would you want your work falling into the hands of the Germans?"

She thought once more of Dietrich, showing her work to Paul Rosenberg with quiet pride. "Of course not."

Sophie nodded. "Göring's agent is selling off whatever he can, and there's a real chance that whatever he sells will be lost forever to the original owners. As for the artwork that he doesn't sell... I fear they're going to destroy it like they did the public collection in Germany. They're already complaining about not having enough space in the museum as it is." They'd reached the side door of the department store and stepped back out onto the sidewalk. Down the road, Pont Neuf was still visible, and Sophie swept her arm out toward it, encompassing the Seine, Île de la Cité and everything beyond. "People keep talking about when the Allies take back France. Do you think the Germans will give up Paris so easily? They will destroy it before letting it go. If that happens, what remains?"

Fabienne didn't answer. Paris had been spared the violence that had ravaged the rest of Europe; spared, in the still and frightened days of the phony war, by politicians who believed the city's buildings to be worth more than the lives of the people who lived there. Had it been worth it? The salvation of the architecture, the monuments to France's glorious past, in exchange for the cowardice of the present?

Or had it been hope, rather than cowardice, which had

driven their actions—hope for a future in which the Germans would one day be driven out? Perhaps so, but there would be long nights, still, before that golden morning. What would happen, in the dangerous days before peace returned to France? Bloodshed in the streets, bombs and riots.

Sophie continued. "What will remain is whatever we can save. Our art. Our culture." She nodded once, decisively. "*That's* Paris. They can destroy the city, tear it all down to rubble—but if we can save one work of art and return it to its owner, is that not worth it?"

She stepped forward. "I'm not a brave person, Fabienne. I'm not going to change the world or plant a bomb in the museum... I'm not Bonsergent, insulting the *Wehrmacht* in the open." She smiled. "I work in a museum. There's very little I can do, but I can do this." She paused. "*We* can do this."

Fabienne could hear the echo of Dietrich in Sophie's words, that same idealism, that same noble pursuit of principle that she'd once admired, encouraged.

She stepped forward and took Sophie's hands in hers. "You remember what Dietrich used to say," she said, "back in those speeches he used to give. How everyone must do what they can to fight back." She released Sophie's hand. "Where do we start?"

33

May 1941

The grand gallery was full to bursting, curators and soldiers and officers wending their way between stacked packing crates that gave the room the temporary appearance of a dockyard. Standing halfway up the staircase, Sophie watched as Colonel Bohn nailed down the lid to a crate containing a Rodin sculpture from Paul Rosenberg's collection. He affixed a label, marking it down as destined for Göring's country estate, Carinhall.

How can one home possibly have room for it all? By Sophie's count, at least seven crates had already been filled with works by Velázquez and Tintoretto, Renoir and Goya: dozens of paintings and sculptures, packed away and waiting to be whisked into Germany on Göring's private train.

She reached the bottom of the staircase and made her way past the packing crates, smiling at Bohn as she went. In recent weeks, Bohn's position at the museum had become largely ceremonial. Richter, acting on Göring's behalf, was the real authority at the Jeu de Paume, his every action sanctioned by Göring in elegant, handwritten missives. Bohn, it seemed, had taken his reduced responsibilities with some measure of relief, though he still directed the ERR's raiding teams as they plundered homes and bank vaults across the country.

Sophie descended into the basement which, like the grand gallery, was full of artwork. Down here, caged light bulbs swung from electrical wires, illuminating the ghostly backs of paintings that had been propped against dark walls. She ran her hand along one of the packing crates, stamped with the initials of the *Einsatzstab Reichsleiter Rosenberg*, the tidy lettering a feeble attempt to erase the provenance of the original owners with bloodless, modern bureaucracy.

At the far end of the basement, Rose Valland stood with a clipboard in hand over an open crate of artwork.

"Mademoiselle Valland," Sophie called, and Rose started, jerking back from the crate with such force that she dropped her clipboard.

Sophie hastened toward her. "I'm so sorry," she said as Rose planted a hand on the open crate to steady herself. "I gave you quite a fright."

"Not at all."

Sophie bent to pick up the clipboard, glancing down instinctively at its contents—a long list—but before she could make sense of it, Rose snatched the clipboard away, obscuring its contents from view.

"I'm afraid I was miles away. There seems to be a never-ending list of tasks to do down here. And the boiler's acting up now, on top of everything else." Rose hugged the clipboard to her chest. "How is everything progressing upstairs?"

"It's looking like the Gare du Nord," Sophie replied.

"I suppose that's hardly surprising. The Vermeer, has it been packed up? Shame, I'd liked to have seen it once more. But I suppose Bohn is filling these walls as quickly as Richter is emptying them." Though Rose always had an air of reserve about her, something in her demeanor had changed. She met Sophie's gaze with bright eyes, looking energized rather than exhausted by her duties.

The realization irked Sophie. How could Rose be happy here, helping the Germans carry out their crimes?

She swallowed her disapproval. "Was there something you wanted my help with?"

"Yes." Rose consulted her clipboard, crossing something off with measured efficiency. "Several of the works we received from the Bacri collection were damaged in transit. I keep telling Bohn to take more care, but men never seem inclined to listen." She rifled through the pages on her clipboard and pulled out a short sheet of paper that listed several works, handing it to Sophie. "If you could take that Picasso up to the storeroom as you go, I'd very much appreciate it." Then she took off in the direction of the boiler.

The painting was a piece from Picasso's Rose Period, depicting a Harlequin standing on a beach, looking maudlin despite his colorful attire. *A worthy addition to our list of candidates*, she thought as she set it down in the overflowing Room of Martyrs. It was easy, here, to grow jaded by the display of remarkable excess, to allow one's eyes to lose focus, let the colors of the paintings run together in a beautiful blur. But each and every painting deserved to be admired on its own merit; each work of art, celebrated.

Saved.

She turned at the sound of footsteps in the hall, and plastered a smile on her face as the lanky figure of Konrad Richter lifted the damask curtain.

"Good afternoon, Dr. Richter." She clasped her hands behind her back. "I was just leaving. Mademoiselle Valland had asked me to bring up a painting from the Bacri collection."

"Picasso?" He crossed the room in a few easy strides, tilting his head to examine the canvas. "A lovely piece." He sighed and turned his attention to the walls. "You know, Mademoiselle Brandt, I'm not comfortable with all this. This—this vilification of art. I'm an educated man. I just don't see the danger in artwork that others do. Neither does my employer, truth be told." He smiled wolfishly and dug in his pocket for his cigarettes as Sophie bit back a retort. The vilification of art was bad enough, but what about the vilification of the people who owned it? "I'm in here on his account. His wife is very fond of Impressionism. You wouldn't tell anyone if a few pieces happened to find their way onto the *Reichsmarschall*'s train, would you?"

"Of course. Your secret is quite safe with me, Doctor."

Satisfied, Richter began to parse the works of art. *Make friends with him*, Hausler had advised her when they'd discussed their plan to forge more of the works of art within the Room of Martyrs. *Richter has been known to like a pretty face.*

The prospect of friendship with the likes of Konrad Richter made Sophie's skin crawl, but she saw merit in the notion. Their task would be easier to accomplish if Richter believed her to be friend rather than foe.

She moved closer and began to search through the canvases piled against the wall. "There's a rather lovely piece by Diane Esmond... Here." She pulled it out. The painting, unframed, depicted an evening at a cabaret, the highly detailed figures in the foreground dissolving into sketch and suggestion as her eye moved further into the canvas.

Richter considered it briefly before dismissing it with a shake of his head. "It's a little louche for dear Emmy's tastes." He pulled out a nearby landscape by the same artist, forests and fields rendered in brilliant jewel tones. "This one, however..."

"An excellent choice," Sophie replied. "You've a remarkable eye, Doctor."

"Well, I should hope so," he replied gruffly, though he looked pleased at the compliment. "Mademoiselle Brandt, I'm sure that you've got plenty of work to get back to, but would you help me find a few more pieces for the *Reichsmarschall*'s wife? I'd appreciate the company."

Sophie's smile sharpened. "I'd be delighted, Doctor."

34

Rain drizzled onto the black awnings that covered the stalls in the Marché aux Puces, trickling over the lip of the tarpaulins to catch, unawares, anyone unwise enough to linger on the edge of a seller's storefront rather than step within. Beneath the expansive canopy of her umbrella, Fabienne needed no such refuge from the rain: the flea market had long been a favorite haunt of hers, with its labyrinthine avenues selling everything she could ever possibly want to buy. Given the weather, it was less crowded than usual, and as she threaded between the vendors' stalls, she savored the mismatched elegance of it all: the brass candlesticks piled in a wicker basket, displaying various degrees of tarnish; old books and birdcages and binoculars; teetering towers of fine china, balanced precariously atop rickety tables; worn fur shawls and desiccated powder puffs.

She paused in front of a stall to admire a display of colorful silks where the shop owner, an older man with an empty sleeve pinned to his jacket, was carefully arranging a red-and-white-checked scarf around the neck of a royal blue jacket displayed on a hanger. *The tricolore*, she thought, meeting the man's defiant gaze with a smile. The colors of the French flag had been outlawed since the beginning of the occupation: to see them here, now, felt like a glimmer of hope.

She carried on, passing stalls offering men's jackets and stout coffeepots. In the distance, she could hear the sound of someone playing an accordion. She held her handbag closer to her side, watching child pickpockets weave through the sparse crowd like silverfish, but could she really judge the little urchins for doing what they must to survive?

With a pang, she thought of Lotte and how empty her apartment felt without her. She would be a mother by now, if all had gone well with the pregnancy. Despite everything that had passed between them, Fabienne hoped that Hans had done right by her, that she was pushing a blond-haired child down the Champs-Élysées in a pram, trading on her lover's prominence to feather a nest where she could shield herself from the harsh realities of the world around her.

Fabienne turned a corner and found herself in the heart of the market, where stalls were packed with paintings and works of art, sculptures and picture frames, and costume jewelry set with stones too large to be anything other than glass. This was the reason Fabienne had come to the Marché aux Puces: vendors offered cheap paintings of a similar vintage to those residing in Sophie's Room of Martyrs.

She entered the foremost stall, nodding to the shawl-enfolded woman who sat on a nearby stool keeping a beady eye on her wares. The stall's thin walls were filled with paintings, some decent and some terrible, but Fabienne hadn't come to pass judgment on artistic merit. Instead, she inspected the canvases, picking up those which looked to be the right age to pass as Post-Impressionist, Expressionist. The canvas itself was Fabienne's quarry, canvas that she could scrape down and paint over to help give a convincing age to the backs of her forgeries.

She held up a pretty little painting of children playing in what appeared to be the Bois de Boulogne. "How much?" she asked, feeling a pang of regret for the artist whose work she would have to destroy.

The woman in the shawl replied without looking up. "Ten centimes."

Fabienne picked up another piece. "This one?"

"Seven."

Slowly, carefully, she inspected the stall's offerings. She needed as many canvases as she could afford, and though Sophie hadn't yet shared the details about how she was going to get the paintings in and out of the museum, Fabienne knew that if anyone was to manage it, it would be Sophie, careful, meticulous Sophie, who'd already brought Fabienne her second commission, a van Gogh, concealed in the hollow of her briefcase.

Fabienne, meanwhile, needed to be meticulous too. Although Sophie would supply her petroleum paint as before, Fabienne would need to make the forgeries convincing, not only in terms of the paintings themselves but the canvases as a whole. *The paint is only one aspect*, she thought as she picked up a painting. The varnish had browned with age, fading in whatever conditions of light and smoke it had once been kept, leaving a small, bright border of color that had once been concealed by a picture frame: how could she recreate that convincing stripe of detail? She turned the canvas to inspect the rusting nails that held the canvas in place. This was another element she couldn't possibly overlook: the rust, transferred around each tiny nail onto the canvas.

She would have to be meticulous, too, in hiding the originals. Though she'd not planned to return to Château Dolus, she knew with uncomfortable clarity that it would be the safest haven for the artworks. Her heart sank at the prospect of confronting Sébastien properly, but what other choice did she have?

"How much?"

"Eight."

She set another painting atop the first two. Confrontation had never come easily to Fabienne, and she hated the thought of further digging up a past she thought she'd buried. But it wasn't just Sébastien she'd hurt by her actions: she'd cut away her parents, too, in the same brutal sweep of a knife.

It had been a coward's way out of a difficult situation. Was she a coward still?

She turned her mind back to the task at hand and took the pictures she'd chosen to the woman with the shawl to haggle for the best possible price. She would sand down the paintings' surfaces, obliterating the layers of varnish and impasto, then paint over whatever remained with a new, shining white ground upon which to work, destroying the paintings beneath to make way for her necessary deceptions. But the remnants of the original paintings would still be there, concealed beneath the surface: a history hidden, but not forgotten by those who knew where to look.

35

Sophie bent over her worktable, staring intently through a magnifying glass as she coaxed the fibers of a split canvas back together. The piece, a large portrait of a woman by Frans Hals, had been earmarked by Richter as worthy of inclusion at Carinhall but for the small rip down the sitter's face. Earlier, Sophie had patched the tear by gluing a small piece of linen down on the back of the painting. Now, she worked on the front of the piece to knit the frayed edges of the tear into the canvas patch with tweezers, the better, she hoped, to make the torn edges lie flat.

She finished setting the fibers in place and straightened, arching her back to ease the aching tension that had settled there over the course of her careful work. There was little more she could do for the piece now. Time was needed, time for the patch and fibers to dry in place.

Across the studio, Gerhardt was retouching a landscape painted on wood by Charpin, infilling repaired cracks in the panel with fresh paint. His signet ring glinted as he tapped along on his palette to Maurice Chevalier on the wireless.

He looked up from his easel and nodded. Without a word between them, Gerhardt set down his palette and turned down the volume on the wireless, reducing the laboratory to silence as Sophie circled to the front door. She leaned against the doorframe, frowning as she listened for the sound of footsteps outside. Hearing none, she removed her overcoat from its hanger and spread it out on her empty table.

Working quickly, she pulled open the hidden snaps that Gerhardt had sewn into its hem and pulled out a linen canvas that had been taken off its stretcher and sandwiched between two layers of Japanese mulberry paper.

She set it on the table as Gerhardt drew closer to study the painting over her shoulder.

"Your artist did wonderfully," he said quietly. In just two weeks, Fabienne had meticulously copied the van Gogh she'd been given, recreating every lift and swirl in the paint with such precision that, seen side by side, even Sophie might have had trouble identifying the original. Fabienne had managed to source a canvas of similar size and age to the original, but she'd painted her initials beneath the shade of one sunflower petal, so small that they looked like stray splotches in keeping with van Gogh's own style.

"So that there are no questions, after the war," she'd told Sophie, after pointing out the minuscule discrepancy. "If it were to end up with some horrible art dealer, I wouldn't want there to be any ambiguity over which one was the original."

Sophie pulled the painting's original stretcher from beneath her worktable and flipped Fabienne's forgery so that she could tack it to the wood. "You'll need to take it downstairs." She pinned down the corners of the canvas. "Rose had been lurk-ing around the last few times I went to the storeroom. I don't want her getting suspicious."

"Of course. Leave it there, and I'll take it down at the end of the day." Gerhardt turned the wireless back on, flooding the laboratory with music to mask their words. "Was there anything else? You seem tense, today."

Sophie rubbed at her temples, attempting to dispel a blos-soming headache. "My artist is running out of paint. My petroleum-based paint."

"Can you not make more?"

"Not without the requisite ingredients." She leaned back on the table, crossed her arms. "It was simple enough to get petroleum before the war, but the French army burned the petroleum reserves at the start of the occupation. And I've a little acrylic resin put by, but it might be difficult to get more."

"I see." Gerhardt circled back to his easel, paintbrush twitching in his hand "Where might one find acrylic resin?"

"I don't know." She'd run through the issue in her head countless times, lost sleep over it. "An industrial warehouse? Most acrylic resin is used to make plexiglass, and as for petroleum—"

"Both are needed for the war effort." Hausler let out a breath. "I'm not saying it's impossible, but I can make inqui-ries through the party…"

"And risk our entire operation? What use would an art restorer have for petroleum? No, if you were to ask around, you might risk raising questions we'd rather not answer." She sighed. "So what do we do?"

Hausler fell silent as the sound of Chevalier's voice crack-led over the wireless.

"You told me that you learned about the paint from the pa-pers of a restorer based in Stuttgart," he said slowly. "Could we reach out to him? He might be able to provide us with some insight."

Sophie hadn't told Gerhardt that Martin Dix was her father—and she wasn't sure whether it was wise to enlighten him. She'd not spoken to Papa in years, not since she and Dietrich had fled from Nuremberg. Was he still alive, all these years later? Or had Sophie and Dietrich's defection condemned him in absentia?

"I knew Dix once, long ago," she said slowly. "He's a party member. If we reach out, it must be with the utmost discretion."

Hausler nodded. "I'll make contact with him, party member to party member," he began, but Sophie shook her head.

"It ought to be me." She looked up. "If we need his help, it ought to be me."

36

July 1941

Fabienne stepped off the train, crooking her carpetbag on her arm as she lifted her hand to look down the platform. Steam drifted through as she watched a handful of other passengers descend from their compartments and disappear into the station. A moment later, a piercing whistle screeched through the air, and the train lurched onward, leaving Fabienne alone on the platform.

Her heart sank at the realization that Papa hadn't come to collect her; that despite sending a telegram to her parents two days ago, she would have to make her way to Château Dolus alone. She went into the station and knocked on the station-master's door, hoping for the use of his son's bicycle, but there was no reply. Disheartened, she snugged the painting she carried beneath her arm and carried on.

Outside, the July sun beamed down on the green fields and

stone buildings that made up the outskirts of Bar-sur-Aube, and although she started sweating almost immediately, she didn't remove her trench coat. Instead, she began to walk toward the far-off steeples of the town square.

A fitting welcome, she thought grimly, *given that no one asked me to come.*

She crossed the street and passed a garage with a rusting Citroën in the drive, wishing for a gallant young mechanic to emerge from within the building and whisk her away on his motorcycle—but most of the region's young men had been carted off to labor camps in Germany. No, judging by the state of the car, as well as the petrol shortage that had impacted all of France, the garage hadn't been open for some time now.

She turned at the sound of hooves clattering on the road. Motorcars might be out of the question, but all a cart needed was a horse and two wheels. Her heart lifted at the prospect of a ride, but then she set down her carpetbag with a thump. *Hardly a gallant mechanic*, she thought as Sébastien, his tall frame slouched over the reins of the chateau's elderly horse, Lutin, pulled to a stop.

"Thank goodness," she said, waving her free hand to dispel a cloud of midges as Sébastien jumped down from the chassis. "I'd started to think that no one had received my telegram."

He picked up the carpetbag and flung it into the back of the cart. "Had to make another stop," he said as Fabienne shrugged out of her coat. "And your train was early."

"Well, I wasn't in charge of the schedule," she retorted as she laid the coat gently atop the carpetbag. She circled to the front of the carriage to greet Lutin, pressing her forehead to the horse's long nose. "Hello, old friend," she murmured as Sébastien climbed back up onto the seat.

"Are you coming?"

Biting back a snarky retort, Fabienne opened her eyes and crawled up beside him, hugging the painting close to her chest.

Her arrival at Château Dolus was no more ceremonial.

"Your parents are in the vineyard. I've got to go join them," Sébastien said as Fabienne climbed down in front of the chateau's crumbling front steps. His calloused fingers twitched around the reins as he waited for her to collect her things, his dark gaze fixed on the limestone walls. "You can let yourself in, yes?"

Fabienne settled her trench over her shoulders as he drove off in a rattling cloud, leaving her alone in the courtyard—although, as he'd said barely two words to her on the ride in, she couldn't exactly feel his absence as a loss.

She let herself into the house, the hinges groaning a half-hearted welcome as she muscled her way past the rusty doors. "Hello, yourself," she muttered, before making her way upstairs. She didn't mind Sébastien's abrupt departure, not when it gave her an opportunity to roam her old home unaccompanied.

She climbed to the second floor, panting slightly with the effort as she deposited her bag on the landing and continued her ascent. Unlike her apartment in Paris, where she could always hear the sound of people, here the chateau spoke for itself in the creaking floorboards, the sigh of old bones settling. The silence felt almost friendly, and though she knew the illusion would shatter the moment her parents came back from their work, she savored it nonetheless.

The fifth floor, originally intended for servants, was sparsely decorated, periwinkle wallpaper peeling from the narrow hallway as she walked along toward the easternmost turret. Here, she opened a door to ascend another, smaller wooden staircase. Even as a child, she'd avoided the attic, with its dark and dusty corners, its oppressive heat. Filled with several centuries' worth of discarded furniture—old wardrobes and commodes, couches and candelabras—the attic was a repository for the chateau's forgotten things. She doubted anyone but herself had come up here in decades. She sidestepped an ancient marble bust with half of the subject's face sheared off and thought of the building's curse: such a relic might have paid for necessary repairs to the chateau's foundation, had it not been ruined in some long-ago accident. Dust swirled in a beam of light shining down from a poorly repaired hole between the ceiling's ancient trusses, and although she knew she was alone, Fabienne couldn't help feeling as though she was being watched.

She looked around the crowded space, trying to get her bearings. She was facing the front of the chateau, surely—but if that were the case, shouldn't there be a small half-moon window somewhere?

She took off her coat and laid it out carefully on the floor, then removed her hat and hatpin. Quickly, carefully, she unpicked the seam that made up the back panel of the coat, scarcely daring to breathe as she reached into the hollow between the gabardine and the silk lining and pulled out a large, flat package wrapped in mulberry paper.

She lifted the paper, sighing with relief as the van Gogh, taken off its stretcher but mercifully undamaged, came into view.

"Hello, beautiful," she whispered, lifting the canvas to admire it in the stream of sunlight. She set it aside and turned her attention back to the paper the van Gogh had been resting on and lifted it to reveal a Chagall; beneath it, a work by André Masson which belonged to the Arpels family.

When Sophie had turned up at her apartment wearing an unseasonable overcoat, Fabienne had assumed that it had everything to do with her sister-in-law's lack of fashion sense, but she'd been impressed when Sophie had pulled several canvases from the lining. Fabienne had borrowed the idea and refashioned her jacket to transport no fewer than five canvases to Château Dolus. To her relief, all five of them had survived the journey intact.

They'd survived the journey—now, they had to survive their stay. Given the humidity of the champagne region's chalky ground, Fabienne had reconsidered her earlier hiding place in the chateau's cellar: the attic, with its drier conditions and clutter, was a more suitable hiding place for works of art. She planned to retrieve the Kirchner as soon as she could, hoping that its sojourn hadn't been long enough to damage it. Here, the paintings would look like so much more discarded junk: relics of a long-gone aristocratic past. *Hide in plain sight*, she told herself as she rolled the canvases and leaned them against an ancient wardrobe.

Fabienne returned to her room after leaving the attic to tuck her limp curls beneath a turban and freshen up her lipstick. She exchanged her tidy burgundy suit for a set of silk trousers she'd worn once on holiday with Dietrich. They were criminally out of date, but the heat of the afternoon made the outfit too hard to resist. Feeling like a hothouse flower in a vegetable plot, she descended the staircase, carrying the last painting she'd brought from Paris still on its stretcher.

Fabienne's trench coat could conceal five paintings at once, but the lining looked suspiciously bulky with the addition of a sixth. As a result, she'd decided to bring the final canvas she'd replicated to Château Dolus by hand.

She followed the sound of voices onto the flagstone terrace out the back of the chateau and found Maman and Papa sitting at a wrought iron patio set, accompanied by a cheese board and a baguette, and a sweating bottle of champagne in a bucket. In the courtyard below, Sébastien was unhitching Lutin from his harness, the back of the cart now filled with vine offcuts and soil.

"Maman," Fabienne said, and Maman, unsmiling, offered Fabienne her bony cheek.

Papa was more effusive in his greeting. "Fabienne, *ma chère*." He stood and Fabienne sank into his embrace. "What a pleasant surprise."

"Not too much of a surprise, I hope," Fabienne replied as Papa held out a chair. "Sébastien was kind enough to fetch me from the station."

"And put us all behind in our work in the process," Maman retorted, pouring Fabienne a glass of champagne before she could refuse.

Fabienne watched Sébastien lead Lutin toward the stables. "Should I go help him?"

"Don't be ridiculous."

"You'll join us for a glass, Sébastien?" Papa called out, and Sébastien threw up his hand in response.

"I brought you something," Fabienne said, more to ease the tension than anything else, and she passed the painting across the table. "I thought it might be a…fresh start." She smiled as Sébastien emerged from the stables and disappeared once more around the side of the chateau. "For all of us, I hope."

Maman and Papa examined the piece. "You painted it?"

"I did, as a matter of fact." Though Fabienne had brazened her way through the Gare de l'Est with a Kirchner in hand once, she didn't much fancy repeating the process; instead, Sophie had come up with a rather ingenious method of concealing one painting beneath another by facing the existing painting with mulberry paper, applying a new canvas over the old one and painting something entirely original on the new.

For all intents and purposes, the painting that Maman and

Papa were looking at was an original painting of Château Dolus—but only she knew that a Picasso lay hidden beneath her canvas.

Several minutes later, Sébastien pulled up a chair, its iron legs scraping across the flagstone as he set a second bottle of champagne in the bucket. He'd had a shower, or at least a swim in the estate's pond, and had changed his shirt. *Nice of him to make an effort*, Fabienne thought wryly, casting a glance over his too-long hair and stubbled jaw.

"The upper fence has been cut again," he mumbled as he filled a tumbler. "We'll need to repair it before harvest. I don't want anyone injuring themselves on the wire."

Maman set down the painting. "Again?"

So much for Fabienne's attempt at a tender moment. But she'd resolved to make a new start, and a new start involved showing interest in the vineyard. "Who would do such a thing?"

"These days, it could be just about anyone," Papa began. "There are all sorts of activities taking place in these parts that have nothing to do with wine-making."

"Maurice," Maman said sharply, and Papa fell silent.

"Doesn't matter who's doing it. What matters is that it's been done." Sébastien pulled the cheese board toward him and knocked a corner from the wedge with a tarnished knife. "It won't be a quick repair. Wire isn't easy to come by these days."

Fabienne smiled her thanks as Sébastien pushed the board over to her, knowing better than to wade further into a conversation she wasn't fully apprised on. She twisted the baguette in her hands and broke off a piece. Unlike the increasingly adulterated loaves on offer at her neighborhood boulangerie, this bread was flavorful, meant to be savored. The cheese, too, was plentiful, as were eggs from the chickens that scratched in the dusty courtyard. Here, food was in abundance, but that didn't mean the countryside didn't have its own share of shortages. Wire, lumber, metal, petrol: all the materials needed to produce the food so desperately needed in the cities.

"I'll speak to de Vogüé about it," Papa replied. "He's got a meeting with Klaebisch on Tuesday. He might be able to put in a good word."

"Who's Klaebisch?" Fabienne asked.

"Otto Klaebisch. The *Weinführer*." Papa's features tightened. "He's in charge of champagne production for Germany."

She frowned, the man's title sounding vaguely familiar. "What do you mean, *in charge*?"

"It's exactly as it sounds. He supplies champagne to the Third Reich." Sébastien took a sip of wine, his shoulders rounded as he planted his elbows on the table. "He was a brandy dealer before the war, which I suppose makes him qualified to tell us all what to do. He wants four hundred thousand bottles of champagne, shipped every week, to the Nazi high brass. *Requisitioned*, he tells us, as a wartime necessity." Sébastien looked up with a twisted smile. "Apparently their *Sekt* doesn't quite measure up."

The numbers were enough to make Fabienne dizzy. Hundreds of thousands of bottles, each week? Most champagne houses had entire vintages held in reserve, which they sold off to customers across the world while their newer vintages matured in the bottle. For the Germans to create such staggering demand all at once represented a near-fatal threat to the region. Not only would it deplete the long-held stores of champagne houses across the region, but it also risked leaving them bankrupt: *requisition*, after all, suggested wholesale looting, couched in terms that implied, but stopped short of promising, payment at some later date.

Furthermore, the champagne region was small, with only

so much capacity to produce new vintages—and not all vintages succeeded.

"How can Klaebisch possibly expect such numbers?"

"I suspect he has little choice in the matter. He receives his orders from the Nazis, like everyone else." Papa sighed, setting down his glass. "De Vogüé set up a committee on behalf of all the growers, and he advocates on our behalf with Klaebisch to get the supplies we need to produce what he's asked for—sugar, copper sulphate, yeast, petrol, bottles. But it's a daunting task, no matter how you look at it."

She let out a breath, watching bubbles fizz across the surface of her glass. As a contract grower, rather than a champagne house, Château Dolus's needs were slightly less pressing than those of the larger champagne houses—but only just. They might not have needed yeast or bottles to transform their yield into champagne, but they needed to grow their grapes just the same.

"Well, I suppose your hands are tied," she said. "But for what it's worth, this is a lovely vintage. Is it a Moët?"

"As a matter of fact, it's a Dolus." Papa clapped a hand paternally on Sébastien's arm. "A 1938. He's determined to make us a champagne house once again. He's held back a little of our yield these past few years to bottle our own champagne."

"It's all stopped now, of course," Sébastien conceded, as Maman topped up their glasses. "The last time we could do it was 1938, and 1939 was shit."

Maman raised her glass. "God sends a poor crop to herald war."

Papa raised his own. "And a fine harvest to mark its end," he replied solemnly. "One day, this chateau might return to its former glory."

One day, one day. Fabienne lifted her glass to her lips, thinking that perhaps the curse of Château Dolus lay in the unrelenting, hopeless optimism of its inhabitants. *One day we might all be millionaires. One day, Dietrich might come back from the dead.*

"I wish you every success," she said.

"Wishing can only go so far." Maman set down her glass. "Hard work is the only way to endure hard times. You ought to know that well enough."

"I do, as a matter of fact, and that's why I've come." Fabienne glanced at the painting she'd given to her parents, now leaning against the chateau's wall. "I've been thinking about you. About all of you, recently." She glanced down, tracing the flowered pattern of her trousers on the top of her thigh. "When I came here last time, I'd not intended to stay. The war, I suppose…" She looked up with a delicate shrug. "One never knows what to believe, in the city, and what with the occupation… I want to start over. With…with all of you." She glanced back down, feeling, rather than seeing, Sébastien's eyes on her. "None of us know what this war might bring, and I already know the pain of losing somebody to it. We can't go back to the way things were, I know that, but I can make amends, for how I left. I'd like to make amends."

She fell silent. She'd prepared the start of her speech on the train, feeling a twinge of regret at the thought of deceiving her parents. But for the artworks from the Jeu de Paume, Fabienne would have never stepped foot onto the chateau's crumbling grounds again. But as she spoke she was surprised to find that she meant what she'd said: the thought of repairing her relationship with her family was more important than she'd known.

Perhaps the war had changed her perspective after all. Or perhaps she was simply caught up in the moment.

Maman and Papa exchanged a glance. "I don't understand," Maman said. "Do you intend to move back home?"

"No," Fabienne replied, too quickly. "I just want to visit. To spend time with you."

Maman and Papa glanced meaningfully at Sébastien. Fabienne couldn't blame them for letting the final decision rest with him. They owed Château Dolus's survival to his hard work.

She picked up the bottle and refilled Sébastien's glass. His eyes flickered to meet hers, but then he looked away once more.

"There will have to be concessions," Maman said finally. "We'll expect you to work when you're here. And we'd need you for the harvest. It's not easy, when so many of our laborers were taken away by the Germans."

She nodded, already dreading the thought of it. The harvest was two grueling weeks of work where all the region came together to harvest grapes on behalf of all the champagne houses. *Manual labor.* She'd vowed to leave it all behind when she moved to Paris. "I'm happy to help, however I can."

Sébastien huffed, and it was clear he'd not forgotten Fabienne's hatred for field work. "How often do you plan to come? I can't be expected to come into town at the drop of a hat to pick you up from the station."

"I'll come for the harvest," she said quickly. It was two months away. How many paintings could she complete in that time? "And after that, every few weeks, maybe? Once a month?" She glanced at Papa. "Just for a couple of days at a time. I wouldn't want to be an imposition."

Though Maman still looked guarded and Sébastien fed up, Papa beamed. "You could never be an imposition, *ma chère.*"

She smiled, relieved. Then Sébastien stood.

"Welcome back, Fabienne," he said. "We'll be starting tomorrow at five o'clock in the morning. I'm sure you remember our schedule."

He stalked off toward the stables, and Papa leaned forward to pick up the second bottle of champagne.

"That went as well as could be expected, I think," he said and pulled the cork from the bottle with a practiced hush.

37

Sophie walked down the pea-gravel pathway in the Bois de Boulogne, light-headed with anticipation. She held a note from Martin Dix in her hand as a talisman, the thrice-folded page creased countless more times, thinking of the letter she'd sent that had prompted his response. *Dr. Dix, I'm writing as an admirer of your work and the glory it brings to the Reich…* In the end, she'd decided against revealing herself too soon; rather, she'd let letters do the work, several weeks of careful flattery leading to here, now, in the shaded groves on the outskirts of Paris.

She paused before reaching their appointed meeting place at the westernmost tip of the Mare Saint-James. Though the pond had once been filled with feeding ducks, now it sat empty, the barest breath of wind gently rippling the surface of the water. *Duck à l'orange*, she thought quickly, absurdly, before her attention turned to the slight figure sitting on a bench beneath a willow, his face hidden beneath the brim of a fedora.

Her heart quickened.

Dr. Martin Dix had always been a small man, made smaller by the circumstances of his youth which Sophie had known only too well. Rickets, as a child, had stunted his growth and left him knock-kneed: small enough to be teased as a boy, but not so slight that he'd not been called up, at eighteen, to serve as a tunneler in the Great War. It was a time he'd seldom spoken of to Sophie, changing the subject whenever the conversation strayed too close to his wartime service. For years, Sophie had watched as he'd steered conversations away from the rocky shores of confrontation with the navigational precision of a helmsman, and perhaps it was in deference to his service that his family had allowed him to avoid the sorts of conversations that ought to have been the purview of a father: conversations about ambition and expectations, fights that any family encountered at some time or another. No, instead of confrontation, Sophie and Dietrich had learned to swallow what they'd truly needed to say, allowing Papa's discomfort, Mama's reverence, to set the tone of their lives—until their obedience to their parents' peace of mind had become too much to bear.

She sat down beside him, keeping her gaze fixed on the pond. "Papa."

Six years had passed since she'd seen him last, six years of pain and heartbreak. Had they been as difficult on him as they'd been on her?

He shifted closer; belatedly, he removed his hat, working the brim between his fingers. "My dear. My darling. If I'd known it was you—"

"I hope you can forgive the deception." She turned and met his gaze with a shaky smile. "Difficult times, you know."

Papa swallowed heavily. This close, she could see the toll that their separation had taken on him in the pallor of his lined cheeks, in the patch of white stubble he'd missed, just below his ear. She'd pictured his face in her mind so many times that she'd long ago forgotten the physical reality of who he was, her imagination altering his features, ever so slightly, in her mind's eye. The hollow at his temple, the notch in his upper lip—all imperfections, smoothed over in six years' worth of dreams and memories. But he pushed up his wire-rimmed glasses in a gesture that was all too real, and Dietrich's blue eyes stared back at her from behind the glass.

"My darling, I can't tell you how…how happy I am to see you," he said finally. "Your mother and I… Not a day has gone by where we haven't thought of you." Sophie allowed him to clasp her hands in his. He looked up hopefully, searching the park for another familiar face. "Dietrich?"

She'd dreaded this conversation for so long that she'd fooled herself into thinking she would never have to have it. "Papa, Dietrich…he died. Two years ago."

His grip on her hands weakened as shock rippled over his face, pinning his smile in place for the span of one heartbeat, two, before faltering.

"They…they found him, Papa. His former unit with the *Wehrmacht*. They learned that we were living here, cornered him after a…after a speech he'd given, speaking out against the Reich. They told him he'd been tried in absentia as a…a deserter." She squeezed her eyes shut, wishing she could block out the image of Dietrich's final moments, trapped in the back of an alley no different than the one he'd rescued her from in Nuremberg, all those years ago—but this time there'd been no escape.

She squeezed Papa's hand, hoping to offer him some cold comfort. "It…was quick. He's buried in Montparnasse."

Papa's jaw tightened, tears tracing silently down his cheeks. It would be too cruel, to tell him the truth: how the soldiers, drunk on their own power, had held Sophie and Fabienne back, had beaten Louis senseless when he'd attempted to intervene. How they'd hung Dietrich from a lamppost, his legs kicking, jerking, as his life drained away. How, beer heavy on their breath, they'd made Sophie and Fabienne watch to the bitter end; how, sobbing, she'd cut Dietrich's body down, once the Germans disappeared into the night.

How Fabienne had tried to save him, breathing air back into his lifeless lungs as Sophie pummeled his chest, willing him to wake. Sophie had been the first to know it was too late; she'd pulled Fabienne off, dragged her down the dark alley toward whatever light could be found in the street.

What purpose would it serve, to relive it all again for Papa?

Papa cleared his throat. "Your...your mother and I, we had no idea. No idea that you were so unhappy. No idea—"

"Didn't you? Dietrich told you often enough."

Papa slumped forward and wiped his eyes. "That's as may be, but what child doesn't rebel? What boy doesn't grow discontented with his lot? He didn't understand—"

Sophie's heart broke. After so long, was Papa truly still in denial? "It was so much more than discontentment, Papa. He could see what the party truly was." She paused. "So did I, when I started to look properly."

"He never understood," Papa retorted fiercely. "He never saw the purpose of it all, he never—he never had to. We protected you from what life was like before the Führer came into power. We protected you from poverty and misery—"

"*Thugs and bullies*, you called them once," Sophie said. "Thugs and bullies. And you made us part of it."

"They're thugs and bullies still." He straightened with a sigh. "But you must understand, they offered us a better life,

Liebchen. We only wanted what was best for you. We were only thinking of your future."

Even now, Papa was refusing to see what the party had cost him, and the realization broke Sophie's heart anew.

"What future, Papa?" She stood, trembling. "What future could we ever have had? The only future they ever promised was yours—comfort for Mamma, advancement for you. The future they promised me was a life of bearing children I didn't want for men I didn't love. The future they promised to Dietrich was death at the end of a bayonet. But so long as you and Mamma were given what you wanted…"

"We didn't know." Papa looked up. "We didn't know."

"You knew that my one dream was to follow in your footsteps. To attend university, to become an art restorer, like you. I was denied that dream, but still you and Mamma made excuses for supporting the party." She shook her head. Papa's attempts at justifying his allegiances were just as feeble as they'd ever been during her childhood. How had she not heard it, all those years ago? "You were always thinking about what was best for yourself. Never about what was best for Dietrich and me."

Papa looked down. "Regardless of how you feel about the party, *Liebchen*, they're winning this war. They're unstoppable."

"Only if we refuse to fight back. Only if we let them win." She sat down once more. Papa had disappointed her, profoundly. Would he disappoint her further? "Papa, I need your help."

38

Fabienne eased herself out of a crouch, letting her secateurs fall to the ground as she squinted into the afternoon sun. Across the fields that made up Moët et Chandon's vineyard, dozens of other workers—women, mainly—were dotted between the vines, dropping carefully cut clusters of grapes into wicker baskets; although, unlike Fabienne, who was several years out of practice, none of them needed to take frequent breaks from the hard work of the harvest.

Several rows away, she watched as Maman, standing out in a bright red blouse, lifted a basket brimming with black-skinned grapes and carried it to the end of her row where Papa, leading an ox-drawn wagon, waited to deposit the grapes into a larger *mannequin*; he relieved her of her basket, leaning forward to sneak a kiss before stepping onto the cart's wheel to shake the grapes into the wooden crate. Once the *mannequin* was full, Papa would lead the ox down to Moët's winepress, where the grapes would be pressed into juice and stored in vast barrels for their first fermentation.

During harvest, precision was of the essence: champagne grapes were only at their peak for a short window of time, the balance between sweetness and acidity perfect for mere weeks before they tipped into oversweetness. It was for this reason that everyone in the region had to be put to work harvesting grapes by hand from all the producers across the region, sweeping like a well-oiled machine from one vineyard to the next in quick, efficient succession. Such was the urgency of the harvest that Lev and Dufy had given Fabienne leave from the atelier to help. She'd gone, but not before pressing two sets of forged papers, finally, into Sylvie Lowenstein's hand.

She looked at her pitiful output: only half her basket was full, whereas Sébastien, three-quarters of the way to the end of the vine opposite, was dropping grape clusters into his second overflowing basket. She knelt and picked up her secateurs, her knees groaning in protest as she cut another cluster of plump grapes from the bottom of the vine. She'd put this life of aristocratic poverty behind her long ago—this life of leaving the fields exhausted and tired, only to return to a moldering chateau in need of every manner of repair; returning to the fields the next day, sunburned and bug-bitten. But there was muscle memory in her movements, and slow as she was, she remembered the cadence of the work: bend, snip, drop, carry.

Once she'd finished filling her basket she straightened, lifting it onto her hip to carry it to the end of the row where Papa, still several acres away, would soon return with his ox and cart. Ahead, Sébastien was reaching into the foliage, snipping clusters from branches with surgical precision. They'd once been a team at harvest time, working down a length of vines in synchronous movement, using the cover of activity to flirt, unnoticed by Maman and Papa. Back then, Sébastien had been the one thing that had made the monotony of harvest bearable: his jokes, his good company. Today, Sébastien had resisted any attempts by Fabienne to coax him into conversation, and though she wasn't so arrogant as to think that her rejection was the only thing weighing on his mind, she hated to see how bitter, how sullen, he'd become in her absence. Had life on the vineyard become as oppressive for him as it had once been for her?

Or was it simply the prospect of ten more days spent in Fabienne's company that had him so out of sorts?

She repositioned the basket on her hip and stepped forward. *If we can't be friends*, she thought with determination, *at least we ought to become something more than enemies.*

She let out a musical whistle, and he looked up.

She smiled brightly and held up her basket to show him the fruits of her labor. "Feels a bit like riding a bicycle, you know. Hard to forget the motions, even if I wanted to."

He grunted, pushing a lock of dark hair back from his face while still holding his secateurs, and looked back down at his vine.

Oh no you don't, Fabienne thought grimly, clenching the handles of her bucket. "You don't happen to have that old flask of yours handy, do you? It's such thirsty work, and as I recall a drop of brandy helps to make the hours pass a little quicker."

He dropped a cluster of grapes into his basket and sat back on his heels. Wordlessly, he reached into the breast pocket of his worn shirt and pulled out a battered silver flask; she took it, running her thumb over the worn insignia of Château Dolus before taking a healthy swig. She'd given him the flask for his seventeenth birthday, having found it among the contents of the chateau's attic, shined it up carefully and taken it to a silversmith to have the hole in the bottom repaired.

"You switched to calvados," she said, handing it back across the vine.

"A few years ago," he replied, taking advantage of the flask's open lid to take a drink himself. "Ever since that blowhard brandy merchant Klaebisch started picking our pockets, I've not felt particularly inclined to line his."

A full sentence! He offered the flask once more, and she took it, more from a desire to keep him talking than from any real inclination to drink. "What do you think of him? The *Weinführer?*"

Sébastien sighed. "I suppose I ought to be grateful to him," he said. "He kept me from being hauled off to some work camp, but I suspect de Vogüé was the one who put in a good word. Had me declared an essential worker, said Château Dolus wouldn't be able to contribute to Moët et Chandon's harvest without me."

"And he's left you one of the most eligible bachelors in Champagne, I would imagine," Fabienne teased. "You and François Tattinger."

"Yeah. Well, I'm pretty sure every woman in these fields would sell me for spare parts if it meant the return of their husbands." He gestured back at the row. "How far along are you?"

She grimaced. "I've gotten a little rusty in my time away… I'm only about halfway down."

Sébastien nodded as Papa came forward to take her basket. "I'll finish up here and then come help you," he said gruffly. "We're better off to work on one vine at a time rather than starting to stagger."

The chateau was dark, the sitting room empty despite the fact that it was only just past midnight, but given that the entire household had risen before dawn, it was perhaps not surprising that her parents had turned in early.

The darkness suited Fabienne, and while she longed for nothing so much as her bed, she found herself wrapped in an ornately patterned dressing gown, tiptoeing through the kitchen and down the winding staircase into the cellar.

She'd not yet had a chance to remove the Kirchner from its hiding place, and it had already spent far too long in the limestone cellar. On her last visit, she'd focused on finding a suitable space in the attic for the other paintings, and over the last few nights she'd been too exhausted to do anything other than collapse atop her threadbare comforter. Tonight, she'd fought to stay awake until the sounds of silence enveloped her, determined to move the painting to safer environs.

She reached the bottom of the staircase and turned on her torch, not daring to switch on the overhead light. As he'd done on her earlier visit to the chateau, Sébastien had left for the village shortly after they'd returned from the harvest, but there was always a chance that Maman might come down to the kitchen for a warm glass of milk and notice a light on in the cellar. Her torchlight glinted off the tops of wine racks, her footsteps falling too heavily, too loudly, in the dark. Irresistibly, she thought of her grandfather's ghost stories about the executed nobleman who'd owned Dolus once, carrying his head beneath his arm as he stalked through the halls he'd once owned—

Stop it, she told herself sternly. She trained the beam of light straight ahead, but her imagination had taken root and flowered, making her hear ghostly voices in the dark. *Stop it*, she told herself again, even as she raced back to the foot of the staircase and flipped a switch, flooding the cellar with a faint orange glow from a handful of overhead bulbs.

She breathed heavily, giving herself a moment to settle her nerves. The last time she'd come down, she'd navigated the space by candlelight alone, racing past ancient riddling racks that she'd assumed at the time were empty. Now she could see that wasn't the case. Dozens of bottles, set at a customary forty-five-degree tilt, rested in the racks, capped with temporary triage stoppers as they underwent their second fermentation.

Château Dolus champagne, she thought, breathing in the heavy, yeast-filled air of the cellar. Behind the still-fermenting bottles, she could see an alcove filled with a modest collection of bottles, all corked and caged, maturing in the darkness. These, then, were the voices she'd heard. Maturation was a living process, after all, each bottle carrying the story of the soil and the grapes, the sunlight and yeast that transformed juice into gold. With some difficulty, she reached up and took a bottle from the top of the pile, blowing away a thin layer of dust to read the date chalked on the glass: 1938.

She smiled, grudgingly impressed at Sébastien's determination. Though her parents' insolvency meant that they still sold most of their grapes to Moët et Chandon, Sébastien had succeeded in bringing champagne back to Château Dolus—in small quantities, to be sure, but champagne nonetheless.

"That's the best vintage," came a voice behind her, and Fabienne nearly dropped the bottle. She turned to find Sébastien standing at the foot of the staircase, an inscrutable expression on his face. "I told you already that the '39 was shit."

"You scared me." Fabienne set the bottle back down and smoothed her shaking hands down her front. "I thought you were—"

"Don't tell me: *the nobleman's ghost*." Sébastien smirked. "Still believing in fairy tales, are we?"

"Well, who else would come down here in the middle of the night?" Fabienne snapped. She tightened the cord of her dressing gown. "I thought you'd gone to town."

"I came back," he retorted. "And I needed to riddle the

bottles before I turned in. Unlike you, my workday doesn't finish after harvesting. What are you doing down here?"

"I couldn't sleep," she replied. "Papa had mentioned that you'd begun bottling, and I thought—"

"You shouldn't be down here on your own. It's dangerous." He stalked past her to the riddling rack and began to turn the bottles, jostling the sediment to make the champagne's characteristic bubbles. "Go back upstairs. We've an early start tomorrow."

"You as much as anyone else," Fabienne protested, thinking that once he'd finished his task she might be able to give him the slip in the kitchen and double back for the painting. "Let me help you—"

Sébastien clunked a bottle into place with more force than he needed to. "Your parents might enjoy your complete disregard for the rules around here, but it's wearing awfully thin with me. Go upstairs, Fabienne. Why can't you ever just do what you're supposed to?"

It was clear that the Kirchner would have to wait another night.

"Look, I understand how difficult this must be for you," she said, "and I appreciate how hard you're trying. I see it, truly I do. But I want to be here. I want to build a relationship with my parents again."

He continued riddling the bottles, setting down each one after a quarter turn with a heavy thunk.

"I lost my husband. This war…it's made me realize I don't want to lose my parents, if I can help it."

His back was still to her, but the clunking sound of the bottles had slowed.

"I know that asking for your friendship might be a step too far. But please, Sébastien, please don't be my enemy."

He bowed his head, and in the orange light she watched

him turn, one of the half-fermented bottles of champagne still in his hand. "I don't want to be your enemy," he said softly. "But what you did...how you left... I don't know how to move forward."

She nodded at the bottle he was holding. "How about we start with a drink?"

39

Sophie measured out yellow pigment onto a glass slab, carefully pushing the dry powder into a small mound with a palette knife before slicing through it to disperse any clumps. In its powdered form, pigment was a fine thing: though each and every pigment had once been part of a component whole—animal, vegetable or mineral—were she to pinch it between her fingers, she knew she wouldn't feel a single grain. This was color in its purest form: yellow ocher, clay and iron oxide transformed into prime, brilliant hue.

Pigment alone, however, was merely dust without a binding agent. She picked up a bottle of linseed oil and drizzled the smallest amount over the powder, then began to push the two substances together with her palette knife. The binding agent was what gave the pigment its form, suspending the particles of color to hold them fast.

She set aside the knife and began to work the mixture with a heavy-bottomed glass muller, spreading it across the plate in a smooth figure-eight motion. Artists had made their own paints using this same method for millennia, grinding down their pigments into power and mixing them with oils, or with tempera—egg yolk—to create paints that would stand the test of time. And the ancient methods still held true, in this day and age when technology took precedence over all else. This was an age of the production line: of laboratories filled with men in white coats; of airplanes and wireless radios; of iron, petrol, coal. Elements pulled, like the minerals in her paints, from the earth and transformed into something else, something beautiful or terrible, depending on the hands that shaped it.

She finished mulling her paint and sighed, wishing that the binding agent she used was that which she'd sought from her father, an acrylic resin made with a petroleum base. Every day that passed was one where Fabienne's supply of paint dwindled, but Sophie hadn't gotten any firm promises out of her father for more.

"You've no idea," Papa had said after Sophie explained what she needed from him in the Bois de Boulogne. "No idea what it's like at home. Your mother and I have everything to lose in opposing the Nazi party."

"And nothing to gain," Sophie replied bitterly. *Other than a relationship with your daughter.*

They emerged from the trees onto the Boulevard Maillot, the handsome apartment buildings of the 17th arrondissement overlooking the endless green canopy of the park.

"I wish I could help you, *Liebchen*," Papa said. As if to prove his point, an immense black Daimler trundled past, its bonnet fluttering with red-and-black flags. "It's just that there's no use in fighting. Not when they've already won."

Sophie didn't follow Papa into the metro station, not when

it was clear that he had already made up his mind. "Promise me that you'll think about it, at least," she'd said. "We have a duty to put right what we can, in whatever way we can."

Papa smiled. "You're an idealist, *Liebchen*. You and your brother both." He paused, and Sophie knew he was thinking of Dietrich. "Be careful. When the war is over... I hope you know that you'll always have a place with us, if you ever need it."

He'd taken his leave, then, melting into the metro as Sophie waited for him to disappear. How blinkered had his world become for him to truly believe that life could continue as before? How could he still turn a blind eye to the Nazis' atrocities, knowing what had happened to Dietrich? To his Jewish neighbors? To those who'd spoken out within his own university?

She scraped down the muller, sickened at the thought that her father had lost his will to stand up for what was right—or that, perhaps, he'd never had such a will the first place.

"Hard at work, I see." She looked up as Konrad Richter stepped through the door of the laboratory.

"Dr. Richter. How are you?"

He leaned against the doorframe, nodding at the mess she'd made. "You know, we can order paint for you," he said. "From the finest art stores in Paris. From anywhere in the world. Anything you like can be here, in this laboratory, with one well-placed telegram."

She pulled a jar of solvent from the glass bottles arrayed on her station. "That's as may be, but I prefer mixing my own." She added a drop of solvent to her concoction and watched, satisfied, as the paint smoothed further beneath the progress of the muller. "It gives me better control over my work, you see. And besides, I enjoy it."

"Aha." Richter stepped closer to watch. "The elusive Mademoiselle Brandt admits that there's something in this world she likes to do." He grinned. "Tell me, Mademoiselle Brandt, what else do you enjoy?"

Deceiving you, you arrogant bastard. She scraped down her muller one final time. "Oh, I don't know, Dr. Richter…what does any young woman enjoy? Walking through the Jardin des Tuileries, I suppose. Wandering along the Seine. Spending time at the Louvre."

"Enjoying the company of friends?"

She paused, then picked up an empty tube and began scraping the paint into its open top. "Who doesn't?"

Richter stepped forward. "In that case, might you permit me to walk you home this evening?" He glanced out the picture window at the tops of the browning trees, the sky still bright beyond. "It's a beautiful evening. Surely you don't intend to stay late. Let me walk you home and share in one of your simple pleasures."

She suppressed a sigh but nodded at the plate glass. "Let me clean all this up, and then we can go."

They wandered along the Rue de Rivoli, the manicured trees of the Jardin des Tuileries casting shade onto the sidewalk from behind the wrought iron fence. Across the street, armed guards flanked the footmen at Le Meurice, watching passersby with their hands on their rifles as SS officers streamed in and out of the hotel's revolving doors.

Richter jerked a thumb at the door. "Have you ever been?" Sophie shook her head, and Richter chuckled. "I have. Drinks with the *Reichsmarschall*… We both prefer the Ritz, but Le Meurice does make a mean martini."

"What's he like?" Sophie couldn't help asking. "*Reichsmarschall* Göring. I see him in the museum, but I've never spoken to him properly."

Richter continued walking. "He's…formidable. I know he can come across as extravagant, frivolous even, but he's a brilliant tactician. There's a reason Hitler chose him as his right-hand man. You didn't have cause to see it in Paris, but his *Luftwaffe* is capable of reducing whole countries to ashes." They reached the end of the Jardin des Tuileries, and Richter put a hand on the small of Sophie's back to escort her across the street. "I wouldn't be one to cross him."

Sophie shuddered, both from the feel of Richter's hand on her as well as his inadvertent warning.

"He's taken rooms at the Ritz. The Imperial Suite," Richter was saying. "He's got a beautiful view overlooking Place Vendôme." He paused. "My own rooms don't quite measure up, I hate to say. I don't mind staying there, of course, but I've begun searching for my own apartment. I find living in a hotel so impersonal, even one as lovely as the Ritz."

Sophie nodded, picturing an apartment stuffed to the brim with paintings pilfered from the Jeu de Paume. She wouldn't put it past Richter to try such a stunt, not when he was already doing so on behalf of his benefactor. "But surely the Ritz has its advantages."

"Indeed. Why, the other evening I was dining in the salon and had a most agreeable exchange with Mademoiselle Chanel." He paused, with the air of someone about to bestow a present from Father Christmas. "I would be happy to make an introduction, if you like."

"To Chanel?" Sophie stuck her hands in the deep pockets of her overcoat. "I don't know. What would I do with haute couture?"

"Wear it." Richter smirked. "Your dedication to the Jeu de Paume is admirable, *mademoiselle*, but don't forget that there's a world outside the museum. A rather lovely one, too, if I may say so."

And isn't that a matter of perspective? Sophie thought bitterly. "I appreciate the sentiment, Dr. Richter, but I don't really think it appropriate to spend money on luxuries when there's a war on, do you?"

"Ah…no. No, of course not," Richter replied as Sophie used the rush of an intersection to skip briskly ahead. He caught up, straightening his tie. "Of course you're right. I wouldn't want you to think me unfeeling."

She paused, enjoying the sensation of having put Richter on the back foot. "Of course not, Doctor."

They carried on down the Rue de Rivoli and through Les Halles. Feigned friendship with Richter was a rather easy thing to cultivate: a well-placed nod or a leading question seemed guaranteed to send him into a lengthy observation or story that Sophie only needed to half listen to. He was someone who liked the sound of his own voice and the sense of his own importance. In fact, so long as Sophie agreed with him at appropriate intervals, she seemed able to get by without saying much at all in return.

"Are you sure you wouldn't prefer to walk along the Left Bank?" Richter asked as they passed the Gothic spire of the Tour Saint-Jacques. "It seems so much more your style."

Setting aside the fact that she didn't want to share her usual walking route with Konrad Richter, it hadn't escaped Sophie's attention that they'd entered the outskirts of the Pletzl, a predominantly Jewish neighborhood.

"Or perhaps we might go down to the *quai*, cross onto the Île de la Cité—"

"Dr. Richter, don't tell me you're uncomfortable." She took his arm. "Besides, isn't it lovely, sometimes, to wander somewhere new?"

He glanced down, pleased at the sight of Sophie's hand on his arm. "Well, it's all new to me, I suppose," he said. "Even if I visited Paris a thousand times, it would still all be new to me."

They passed Hôtel de Ville, leaving Île de la Cité behind as the Seine snaked around the tip of Île Saint-Louis. Richter was prattling on about the 1936 Olympics when Sophie noticed a disturbance in the road ahead.

The intersection of Rue de Rivoli and Rue Pavée had been cordoned off, gendarmes and German soldiers milling about as they tried to dispel small handfuls of curious onlookers. Sophie frowned, the heavy smell of gunpowder thick in the air.

She broke away from Richter and approached a gendarme. "Excuse me, Officer. What happened?"

He held out his arms, attempting to obstruct Sophie's view up Rue Pavée. "Nothing to concern yourself with, *mademoiselle*."

"Sophie?" Richter rested a proprietary hand across her shoulders. She shook him off, and as the gendarme turned she saw behind him debris in the narrow street, officers and firefighters gathered in a tight huddle. "I don't think we should get involved, perhaps—"

"What happened?"

The gendarme glanced over his shoulder. "It's the synagogue, *mademoiselle*. Bombed early this morning. I wouldn't want you hurting yourself on the broken glass—"

Sophie froze. "Bombed? By whom?"

The gendarme exchanged a glance with Richter. "Our investigation is still ongoing."

"Sophie." Richter put his arm around Sophie's shoulder once more, and she didn't bother to fight him off. "We need to do as the officer says. It's unsafe."

He steered her across the street and partway down Rue de Fourcy, where he found a vacant bench. Numb, she sank onto it, and though she knew she had to conceal her thoughts from

Richter, she couldn't stop them racing though her mind. How many times had she seen Jewish businesses, Jewish houses of worship, desecrated or destroyed in Stuttgart? How many times had she seen police officers turn away with a shrug— or, worse, take part in the attacks? *It's all happening here*, she thought, and though she'd seen the spoils of such destruction make their way through the Jeu de Paume, she'd somehow managed to block out the thought of the brutality that had no doubt resulted from it: the pain, the anguish, of the city's Jewish families.

It's all happening here, and there's nothing I can do to stop it—

"Sophie." Richter took her hands in his. "Sophie, are you all right?"

She looked up. Belatedly, she realized how dangerous a position she was in. What would Richter think if he knew the extent of her distress?

"I… I didn't expect to see…to see a bombing in the city," she said, and Richter pressed his advantage, drawing her closer.

"I'm so sorry. If I'd known the city better, we might have avoided—"

Sophie looked up. "You knew about this?"

Richter sighed. "I'd heard about it, yes, but I didn't realize we were so close to one of the sites. There were six in total, I believe. It was a coordinated operation."

"Coordinated by whom?" She willed herself to stop trembling. "There might have been people in there."

"There weren't," Richter replied quickly. "The bombings took place in the middle of the night. It was meant as a warning, that's all."

"A…a warning?"

He shook his head, looking back up at the Rue de Rivoli. "You would think they would understand by now that they're not wanted," he said bitterly.

Sophie stiffened at the annoyance in his voice. To Richter, the consequence of the bombing didn't lie in the terror it meant to instill in the city's Jewish population, nor even the clear insinuation that the city's police force had been behind it. No, to Richter, the real trouble with the bombing was the fact that it had interrupted his attempt at a romantic walk.

Outraged, Sophie drew herself up to face Richter, and Dietrich's voice echoed in her head. *Be careful.*

Richter squeezed Sophie's hand. "You've had a nasty shock, just now," he said. "War's a terrible thing to see. Why don't we stop somewhere for a drink, help to settle your nerves?"

"No." Sophie stood, still trembling with rage as she turned away from Rue de Rivoli. "No, take me home, please. Now, Dr. Richter."

She walked through her building's courtyard soon afterward, feeling as though she were moving through quicksand as she crossed to the base of her staircase. She'd left Richter at the door, having declined his suggestion of a cup of tea. To her relief, he'd not pressed the issue, though Sophie very much doubted she'd heard the last of such offers from him.

Here, within the privacy of her apartment building's walls, Sophie braced herself on the banister and doubled over, pressing her free hand to her mouth to stifle her sobs as she thought, once more, of the ruined synagogue. The silence surrounding Rue Pavée had been most chilling of all: though dozens of other people had crowded the intersection, no one had been crying, no one shouting or protesting, no one had stormed the street, trying to hold to account those who'd committed such an act of violence. No, the faces of those around her had been grim—grim because, like Richter, they'd felt the destruction beneath their notice or because, like Sophie, they knew that their outrage would put them in danger. Had there been members of the synagogue's congregation standing there on Rue Pavée, watching as the city's gendarmes refused to investigate the crime? Perhaps they'd known that any reaction would be taken as a victory on the part of the perpetrators. Perhaps they'd known that there was little justice to be had in a city where their neighbors had already stood by, silently, as they'd lost their businesses, their possessions.

She turned at the narrow landing, and her mind turned to the couple whose photographs she'd passed on to Louis for false papers: the man, with his lined cheeks and kindly eyes, the woman, staring at the camera with fierce grace. Louis had given her the papers nearly a month ago now, and Sophie had smuggled them to Fabienne in the lining of her overcoat, along with a masterful Matisse. Had Fabienne given them to their owners?

"Whoever they are, tell them to make use of these papers sooner rather than later," Louis had muttered when he'd handed Sophie the forged documents within the fold of a newspaper. "My sources tell me that it's only just beginning, for their lot."

Was this what he'd meant?

She took a breath. What could she do in the face of such hatred?

She reached her landing and paused at the sight of a battered package propped against her door. It looked as if it had been delivered by hand, the label bearing no return address nor stamps, only her name, written in her father's cramped handwriting.

The right thing. She picked it up, relieved to feel its substantial weight, to note the faint smell of petrol through the paper. *We can strive to do the right thing.*

40

Sébastien led Fabienne up the winding staircase. The kitchen—
a hasty Victorian addition cobbled together in a room that had
once been a parlor—was cramped but welcoming, with slowly
oxidizing copper pots hung over an ancient stove. The sink,
piled high with the evening's unwashed dishes, was positioned
beneath an immense window hung with painted curtains—
one of Fabienne's early art experiments—and though the window was closed, the curtains still billowed in the evening
breeze, thanks to a crack in the windowpane. If they were in
Paris, that sliver of light pouring out into the grounds would
be enough to warrant a visit from the local constabulary, but
here in the countryside blackout restrictions seemed to matter
less. Sébastien, certainly, seemed unconcerned as he crossed to
the cupboard with a champagne bottle in hand. He glanced

at the empty cupboard, then set down the bottle to rinse two glasses from the pile in the sink.

Fabienne sat at the small harvest table wedged between the icebox and the stove, uncertain what to say but knowing that the silence was hers to break. Sébastien wanted an apology, that much was clear. But how could she give it to him, knowing that if she were to go back in time, she would do it all over again?

He set the glasses down and uncaged the bottle of champagne, muffling the sound of the cork with a tea towel. Without his ever-present scowl, Fabienne could see that the years had been good to him: he'd matured into his features, his cheeks hollow beneath the stubbled growth of a several-days-old beard. His shoulders were broad beneath the worn linen of his rolled-up shirtsleeves, while his dark hair had only just begun to gray. She thought back to what she'd teased him about earlier, in the fields. No doubt he'd had plenty of sweethearts over the years. Was there any girl in particular to account for his nightly disappearances?

But those were thoughts to which she no longer had a claim. She cleared her throat and watched as Sébastien filled her glass, the bubbles rising precariously close to the rim before subsiding.

"You know," she said when he'd finished, "I hardly ever drink champagne these days. When I moved to Paris, I promised myself I would never—what?"

Sébastien sank into a chair, rolling his eyes in a gesture so overdrawn it belonged on stage.

"There it is," he said. "We've barely sat down and already you're complaining about this place." He leaned forward, planting his elbows on the table. "Did it ever occur to you that your constant whining hasn't exactly lent itself to a warm welcome home?"

She sat back, feeling the sting of Sébastien's rebuke. In her mind, she'd always been so stoic about her dislike of Château Dolus—but then, she'd always had a habit of ignoring traits of hers that she preferred not to confront.

"I suppose you might have a point." She lifted her glass to her lips. "If it's any consolation, this is quite good. I don't think any of us thought our grapes would ever be worth bottling on their own."

He scoffed again. "I didn't do anything particularly ground-breaking," he replied. "I think we'd been selling our grapes for so long that we'd lost sight of what we have here, but it's the soil, the environment, that makes them special. I just happened to harvest them."

"You never did give yourself enough credit," Fabienne retorted, and it was Sébastien's turn to look chastened. "I know people say that humility's a virtue. But really and truly, have some pride in what you've accomplished." She held up her glass, watching the bubbles dance and fizz. "You've done what generations of my family couldn't. You've made proper champagne. Out of our pinot noirs, our chardonnays." Though Sébastien hadn't lifted his champagne, she reached across the table and tapped her glass to his. "Combined as they were meant to be, in service to Château Dolus."

He looked down, digging dirt from beneath the half-moon of his thumbnail. "Maybe so," he conceded with a shrug, "but there's no guarantee it will ever amount to anything. Selling grapes to de Vogüé—that's a sure bet. But making champagne on our own? Less so." He met Fabienne's eyes for a split second before looking back down at his broad hands. "Anyway, it's all immaterial, now. It's not worth the risk when everyone is under such pressure from Klaebisch."

"Isn't pursuing your dream worth taking the risk?"

"Well," he replied with a smirk, "you'd know a thing or two about risking it all on a dream, wouldn't you?"

The observation hurt, more than Fabienne was willing to let on. She'd taken the risks, yes, but she'd not been brave enough to face the consequences of her actions. Was it any wonder that Sébastien resented her now?

She set down her champagne. "I never meant to hurt you, Sébastien. But the thought of living here, in a life that had been all planned out from the start… Didn't it scare you, too?"

"You think it wasn't obvious to all of us that you wanted a different life from your parents? That you had dreams you wanted to chase?" His stern expression crumbled, before he shored himself back up again. "Did it ever occur to you that if you'd spoken to me about it, I would have been happy to build that life with you somewhere else?"

Though her answer rang clearly in her head, she had the presence of mind not to say it out loud; it was evident, however, that Sébastien knew exactly what she was thinking.

"The thing I find so hard is that you never spoke to me— *really* spoke to me—about it," he continued. "You made so many assumptions. In the years after you left, I had to wonder…had you ever truly given us a chance? Or were you always too worried about what other people wanted?"

"How could I not be?" Fabienne stood. "Maman and Papa were always there, putting so many *expectations* on us. They were so proud, when you showed an interest in the vineyard, so happy, when we began courting. How could I not take their wishes into account? And you…" She thought back to Sébastien as she'd known him, gawky and beaming. "You love this life, the vines, the chateau. Farming. Who was I to take you away from that?" She buried her face in her hands, feeling that same sense of exasperation, frustration, that had driven her in those long years before Paris. "You'd all made so many plans

for me. How could I go through with our wedding, knowing that I'd disappoint everyone in the end?"

"Your parents never expected anything from you beyond
your love, Fabienne. God knows, neither did I." He let out
a breath, and Fabienne could see the effort it had taken for
him to hold onto this pain for so many years, his anguish, in
finally saying what he'd no doubt thought of saying countless times, or otherwise resolved never to tell her. "From the
time we were kids, all I ever wanted was to make you happy.
You, Fabienne. Not Château Dolus. Not your parents. I would
have gone to Paris with you, if you'd given me the chance."

"And left my parents without someone to rely on?"

"They would have found some other way to cope." He
sighed, draining the last of his glass. "But it's too late now."

Fabienne sat back down and rested her hand over his. "I'm
sorry," she said gently. "You deserved more. And I know it's
not what you want to hear, but I found the life I was meant
to live. In Paris."

"And the man you were meant to live it with." Sébastien
didn't remove his hand from beneath hers, and something in
Fabienne's heart tugged, ever so slightly, as his eyes met hers.
"Tell me about him. Dietrich."

The sound of her husband's name out of Sébastien's mouth
was almost too much to take. Under the pretense of sitting
back in her seat, she slid her hand away. "What do you want
to know?"

"What was he like?"

Fabienne knew what he wanted her to say: that Dietrich
was a brute, that he'd been a bad husband. "He was a good
man," she replied simply. "A good man who believed in fighting back against injustice."

Sébastien refilled their glasses, his expression hardening.

"A German," he replied, as though that alone condemned Dietrich.

"He couldn't help where he was born, no more than you," she shot back. "But Dietrich refused to let it define him. He left Germany. He did everything he could to warn people against Hitler."

He raised his eyebrows. "A man of principle, then."

"Yes." Fabienne quietened. For a brief, shining moment—from the day she made her marriage vows to the day she stood over her husband's grave—she'd been a good person. But what of her actions before and since? Had Dietrich been the only thing tethering her to a life of principle? "He was a good man. And a good husband."

"And he loved you?"

She bowed her head. "Yes."

Sébastien sighed. "I'm glad for that, at least." He set down his glass and stood. "We've an early start tomorrow."

"Oh…of course." She got up and took their glasses over to the sink, twisted the tap to let water cascade over the mountain of plates her parents had left behind. "You go on upstairs. I'll… I'll just finish up these dishes." She ran her hand under the water, letting it darken the sleeve of her dressing gown before she pushed the fabric up her arm. She smiled, searching for a lighthearted note on which to end their conversation. "We might never get back to friendship, I know, but perhaps this is a first step toward something other than active hatred."

She could hear his footsteps behind her, a gentle thud as he set down the empty champagne bottle. "Once again, you've added two and two and somehow ended up with twenty," he said softly. "At what point did I ever say I hated you?"

She whirled round, but he'd already disappeared into the dark hallway.

41

The grand gallery was quiet, the potted palms gleaming in bright sunlight that streamed through the picture windows. In the center of the room, Hermann Göring sat before a shrouded easel, his ring-laden hand curled over the head of a jeweled cane. He watched as a dark-suited dealer lifted the curtain from the easel with a practiced flourish to reveal a painting of a thatched house nestled in the lee of a lush valley.

"Karl von Blochen," the dealer announced, and Göring leaned forward. *"Mill in Saxony."*

"Magnificent," Göring breathed, his blue eyes glittering. Readying two more covered easels behind him, Sophie studied the painting. Personally, it wasn't to her taste, the vivid greens and yellows of the saccharine forest putting her in mind of "Snow White and the Seven Dwarfs"; however, it hardly surprised her that the fairytale-like painting would appeal to Göring's love of myth and grandeur.

He tilted his head to glance at Richter. "Well done, Konrad," he said, then turned back to the art dealer. "And you, my dear von Frey. I so appreciate you making the trip from Lucerne in such difficult times."

"I only hope it was worth your while," von Frey replied smoothly. The dealer—thin and tall, with slicked-back hair and a feeble moustache—had brought the von Blochen, along with a painting by Makart, from his Swiss gallery for Göring's consideration. "Being, I'm sure, so preoccupied with events in Russia."

Göring's smile froze. It was no secret that after so many early victories, the mighty *Reichsmarschall* had experienced his first true military failures. In Russia, the German army had hemorrhaged men and supplies on a doomed invasion of Moscow and Leningrad; in Britain, meanwhile, Churchill's RAF had fought the *Luftwaffe* to a standstill. "Preoccupied for certain, my dear von Frey, but a man of culture can always make time for art. Konrad?"

Richter stepped forward and nodded sharply at Sophie. One by one, she lifted the sheets covering the extra easels to reveal two paintings from the Room of Martyrs: a landscape by Cézanne, and a portrait of a young woman by Renoir.

Von Frey's smug composure faltered slightly at the sight of the masterpieces. "My goodness," he said as Göring hefted himself to his feet.

"Quite the pair, aren't they?" Göring put his mitt of a hand on von Frey's rounded shoulder. "And they could both be yours."

Sophie folded the sheets over her arm as the three men began to haggle. She'd assisted Richter in more exchanges than she could count, usually within the discreet confines

of the Room of Martyrs; however, Göring's arrival had ne-
cessitated a little more in the way of pageantry, which was
why Richter had opted to move to the grand gallery. The
shrouded easels had been Sophie's suggestion, ostensibly to
appeal to Göring's flair for the dramatic, but in reality they
were a convenient means of ensuring that she had a front-row
seat to the negotiations.

"The Makart and the von Blochen, then, for the Cézanne
and the Renoir," Richter was saying as he poured three glasses
of cognac from a crystal decanter.

"A Cézanne and a Renoir of dubious provenance," von Frey
replied doubtfully as he accepted one of the snifters.

"But a Cézanne and a Renoir, nonetheless, my dear fellow!" Göring cried. "Their value is certain only to grow."

"You can't deny you're getting the better end of the deal,"
added Richter.

"And think of the service you would be rendering the
Reich." Göring smiled, bestowing upon von Frey the full
force of his charm. "Makart and von Blochen are renowned
Aryan artists, showcasing the true mastery of our illustrious
culture. Is it not your duty to return these works of art to their
homeland?" He stepped back, looking at the von Blochen with
barely restrained glee. "In fact, I shall make a present of the
von Blochen to the Führer. A scene to remind him of what
he is fighting for...and I shall let him know the name of the
dealer who rendered him such a service." He rested a hand on
the rise of his belt. "What do you think of that?"

"I should think it would increase their value to you, *Reichsmarschall*," von Frey replied evenly, and Sophie looked up with
surprise. Perhaps he wasn't as milquetoast as he appeared.

Richter stiffened, but Göring chuckled. "You drive a hard
bargain, von Frey. I admire that," he said. "Konrad, perhaps
your lovely assistant might fetch our third offering."

Sophie nodded and doubled into the adjacent gallery where a third painting from the Room of Martyrs waited on a table. Richter had held the piece back, no doubt hoping to make an even deal—two paintings for two paintings—but he wasn't such a fool as to negotiate without an additional card up his sleeve.

She returned to the grand gallery, and Richter let his fingers brush against hers as he took it.

The Picasso was, without doubt, the most masterful of the paintings in the room. It was a soft, almost sensual painting of an apple, the shape of the fruit mirroring the curves of a woman's backside.

"Now," said Göring, nudging von Frey with the expression of someone who'd just turned up trumps. "What red-blooded man would say no to a painting like that, eh?"

Von Frey nodded. "The Renoir, the Cézanne and the Picasso," he replied, offering his hand to Göring. "In exchange for the Makart and the von Blochen."

Göring drained his glass of cognac. "A pleasure doing business with you, my good fellow. Now, there's a hotel not too far from here that does a marvelous *steak frites*. What say you and I go make the most of this fine afternoon while Konrad sorts the paperwork?"

Richter showed the two men out the door with smiles and obsequiousness, but when he turned back to the grand gallery he let his elegant expression drop.

"Odious man," he muttered. He took out his cigarette case and flipped it open. "That stunt he pulled with the von Blochen..." He sighed, jamming a cigarette into his mouth. "Shame about the Picasso. I had hoped to take it for myself."

Sophie stepped forward, took his lighter and flicked it open for him. He leaned in, looking mildly surprised at the gesture, but Sophie's mind was racing. Richter had been stealing on Göring's behalf for months, each transaction carefully recorded to give them a feeble gloss of legitimacy, but if Richter was stealing from the Room of Martyrs for his own edification, she very much doubted that any records of his own thefts would exist.

She'd kept track of all the exchanges that Richter had made on Göring's behalf. But if Richter was simply tucking paintings under his arm and walking out of the museum, how could she know what he'd stolen?

"There will be other artworks," she said as she flipped the lighter shut. "Other Picassos."

"Of course you're right," Richter replied. He ran a hand down Sophie's arm, sending a shiver of displeasure rippling in its wake. "But that was a particular favorite. I would often see it in the storeroom and think of you…" His eyes were dark with lust, and Sophie twisted out of his grasp.

"You've had a hard day, Konrad. Why don't you finish up early?" She glanced at the von Blochen. "I'd be happy to write up the bill of sale, if you'd like."

For a brief, terrifying moment, Sophie was certain she'd overplayed her hand, expressed too keen an interest in his dealings.

"No, but I appreciate the offer." He smiled, pinning his cigarette between two fingers. "You're too good to me, Mademoiselle Brandt. My work is…complicated, and you somehow make it easier to bear." He paused. "I don't suppose you'd let me take you to the opening of the Arno Breker exhibition next week? At the Orangerie?"

His expression was so hopeful that Sophie almost felt bad for leading him on, but allowing Richter to take her to the exhibition would give Gerhardt valuable time alone in the Room of Martyrs to determine what Richter had taken for himself. "I'd be delighted."

Richter leaned closer, the scent of his cologne cloying and expensive, and Sophie resisted the urge to step back as he set his hand on the small of her back to coax her toward him. Panic flooded through her as he closed his eyes, his features blurring as she felt his breath, hot and warm, on her cheek—

Somewhere nearby a door opened, and Richter pulled back.

"Scheisse," he muttered bitterly, running a hand through his hair as Bohn's secretary scuttled past.

Sophie took advantage of the moment to slide out of his grasp, but she knew that her reprieve was only temporary. Soon, Richter would tire of her keeping him at arm's length.

"The Breker exhibit, then," she said breathlessly, pausing at the door. "I look forward to it."

42

Fabienne worked a Bakelite bracelet, admiring the vibrant green of the resin as she carved a geometric design into it with a minuscule electric saw. Months ago, she'd been given Myriam's vacant desk, but she still only worked on the most basic of the atelier's commissions. Given Myriam's continued absence, Beatrice was now the most skilled artist at Atelier Dufy, her work more intricate than anything Fabienne could turn out. It seemed that her skill with a paintbrush didn't translate into jewelry manufacture, but on her lunch break Fabienne sketched designs nonetheless, hoping to better understand the material with which she worked.

That said, there was something enjoyable about creating the simpler designs. It allowed her to turn her mind to other concerns: the canvas she'd primed so she could recreate a work by Chagall; the three originals, a Dalí, a Masson and a Franz Marc, hiding beneath the floorboards in her kitchen.

She'd take them to Château Dolus once she'd finished the Chagall. This next arrival would bring her count to fifteen— fifteen paintings she'd successfully replicated and hidden. In the grand scheme of things, it wasn't much of a contribution to the war effort—she was hardly blowing up railway lines— but it was something. She thought back to that first conversation she'd had with Sophie, back when she had arrived at Fabienne's apartment with a stolen Kirchner, about the concept of legality in times of war.

How easy it was to break the rules, when they were being made by those who lacked any sort of moral compass.

She'd forgotten, in those long months after they lost Dietrich, how much she'd once enjoyed Sophie's company, how much she'd missed her not only as a sister-in-law but also as a friend. The last time she'd come with a painting, Sophie had actually stayed longer than fifteen minutes, their shared mission meaning more to them both than their shared grief. Though Dietrich's memory would always stand between them, it felt as though the sharp edges of the past were softening into something less prickly than before.

She made the final cut in the bracelet and set down the electric saw, blowing resin dust out of the grooves to inspect her handiwork. She'd created a crosshatch pattern in the bracelet and was satisfied with how it turned out. Once she'd sanded down the rough edges and polished it, it would be ready for the jewelry case.

She slipped the bracelet on her wrist, wondering what Sébastien would say if he saw it. He'd roll his eyes, no doubt, at the unnecessary ornamentation, but she suspected that he would respect the skill it took to make it. He'd never been one for fashion. While Fabienne used to dig through the chateau's closets to find moth-eaten dressing gowns and brocaded curtains she could transform into blouses and skirts, Sébastien would wear whatever was easiest: dark trousers, worn linen shirts. On her most recent visit to Dolus, Fabienne was certain she'd even seen him in a shirt she recalled from their teenage years—but there was something about his lack of pretension that struck her, something solid about his steady approach to life.

Perhaps that steadiness was what she'd found attractive, when they were young: a steadiness to balance out her impulse to fly. Hadn't Dietrich shared that very quality?

She took the bracelet off and set it to one side of her workstation, listening to the whirring of machinery around her. It was getting harder and harder to think of Dietrich—when she couldn't deny that there was still something there with Sébastien. Some latent spark, long buried, reigniting. She'd felt it on her last trip to Château Dolus, when he'd come in a *gazogene* lorry to pick her up from the station, and she'd laughed at a joke he'd made, and his lips had curled up in a grudging smile. She'd only stayed the one night, but she'd felt it again when she'd gone down to retrieve eggs from the nesting chickens the next morning and caught sight of him trudging up into the vineyard, watched him turn and look back at the chateau, as if waiting for a twitch of curtains at her window.

Don't lead him on, Maman had said, her expression hard as Fabienne returned to the chateau with a basket of eggs. *Don't break his heart.* She had no intention of doing so, not when the thought of taking up again with her once-fiancé felt like a rejection of everything she'd had with Dietrich.

For that's what a life with Sébastien would be: a rejection, given that he was tied heart and soul to Château Dolus. She wouldn't allow herself to go back to a life of hard scrabble and disappointment, a life devoid of the art that gave her breath. Her attraction to Sébastien was a reaction to the uncertainty of the war, she was sure of it; a tempting return to the predictability of the past. What she felt was the ghost of a memory—a sweet reminder of a love long since gone. She wouldn't allow herself to indulge such feelings, not when they carried so much risk.

She sighed and began working on a second bracelet to match the first. After several minutes, she felt a small, wet nose nuzzling her ankle, followed by the warm swipe of a tongue, and looked down to see Hugo, Lev's poodle.

"Here to inspect my handiwork?" She leaned down and plunged her hands into the poodle's black and white fur, enjoying the feel of his curls between her fingers.

From behind her chair she heard Lev's amused chuckle. "As is his duty. Every floor needs a foreman." He reached past her shoulder to pick up the bracelet she'd finished, holding it up to examine the craftsmanship. She twisted in her seat to gauge his reaction, and her stomach lurched violently: there, sewn to the front of his jacket, was a yellow star.

She'd read in the papers about the new law requiring all Jews to wear the Star of David, an identifying mark intended, no doubt, to make their ongoing persecution easier for the authorities. She'd seen the ugly things appear in the streets, but never up close. It was a slap in the face, an undeniable expression of hostility on the part of those who'd taken control of the city. Her heart broke at the thought of Sylvie Lowenstein, sewing the hateful patch onto the Chanel jackets she wore with such dignity.

He lowered the bracelet, and Fabienne, horrified, realized she'd been staring.

"Beautifully done, my dear," he said. "I must say, you're gaining a steadier hand."

"I'm afraid I still find my hand steadier when wielding a

paintbrush." She met his gaze, refusing to look down at the flash of yellow still persistently visible out of the corner of her eye. It was what the Germans wanted: for people to see the Jews of France as different, lesser. But they were sorely mistaken if they thought a patch of fabric could destroy friendships and families so easily.

It was clear that Lev knew what Fabienne was thinking. He leaned down and patted her wrist with a warm hand. "This too shall pass, my dear," he murmured. His brown eyes crinkled. "This too shall pass."

43

May 1942

Like its sister institution, the Musée de l'Orangerie was located within the grounds of the Jardin des Tuileries, its slender stone façade mirroring the Jeu de Paume with its pleasing, careful symmetry. After Dietrich's death, Sophie had often found comfort here in the oval rooms that housed Monet's *Water Lilies*. She'd sit for hours, watching the paintings as the sun tracked its way along the skylit ceiling, hoping, by some unknown process, to absorb some sense of the calm in Monet's brushstrokes: to set aside the howling grief within her; to forget, for a moment, that she had been left alone in the world.

Perhaps Monet, too, found the world outside too overwhelming, too subject to change, for he'd had his paintings permanently affixed to the museum's custom-built walls, offering a place of respite to Paris's citizens with a guarantee that, although their own circumstances might shift on the sands of change, his water lilies would always be here, waiting to soothe their troubled souls.

What sorrow would he feel, then, to see his water lilies concealed from view, covered over with heavy red curtains, the quiet solitude given over to a din of dignitaries and artists, swastikas and flashbulbs? Rather than the gentle greens and blues of Monet's linen canvases, the Musée de l'Orangerie now boasted the harsh marbles and bronzes of the German sculptor Arno Breker, whose immense statues and reliefs gave the buildings of Nazi Germany their forceful, merciless character.

Standing arm in arm with Konrad Richter, Sophie looked up at an immense bronze of a seated man, his nude body impossibly perfect, impossibly muscled: indomitable perfection, obliterating the classical lines of Greek sculpture and replacing them with something more, something unattainable. She lifted her gaze higher to focus on the figure's face: its strong jaw and jarringly modern hair; its eyes two blank, serene discs. This, then, was the German *Übermensch*: the ideal human, the Aryan elite. Hitler's monstrous hope for what a pure German bloodline could produce. At once, Sophie was transported back to Nuremberg, listening to Ella explain the importance of giving the Reich a child who could be molded into this impossible conqueror.

"Magnificent, isn't it?" Richter trapped Sophie's hand between the crook of his elbow and his free hand. Was it her imagination, or was he standing taller among these examples of human perfection? "It's not for nothing that Breker is the Führer's official state sculptor."

Sophie nodded, uncomfortably aware of the crush of people around her: Göring, holding court before an imposing bust of Hitler; Breker himself, handsome and dark-haired, casting a satisfied eye over all his admirers. "It's all very overwhelming," she replied. "Sculptures like these belong outdoors, where the elements might add to their beauty."

Richter watched her for a moment. "I keep forgetting how much you dislike crowds," he said. "Why don't we find somewhere a little quieter?"

He led her into the Luxembourg wing. Here, the gallery was still busy, but at least there were windows, set all along the southern façade of the museum, which let in the opalescent light of a drizzling afternoon.

She stopped walking and stared out at the rain. She'd come here once with a particular friend, shortly before Dietrich's final days: a young Socialist from Louis and Fabienne's circle of firebrands, beautiful and lithe and ferociously smart. They'd sat down, side by side amid the water lilies, let their hands drift together when they found themselves alone with the artwork...

But she'd let the acquaintance lapse in the dark days that followed.

Richter called to her from beneath a bronze relief, two flutes of champagne in his hand.

"Apollo und Daphne," he said, handing her one of the glasses. Unlike Breker's other work, this piece was genuinely beautiful: a softer portrayal of a woman fleeing from the attentions of a man, holding a bough of laurel leaves above her head.

He waited a moment, watching carefully as Sophie took a sip of champagne. "Better?"

"Much." She looked up, letting thoughts of the firebrand slide away as she studied the relief: Apollo, urgent and wanting; Daphne, rejecting his advances. "It's silly, I know. Ever since I was a little girl, crowds have made me nervous."

"It's not silly at all," he replied. "I suppose that's why you prefer art restoration to gallery openings."

"I suppose so," she said, honestly. "You can engage with art however you like. It doesn't...push itself upon you. Unless that's the intention of the artist, and then you can just turn away."

He smiled. "There it is," he said, holding up a finger triumphantly. "Something else I've learned about Sophie Brandt." He leaned close, and she fought the urge to flinch. "If we keep up this rate, I might just know five things about you by Christmas."

She put a hand on his arm with a demure smile. *Here's one thing you don't know*, she thought viciously. *Gerhardt Hausler is inventorying the Room of Martyrs as we speak, to determine which paintings you stole for your grubby little apartment.*

Laughter rang from the other room, and Sophie watched as Göring, his ice-blonde wife, Emmy, on his arm, sailed into the Luxembourg wing. He was flanked on all sides by people: Breker and Albert Speer, Jean Cocteau and Maurice de Vlaminck.

Göring made his way to Richter as though he were parting the Red Sea.

"Not quite up to your usual standard, Konrad," he muttered in German, looking at Sophie with a bright smile, and though Richter winced, Sophie refused to allow herself to feel a moment's pain at an insult from such a loathsome man. "But then, I consider your taste impeccable in all things, so I must be the one missing out on the charms of your lovely companion. *Fräulein Brandt*," he continued, switching smoothly into French. "Please permit me to pull you and Konrad away from the delights of Arno's work and come join us for a drink at the Ritz. I always say my dear Konrad works far too hard. Help him to have some fun, would you?"

Göring's wife tilted her head, pursing her lips in a pouty moue before draping her arms around Göring's neck in a gesture that belonged to a young silver-screen ingenue rather than a middle-aged matron. "I always say the same thing to my dear Hermann," she purred.

"Thank you, *Reichsmarschall*, but I'm afraid I must decline," Sophie replied. "But Dr. Richter shouldn't miss out on my account."

Göring's smile dropped with almost comic disappointment. "A woman who knows her own mind," he said approvingly, "but not too much so, I hope, for Konrad's sake! Very well, *Fräulein*, we shall say good-night."

He sailed on with his retinue, leaving Sophie alone with Richter once more.

"You don't mind if I go?" Richter asked, staring after Göring like a son might a father. "He's had a ghastly time of it over the past few days. Apparently, the head of the ERR caught wind of our work at the Jeu de Paume, and Göring received rather an earful about it. We're not to sell on any more works of art from the degenerate collection." Richter grimaced. "I suppose we weren't being particularly discreet with von Frey."

Sophie began to walk toward the exit. "What does that mean for…for our work together?"

Richter retrieved her coat from the attendant at the front door and held it out so she could slip her arms into the sleeves. "Oh, we'll carry on, of course. Typical bureaucratic nonsense. But what else are we to do with the degenerates? That storeroom is getting too full as it is. We need to find some kind of solution for it all." He rested his hands on her shoulders. "Are you sure you don't mind my going?"

"Don't be silly." Sophie walked out into the Jardin des Tuileries under cover of Richter's umbrella. In fact, she was relieved that Göring had provided a natural end to her date, but she wasn't about to admit it—particularly when she wanted time to think over what Richter had revealed. There wasn't much to be done with the information, she supposed, not immediately, but Richter's throwaway notion of finding a solution for the Room of Martyrs unsettled her. "Of course you must go! I'll be perfectly all right walking home."

"Along the Rue de Rivoli? Or the Seine?" Richter asked. Over the sound of wind and traffic, she could still hear Göring's booming voice as he walked down the horseshoe path toward the Rue de Rivoli.

"The Seine, I think." She clasped her hands. "Thank you, Konrad, for inviting me to the exhibition. I found it most illuminating."

"As did I," Richter replied as he handed her his umbrella. "And so, this Apollo will say good-night to his Daphne."

He pecked her on the cheek and then set off at a jog toward the heavy iron gates that separated the Jardin des Tuileries from the Place de la Concorde. Sophie, meanwhile, let herself out the side gate of the Jardin des Tuileries, thinking on Richter's parting words. *You seem to forget your Greek mythology, Dr. Richter. In the end, Daphne would rather transform into a tree than submit to Apollo's advances.*

44

July 1942

Flies buzzed lazily in the air above the vivid green of the vineyard. Crouched before the vines, Fabienne gently pushed aside a cluster of underripe grapes to clip away at the leaves that surrounded it. Trimming the foliage would allow the grapes to better soak up the summer sunlight, causing the sugars within each grape to ripen to sweet perfection—or so the theory went. She finished pruning and sighed, staring back up along the tidy vines. Though there were indeed small clusters to show for the chateau's careful efforts over the past year, almost half the grapes had already withered on the vine. She left the cluster where it was, knowing that the next vine would be similarly affected. How much of the harvest would be salvageable come autumn?

At least her efforts with Sophie were proving more fruit-ful. She thought of the steadily growing cache of artwork in the chateau's attic, hidden in plain sight among the building's forgotten relics.

She clipped a withered cluster and held it aloft. "The curse of Château Dolus," she announced.

"For once, Fabienne, I disagree," Sébastien replied, pruning the other side of the vine with neat precision. "I visited Tattinger, and they've got the same problem with their vines. Moët et Chandon does too. The whole region has been affected by all the heavy rain." He leaned back on his heels. "The Germans have requisitioned the copper sulphate we use to treat mildew. But how can Klaebisch expect us to fulfill his orders if we don't have the chemicals we need?"

"Requisition, requisition," Fabienne replied crisply. "If I never hear the word *requisition* again, it will be too soon."

"You can cover your ears all you want, but requisitions will happen regardless." Sébastien sighed, watching as Maman attempted to persuade an implacable ox to drag a heavy plow between vines. "France is just a department store to Klaebisch and his cronies. They don't care about the effort it takes to make the products they want, so long as they get them."

Fabienne thought darkly of the future the Nazis aspired to: a future built on slave labor and the subjugation of entire populations. What did it matter to them if each and every champagne producer went under, so long as they got the bottles they wanted? What did it matter if the art they wanted belonged to another, when they could take it regardless?

"Why worry about tomorrow, when you can have everything you want today?" she said darkly.

Sébastien shot her a sidelong glance. "Just so," he began—but then a shriek split the air.

Fabienne looked up sharply. Several rows away, Maman was standing before the ox, who'd not moved an inch in the last several minutes. She dropped the ox's lead, cursing wildly as the creature stared at her dully. Maman might as well have been yelling at a brick wall for all it was doing. Eventually, she ran out of steam. She dropped her arms, chest heaving, and pressed a hand to her face.

"You'll have to forgive her," Sébastien said quietly. "We had a visit from Klaebisch yesterday… Apparently, he's been asked to find room and board for another regiment of soldiers."

Fabienne frowned. "You think he means to use Dolus?"

Sébastien exhaled. "It would certainly complicate matters for us."

The prospect of exploring a chateau would be too much to resist for a group of German soldiers relegated to the uneventful French countryside. Surely all the works of art she'd hidden for Sophie would be discovered. Was there somewhere else on the estate she might take them—some other hidden corner, unnoticed and overlooked?

"There has to be some way of putting him off," she said, without any real hope. "He called the chateau uninhabitable before, and nothing's changed—"

"Nothing's changed other than the number of soldiers in need of billeting. But I'm afraid the decision won't be ours to make." He picked up his secateurs, glancing down at Maman. "The chateau, the war… It all weighs so heavily on her."

Fabienne followed his gaze. Maman had given up on her tirade and instead was leaning against the ox's broad side to light a cigarette. Things had always weighed heavier on Maman than Papa, or so it seemed to Fabienne. She was the one who attempted to balance the estate's accounts or called creditors to extend on the chateau's loans. Papa, of course, had his own share of worries, but he seemed more capable of a sound sleep. Maman, Fabienne suspected, hadn't enjoyed a full night's rest in years.

Perhaps it was because the chateau had been Maman's life's

work before it was ever Papa's. Like Fabienne, she'd grown up in its crumbling shadow, passed down to her by her own parents. Perhaps it was a sense of duty to the past which drove her, just as much as her duty to the future.

Or perhaps the thought of billeting German soldiers is simply too much to bear, Fabienne thought. She'd not been fair to Maman. In returning to Château Dolus time and again, she'd added another complication to her mother's life at a moment when she could least afford it.

She stood and tightened the silk kerchief she'd tied around her head. "You don't mind finishing this on your own?"

Sébastien shrugged and indicated his assent with a wave of his shears.

She walked to the bottom of the row and made her way along the vines. Maman had managed a few furrows before the ox—named Otto in mocking tribute to the *Weinführer*—had given up on her, and the smell of freshly turned earth scented the air with memories of years past.

Maman stood facing the vineyards behind Château Dolus's modest acreage, and though her hair was now shot through with gray, she could still pass for thirty. The realization made Fabienne feel fifteen years old again. She watched her, sun-browned and beautiful in her oversized trousers and linen shirt, put a steadying fist on the ox's shoulder.

"Not your favorite creature on earth at the moment, is he?" Fabienne called out.

Maman wiped her cheek hastily before turning to face Fabienne. "You know, some creatures are just put on this earth to test us."

"I feel like that's directed more at me than at Otto," Fabienne offered.

She chuckled. "Some days, perhaps, but my quarrel isn't with you at this particular moment."

"Give it time, Maman." Fabienne picked up Otto's lead. "I assume that Otto's not the only one you've quarreled with recently."

The older woman closed her eyes and let out a shuddering sigh. "I only wish it were the case," she muttered. "Between the rain, the mildew, the *Weinführer*… Everything seems poised to break down all at once."

Fabienne stroked Otto's broad head. "Well, that's hardly a change from what we're used to," she replied. "How many times have we been on the brink of disaster? It's the chateau's curse, come back to haunt us again. But we carry on."

Maman ground out her cigarette on the corner of the plow. "It's come back far too many times for me to want to carry on," she replied quietly, and the despair in her voice was something Fabienne hadn't heard before. "I wish it were the curse alone. That might be manageable. Sébastien might have told you already, but we had a visit from the *Weinführer* recently."

"Yes, he mentioned it," Fabienne replied, striving to sound as though it was nothing of real consequence. "Something about billeting soldiers?"

Maman shook her head. "It's nothing to do with billeting soldiers," she began. "You recall Sébastien's friend, François? He was arrested three days ago for selling an inferior vintage to the *Wehrmacht*."

Fabienne looked up in alarm. François Tattinger belonged to one of the most prominent families in Champagne. If Klaebisch could have him carted off to prison, no one was safe from his influence. "Arrested?"

Maman nodded grimly. "Klaebisch sees François's actions as a form of defiance he's determined to put down. He's determined to make an example of him…along with all of his friends."

★ ★ ★

Fabienne sat on the front steps of Château Dolus, her house robe wrapped around her as she watched the darkness. The night was alive with sounds: insects buzzing through the tall grass beyond the drive, and wind breathing life into the vines.

But she was listening for something else. After what felt like hours, she finally heard bicycle wheels, and though she didn't draw attention to herself she watched as Sébastien drew up to the chateau. He hopped off the bike, resting heavily on a pedal before untying a wicker basket from the handlebars, then moved quickly toward the door.

"Where do you go?" she called out, and Sébastien started violently, diving behind the heavy balustrade of the stone staircase.

She wrapped her arms around her knees. "When you leave after dinner? Where do you go?"

"*Merde*, Fabienne," he said shakily, drawing back up to his full height. "You could have warned me you were sitting there."

"Oh, you know me." She tilted her head to admire the dizzying array of stars, listening to the thump of his boots as he came up the stairs. "I prefer the element of surprise."

"I know," he replied gruffly. He sat beside her and unscrewed the lid of a flask, the smell of whiskey mingling with the scent of sweat and soap. "Shouldn't you be asleep?"

She'd slept long enough, tossing in the unbearable heat of the evening. "I should," she said after taking an offered sip. "So should you. Where do you go every night?"

He leaned back. "Don't ask questions that I can't answer," he replied. "It's safer for everyone these days if we all keep to our own business."

Fabienne had suspected that his absences had something to do with the burgeoning Resistance movement that she'd heard about, but she couldn't deny that she felt relieved, just a little bit, to know that he wasn't going to see another woman.

"It was nice, what you did for Annette today," Sébastien said. "Helping her with that blasted ox."

"He's not so bad." She'd sent Maman back down to the chateau after they'd finished talking and spent the rest of the afternoon persuading Otto to move, one steady foot after another, through the vines. "He just takes a little convincing."

She watched Sébastien's dark silhouette as he lifted the flask to his lips.

Fabienne stared out at the lines of darker and lighter night that made up the grounds and the horizon. "Maman told me why Klaebisch was here today," she said finally. "He wants to requisition *you*, it seems."

Sébastien cleared his throat, fingers drumming on the flask. "For the STO, the *Service du Travail Obligatoire*," he said. "The Nazis have already sent thousands of other Frenchmen into Germany to work in their camps and their factories. Why wouldn't they come for me too?"

"Because Klaebisch exempted you from service," Fabienne replied. "You're an essential worker. This place would fall apart without you."

"I *was* essential," Sébastien corrected her. "I'm not sure that I will be for much longer. But it could still all blow over. Klaebisch is just trying to throw his weight around the village. He wants to make a big scene, remind us that he holds all the cards." He held out the flask. "For now, at least."

She hated the thought of Sébastien pulled away from his life's work, his home, just so that the *Weinführer* could make a point. "Be careful," she said. "Don't give him any reasons to make good on his threats."

"Well, I'm touched by your concern. It wasn't that long ago you didn't care whether I lived or died."

"Don't say that," she replied softly. "I care. Very much. It's why I couldn't bear to end our engagement face to face."

Sébastien looked up, and even in the darkness she could see the look of surprise on his face.

She hugged her knees closer and held out the flask. "Bet you weren't expecting me to say that."

Sébastien took the flask. "No," he said finally. "No, I wasn't."

There, she thought. *Now you know.* She didn't need anything from him—no further questions, no attempt to put things right. But it felt right, somehow, to tell him now, to let him know, in some small part, the feelings that she'd tried for too long to deny.

He knocked the flask against her leg, and she took it without drinking. "You know, this war being what it is, there are…hidden dangers, hidden risks, that we all take," he said, looking up, and though she couldn't see the color of his eyes, she knew they were green, impossibly green, unfathomably green. "And whether I get taken away from here to join the STO or…or, if anything else happens, I want you to know that I thought about you every day that you were gone. Every single day."

He glanced back at the door of the chateau, as if expecting Fabienne's parents to come storming out to defend her honor. But what honor did they have to defend?

"I spent every day hoping that you would walk back through that door," he said, "and when you did…it took every ounce of resolve within me to hate you rather than fall to my knees and beg you to stay." He looked down. "I don't expect this to…to change anything between us. But if something were to happen, either to you or to me, I wouldn't forgive myself for not telling you this now."

It was everything she longed to hear; it was everything she

didn't deserve. Perhaps, like for her, the darkness made it easier for him to say what he truly felt.

She looked across the grounds of Château Dolus. Chateau Deceit.

She was deceiving him now—deceiving her parents, too, by bringing priceless works of art here without their knowledge, putting them in danger, without ever truly considering the risks.

She gripped her hands together, willing herself not to reach out and thread her fingers through his.

"I'm not a good person, Sébastien," she whispered, feeling as though she were on the edge of a cliff, waiting to throw herself over. "I'm not the girl you fell in love with all those years ago."

"You were the girl I loved then, and you're the woman I love now." Sébastien twisted on the stair and put his hand on her cheek, setting a small trail of fire in the wake of his fingertips, familiar and new, all at once. "I won't pretend the past doesn't matter, and neither of us can guarantee the future. But we're both here now. Today. And for me, that's enough."

He pulled her close and pressed his forehead to hers, waiting for an answer to the question he'd asked with everything but words. With Dietrich's memory still so vivid in her mind, was Fabienne willing to answer it?

She lifted her hands and ran her fingers over the breadth of his chest, feeling the muscles beneath his shirt respond to her touch as they'd once done so many years ago.

"It's enough for me too," she whispered and pressed her lips to his.

45

Sophie jolted awake to the sound of fists hammering against her door. Heart pounding, she felt around on the nightstand for the lamp, the room a dim blur in the half-light. What time was it? She turned it on and threw off the covers, still struggling to pull herself out of a dream.

They'd found her—Bohn and his men, they'd discovered a forgery in the Room of Martyrs, traced it back to her. It was too late to save herself, that much was clear, but what about Fabienne? Gerhardt? She would keep the wolves from their doors if it cost her her life.

She lurched out of bed, but as she grew more alert she realized that the hammering in the hallway wasn't being directed at her door. She crept toward it nonetheless, hearing the sound of voices. She opened the door a crack, barely breathing. On the landing, two gendarmes stood in pressed uniforms, hands on their sidearms as they addressed Monsieur Nowak, Sophie's across-the-hall neighbor.

Like Sophie, Pavel Nowak was dressed in his pajamas, having no doubt been jolted out of a restful sleep. Being a young academic, Pavel was used to late hours, and it was his bookish nature that made him such an ideal neighbor. Like Sophie, he'd come to Paris to attend university, and he would often tell her stories of his upbringing in Poland or else wax eloquent about his dissertation on bridge trusses.

In recent months Pavel had lost his position at the university, newly imposed quotas against Jewish students forcing him into a factory job which would allow him to provide for his wife and infant daughter. His late nights had been exchanged for early mornings, and Sophie missed their quiet conversations.

Pavel shielded Anna, his wide-eyed wife, with a protective arm over the doorframe. "What is it? What do you want?"

"Pavel and Anna Nowak, you need to come with us."

"Why?" He looked from one gendarme to the other. "On whose authority?"

The gendarme sounded almost bored. "If you refuse to come willingly, we are authorized to use force." He tightened his grip on his sidearm. "Bring food and clothing for two days, but nothing more."

"Where are you taking us?" Anna sounded terrified but steady as she pulled the neck of her house robe tight.

"A processing facility for Jews." With his hand still on his sidearm, the gendarme brushed Pavel aside, sending him and Anna stumbling back into the vestibule so that he could enter their apartment.

Sophie remained at the door, rigid with fear, listening as other gendarmes questioned Jewish residents on the floors above and below her flat. It was *Kristallnacht* all over again, but much, much worse. *Kristallnacht* had been a night of riot and looting, when the police had lost control of cities across Germany and allowed brownshirts to run roughshod over the businesses of Jewish inhabitants. Here, now, it was the police themselves who were pulling people from their beds with controlled chaos.

Memories from Stuttgart came crashing back into her mind, memories she'd long tried to bury: of violence and hatred, persecution and blame.

She could hear lorries idling on the pavement outside—a spill of sounds, screams and protests. This was a coordinated attack against the city's Jewish residents: a coordinated disappearance, with the unpleasantness meant to be concluded before the German officers at the Ritz sat down for their morning coffee.

There was little she could do on her side of the door, but Sophie knew one thing: if Pavel and Anna Nowak left for that so-called processing facility, they would never return to the Latin Quarter.

Pavel reappeared in the hallway first, dressed in trousers and an overcoat emblazoned with a yellow star. He carried a heavy suitcase, glancing back as Anna carried baby Isobel into the hall.

There was nothing Sophie could do: nothing, when the gendarmes both carried pistols at their sides; nothing, when she could hear police officers on each of the other floors, rounding up similarly bewildered Jewish families.

Nothing, when she so completely lacked her brother's bravery.

Somewhere in the open stairwell, someone let out a piercing scream. The gendarmes paused, then strode over to the stairwell to see what had happened. Sophie took advantage of the split second to push the door wider.

She looked at Anna and mouthed a single word: *Run*.

Already, the gendarmes had turned back to Anna and Pavel, clamped heavy hands around their upper arms. Pavel was still stammering protests as he descended the staircase, but Anna was thinking, the whirring of her brain almost audible to Sophie as they were led to the staircase. There was no hope for escape within the walls of the apartment building, but perhaps once they reached the courtyard, the street...

The gendarme behind her prodded her in the back with his pistol, but Anna turned, searching the hall, and Sophie opened her door. Anna met her eyes and nodded once—decisively, defiantly—then she carried baby Isobel down the stairs.

Sophie closed her door and sank to the floor, wishing with all her heart that it had been Bohn and his men in the hall instead, that they'd taken her, rather than a young family who'd done nothing to deserve their fate.

Outside, the screams grew louder.

46

Fabienne ducked into the metro as the doors were closing, relieved to find so many empty seats to choose from as it started to move away from the Gare de l'Est. She sat her carpetbag on the seat beside her, pleasantly surprised: she'd expected to have to fight for space on the handrail, given that it was Friday afternoon, but she wasn't about to complain about the luxury of having the compartment almost entirely to herself. No Parisians crowding her, no soldiers harassing her, just Fabienne, still basking in the glow of what had occurred at Château Dolus. There was little to complain about today, not when Maman had given her a genuine hug upon her departure, nor when Papa had tucked a wire cage of freshly laid eggs in her bag. And not when she'd awoken this morning in Sébastien's arms.

She smiled, recalling the taste of his lips on hers, the feel of his stubble, rasping against her skin. There had been a familiarity with him, of course, but also a novelty, in discovering things about Sébastien that she'd only ever imagined: their bodies, moving in motion together; the sound he made at the peak of it all. She'd dreamed of such a moment in her younger years, but the reality was so much better than she'd ever thought possible.

The metro banked along a rail, jostling as it snaked beneath the Seine. She'd left Sébastien's room late this morning, after he'd gone down to breakfast with Maman and Papa, relying upon her outdated reputation for sleeping in to shield her from awkward discoveries in the hallway. Sébastien had agreed to keep what had happened between the two of them a secret—for now, at least.

"After all," Fabienne had said as Sébastien rested his head on her stomach, threading her fingers through his dark curls, "Maman will have my hide if she thinks I might break your heart again."

He'd turned his head to meet her gaze, sweeping his lips across her navel with a deliberate, agonizingly slow movement. "I don't care if you shatter it, so long as we can do all that again."

The train pulled into the station, and she sailed out onto the white-tiled platform, feeling as though she were walking on air. Perhaps they would break each other's hearts, in the end; perhaps they were only clinging to the comfort of the past. There might not be a tomorrow, but Fabienne knew that she would never regret what had passed between them.

The sound of the departing train echoed through the tunnel, screeching along the rail lines as she reached the top of the stairs. Something about the empty platform reminded her, somehow, of the early, uncertain days of the *drôle de guerre*: those long weeks after Germany declared war but before it invaded, when people stuck to their flats for fear that a bomb might fall from the sky and flatten them all.

Though the platform was empty, the entrance to the metro station was busy. Gendarmes and German soldiers stood, stern-faced, in groups of three and four as though expecting trouble to break out at any moment. She paused, uneasy, beside the ticket-taker's booth. Had something happened, in the two days she'd been at Château Dolus?

As she walked toward the staircase that led to the street, a gendarme stepped forward.

"Papers," he said, and Fabienne set down her carpetbag and handed him her identity card. As he studied it, Fabienne read a poster newly plastered to the wall behind him.

By order of Military Commander Carl-Heinrich von Stülpnagel:
-The nearest male relatives, brothers-in-law, and cousins of trou-blemakers above the age of 18 will be shot.
-All women relatives of the same degree of kinship will be con-demned to forced labor.
-Children of less than 18 years of age of all the above-mentioned persons will be placed in reform schools.

Fabienne's blood iced over. "Excuse me, officer. Has some-thing happened?"

The gendarme handed back her papers. "Nothing for you to concern yourself with, *mademoiselle*."

Outside, Fabienne's sense of unease grew. The streets and café patios were nearly empty, shop owners watching out the windows as Fabienne scuttled past. She walked quickly, want-ing nothing more than to get indoors, take refuge—but from what, she didn't know. In the streets, dark autobuses drove past, emblazoned with the insignia of the *gendarmerie*; litter choked the gutters, papers and clothing and the occasional suitcase, abandoned at the foundations of shuttered apartment buildings.

She crossed the street, and a flash of metal on the ground caught her eye. She looked down and saw a photograph of a child smiling back at her from within the remains of a smashed frame.

Something had happened here—and whatever it was, the anguish of the moment lingered in the air like pollen.

Within the courtyard of her apartment complex, Madame de Frontenac was bent over her little garden bed, tending to her carrots. She pulled weeds from the soil with single-minded determination; beside her, Monsieur Minci's rabbits twitched in their hutch as they devoured whatever greenery Madame de Frontenac pushed inside.

"Good morning," Fabienne called out, and the older woman looked up. "What happened?"

"Oh. It's you." Was it Fabienne's imagination, or did Madame de Frontenac sound disappointed? She turned back to her carrots, sweat staining the back of her worn apron as she pulled out the weeds with steady determination. "Where were you? Hard to have missed all the commotion."

"I was in the country," Fabienne replied, "visiting my parents."

De Frontenac's scarf-clad head lifted. "The countryside, you say?" She looked over her shoulder at Fabienne, her brown eyes glinting as she tossed a handful of weeds closer to the hutch. "Must be nice, having someone to visit in the countryside. I bet you ate like a queen."

Fabienne sighed, then reached into her carpetbag. Careful not to show Madame de Frontenac the extent of what Papa had given her, she extracted two eggs, then waited as her neighbor scrambled to her feet.

De Frontenac took the eggs, weighing them in her hand as

though doubtful of their contents; then, pursing her lips, she tucked them in the pocket of her apron. "It was the Jews," she said dispassionately. "The gendarmes came for them at dawn." She shook her head, her eyes hard. "They made such a racket, they woke poor Monsieur de Frontenac straight out of a dead sleep."

Fabienne's knees turned to water. "Th–the Jews? Who? How many?"

Madame de Frontenac shrugged. "Who's to say? Foreigners, mostly, I think. Monsieur Minci and his son, they were carrying on like you wouldn't believe, but I suppose that's the Latin in them... Monsieur de Frontenac's nerves couldn't take it. He's been in bed all day."

Horrified, Fabienne thought of the poster she'd seen at the metro station. What had Monsieur Minci done to deserve such a fate? And his son, only seven years old...

"How many?" Fabienne asked again, interrupting de Frontenac's tirade about her husband's discomfort.

Madame de Frontenac gaped for a moment, outraged at what she clearly perceived to be Fabienne's lack of tact. "I don't know," she replied peevishly. "A few hundred, I suppose, from this neighborhood, but I'm told there were roundups all over the city. They took the families all together, so at least they'll have each other, wherever it is they're going."

Hundreds. Thousands. Jewish people pulled from their beds, women and children among them, rounded up like criminals, guilty of nothing but sharing a faith and ancestry. "Where...where did they take them?"

"How should I know?" Madame de Frontenac had already resumed her weeding. "It's not like we weren't all expecting something like this to happen. Now, I've got nothing against *those people*, but there's a silver lining in all this. We'll have more selection at the boulangerie..."

Fabienne took off at a run through the courtyard. She vaulted up the stairs that led to her apartment, feeling as though she might throw up—but she couldn't stop, not until she reached the second floor.

Foreigners, mostly, Madame de Frontenac had said.

Mostly, but not all.

She reached the Lowensteins' apartment, hoping against hope that she would find it locked, that Lev would have taken the day off work, that he and Sylvie would be sitting at their balcony, overlooking the street through open French doors. But she knew in her heart that such a hope was futile, even before she saw that their door had been left ajar.

She pushed it open and dropped her bag, choking back a sob as she walked through their hall. The handsome apartment was in tatters, the elegant furniture—so carefully curated by Sylvie Lowenstein—overturned, as though the place had been the scene of some violent crime. Paintings hung drunkenly on the walls, slashed to ribbons. Books, pulled from alcoved bookcases, had been thrown across the room, their spines split and pages torn out. Feathers floated in the air, and when she went into the bedroom Fabienne could see why: the pillows had been torn apart, their innards shaken loose as though someone had been searching for valuables within the seams. As she moved from room to room, she hoped that she wouldn't find what she most dreaded seeing: Lev and Sylvie, injured, or worse, amid the ruin.

She left the empty apartment shortly thereafter and shut the door with trembling hands. *They might have escaped*, she told herself. She'd given them the false papers, after all—maybe Sylvie had finally convinced Lev to leave, to get out under cover of darkness, flee to Switzerland or farther afield. They might have received warning about the roundup from some well-placed friend or another, gotten out before the gendarmes had pounded on the door. Perhaps the gendarmes had destroyed the apartment in retaliation for the Lowensteins' absence, rather than as the result of a struggle.

She reached the final turn in the staircase and paused to wipe her eyes—then looked up at the sound of whimpering from above.

Hugo, Lev's poodle, was sitting at the top of the stairs, his lead looped around the balustrade. He got to his feet and barked, the sound frenzied and desperate as he launched himself into her arms.

She pressed her nose into his fur, biting back further tears as the dog howled miserably. "Where's Lev, *chérie*? Where's Sylvie?"

She didn't put the dog back on the floor as she fumbled for her house keys, opting instead to cuddle him, one-armed, as she opened the door with the other. How long had Hugo been waiting for her, here at the top of the stairs? Had Lev left him here for Fabienne to find—or had it been a gendarme, attempting to make the dog scarce as they looted the apartment?

Regardless of how he'd gotten here, Fabienne shut the door behind her and collapsed onto the couch, letting Hugo frantically lick her cheek. She pictured Lev and Sylvie where she hoped they were: on the prow of some steamship, watching the smoking remains of Europe recede behind them. Sylvie, her head on Lev's shoulder; Lev, no doubt, worrying for those he'd left in Paris.

"Don't worry," she whispered as Hugo curled himself into a ball on her lap. "We're family, you and me. I'll keep you safe until your papa comes home."

47

May 1943

The vineyard was an explosion of green, months of steady temperatures and regular rainfall having contributed to a burst of foliage which, if properly tended, would result in a spectacular harvest. Standing at the end of a long row of vines, Fabienne lifted a shoot heavy with hard clusters that would one day become grapes. Unlike last year's dismal crop, this year's clusters were small and perfectly formed, and she smiled as she pinned the shoot to a long wire running horizontally across the top of the trunk, allowing the nascent clusters to hang gracefully from the wire. Done correctly, lifting the vines would promote air circulation and train the new growth of the vine shoot to grow upward, better positioning the grapes to grow fat and sweet in the spring sunlight.

She finished attaching the shoot to the wire and looked up. It had been nearly two years since that first harvest, and Fabienne had returned to Château Dolus on an almost monthly basis with concealed paintings, each short trip a welcome respite from the increasingly hostile atmosphere in Paris, and an opportunity to improve her relationships with the chateau's inhabitants. Maman and Papa were on the other side of the long line of grapevines. Sébastien, meanwhile, was down in the courtyard. To her intense relief, he'd not yet been called up to serve in the *Service du Travail Obligatoire*, though she knew that his reprieve rested on the continued good graces of the *Weinführer*. He rested an elbow on Otto's back as he hitched him to the cart; nearby, Lev's dog, Hugo, dozed in the long shadow cast by the barn.

Fabienne still found it impossible to think of him as anything other than Lev's dog. In the weeks that followed the horrible events of the roundup, Hugo had whined at the door to her apartment, scratching to be let out to find Lev and Sylvie. She'd brought him to the vineyard shortly after, hoping that a change of scenery might help to ease his troubled mind.

Her heart broke at the little dog's faithfulness. Her own attempts at locating Lev and Sylvie had fallen short, as had Dufy's constant inquiries after their welfare at the police prefecture. Lev's stout business partner had pursued Lev and Sylvie with the dogged determination of a lawyer until the *Milice* paid him a visit at the atelier after work hours. Fabienne and Beatrice had found him in the wreckage of the workroom the next morning, so badly beaten that he'd slipped into a coma from which he'd not yet recovered.

Perhaps it was for the best that Lev and Sylvie had disappeared into thin air—at least their names hadn't appeared on any of the lists of people who had been deported from the Vélodrome d'Hiver in cattle cars. It gave Fabienne hope that one day Hugo might be reunited with Lev; that, one day, she might see Sylvie again.

Papa appeared on the opposite side of the vine. "You look like you're miles away, *chérie*," he said. "Is it anything I can help with?"

She sighed, turning her attention away from Hugo with a perfunctory smile. "Not particularly," she replied, bending down to pick up another long shoot, "but thank you for asking."

She lifted the vine and Papa took it, wrapping the end around the long wire. "I remember planting all this rootstock after the last war," he said, running his hand along the leaves with a careful caress. "The Germans had decimated the region entirely. Reims, flattened... Trenches and barbed wire, as far as you could see." He looked down at Château Dolus, and Fabienne followed his gaze. Sébastien, still in the courtyard, had climbed up into the ox-drawn cart. He let out a sharp whistle and patted the seat. Hugo, who'd until that moment looked as though he'd been fast asleep, leaped to his feet and jumped into the cart. "I remember coming home after the war, wondering whether we could ever come back from it all. It's a miracle that Dolus survived. A miracle that we got the vines to grow again."

Fabienne had heard many times before the story of how the Great War had changed Château Dolus's fortunes. "You had to start it all again from nothing," Fabienne offered, knowing that it was what Papa wanted to hear.

"We had to start from scratch," he agreed. "And we needed the money to do it. We sold off acreage, furniture...whatever we could. We decided to sell our grapes to Moët et Chandon, rather than bottle them ourselves."

"I remember," Fabienne said, thinking of the lean years from her own youth. "You could have taken on a smaller farm, a different crop. What prompted you to stay?"

Papa chuckled softly. "What prompted you to leave? It's

317

what we love, your mother and I. It's our life's work." He looked down at the chateau, its slate roof golden in the ripening sunlight. "The entire process of making champagne is steeped in adversity. So much of it is beyond our control. Crops fail, the weather turns. It's years before we can taste a vintage and know whether we've succeeded in creating something worth having. But look at us now." He lifted another vine to the wire. "Sébastien and I have decided that we're going to hold back our entire harvest this year rather than sell it on to Moët et Chandon."

Fabienne paused. "What do you mean, hold back the harvest?" The prospect was mad: Château Dolus's survival relied upon the regular income they received in exchange for their grapes.

"We're going to bottle our own vintage. Sébastien believes that this year's crop is worth selling under our own label." Through the lush green of the leaves, she could see Papa's satisfied smile. "It's our chance to become a proper champagne house once again, rather than a producer. We've got enough put aside to make it worthwhile."

"And what of the *Weinführer*? What of Moët et Chandon? Won't de Vogüé be relying on us to help him make up this year's yield?"

"We've spoken to de Vogüé. He agrees that this is the year to do it. As for the *Weinführer*...we'll cross that bridge when we come to it."

It was madness, to hold back the harvest, to stake their survival on such a thing during a year of war. Holding it back would mean waiting three years before they would see any return for their investment.

But Papa was too proud, too set in his decision, for Fabienne to warn him off.

"If you're sure," she said, and Papa nodded.

"I'm sure," he replied. "My dearest, you know as well as I do that a harvest can succeed or fail based entirely on factors outside our control. And of course, the curse of Château Dolus might turn against us. But there is one thing that is needed above all else, in order for us to succeed at what we wish." He parted the leaves, his brown eyes shining. "Hope."

The tantalizing smell of roasting pigeon lured Fabienne downstairs that evening, once she'd scrubbed away the dirt and dust of the vineyard. In the kitchen, warm light made the room glow amber. Maman, facing the window, pulled a bubbling dish from the oven while Papa, humming an unfamiliar tune, washed dishes.

Unaware of Fabienne's presence, Maman, too, started humming along with Papa. She picked up a dish towel, letting her head fall gently onto Papa's shoulder as she began to dry a teacup.

Fabienne paused in the doorframe, not wanting to interrupt her parents in this rare moment of intimacy. She didn't remember them being so close when she was younger. But then, as a girl, she'd been so wrapped up in her own preoccupations, her own sense of injustice, that she never truly paid attention. Now, she could see in Maman and Papa an echo of the life she'd led with Dietrich, and to her surprise the reminder wasn't saddening. Instead, she could admire the love between them, so palpable and rare; the life they'd built, modest and beautiful all at once.

She stepped into the room, and Papa turned around. *"Chérie,"* he said. "Dinner's just about ready. I think Sébastien is downstairs. Would you go get him?"

She descended into the cellar, led by the yellow light that hung over the empty riddling boards. In the basement, Sébastien was stacking crates of empty bottles one atop the other, and Fabienne paused at the top of the stairs, imagining the riddling boards groaning beneath the weight of full bottles. Were they truly ready to bottle their own vintage? The idea still gave Fabienne pause, but she watched as Sébastien counted bottles, holding them to the light one by one to ensure that they were sound.

"You know, François and his brother have a machine that riddles the bottles for them," he said. He set the bottle in a crate, wiped his hand along the sleeve of his worn shirt. "A machine that turns the bottles, freezes the deposit, corks the bottles." He cast his gaze down the empty cellar, and Fabienne knew that he was seeing the future, its promise shaped by thousands of brimming bottles collecting dust as their contents ripened. "All sorts of efficiencies, accomplished at the press of a button."

Fabienne looked at the empty bottles and saw the inescapable present: mismatched and brown, they were clearly not champagne bottles of the highest quality. But they would hold wine, and that was what mattered.

"I think that Tattinger's yield is somewhat higher than ours," she replied wryly.

Sébastien shrugged. "Not forever, I hope." He stepped over one of the crates. "Maurice told you, then? What do you think? Can we bring Château Dolus back?"

"I think it's admirable that you want to," Fabienne replied. "But are you sure the timing's right?"

He pulled Fabienne into his arms. "Is the timing ever right for a new venture? But I believe in this year's harvest. It might be years before we get another opportunity to put out a vintage like this one." He paused. "Though, I can't pretend it will be easy. Most of the men in the village have been taken away by the STO. We'll have to work hard to bring in the harvest."

Fabienne allowed her hands to meet his. The *Service du Tra-*

vail Obligatoire had long been a scourge on the village, hauling away most of France's able-bodied men to labor camps in Germany; however, Sébastien had been given a reprieve because the grapes he sold to Moët et Chandon helped them meet the insatiable German quotas. Would the reprieve still hold if he kept the harvest back for Château Dolus?

Fabienne ran her fingers along his sunburned forearm. "What will you do if you get called up?"

"Run, I suppose," he sighed. "Lots of people would rather join the Resistance than the STO. But it's risky either way... and whether we keep it for ourselves or sell it on, I hate the thought of leaving your parents to bring in the harvest on their own."

Fabienne was silent. She didn't mind visiting Château Dolus—but what responsibility would she have to her family if Sébastien were to be taken away?

It was midnight before Sébastien stirred beside her, his heavy arm lifting from her waist. She felt the chill breath of the night air on her skin and instinctively turned beneath the covers, reaching for his warmth.

"Must you go?"

He kissed her cheek. "No questions, no lies," he whispered. By now, she was used to his evening departures, certain that they had something—everything—to do with the regional Resistance movement.

She turned back over in the sheets, letting his kiss drift across her shoulders. In the moonlit room, she could see his face in profile and felt the urge to pick up her paintbrush. Whereas she'd always painted Dietrich in the brightest shades of her palette, cornflower blues and vibrant yellows, Sébastien was darker—moody purples and mossy greens, tempered with gray.

"Come back to me," she murmured.

She listened until his footsteps receded down the staircase, then pulled off the covers. She wrapped herself in a house robe, then snapped open the lining of her trench coat and pulled out two canvases wrapped in mulberry paper. She tucked them beneath her arm, then tiptoed out into the hall.

The chateau was silent as she made her way upstairs to the servants' wing, and she winced as a floorboard squeaked beneath her slippered foot. She didn't dare turn on a light, but then she'd never needed to—not when she'd made this journey so many times before, up through the hallway and toward the rickety staircase to the attic. In the darkness, the chateau's abandoned furniture looked alive, candelabras and wardrobes transforming into the gargoyles that graced the building's gutters. She hurried on, past the bric-a-brac toward the heavy armoire where she'd stored dozens of works of art—

A torch switched on behind her, and Fabienne whirled around. In the unforgiving glare, she couldn't make out who was holding it, but her heart nearly stopped at the sound of Sébastien's voice—no longer tender and loving, but harsh, brutal.

Furious.

He leveled a pistol at her chest, his aim steady and sure. "You need to tell me what you're doing up here. Right now."

48

Sophie was attempting to coax a spent light bulb into working from atop a stepladder when Konrad Richter burst through the door of the restoration lab.

"It happened," he said, holding out a bottle of Dom Pér-ignon with a flourish. "It finally happened!"

Sophie steadied herself on the ladder, the bulb flickering light and dark above her. "I beg your pardon?"

Richter offered her his hand, and she descended, exchang-ing a bewildered glance with Gerhardt Hausler. "After three long years of searching, Sophie, it's finally happened!" He pulled her into a hug, the bottle of champagne cold against the thin fabric of her blouse.

She stepped back, patting Richter on the chest in an attempt to make the movement seem less like the recoil that it was. "My goodness," she said lightly. "What's got you so excited?"

Richter set the champagne down. "The Schloss Collection," he replied. "We found it. Couldn't scrounge up some glasses, could you, Hausler?" He pulled a chair out from beneath Sophie's worktable and sat down, folding his long legs one over the other.

Sophie perched on the edge of the table as Richter began to work the cage atop the champagne cork. Since his arrival at the Jeu de Paume three years earlier, Richter had been searching for Adolphe Schloss's renowned collection of Dutch and Flemish old masters—a priceless selection of over three hundred works of art, including the finest examples of old masters in France—finer even than the artworks amassed by the mighty Rothschild family. If it had fallen into Nazi hands, Sophie knew that the Schloss family would likely never again see the works of art their patriarch had so painstakingly assembled.

She flinched as Richter sent the cork flying with a flick of his thumb. "It was in the unoccupied zone—well, what used to be the unoccupied zone," he explained as the cork hit the far wall with a thud. "Wait until you see it, Sophie. Rembrandt, Christus, de Velours… Truly, it's sublime."

Gerhardt slid three teacups across the table. "How on earth did you manage to track it down?"

"My contacts were able to provide some intelligence on the collection's whereabouts." Richter leaned back in his chair, allowing his leg to brush against Sophie's knee as he filled the teacups, brimming with champagne. "I have well-placed individuals in some *seedier* channels… They were able to confirm that the collection was hidden in a chateau near Laguenne."

Sophie shifted, pulling her leg a scant inch farther away from Richter. "And there aren't any issues with getting hold of it?"

"Well, there are some legal niceties we have to observe." Richter sighed. "Jaujard over at the Louvre has been bleating about jurisdiction, but we all know who holds the true authority in these sorts of matters." He looked up at Sophie and ran a long finger down the seam of her stocking from knee to ankle. "I hope you might permit me to take you to dinner to celebrate properly."

Sophie glanced at Gerhardt, who was studying his teacup with single-minded focus. She'd managed to keep Richter dangling at the end of a string for over a year, allowing him to walk her home or escort her to a museum but stopping short of letting him take her out for dinner or dancing. She could tell, however, that his patience was running short and that the triumph of today's discovery had emboldened him like never before.

"I was thinking, perhaps, Maxim's," he continued. "Oysters to start, and a bottle of 1937 Salon. We'll raise a toast to old man Schloss and his impeccable taste."

She lifted her cup of Dom Pérignon, knowing that there was only one answer she was permitted to give. "And to your impressive powers of investigation," she replied. "How could I possibly refuse?"

Gerhardt cleared his throat. "You make me quite jealous," he interjected mildly. "Might there be space for one more at the table?"

Richter stared at Sophie with the expression of a cat toying with a mouse. "I'm afraid not," he said, and his gaze was as unbearable, unendurable, as his fingers around Sophie's ankle.

She jumped to her feet.

"Maxim's, my goodness, what a treat," she said, her cheeks burning. "I'll have to raid my wardrobe for something smart to wear."

"You'll be the best-looking girl in the room no matter what you have on—although I do hope you'll decide to leave that old overcoat of yours at home." Richter drained the last of his teacup and stood. "Well, lots to do. The *Reichsmarschall* wants a full written account of everything that's transpired today, but I couldn't resist celebrating. I'll let you know once I've settled the reservation, shall I?"

He winked and left the laboratory, shutting the door behind him with a soft click.

"Maxim's," Gerhardt muttered as Sophie ascended the ladder once again. "Are you sure you want to go on your own?"

"It's fine, Gerhardt." Sophie fiddled with the light bulb a moment longer before finally pulling it from the socket with a snort of frustration. "I could hardly keep putting him off, could I?"

"I don't like it." Gerhardt set down his cup. "You do know that a swift kick to the bollocks will take him down like a tranquilized bull elephant?"

Sophie smirked as she made her way down the ladder with the spent bulb in hand. "Thanks for the advice," she replied, "but I doubt it will come to that. He prides himself on being a gentleman."

"Still. Better to know and not need it."

Sophie strode to the door. "You know I grew up with a brother, don't you? It wouldn't be the first time I've kneed a man in the stones."

He returned to his workstation. "What happened to that timid little mouse I used to work with?"

She shot Gerhardt a sad smile. "She toughened up, I'm afraid."

She slipped across the hall and down the staff staircase, bulb in hand as she descended into the museum's basement. Though Rose Valland had initially moved into the curator's office, she'd given up her desk to Bohn upon his appointment as head of the ERR and returned to her broom closet in the basement. Sophie recalled Rose's insistence that war made strange bedfellows, that it might prove an opportunity to vault up the ranks of success. How had it worked out for Rose or for Sophie? Rose, a glorified housekeeper; Sophie, an ornament on Konrad Richter's arm. Was that what Rose had meant when she said they could make a difference?

She reached Rose's office and knocked on the door, then, hearing only silence, she walked in.

Rose's office was small and efficiently proportioned, with barely enough space to squeeze past the desk to the filing cabinets banked behind. Sophie felt in the darkness for a swaying tendril of string, which she pulled to turn on the overhead light, and a single bulb burned into being, filaments buzzing yellow in the dark.

She squeezed past the desk and opened the topmost drawer, hoping to find a spare set of light bulbs. In recent months, Rose had taken over responsibility for the museum's day-to-day maintenance, including fixing the building's finicky boiler. Given her work, Sophie suspected that a light bulb wouldn't be beyond her purview. However, the drawer yielded nothing other than spark plugs and a few open envelopes, scattered in a surprisingly untidy mess.

She opened the next set of cabinets to find more orderly chaos, files lined neatly in a collection that the finest librarian might find enviable. Despite herself, Sophie couldn't help nosing, just a little bit. She ran her fingers up the tabs, reading Rose's neat lettering: *Gallery One*, *Gallery Two*, *Gallery Five*.

Her finger stopped as she reached a file labeled *Entartete Kunst*.

She glanced back at the door, her heart pounding. Surely, this file pertained to the works of art in the Room of Martyrs? She pulled it out from the cabinet, listening for the sound of footsteps in the hall as she opened it.

The file was thick, sheets of loose-leaf paper threatening to spill out beyond the bounds of the manila folder. She'd seen the information contained within the file before, typed out in duplicate by the careful typists of the ERR. Here, however, each work of art within the Room of Martyrs had been recorded in Rose's delicate hand: artist, type of artwork and brief description, meticulously recorded, along with the purchase details of any of Richter's so-called exchanges.

Sophie frowned. Was Rose passing this information on to the Resistance?

If so, she would do better than to keep records within her office. Sophie flipped through the pages, looking for the record pertaining to the first Kirchner she'd given to Fabienne.

She found it and let out a deeply held breath: nothing in the record indicated that Rose knew the Kirchner was a forgery. The work had been categorized by size, provenance, artist, medium. Each column a talisman, a comfort, as she breathed in the words.

Then her breath caught in her throat as she saw an additional, small column welded to the record.

The column was narrow, with space enough for a single mark, a check or a cross. She ran her finger to the top of the page, bile pooling in the pit of her stomach as she read the header:

VERNICHTUNG.

Slated for destruction.

The Kirchner had a small check mark beside the record, a tidy annihilation. She flipped through the records, not caring that she was upsetting the pages as she found check mark after check mark.

VERNICHTUNG.
VERNICHTUNG.
VERNICHTUNG.

49

Sébastien lowered the torch, sending a long arc of light skit-
tering across the grime-covered floorboards. In the silence,
Fabienne listened to her own heart thudding loudly in her ears
as she met his brittle gaze. What was so important that he was
patrolling the chateau with a sidearm in hand?

"You nearly frightened the life out of me," she said. "What
on earth possessed you to—?"

"I'll ask you again." The pistol twitched in his hand, light
glinting off the barrel. "What are you doing here?"

She didn't want to tell him about the paintings, not when
it was clear that Sébastien had allegiances that lay somewhere
other than Château Dolus alone. Was he a member of the Resistance? Fabienne suspected so, but she had no guarantee that
he wasn't part of some other, more sinister organization: the
Milice, perhaps, ratting out men and women to the Germans

in exchange for preferential treatment. Her mind flashed to his sudden resolve to bottle his own vintage, his breezy confidence that it wouldn't pose a problem with the *Weinführer*. Could that be the price he'd named in exchange for his cooperation?

"*Fabienne.*"

"Could you lower that…that thing?" Fabienne squinted into the torchlight. "*Mon Dieu*, Sébastien. We're sleeping together. I hardly think the pistol is necessary."

"That depends on what you have to tell me." She'd never seen Sébastien so angry. He crooked the pistol to his side but kept it steadily trained on her.

He might not be a *Milice* informant, but even if Sébastien were a member of the Resistance, that could pose its own complications. The Resistance was a hardscrabble group without regular funding or leadership. If they were to get their hands on the paintings, how could Fabienne be sure that they wouldn't sell them to pay for the weapons and provisions that the growing movement required?

"Look, I couldn't get back to sleep after you got out of bed," she said finally. "I fancied a walk. Is that a crime? I wanted to remember old places we used to go—"

"Bullshit. We never spent time up here." He took a step toward her, and she flinched as the torchlight beam fell onto her face. "What are you searching for?"

"*Searching* for? I'm not searching for anything."

"I don't believe you. I found you lurking in the cellars once too, remember? And at the door, the night we—" He broke off and lowered the pistol, holding it slack at his side. "You've been searching the chateau, haven't you? Room by room, hoping to find—" He reddened, contempt and anger and dismay commingled on his features. "So, what? You're an informant? A radio operator?" He gestured to her with his pistol, taking in her dressing gown, the canvases rolled up beneath her arm. "Passing along information to your husband's countrymen—"

Fabienne's jaw dropped. "To the *Germans*?"

"Who else? I made inquiries through my contacts in the Resistance, and they had quite the story about you. Imagine my surprise when they told me that you spent the early days of the war as a bed warmer for German officers…" He chuckled humorlessly, setting the torchlight trembling. "I ought to have known from the start. A German's husband, then a German's whore."

Without regard for the pistol he carried, Fabienne crossed the space between them and slapped Sébastien across the face, hard. Had he been planning to confront her all this time? When she'd been in the cellar with him? In his bed earlier this evening? Waiting, hiding, concealing his disgust over conclusions he'd made based on conjecture?

"You don't know the first thing about me," she spat as Sébastien raised the pistol once more. "They killed Dietrich. *Killed* him. You think I would betray my country to them after that?"

Shock rippled across Sébastien's features. "He…he was killed by Nazis?"

"Because he'd defected from the *Wehrmacht*."

Sébastien lowered the pistol. "I didn't know."

"Yes, well, I'm not exactly keen on talking about it," Fabienne replied. With Sébastien's pistol no longer at the ready, she leaned against a nearby table to hide her shaking knees. "He was hanged in the street by members of his former regiment. They tracked us down in Paris." She closed her eyes, picturing the darkened alley she'd never truly left. "I did what I had to do after I lost him in order to make ends meet, and I'm not proud of it. But Dietrich was never a Nazi. And neither am I."

Sébastien was silent. There was more to tell him—there

would always be more to tell him than she could ever say, but silence hadn't served her in the past, nor was it serving her now. She'd put Sébastien and her parents at risk by bringing the paintings to Château Dolus. Was that not reason enough to tell him the truth?

She straightened. "Let me show you what I'm doing up here."

Sébastien followed her to the armoire, his torch held at the ready as she unlatched the wooden door. She opened it and stepped to one side, allowing Sébastien's torchlight to shine on the canvases, standing in rolled columns within the armoire's cavity, dozens of them, awaiting an audience.

She allowed him a moment's inspection, then went to open a nearby steamer trunk emblazoned with Château Dolus's insignia to reveal a dozen more rolled canvases. She circled back to the table she'd been leaning against and, feeling like an explorer unfurling a map, unrolled the two canvases she'd carried up to the attic.

Sébastien came closer, letting his beam of light shine on the hatched lines of a painted haystack. "What am I looking at, exactly? Is this one of yours?"

"This is a painting by Vincent van Gogh," she said, irresistibly recalling the moment when Sophie first walked back into her life with a Kirchner under her arm. She smoothed back the edges of the painting, letting her fingers drift over a hole in the edge of the canvas where it had once been nailed to its stretcher. "It belongs to a man named Louis Weinburger."

Sébastien bent down over the table, his fringe falling loose over his eyes. "If it belongs to Louis Weinburger, what's it doing here?"

She leaned heavily against the table. "The Germans stole it from Monsieur Weinburger and put it in a museum called the Jeu de Paume," she explained. "Thousands of Jewish people

throughout France have had their art stolen by the Nazis."
She gestured to a sagging armchair. "Sit down, and I'll tell
you everything."

50

Red light glinted off the death-head insignia of SS officers seated within plush banquettes, their gray arms draped over the artificially squared shoulders of women dressed in black and chrome. Walking with Richter's hand on the small of her back through the exclusive dining room at Maxim's, Sophie stared up at the mirrored walls, watching her reflection sway beneath the stained glass ceiling: from their pastel-painted idylls, soft murals of bare-chested river nymphs watched as Richter led her to their table. In a room such as this, women were meant to be ornamental, beautiful accessories, smiling dumbly as their companions reshaped Paris in their own monstrous image.

Richter tucked her chair into the edge of the linen-covered table, then circled to the banquette opposite. He sat down, touching the knot of his tie as he looked over the dining room.

With his movie-star looks and dark tuxedo, Richter looked at home, nestled beside Nazi tastemakers and thugs.

He lifted his hand in the air; seconds later, an elderly waiter materialized behind Sophie's chair.

"We'll start with the caviar and blanched asparagus," Richter said without preamble, "and the roast beef for our main course, rare but not too pink. And a bottle of the '37 Salon." The waiter scuttled away, and Richter leaned across the table. "You do like caviar, yes?"

"I've not tried it," Sophie replied.

A smile crept across his face. "Just you wait. It's a rare delicacy."

The waiter returned with a bottle of champagne and a bucket of ice in a spindly, three-legged stand, and Richter watched as he began to twist the wire cage from the neck of the bottle with arthritic fingers.

"May I?" He held out his hand, and the waiter, his lined features trained into an expression of serenity, handed him the bottle.

Richter lifted the bottle to the red light of the lamp set on the edge of the table and rubbed at the dust that had accumulated on the label. "The French think we Germans are philistines when it comes to the finer things in life—that our tastes run no further than pilsner and pretzels in a beer hall." Above him, the waiter stood, hands clasped behind his back as he watched Richter inspect the bottle. "I'm told some restaurants have even tried passing off their cheaper swill as fine vintages. They change labels and sprinkle carpet dust over the bottles to impress us, make the bottles look older than they are." He passed the bottle back to the waiter, his smile hardening. "Some of my compatriots might be taken in by such parlor tricks, but I've spent enough time in Paris to refine my palate. Pour, monsieur. Let us see whether I'll have a tale to tell to *Reichsmarschall* Göring tomorrow about French hospitality."

Sophie held her breath as the waiter, pale-faced, eased the cork from the bottle and poured a splash of champagne into Richter's glass. Surely, a restaurant as illustrious as Maxim's wouldn't be foolish enough to attempt such a thing?

Richter lifted his glass to his lips and took a sip. "Excellent," he said and with a graceful wave permitted the waiter to finish pouring. "But then, one can't be too careful."

Once the waiter had plunged the bottle of champagne into the ice bucket and retreated, Richter lifted his flute. "To the Schloss Collection."

"To...Schloss." Sophie tapped her glass against his. "What will happen to it now?"

"The *Reichsmarschall* is on his way from Berlin as we speak," he replied, stretching a long arm across the top of the banquette, "to lend his support as we do battle with the Louvre. Jaujard believes the collection ought to remain within the French national collection's sphere of influence."

"And shouldn't it?" Sophie replied.

Richter shook his head with barely concealed irritation. "It's a collection previously owned by a stateless individual, and as such it falls within the purview of the ERR. The law couldn't be clearer on this."

A corrupt law, Sophie thought as she took another sip of champagne, but she knew better than to voice her opinion out loud. "And once the wrinkles are all smoothed out... where will it go?"

Richter frowned. "Into Hitler's museum in Linz, of course. The collection will belong to the German people."

"With a few exceptions." Sophie edged her foot across the floor to nudge Richter's leg, and his petulant expression lightened.

"Perhaps one or two," he conceded. "The *Reichsmarschall* has his eye on a few pieces for Carinhall. There's a van Ruysdael, in particular, that I know he'd like for his dining hall. And I'm hoping I might acquire a certain van der Neer, as a token of appreciation for all my hard work." He looked pleased at the prospect. "You've not seen my new apartment on Avenue Matignon, have you? You ought to come for tea. A connoisseur such as yourself would appreciate my collection."

Richter ran his toe up Sophie's calf, and she pulled her leg away. "Tell me about Carinhall," she said, hoping to steer the conversation toward safer shores. "Göring's country home. Is it truly as grand as people say it is?"

"More so," Richter replied as the waiter returned with a plate of blini topped with glistening caviar. "It's a hunting lodge, though I don't think the *Reichsmarschall* does much in the way of hunting these days. All timbered beams and roaring fireplaces. But the artwork… It's a shrine, Sophie. Truly, it puts the Jeu de Paume to shame." Richter smiled and picked up a blin. "And then there's Hermann, sat with all his treasures, looking like the very picture of Bavarian splendor."

A shrine and a mausoleum, thought Sophie. Göring was all opulence and ambition, greed and rage. She pictured Göring's selections leaving the Jeu de Paume: crates upon crates of artwork, piled endlessly onto a snaking train leading into the hollow heart of Germany. Did it soothe him, to walk among beauty while his lieutenants carried out atrocities in his name?

"He's…formidable," Sophie conceded.

"He's a great man. It's a privilege to work beneath him." Richter held out the tray of caviar. "I'm being rude. I'll have this whole plate myself if I'm not careful. Please."

She took a blin and crammed it into her mouth: the taste was overwhelming and salty, not at all what she'd expected, and not to her taste. Richter watched expectantly as she chewed, swallowed—

"It's sublime," she said, washing it down with a generous swig of champagne.

He nodded his approval. "I knew you'd like it." He settled back in the banquette, and Sophie resisted the urge to follow his gaze over her shoulder to look at the room behind her. "Now, tell me, how does someone such as yourself become a fine-arts restorer? It seems a rather unique occupation for a woman."

Sophie swallowed down his condescension with a second blin. "Well, I've always been drawn to art," she began slowly, "but I never fancied myself an artist."

"Too bohemian for you?" Richter guessed with a grin.

"Too unpredictable," Sophie replied. "I don't think I possess the creativity to create something entirely original. But preserving another person's originality, their vision...there's something valuable in that."

"Come, now, don't sell yourself short," Richter said, and Sophie took another sip of champagne. *I wasn't aware that I was*, she thought, and he continued. "There's real artistry in what you do. Don't you want people sitting in awe of your talents? Don't you want everyone in this restaurant falling over themselves for the opportunity to have a Sophie Brandt hanging on their walls?"

"Careful, now, Konrad. Your Führer might have something to say about a woman whose ambitions lie outside the home." Too late, Sophie realized that the champagne had loosened her tongue to the point of bitterness. She looked up, alarmed, but Richter was smiling.

"It might surprise you to learn that I don't share Herr Hitler's views on all matters—least of all, on a woman's place." He reached across the table and trapped Sophie's hand beneath his long fingers. "I think it's admirable that you've found work in a field that makes you passionate."

It would be easy, she thought as she stared into Richter's blue eyes, to get taken in by his pretty words; easy, to fall, headlong, into his handsome smile and the security it promised—if she were not also privy to the beliefs of the Führer that he *did* share.

"I'm glad you think so," she replied. Not a moment too soon, the waiter returned with the asparagus, and Sophie pulled her hand away to make space for the plate. "Tell me, how did you come to work for the *Reichsmarschall*?"

She could tell that she'd hit upon a preferred topic of conversation. "I was in the right place at the right time," he said, "and I happened to possess a skill set that was of value to a great man. I can't tell you how much the *Reichsmarschall* has come to rely upon my expertise. Why, only the other week, he was nearly taken in by a forgery."

Sophie cut into her asparagus, dragged the spear through hollandaise sauce. "Is that so?"

"Indeed." Richter waved his knife in the air, his attention focused on his plate. "Some dealer in Poland, trying to pass off a supposed Cranach. Hermann would have paid through the nose if I'd not been there to offer my expertise." He smiled as he chewed. "But we all lend our talents to the Reich in whatever way we can, I suppose."

"Extraordinary," Sophie murmured. "Do you come across a lot of artworks like that? Forgeries?"

"Not so many. The occasional ostensible Vermeer, turning up in some old woman's attic. But I suppose everyone is trying to make their money these days. Besides, it's a small inconvenience, when I spend my days surrounded by true works of art."

"True works of art," Sophie echoed, thinking of the Room of Martyrs. "Tell me, Konrad. Just between the two of us, what do you really think of the…degenerates? The art we've been cataloging in the storeroom beneath the restoration lab?"

Richter sighed and set down his knife. "You know I don't agree with the Führer's views on modern art," he said, "and nor does the *Reichsmarschall*, truth be told. But I know my duty. I'm a good soldier. I follow the orders that are given to me, much though it might pain me to do so."

Sophie paused. "What do you mean by that?"

"Between the two of us, I'm afraid the ERR's patience is wearing thin," Richter said. "We've received orders from Berlin that we're to make room at the Jeu de Paume for future acquisitions. I'm afraid we'll no longer be able to house the degenerate collection." To his limited credit, Richter looked troubled. "Why do you think I've been so focused on selling off works from the storeroom? They're going to destroy it all. Everything that doesn't stand a decent chance of being sold on. Sooner rather than later, I hate to say."

He looked up, seemingly oblivious to the gravity of what he'd just imparted. Sophie, meanwhile, sat frozen over her congealing plate, her mind racing in a thousand different directions.

VERNICHTUNG, VERNICHTUNG, VERNICHTUNG.

Richter held up his butter knife, nose wrinkling in disgust. "A restaurant like this, you think I'd not have to worry about water-stains on my cutlery… *Garçon? Garçon*, this is entirely unacceptable—and my companion's glass is nearly empty! You call yourself a fine dining establishment? Really, Sophie, I do apologize…"

51

Fabienne hopped off her bicycle at the gates to Montparnasse Cemetery and paused, looking up at the grim stone walls she'd avoided for so many years. On either side of the gates hung wisteria, fragrant and purple. Had it been in bloom on the day they'd buried Dietrich?

She walked through the gates, steering her bicycle across the pea gravel by the handlebars. There was no rule, strictly, against riding through the cemetery, but she felt it to be disrespectful nonetheless, and she'd already proven herself a disrespectful-enough widow without incurring the disapproval of Montparnasse's ghostly inhabitants.

The narrow avenues were lined by flowering empress trees, which created a delicate violet canopy overhead, and Fabienne watched as women—young and old, wealthy and poor—shepherded small children this way and that along the paths.

How many of them had lost husbands, fathers and sons over the past few years? War being what it was, she doubted that most of the women walking alongside her had proper graves to visit: most, she suspected, had received letters, dated and signed by some bureaucrat, telling them about their loved one's death on some battlefield or in a German work camp. But perhaps it gave them some comfort, to walk here among the tombs, to find peace amid the headstones of strangers.

At least Fabienne knew where her loved one lay. She turned down a final avenue that dead-ended at the cemetery's western wall and rolled her bicycle to a stop.

"Hello, darling," she murmured.

Dietrich's headstone was still sharp with newness, but it had begun to show signs of weathering: lichen had crept, thin and unassuming, into the corners of the grooved lettering. She leaned her bicycle against a tree and crouched down to pick up the withered remains of a bouquet wrapped in newspaper, wishing that she'd thought to bring something, anything, to adorn the stone, to show the women who walked without an anchor for their grief that here lay a man who had been loved, who was loved still. But even as she rebuked herself for her carelessness, she knew that bringing flowers was a gesture meant for the living, rather than for the dead. What good were flowers, when her memories were the thing that truly mattered?

She deposited the spent bouquet in her bicycle's wicker basket, then turned to see Sophie, walking arm in arm with an older man using a slender cane.

Sophie offered Fabienne a half-hearted smile, and Fabienne returned it. She looked well: taller, somehow, less the shrinking violet she'd been in the months after Dietrich's death. Their work had given her purpose, and Fabienne opened her mouth to make some smart comment, but then she shut it once again. Hadn't their work changed her too? Fabienne thought about what her sister-in-law had given her, these past few years: a renewed commitment to art, and a reconciliation with her parents. A relationship with a man she'd thought as lost to her as Dietrich, in his own way.

"Rather a dramatic meeting place." Fabienne looked down at Dietrich's headstone with a smile. "Though I'm sure he would have appreciated being involved."

"Well, I felt it appropriate," Sophie replied. "Far from the museum. I would prefer if we weren't overheard."

Sophie had chosen their meeting place well: this close to the cemetery wall, and surrounded by flat gravesites rather than austere crypts, it would be difficult for anyone to get close enough to listen without being seen.

She gestured to the man at her side. "This is my associate, Dr. Gerhardt Hausler. From the Jeu de Paume."

"You're the artist, I presume." Hausler stepped forward and hung his cane in the crook of one elbow before holding out his hand for Fabienne to take. He had a face too kind for Paris, these days, handsome and craggy, yet softened by his round spectacles. "It's an honor to meet you."

"I'm the artist, you're the engineer," Fabienne replied, instantly warming to Hausler. "I'm told I have you to thank for the rather ingenious alteration to my overcoat."

Hausler dismissed his contribution with a wave of his hand. "An invention borne of necessity," he replied. "But you're the one doing the real work here. I must tell you, my dear, your skills are truly remarkable—"

"Yes, it's all very lovely," Sophie interrupted, "but I'm afraid we've got very little time for niceties. I asked you both here because I've learned that the contents of the Room of Martyrs are to be destroyed."

Fabienne looked from Gerhardt to Sophie. "All of them?"

"All of them." Sophie sank down onto the stone border of Dietrich's plot. "They're going to liquidate the contents of the Room of Martyrs, at some point within the next few weeks. I thought we had more time."

"The next few *weeks*?" Fabienne watched as Sophie worried the worn cuff of her overcoat. They'd gotten dozens of works of art out of the Room of Martyrs, over sixty at least, but their work had been slow, painstaking. From what Sophie had told her, the room contained hundreds of paintings and sculptures, many of which fell far beyond Fabienne's abilities to recreate. "Well, that's it, then, isn't it? We've done everything we can do."

"Perhaps not. Recently I was able to take a look at a ledger containing the records of the Room of Martyrs. There are some five hundred, all told."

"Five *hundred*—?"

Sophie nodded, grim-faced. "Those that aren't marked down for destruction will be removed from the room for exchange, but the rest—" She broke off and rubbed at her eyes as red rose furiously in her cheeks. "They'll likely be burned. To make space for more of the private collections."

Fabienne felt the world dim, the sheer volume of artwork at risk too much to take in at once. Five hundred works of art—five hundred examples of creativity, passion, legacy—all gone in the blink of an eye. She thought of the women walking through the cemetery. What remained of the men they'd lost? Letters, clothing, bank accounts, the pipe they'd smoked, the pen they'd used.

The art that had moved them, a reminder of the person they'd been, where it had hung in their home, how it had given them a sense of the world.

"But what if we could get it out?" Sophie stood. "Early on in the war, I helped evacuate the national collection from the

Louvre. But we had the help of dozens of students from the École du Louvre, and the Samaritaine department store lent us their trucks so we could remove thousands of artworks—"

"Even if we had the entirety of the École du Louvre, we wouldn't be able to replace five hundred paintings," Fabienne pointed out. "There's simply no way we could forge on that kind of scale, not with only a few weeks to work."

"Then, we don't forge." Gerhardt Hausler curled his fingers around the top of his cane and adjusted his spectacles, looking for all the world as though he was discussing a thorny hypothetical in a lecture hall. "We steal."

PART THREE

52

The dance hall's floor was covered in sawdust, people crowding around wine barrels that were too dried out for use in a vineyard but still sufficient as cheap tables. Peering out from behind a burlap curtain that separated the stage from the audience, Fabienne listened to the slowly building crowd. At the door, Louis was taking names down on a clipboard, passing out pamphlets extolling the dangers of fascism.

She felt Dietrich's hand, large and comforting, on her shoulder and instinctively turned her head to kiss his fingers. She hadn't yet grown used to seeing the glint of gold that was his wedding ring and still found herself turning toward it, mesmerized as a magpie, as he pressed his lips to her hair.

"It's a bigger crowd than last week," he murmured.

"It's a bigger crowd than you've ever spoken to before," she replied, letting the curtain fall. "Louis will be elated."

"He'd be elated by anyone offering to take over his role on stage," Dietrich said with a chuckle.

"Yes, well, public speaking isn't exactly his strong suit," Fabienne replied. "Thank goodness it's yours."

Dietrich's smile faded. "Do you really think so? Every time I go up in front of a group I think about what would happen if I made a fool of myself...whether this is the moment they all realize I've got nothing to say."

Fabienne met his worried gaze. "You've got everything to say," she replied. "You've got firsthand experience living under a fascist government. You're the canary in the coal mine. Everyone is here to listen to you speak, and I know that the last thing you'll do is make a fool of yourself. Besides," she added, drawing closer still, "if you do, know that I will never, ever let you live it down."

Dietrich chuckled again and pressed his lips against hers. The sound of the audience faded away, and Fabienne let herself fall, headlong, into his kiss. Would she ever not want him as much as she did at this very moment? She hoped not—she hoped to live every day of her life as in love with Dietrich as she was right now.

They broke apart, foreheads still pressed together.

"To business," Fabienne whispered, playacting a sternness she didn't truly feel.

"To business," Dietrich agreed, letting his hand drift below the small of her back.

"Dietrich!"

Fabienne jumped at the sound of Sophie's voice as she came around the side of the curtain. "Dietrich, there are a lot of people out there. Do you really think it's safe...?"

Sophie had always had her misgivings about Dietrich speaking publicly, the scowl on her face deepening as the size of Dietrich's crowds grew. It wasn't that Fabienne didn't appreciate the risks that Dietrich took in criticizing Germany so openly—but what danger was there, really, in speaking one's mind in a democratic country?

"You say this every time Dietrich gets on stage," Fabienne said lightly. She reached for a glass of champagne on a nearby side table and offered it to Sophie. "Don't be so tense. Your brother is doing good work. Necessary work."

"Work that makes him a target," Sophie shot back. "Dietrich, there are a few faces in the crowd that I've not seen before. I'm not sure—"

"Isn't that what we want? To be drawing in new people?" Dietrich twitched back the curtain to inspect the audience. "Truly, Sophie. We're not in Stuttgart anymore."

"What we're doing here is important," Fabienne added. "We're stopping the spread of fascism."

"By making Dietrich a figurehead! A target! You don't know what it was like in Germany. You have no idea—"

Dietrich took Sophie's hands in his as Louis, still clutching the clipboard, stumped up the stage.

"Are you ready?" Louis asked.

"We're not in Stuttgart anymore," Dietrich repeated firmly. "And Fabienne is right. What we're doing here... If we can change even one mind, it's worth a little risk."

53

Red-and-black flags hung from the arcaded entrance to Le Meurice, fluttering limply in the evening breeze. Five years ago, Le Meurice had been the most luxurious hotel in Paris, rivaled only by the illustrious Ritz; now, as the unwilling headquarters to the German forces in Paris, it had taken on a markedly different clientele. Walking past the bucket-helmeted guards flanking the front door, Sophie thought of the stories she'd heard of Le Meurice's legendary past: entertaining Picasso and his Ukrainian bride on the night of their wedding; footmen receiving five francs apiece from Salvador Dalí in exchange for live flies captured from the Jardin des Tuileries; the Duke and Duchess of Windsor dining *à deux* after their scandalous departure from England; Coco Chanel hosting glittering receptions on the rooftop bar.

With Konrad Richter's hand at the small of her back, Sophie allowed herself to be steered into the lobby, resisting the urge to glance back at the inky darkness that was the Jardin des Tuileries, barely visible in the deepening twilight. Instead, she lifted the sparkling hem of her borrowed evening gown and carried on, pausing to read a modest easel set in the center of the lobby.

The Einsatzstab Reichsleiter Rosenberg *presents an evening with the Schloss Collection. By invitation only.*

Richter leaned close to Sophie, his lips grazing her neck as he whispered in her ear. "Smile, my dear. Tonight is a victory for us both."

It was a victory, but not in the way Richter meant—or so Sophie hoped. She'd agreed to join him at this farce of a reception in order to keep him suitably distracted, and she intended to do whatever she had to in pursuit of that goal: anything to draw his attention away from the events which, she hoped, were happening at the Jeu de Paume this very moment.

She followed Richter into a grand mirrored hall. Corinthian columns held up an immense artificially lit domed skylight, while giant vases brimming full of roses scented the air with their cloying perfume. Throughout the room, guards stood beside easels that displayed the choicest works of art from Adolphe Schloss's collection while assembled guests fawned over the canvases—men and women whose elegant attire did little to detract from the ice behind their smiles.

It was an audacious thing for Richter to have decided to host a reception of artwork stolen from one of Paris's most notable Jewish families; it was more audacious still for the ERR to have approved it. But who in this room would object to such a thing, when the crime had already been signed off by corrupt German lawmakers and the Vichy government alike?

Richter tucked Sophie's hand into the crook of his arm, nodding periodically at some guest or another as he navigated, slowly but meaningfully, toward Hermann Göring. As was his habit, Göring had taken advantage of the occasion to unveil another opulent uniform, this one a pristine white adorned with gold shoulder-boards and a heavy iron cross beneath his collar.

"There, by the bar. That's Heinrich Himmler," Richter murmured in an undertone, and Sophie's stomach dropped precipitously at the sight of Hitler's most terrifying lieutenant, his dead eyes meeting hers for a split second from behind his pince-nez. "And General von Choltitz, over there with the monocle—"

Sophie tightened her grip on Richter's arm, resisting the sudden urge to run. What had she been thinking, walking into a viper's nest such as this?

"And here, of course…" Richter clapped Göring companionably on the back. *"Reichsmarschall!"*

"Richter, my dear boy," Göring murmured, clasping Richter's hand in his. "You've outdone yourself. I'm afraid I was beginning to find your exhibitions at the Jeu de Paume a little stale, but this—" He swept out his hand, taking in the paintings, the soldiers, the guests. "Magnificent."

Richter beamed, his confidence transformed into obsequiousness. "I'm honored by your presence," he said. "Truly, this is a momentous evening."

"A momentous evening, spent in the company of a lovely woman," Göring said, turning his attention to Sophie. He lifted her gloved hand to his mouth, pressed his fat lips against her fingers. "It's a pleasure to meet you, *Fräulein*—"

"You remember Mademoiselle Brandt, from the Jeu de Paume?" Richter interrupted politely.

"Of course! Mademoiselle Brandt." His mildly quizzical expression cleared. "I hardly recognized you out of your tweeds. And with a sparkling new adornment—"

"A gift," Richter interjected, as Göring examined the diamond and platinum tennis bracelet on Sophie's wrist. "To commemorate this wonderful evening."

"Beautiful," Göring murmured. "You know I'm something of a connoisseur, when it comes to fine jewelry—"

"You're a connoisseur in many things, *Reichsmarschall*," Sophie replied smoothly, as Göring pawed at her wrist. Richter had presented the bracelet to her earlier in the evening, and Sophie had accepted it with no small amount of trepidation. To whom had it belonged, before it had fallen into Richter's hands?

"Cartier?" Göring asked, and Richter nodded. "Good." He turned his glassy smile to Sophie, and it was clear in the depths of his eyes that he'd already dipped into something considerably stronger than champagne. "I detest the recent trends toward artificial stones. Nothing but quality, my dear!"

"You're too kind, *Reichsmarschall*," Sophie replied. She could feel a familiar panic rising from deep within her at the feel of Göring's hand around her wrist, and she freed herself from his grasp, her heart pounding, threatening to overwhelm her. "Konrad, if you'd excuse me for a moment…"

She hurried out of the room, past the Rembrandts on display, past Himmler's blank stare. *Breathe*, she told herself. She reached into her evening bag and pulled out Dietrich's old pocket watch, battered but accurate. If all had gone according to plan, the others would be reaching the Jeu de Paume at this very moment.

She walked into the ladies' room and ran a hand towel under cold water before pressing it to her burning cheeks. *Breathe*, she told herself again. It was insanity, what she was attempting to do—insanity, when members of the Nazi high brass were gathered here, just a stone's throw away from the Jeu de Paume. She tossed aside the towel, willing her hands to stop trembling as she ran through the plan in her mind. The distraction of the Schloss Collection was her best hope, her only hope, for spiriting away the contents of the Room of Martyrs. All eyes were on Le Meurice, all attention focused, for one night and one night alone, on the priceless artworks on display here, rather than in the Jeu de Paume. This was an opportunity not to be squandered—and it was for that reason that Sophie had to pull herself together, fake a confidence she didn't truly feel.

Where's the best place to hide something? She stared at her reflection in the mirror, and her hands grew steady. *In plain sight.*

She dried her cheeks and fixed her lipstick, then strode out to rejoin Richter and Göring by the bar.

54

July 1943

Fabienne crouched in the darkness of the Jardin des Tuileries's southern postern, listening to the Seine splashing merrily against its banks. She waved a hand in front of her face and saw little more than the outline of her fingers. Satisfied, she straightened, feeling the darkness settle around her like a cloak. Even if nothing else went to plan tonight, at least the night sky, heavily laden with clouds, had conspired in her favor.

She listened in the dark to the sound of revelry from Le Meurice. She closed her eyes, picturing Sophie, dressed in Fabienne's elegant blue gown, and it felt a special sort of irony that Sophie, not Fabienne, was playing the part of the glamorous distraction. Sophie had always seemed such a wallflower to Fabienne, so fragile, so eager to please. But had Sophie not proven her strength time and again? It was she who'd escaped Germany with Dietrich; she who'd smuggled paintings out from a Nazi stronghold; she who'd developed paints capable of mimicking the qualities of oils; and she who'd masterminded tonight's audacious heist.

She felt, rather than saw, Sébastien slide into the postern beside her.

"There are guards along the Rue de Rivoli," he whispered, giving Fabienne's elbow a reassuring squeeze. "They're focused on the hotel, like Sophie said. There are so many dignitaries there, so many works of art…"

"…who would worry about the Jeu de Paume?" Fabienne finished. She leaned over and kissed his stubbled cheek, grateful for his devotion not only to her but to the artwork she'd made it her mission to save.

He gripped the iron bars that separated the Jardin des Tuileries from the Place de la Concorde. "With any luck, they're all so focused on Le Meurice that they've left the museum vulnerable."

"I wouldn't count on it," Fabienne muttered. The Jeu de Paume was protected not only by the high gates that surrounded the Jardin but also by night watchmen throughout the grounds and beyond. Blue-jacketed members of the *Milice* patrolled Paris's arrondissements, enforcing compliance with the city-wide curfew. German soldiers, meanwhile, prowled outside Le Meurice, the Hôtel de la Marine and the Place de la Concorde.

It was a suicide mission, Fabienne knew, to try and infiltrate the museum, to have come to the 16th arrondissement under cover of darkness, sliding from alley to alley, only to find herself locked outside the Jardin des Tuileries's tall gates. It had been dangerous enough, she knew, to have replaced painting after painting with forgeries, but everything they'd done now paled in comparison to what they were about to attempt tonight.

But she was here now. It was too late to indulge in doubt.

In the darkness, she watched a shadow approach the entrance from within the Jardin. A glint of orange flared up from the end of a cigarette, illuminating the white of a broad, blunt smile.

"Put that out," she hissed as Louis, hefting a heavy set of bolt cutters over his shoulder, reached the postern. "Do you want to alert the *Milice*?"

"Spoilsport." Louis stubbed out the cigarette on the wall. "Besides, they'll just think I'm the night watchman. Who, incidentally, is knocked out cold beneath the Carrousel." He fitted the bolt cutters to the heavy lock on the gate. "The lads did a sweep of the grounds. You should be on your own in there."

"Alone but for the guards within the museum itself," Sébastien muttered as Louis broke the lock.

"We've broken the lock on the door at the end of the Esplanade de Feuillants," Louis said as Fabienne slipped past him and up the stairs. "We'll wait thirty minutes before we start firing near the Louvre. Hopefully we'll draw their attention, and you can slip out unnoticed."

Fabienne paused. "That's not the plan, Louis. You're to cut the locks and leave."

"And miss all the fun?" In the dark, Louis sounded incredulous. "I gathered up a few *friends* to help... We'll cause a suitable distraction, I can assure you."

"I don't doubt it," Fabienne replied, "but what about Eline? Your children?"

Louis lit another cigarette, shielding the ember from view with a cupped hand. "I'm well aware of the risks," he said evenly. "But this is important. Eline understands that as well as I do."

Fabienne pulled Louis into a tight hug as Sébastien sprinted to the looming wall of the Musée de l'Orangerie. "I can't tell you how much it means to have your help. Truly, Louis."

"Well, it was a good reason to get the old gang back together," Louis replied. "And to have a cause to fight for again. I've had my share of scrapes with fascists in the past. I think we'll be able to hold our own tonight. And I feel that we owe it to you, to Sophie…to Dietrich's memory, to help how we can."

Fabienne could see only the outline of Louis's face in the dark, his cap pulled low over his forehead. "You're a good friend, Louis."

"So was your husband." Louis nodded toward the wall of the Orangerie. "You'd best hurry. I'll be keeping watch."

Fabienne crouched low as she ran to catch up with Sébastien. They'd come into the Jardin des Tuileries by the gate nearest to the Musée de l'Orangerie, and Fabienne pictured the steps they had yet to make, across the sloping horseshoe that separated the Musée de l'Orangerie from the Jeu de Paume. She wished she could take a little more time to get her bearings, but she knew the Jardin better than she gave herself credit for. How many times had she walked this very path with Dietrich?

Sébastien took off at a run, crouched double as he darted between the chestnut trees. She followed, her heart pounding wildly in her chest. Though Louis had assured her that the grounds were empty, she couldn't help feeling like someone was standing behind her with a rifle trained at her back. She closed her eyes and moved down the slope, trying to make as little noise as possible as her feet hit the hard-packed earth.

She reached the bottom and leveled out onto the wide bare ground surrounding the octagonal pond that separated the Jeu de Paume from the Orangerie. On one side, the chestnut trees stood in tidy lines; on the other were the gold-topped gates of the Porte de la Concorde. She dashed toward the water, and as she reached it a thin beam of torchlight shone through the gate. She dropped to the ground, praying that the reflective surface and shallow banks of the pond would shield her from view.

Her palms scraped across the pebbled ground as the torchlight raked back and forth across the pond. *Sébastien*, she thought, not daring to look up. Then, after several agonizing moments, the light disappeared.

She got to her feet and sprinted across to the stone steps that led up to the Jeu de Paume's low terrace, where Sébastien crouched behind the shallow steps. He held out an arm and Fabienne ducked into his side, sheltering momentarily in the comforting warmth of his chest.

"Are you okay?" he breathed, and Fabienne nodded. "Not much farther now."

They took the final leg of their route at a run, dashing up the steps and toward the back of the museum. Several canvas-backed lorries were parked outside the museum's back door: no doubt they'd been used to carry the Schloss Collection over to the reception earlier that afternoon. From this side of the park, Fabienne could see the dark outline of the buildings along Rue de Rivoli, all observing the mandatory blackout, but farther down the road, light spilled, bright and audacious, from the open door of Le Meurice.

She turned her attention back to the Jeu de Paume and knocked on the door.

It creaked open, and Gerhardt Hausler, wearing a *Luftwaffe* uniform, beckoned Sébastien and Fabienne into the darkness of the museum.

"It's been madness here today," Hausler said as Fabienne slumped against the wall in relief. He switched on a torch to reveal they were standing in a modest entryway. "Everyone was so preoccupied with the Schloss Collection, no one seemed to notice that I decided to work late." He looked down at his attire and grinned. "Or that I decided to borrow a uniform from one of the guards."

He didn't bother to keep his voice down, and Fabienne glanced at the dark gallery beyond the entrance. "The night watchman...?"

Gerhardt's grin widened. "I still have a few tricks up my sleeve from my service days," he said with something resembling swagger. He threw a gray jacket at Sébastien, badges glinting yellow from the collar. "He's tied up in Mademoiselle Valland's office... He didn't see my face, so we should be safe enough when he wakes. I thought it prudent to relieve him of his jacket. Hopefully it will make for fewer questions as you deal with the vehicle. Fabienne, if you'll follow me..."

Sébastien cut back out the service door, shrugging into the jacket as he went. Fabienne, meanwhile, followed Gerhardt into a narrow hall, and they turned at a doorframe covered by a heavy brocaded curtain. Gerhardt lifted the curtain and ushered Fabienne through.

The Room of Martyrs was everything Sophie had said it would be—everything and more, packed top to bottom with canvases and sculptures and tapestries. The air crackled with some quiet, strange electricity, as though the artworks themselves were the source. Gerhardt swept his torch through the room, illuminating a small canvas, and Fabienne picked it up. It depicted a trio of swans in an alien landscape, their reflections in a serene pond showing three graceful, swaying elephants.

"Dalí," she murmured softly, but Gerhardt was already hefting paintings into his arms.

"We don't have much time," he said, and Fabienne nodded, thinking of Louis's instruction. They only had thirty precious minutes, five of which had already passed. She stacked the Dalí carefully atop a second, a third painting, and carried them out into the night.

Outside, Fabienne followed Gerhardt toward the lorries in the yard, and as her eyes adjusted to the darkness she could see Sébastien in the cab of the nearest one, working beneath the wheel with a pocket torch trapped between his teeth. She heard the muffled sound of him swearing but jumped into the truck's covered chassis, carefully leaning the pictures against the side of the truck bed; then she doubled back and lifted Gerhardt's paintings into the truck as well.

She glanced over her shoulder at Le Meurice before she slipped back into the museum, working quickly, quietly, hoping against hope that they would be able to complete their work before the Schloss reception was over.

55

The crowd within the reception hall at Le Meurice had grown louder and more boisterous, their voices drowning out the sound of the lounge singer whose microphone crackled atop a pianist's rendition of an Édith Piaf song. Standing at Richter's side, Sophie chanced a glance at her wristwatch: it was now past midnight. If all had gone according to plan, Louis would be long gone, and Fabienne and the others would be within the Jeu de Paume by now.

Not that there was any way for Sophie to know for certain, not here, where her every move was made beneath the watchful eye of the *Luftwaffe*.

She ran through the plan in her mind once more, each step simple in theory but no doubt more complicated in practice: Louis, breaking open gates within the Jardin des Tuileries; Gerhardt, securing access to the museum. Fabienne, carting out artworks under cover of darkness; Sébastien, hot-wiring one of the ERR's panel trucks.

Not for the first time, she wondered about the involvement of Fabienne's companion. Was he more than a friend to her? The loyalist in her rankled at the thought, outraged at the thought that Fabienne might have moved on from Dietrich, but the pragmatist in her knew better. If Fabienne had found someone with whom to share her years, who was Sophie to judge?

She turned her attention back to the small gathering of people clustered around her: Richter; Gustav Rochlitz; Hildebrand Gurlitt and his slender wife, Helene. Across the room, Hermann and Emmy Göring were admiring a painting by Cranach the Elder, but Sophie and Richter had gotten roped into a conversation headed by Colonel Bohn.

It was clear that Bohn relished being the center of attention, even if he couldn't care less about the Schloss Collection. For him, with his wife making a rare appearance at his side rather than his mistress, holding court in this seat of Nazi power was all he'd ever hoped for.

Only half listening, Sophie missed the joke that made Richter and the others erupt in peals of laughter; automatically, she followed suit, letting a belated smile cross her lips.

"Really, Bohn, where do you come up with such stories?" Richter chuckled and looked down at his glass as if surprised to find it empty. "I'm afraid we must excuse ourselves. We appear to be in need of refreshments. But what a pleasure it's been chatting with you all. Clara, you must be so proud of your husband." He steered Sophie away, and once they were out of earshot he let fall his pleasant demeanor. "Odious little man. Always toadying up to the *Reichsmarschall*, putting on airs... I don't know what he has to be so proud of. He's little more than a piano mover."

Sophie laughed at the observation, but she couldn't help seeing the similarities between Bohn and Richter himself. Weren't they both doing everything they could to curry favor with those more powerful? Didn't they both take pride in their moral bankruptcy, all for the chance to attain a higher station?

"He's almost as off-putting as that Valland woman," Richter continued, holding up two fingers as he leaned against the bar rail.

"Rose?" Sophie watched as the bartender plucked coupes from a gleaming pyramid, brilliantine glinting in his hair. "I don't know, Konrad. She seems harmless enough to me."

Richter smirked. "She might be many things, but I wouldn't count *harmless* among them."

"Why? What's she done?"

Richter took the two brimming glasses of champagne. "Oh, I don't know. Nothing, I suppose. But there's something about her I just don't trust… She's always lurking around the museum, poking around every corner with her clipboard and hideous shoes."

Sophie accepted the proffered glass, thinking of quiet Rose Valland and the ledger she'd found in Rose's office; standing by Jacques Jaujard's side as he oversaw the evacuation of the Louvre; putting Sophie in charge of the Room of Martyrs. She'd not thought to consider whether tonight's activities risked implicating anyone other than herself and Gerhardt.

"Surely, you're joking," she said. "An old maid like her, posing some kind of threat to the museum? To you?"

Richter watched Göring from across the room. "That's my point exactly—a woman like her," he said. "What do we know about her, really?"

"She takes care of the building maintenance," Sophie pointed out. "She had the boiler repaired, and that was no small feat, given the winter we had. She's also arranged all the loans of furniture from the Louvre for the *Reichsmarschall's* exhibitions—"

"All work an orangutan could do," Richter countered. "I don't know, perhaps I'm being unreasonable, but she's always underfoot. Always *watching*... Göring tells me to leave it alone, but I can't help feeling as though she's judging me. Judging us."

Sophie had accepted the risks that she and her coconspirators had taken tonight, but if her actions ended up having consequences for an innocent bystander like Rose, she would never forgive herself. She sidled closer, knowing that her attempts to dissuade Richter could mean all the difference tomorrow.

"I'm always underfoot too, aren't I?" She looked up at Richter, letting her diamond-clad hand float to the lapel of his tuxedo jacket. "And you don't seem to mind very much."

Richter ran his hand along her wrist. "Yes, but the difference is that I *like* having you underfoot." His hand drifted again, fingers slowly trailing to the fine flesh at the crux of her elbow.

She resisted the urge to shiver. *This is the job*, she told herself sternly, plastering a look of what she hoped was admiration on her face. *Distract. Divert.*

"I hope you don't think me too forward, but I thought we might cut out early," Richter murmured. "What would you say to coming back to my apartment? It's just off the Champs-Élysées... I might just show you my private collection over a nightcap..."

I bet you would. "What a thought, Konrad...but what about the curfew? I rather assumed we would be here until morning."

He smirked. "Curfews don't apply to men like me," he replied, and the chilled edge of his champagne coupe grazed the bare skin of her upper back, compelling her to flinch closer into his grasp. "Nor to women like you, so long as you stick with the right people."

He's going to kiss me, she thought with numbing clarity. As though the experience was happening to someone else, she watched him tilt his head to meet hers. He closed his eyes with an expression of absurd, unbearable softness—

"Richter." He pulled back, and though he let out a soft grunt of frustration, Sophie had never been so relieved to see Colonel Bohn standing behind them. He glanced at Sophie and continued in German. "We're needed in the lobby."

Sophie's heart nearly stopped as Richter and Bohn conversed in terse whispers. "Konrad, what is it? What's happened?"

She half expected him to brush her off, but he cast a quick glance around the room, then took her by the hand. "Come with us."

They walked out of the reception hall slowly, as though not to raise suspicion, and Sophie's mind swirled with worry as she pictured Fabienne and Gerhardt, pinned like rats in a trap within the Jardin des Tuileries's high gates.

She thought of Dietrich in his final moments. How could she have put anyone else at risk of that sort of fate?

They emerged from the reception hall into a narrow vestibule. Beyond, the lobby was filled with soldiers, massed with rifles at the ready, but she only saw them for a split second before the lobby's lights were cut—the better, she assumed, to see what was happening in the darkness beyond.

"Konrad, please," she whispered, tugging Richter to a stop. "What's going on?"

"There are agitators at the Louvre," Richter said, exchanging a glance with Bohn. "Gunshots were heard—"

"Gunshots? At the museum?"

"At the Louvre." Bohn frowned, glancing at the soldiers as

they pointed their rifles into the night. "It seems they're trying to get to the Schloss Collection."

Louis, Sophie thought, her heart sinking with sudden realization. His job had been simple: to ensure that there were
no night watchmen in the grounds of the Jardin des Tuileries,
and then break the locks on two gates so that Fabienne could
get in and out. Had he been caught—or had he taken matters
into his own hands?

Richter ran a hand down Sophie's arm. "Perhaps you ought
to return to the party," he said. "I would never forgive myself
if anything were to happen to you."

"If they're after the Schloss Collection, I want to be here,
with you," she said. "To...to help. I don't want to be somewhere else, wondering what's happening—"

"They won't get within one hundred yards of the hotel, you
can rest assured," Bohn said in a placating tone. He switched
to German. "We don't have time for this, Richter. Get rid
of her."

If Richter stepped outside, there was every chance he would
look to the safety of the Jeu de Paume first—his plunder, his
nest egg. With any luck, Fabienne and Gerhardt had already
gotten away with their takings from the Room of Martyrs,
but what if they hadn't?

Desperate to slow him down, Sophie took Richter's jacket
lapels in her hands and pulled him forward. She closed her eyes
and planted a kiss on his lips, the scent of his cologne overwhelming, the stubble of his chin rough against her smooth
cheek.

She broke away. "Don't leave me here to worry about you,"
she whispered, and despite the confusion of the moment Richter looked dazzled, as though all of his dreams had come true
at once. "Please, Konrad."

He hesitated a second longer, then nodded. Wordlessly, he led her into the darkened lobby.

At the open front doors, six soldiers stood with their feet firmly planted as they aimed their rifles into the dark. Ahead, she could see the manicured trees of the Jardin des Tuileries, black in the dark night; to the east, she could hear the crack of gunfire.

The sound of the skirmish rang off the tall buildings of the Rue de Rivoli, and Sophie realized that Louis was drawing the Germans away from the Jeu de Paume to the opposite end of the Jardin des Tuileries. There was nothing she could do—not here, not now. Her heart broke for Louis's wife and children, knowing that if she'd not reached out he wouldn't be here, laying down his life for a set of ideals that Sophie had asked him to fight for.

Richter addressed the commanding officer. "How many are there?"

"Ten at least, from what we can tell," he replied. "They're Resistance fighters. We've identified two of them already. We've requested support from the *Milice* to help round them up, but we don't yet know whether this is part of a larger Allied plot."

Resistance. She'd suspected Louis of having some involvement with the Resistance—suspected, but never outright confirmed. The revelation that Louis had comrades-in-arms out in the night was heartening, if not entirely reassuring, as was knowing that the team at the Jeu de Paume had some cover while they made their escape.

From behind her, Sophie heard the sound of heavy footsteps and wheeled around as Hermann Göring charged into the lobby.

"What the hell is the meaning of this?" he shouted, before plunging past the unit of soldiers at the front door. Taking advantage of the break in the line, Richter and Sophie followed in his wake, and Sophie took shelter beneath Le Meurice's arcade as Göring and Richter conferred with the commanding officer.

Though the night was still dark, Sophie could see gunfire illuminating the easternmost corner of the Jardin, gilding the distant walls of the Louvre with momentary lightning. She resisted the urge to look toward the Jeu de Paume. Had Fabienne made her escape yet, or was she pinned behind the Jardin's iron gates?

"I want all exits to this building covered and roads blocked all along the Rue de Rivoli," Göring barked, and for the first time Sophie could see echoes of the formidable tactician the *Reichsmarschall* was purported to be. "Your duty, first and foremost, is to the artwork at Le Meurice, do you understand me? Let the *Milice* smoke the miserable bastards out. Concentrate your efforts on defending our position." He paused, glancing round as a heavy spotlight switched on from the roof of the Hôtel de la Marine and trained its beam on the Louvre. Squinting in the sudden glare, Sophie could see Göring's murderous determination, his steely fury. "Limit collateral damage if possible, but do whatever you must to stop them from breaching our position. I will be damned before I let this collection fall into the hands of rebels and reprobates!"

He tightened his grip on his jeweled scepter, his polished boots gleaming as he returned behind the line of soldiers. He made as if to return to the reception hall, and Richter returned to Sophie's side. "You ought to go with him. It isn't safe out here," he began, but then a crack of gunfire from the west caused them both to turn.

Amid the staccato of gunfire, Sophie heard a loud roar as an engine sputtered to life.

"It's coming from the museum," Richter breathed, and

in the backlight from the vestibule she could see realization dawning, terrible and clear, on his face. "It's the museum! The Jeu de Paume!"

She reached for his arm, but Richter was too quick for her. He sprinted out into the street, running as fast as his feet could carry him. Cursing, Sophie kicked off her high heels and lifted the hem of her dress to follow. She could hear soldiers and gendarmes running to catch up, and Göring screaming furiously from the door of Le Meurice. She raced after Richter's dark figure, bullets flying past as the soldiers retrained their fire at the Jeu de Paume.

Overhead, the spotlight from the roof of the Hôtel de la Marine swung round to fix itself onto a small, unmarked lorry—one of the ERR's own vehicles—that was careening through the Jardin des Tuileries. It rocketed out of sight and down the sloping horseshoe, then reappeared in the Allée de Castiglione, up a set of shallow steps and onto the Terrasse des Feuillants.

Gerhardt, she thought, sprinting as fast as she could. Richter wouldn't know Fabienne's face, but he would recognize Gerhardt Hausler's salt-and-pepper hair, his distinctive limp. She redoubled her efforts, lungs bursting as she caught up to Richter, amazed that she'd not been hit by a stray bullet. Richter skidded to a halt, watching, as the lorry accelerated through the Jardin—*It's going to hit the gate*, Sophie thought absurdly—but the vehicle didn't slow down. It struck the gate with a terrific crash, and the gate swung open, its lock already cut by Louis and his men.

Richter stood beneath the arches of a building on the Rue de Rivoli and screamed into the night. "Stop them! Stop them!"

She pulled on his arm, hoping to distract him as the lorry wheeled across the Rue de Rivoli. "Konrad, it's not safe—"

He turned with a terrifying snarl, and over his shoulder Sophie watched the lorry disappear down Rue Saint-Florentin, Fabienne's pale face visible through the window.

56

The lorry trundled through the empty streets of Paris, and Sébastien seemed to steer on instinct alone as they drove without headlights past the city's darkened buildings. Gerhardt was sitting beside him, cursing through gritted teeth at every bump and rise in the road. In their pilfered *Luftwaffe* uniforms, the two men resembled, at a distance, legitimate German soldiers taking a shipment out of Paris. Were anyone to look closer, however, they might notice the sheen of sweat on Gerhardt's ashen face; the woman crouching in the passenger side's footwell.

Fabienne removed her dark sweater and pressed it to Gerhardt's upper thigh to stanch the flow of blood from a bullet wound. It had missed his femoral artery, Fabienne realized with no small degree of relief. In the darkness, she couldn't see whether the bullet had gone clean through, but she suspected not. She shifted on the floor of the vehicle and repositioned the sweater, causing Gerhardt to wince.

"He's still bleeding," she said as Sébastien turned into the 10th arrondissement. "We must stop. He needs medical attention."

"I'm fine," Gerhardt managed. "You think this is painful? You've seen what happened below the knee. Believe me, this is nothing. A scratch."

Sébastien tore his eyes from the road to look at Gerhardt. "You're sure there isn't somewhere I can drop you? A hospital?"

He shook his head. "If we get stopped by the Germans, you'll want me here to speak for us. Wherever we're going, I can take the train back to Paris once I know the artwork is safe."

Fabienne lifted herself out of the footwell to look out the back window, expecting to see a lorry full of soldiers following them, but there was nothing but the empty road behind them. "You're sure? There might be a metro stop where we can let you out."

"And how far do you think I'd get on this leg?" He let out a forced chuckle and gestured to his prosthetic lower leg. "Bad luck they didn't aim ten inches lower."

Twisting awkwardly Fabienne tore the pant leg off her trousers and ripped the loose fabric into strips. "At least they got your bad leg rather than your good one," she joked, attempting to distract him from the pain as she snuck one of the pieces of fabric beneath his thigh. She tied it off as tight as she could manage, thinking that a pair of her pantyhose would have made a better makeshift tourniquet. "It might have been a little difficult tomorrow to explain why you were limping on both sides."

"Looking on the bright side of things, I see," Gerhardt replied with a wry, pained smile. "Are you always such an optimist?"

The rest of the drive to Château Dolus was spent in silence, and Fabienne knew that Sébastien and Gerhardt were as lost in their thoughts as she was in hers. For all her attempts at cheeriness, Fabienne pictured Louis and his Resistance friends, who'd come to their aid in the Jardin des Tuileries. Had they survived? Had they escaped? Sébastien's quiet drive out of Paris suggested that they'd held their own against the Germans. Were they fighting still, or had they scattered into the darkness?

It was nearly four in the morning by the time they reached Bar-sur-Aube, and on the very fringes of the horizon the black sky had begun to lighten. Miraculously, they'd not been stopped, although every turn in the road had prompted new anxiety about coming up against a roadblock. Had it been Dietrich, somehow, clearing their path? Fabienne couldn't know, but as they pulled into the long drive at Château Dolus, she sent up a prayer to him regardless.

Sébastien parked the lorry and jumped out, circling to the passenger door to help Gerhardt. "We need to empty the artwork and get rid of the van as quickly as possible," he said, and Fabienne nodded as she eased herself out of the lorry.

She lent her strength to Gerhardt to help him up the chateau's front steps and into the entrance hall, then made her way up the grand staircase to the second floor. Through the half-moon window on the landing, she could see the night sky was brightening further still, the blackness giving way to a deep indigo that silhouetted the vineyard and the trees beyond. They were losing the advantage of darkness, and much as she'd not wanted to implicate her parents in the night's activities, it was clear that she needed their help if they were to make the theft invisible by the time the sun broke over the horizon.

She opened the door to her parents' room and crept inside.

In the darkness, it looked unchanged from all the long years of Fabienne's youth: large and woebegone, with an ancient four-poster bed pushed against a peeling damask wall. She squinted in the dark, recognizing the shape of the painting hung above the bed. It was the piece Fabienne had brought to the cha-teau as a peace offering, her own canvas which concealed a Picasso. Papa was snoring gently, and she rested a hand on the soft mound that was Maman, deep in sleep beneath the covers.

Maman stirred, and Fabienne risked turning on the bed-side lamp.

"Fabienne?" Maman's voice was hoarse as she squinted in the sudden burst of light. Beside her, Papa cleared his throat and rolled over, his white hair rumpled. "Is everything all right? Are you hurt?"

"Everything's fine, but we need your help," Fabienne re-plied. "In the courtyard, as quickly as you can."

To their credit, Maman and Papa reacted surprisingly well to the scene that greeted them downstairs: to the lorry stuffed full of stolen, priceless art, and to the man bleeding profusely in the front hall.

Papa was first down the stairs, and he crossed to the door, watching as Sébastien jumped into the back of the lorry.

He hesitated. "Is it illegal?"

Whether it was the result of exhaustion or hysteria, Fabi-enne wasn't sure, but she smiled. "I think we can agree," she said, recalling a terse conversation she'd had with Sophie sev-eral years ago, "that legality is something of a fluid concept in times of war."

Papa exhaled as if steeling himself, then nodded. "Best get to work, then."

He started down the stairs to help Sébastien, and Fabienne turned back to face the staircase.

Maman was standing on the landing, her dressing gown

wrapped tightly around her thin frame. Even though she'd just woken up, Maman still looked elegant, somehow, as she stared down at Fabienne in the brightening dawn.

Fabienne stared back, and for a split second she wondered whether she'd done the right thing. Her parents were old; they'd spent their lives at hard work, honest work. Was it fair to implicate them in her own crime? To bring chaos, danger, to their doorstep?

Then Maman began to move. Her eyes fixed on Gerhardt, she descended the grand staircase slowly, the train of her threadbare dressing gown trailing down the steps behind her as if she were about to attend a ball at Versailles.

"Gunshot wound?"

Gerhardt, slumped against the wall, nodded. He had one hand clamped over the sweater Fabienne had used to cover his leg, but blood was dripping onto the marble floor, marring the checkerboard pattern.

Maman lifted her chin. "Very well. Fabienne, I'll need you to boil some water and get some clean linen from the cupboard—not one of my good tablecloths, mind—and my sewing kit. There are tweezers in the bathroom. I'll need those as well." She knelt in front of Gerhardt and gently inspected his leg.

She paused, looking over her shoulder at Fabienne. "What are you waiting for? Really, *chérie*, your friend is in pain!"

By the time the sun had risen, the lorry they'd stolen from the Germans was entirely empty, and Fabienne couldn't help feeling a sense of relief as she watched Sébastien drive it into the woods beyond the vineyard.

"Shame," Papa said as he drew up behind her with two mugs of ersatz coffee in hand. He gave one to her and leaned against the doorframe as the truck disappeared through the trees. "It would have been useful come harvest time."

Together, Fabienne and Papa turned to look at the drawing room. Dozens of paintings now sat lined against the walls, or else flat on the floor: Klees and Picassos and Gauguins, Braques and Dalís. Oil paintings, watercolors, collages, sculptures and even a tapestry.

So many works of art, out of the hands of the Germans. Safe for their owners to reclaim one day.

"I suppose we'll have to rely on Otto," Fabienne replied. They wandered out onto the terrace, and Fabienne, finally allowing herself to succumb to exhaustion, rested her head on Papa's shoulder. "Where's Gerhardt?"

"Your mother is putting him to bed," Papa replied.

Fabienne sighed, thinking of the chaos they'd left back in Paris. "I suppose we ought to get him to the train station," she said. "There will be questions, I'm sure, for all members of the museum's staff."

"On a Sunday?" Papa lifted his mug to his lips. "They'll assume he's gone to church. Or to visit family."

"Even so…"

"Oh, let your mother fuss." Papa looked down, his beard brushing against Fabienne's forehead. "It's been years since she's had a proper guest to take care of."

Far off in the distance, Fabienne could see Sébastien emerge from the woods. She lifted her head from Papa's shoulder, watching as he made his way toward the vineyard. "What are you talking about? I've been coming back to Dolus for the better part of two years, and she never made a fuss over me."

Papa shrugged and finished the last of his coffee. "Well, why would she? You're not a guest." He turned back to the drawing room, stepping carefully over the artwork on the floor. "You're family."

57

July 1943

Sophie chained her bicycle to the gate surrounding the Jardin des Tuileries. She resisted the urge to look at the twisted iron of the gate at the end of the Terrasse des Feuillants, chained and padlocked shut. Instead, she turned to smile hesitantly at the many guards that flanked the Jeu de Paume. Given the events of Saturday night, Sophie wasn't surprised to see that security around the museum had been tripled, that the Germans were determined never to let such an embarrassment happen again.

She walked into the museum and gave her *Ausweis* to the sentry at the door, wondering about the fate of the night watchman who'd let such a theft occur while he'd been on duty. Had he been reassigned, perhaps, to serve as cannon fodder on one of Germany's failing front lines? Had he received a dishonorable discharge—or had he simply been shot, condemned by his failure to stop one of the most significant art heists in history?

Within, the museum looked as orderly as it usually did before a visit from Göring, paintings hung neatly on the gallery walls. ERR curators wandered the halls, and Sophie nodded her hellos as she made her way to the restoration lab. Did they know what had happened here on Saturday, or had they been kept in the dark? Solicitously, she avoided the Room of Martyrs, given that, officially, she'd not been made privy to the scale of the theft, nor which works of art had been targeted. She thought back to Saturday night. Richter had been so distraught he'd hardly said good-bye as he piled Sophie into the back of a requisitioned Citroën.

She opened the door to the lab, and Gerhardt Hausler, perched atop a high stool at his worktable, looked up. He was gaunter, grayer, than Sophie had seen him before, his spectacles slightly askew, but he smiled nonetheless and got to his feet.

She shut the door, and wordlessly, Gerhardt limped over to pull her into a long hug.

Just as silently, Sophie gripped back, letting her lips curve into a smile against the white serge of his overcoat. Unlike Richter's touch, which she tolerated only for the purposes of subterfuge, Gerhardt's hug meant everything to her. It was all the hugs she'd ever wanted to give, when she was too shy; all the hugs she'd ever wanted to receive when she'd not felt comfortable enough to share her true feelings. It was comfort and home, and as Gerhardt pulled back, she already knew the answer to the question she'd been burning to ask.

"You're limping," she said lightly as she set aside her briefcase.

"More than usual?" Gerhardt leaned heavily against his cane with a sly smile. "I'm afraid I had a nasty fall on Saturday night…tumbled right down the steps of my flat."

"Those vexing stairs," Sophie replied. "All those steps, all that coordination… It can be tricky." She planted her hands on her table, studying the blue circles beneath Gerhardt's eyes. "Are you sure you're all right?"

Gerhardt returned to his stool and set his cane gently to one side. "I'm fine, my dear," he replied gently. "As are our friends. One hundred and seven of them, to be exact."

Sophie paused, the enormity of Gerhardt's news hitting her like a wave, all at once. "One…one hundred and seven?" she replied faintly. "Truly?"

He nodded, and in his expression Sophie could see a reflection of her own disbelief, her own joy. "We did it," he whispered. "We did it."

One hundred and seven works of art—one hundred and seven cultural artifacts, now out of reach of the Germans. One hundred and seven paintings one step closer to returning to their owners.

"It's not everything," Gerhardt cautioned, even as Sophie's heart felt ready to burst at their accomplishment. "We'd only gotten so far before the Germans caught up with us. But Louis held them off long enough for us to take what we could."

"That doesn't matter," Sophie whispered back, her eyes welling with tears. "It's still one hundred and seven more paintings out of Richter's hands."

"We took them to a chateau in Champagne," Gerhardt whispered. "Château Dolus, outside of Bar-sur-Aube. They're with Fabienne, along with all the other paintings we replaced." He squeezed her arm, and Sophie felt a pang of regret that she wouldn't have a chance to thank Fabienne in person. They'd agreed, before the events of last weekend, that it was safer, both for the paintings and for themselves, to cut off contact with each other until the end of the war.

Sophie took her most recent commission, a work by Bonvin, out of storage. In the gentle silence, she knew that Gerhardt was thinking of his lost love, Willi, just as she was thinking of Paul Rosenberg, of Dietrich, of Greta. They'd made a promise to one another, Sophie and Gerhardt, in memory of people they'd loved: to save what they could from the Room of Martyrs, to prevent such works of art from becoming more victims of the Reich.

It wasn't an end to the war. It wasn't the saving of a life. But it was the preservation of family legacies and the possibility of returning stolen property to those who'd lost too much, to put right, in some small way, a crime and an indignity against France's Jewish citizens.

It was, too, the conservation of a culture, an ideology, that Hitler deemed degenerate, a safeguarding of that which he considered too dangerous to survive. It was the preservation of voices which challenged Hitler's own, which shone light upon those who questioned everything that he and his followers had tried, and failed, to instill in Sophie herself.

It was resistance; it was hope. And if France still held within its borders those who believed in the messages that modern art sought to teach, there was still a chance that they could win this war.

It was just past noon when Richter entered the restoration lab, looking like he'd not slept in days. *Perhaps he hasn't*, Sophie thought. How could he, when his triumphant exhibition at Le Meurice had been so disastrously undermined? She almost felt for him, knowing how much pride he took in his work. He would have seen it as a personal failure, Sophie knew, to have any collection under his authority stolen while Göring watched from half a block away.

"Konrad," she said, injecting her tone with feigned compassion. She circled the table and held out her arms. Richter glanced, distracted, at Gerhardt before offering Sophie a perfunctory kiss on the cheek. "How are you?"

"Fine," he replied, stepping back, and Sophie felt a twinge of unease. Since when did Konrad Richter care about professional propriety? "I'm sorry to interrupt your work, but we're needed downstairs. All of us."

She glanced back at her table, meeting Gerhardt's eye. "Is it really necessary? We've a lot to do—"

"It's mandatory," Richter replied. "Colonel Bohn is insistent."

As Gerhardt removed his laboratory coat and straightened his tie, Sophie stepped close to Richter to address him in an undertone. "Is this about…?"

"I'm afraid I can't say," Richter replied. "Hausler, old man, are you quite well?"

Gerhardt grinned as they followed Richter down the staff staircase. "Right as rain, Dr. Richter," he said. "My old war wound is acting up, but thankfully it's nothing that affects my skills with a paintbrush."

They reached the first floor. Off the landing, the damask curtain covering the entrance to the Room of Martyrs was pulled tightly shut. She turned as if to walk through the gallery, but Richter held open the service door, revealing the brilliant blue of the summer day beyond.

Sophie faltered. "He wants to meet us outside?"

Richter's expression was inscrutable. "Please, Sophie."

She felt like she was walking through sand, her gut twisting with the certainty of knowing what she would encounter in the courtyard but dreading it just the same. Richter put a hand on the small of her back to urge her forward. Whether the gesture was one of coercion or affection, she didn't know, but she resisted the urge to run.

In the space behind the museum where the ERR lorries

usually sat parked, the remaining contents of the Room of Martyrs—everything that Fabienne, Gerhardt and Sébastien had failed to rescue—were stacked high in a terrible, dizzying pile.

"No," she whispered as Richter propelled her onward, toward the line of soldiers that lined the back wall of the Jeu de Paume. From the far end of the museum, the rest of the staff at the Jeu de Paume were trickling toward the pile, some grim-faced, others wearing looks of smug satisfaction.

The sheer volume was overwhelming, so much so that Sophie's earlier satisfaction evaporated entirely. What was one hundred and seven when hundreds more had been left behind?

She blinked, and for an instant she was back in front of the Reichstag, watching the destruction of the *Entartete Kunst* exhibition. She took a steadying breath and glanced at Gerhardt, who nodded grimly. This had long been the fate awaiting every single work of art in the Room of Martyrs—she'd known that horrible fact from the outset. At least they'd saved what they could. That alone would have to be her consolation.

Richter deposited Sophie and Gerhardt next to Rose Valland before going to join Colonel Bohn. Bohn wore his Red Cross uniform, the red-and-gray symbol at his collar indicating a commitment to heal, but a swastika hung over his heart all the same. He turned, and Sophie saw the dark glint of a pistol, tucked into a leather holster at his side and polished to a high shine.

Bohn checked his wristwatch, the muscles in his cheek working hard as he swallowed. "Is this everyone?" He raised his voice, hands clasped behind his back. "Two nights ago, a crime was committed here at the Jeu de Paume," he announced. "Artwork was stolen by Resistance operatives in an act which claimed the lives of four brave German soldiers." He paused, his gaze coming to rest on Sophie before sliding to Rose. "I am pleased to report that before they gave their lives in service to the Führer, our men executed the ringleader as well as several of his coconspirators in this failed attempt at subversion."

Sophie felt as though she'd been kicked in the chest, but she didn't dare show it. Louis, dead?

"After an extensive investigation headed by *Reichsmarschall* Göring himself, it has become abundantly clear that the Resistance did not act alone, they had help from someone within your number, someone with extensive knowledge of the ERR's inner workings." Bohn paused again, an ugly flush rising in his cheeks. "The crimes that they committed have not only put several valuable works of art under our protection at risk, but it is also an inexcusable insult to the Reich, to *Reichsmarschall* Göring, and to the Führer himself!"

A soldier stepped forward carrying a canister of gasoline. Beside Sophie, Rose Valland lurched forward, and Sophie clapped a hand around Rose's wrist in a warning to remain still.

"It is evident that this treasonous act was a Jewish plot, orchestrated by Allied forces to undermine our authority and the hard work we do. We will not rest until we uncover the identities of each and every coconspirator involved." Bohn's hand tightened over the butt of his pistol. "I have done my best to guide this administration in adherence with the principles set down by our Führer, but I see now that I have been lax in my leadership. I allowed baser instincts of profit and gain to derail my commitment to the ideological purity of the Nazi party." He bowed his head, and if Sophie didn't know better, she would have sworn he'd just directed a look of loathing over his shoulder at Richter. "For too long, we have permitted degeneracy to fester beneath our careful watch, and we see now what harvest we have reaped. Deceit. Insubordination." He advanced toward the line of curators, and Sophie's knees turned to water. "But degeneracy has no place within the Greater German Reich. Nor do traitors."

Hold it together. Sophie closed her eyes, waiting for the jab of a gun barrel in her back. *Just hold it together...*

"Mademoiselle Valland," Bohn barked, and Sophie opened her eyes. *No,* she thought. *Not Rose.* "You stand accused of conspiring with Resistance forces to steal valuable property from the Jeu de Paume—"

Rose's disdainful laugh caught Bohn off guard, and Sophie turned in amazement.

Bohn sputtered, his dark eyebrows lifting in surprise. "Do... do you have anything to say in your defense?"

"Of course I do," Rose spat. Behind her round glasses, her gray eyes shone with cold, bright indignation. "Do you honestly believe that I would risk any harm befalling pieces from this collection? Might I remind you, Colonel, that I have repeatedly brought the welfare of this collection—a collection for which you take full credit—to your attention in order to keep it safe from mishandling and rank incompetence. Do you really think I would put any part of it in jeopardy by staging some misguided attempt at sabotage?" She looked down her nose at Bohn, her dowdy skirt suit shining like a suit of armor. "You really haven't the first clue about me, have you?"

Bohn looked as though he'd been slapped. For a moment, Sophie thought he might lift his sidearm and shoot Rose point-blank for sheer defiance. "And you've an explanation, do you, for your whereabouts on Saturday evening?"

"I was at home," Rose replied acidly. "With my housemate. Would you care for her details?"

Bohn looked away. "No," he muttered. "No, that won't be necessary."

He turned his back to Rose and paused, but not before Sophie caught the look of humiliation on his crimson face. *Rose*, she thought with amazement. Who would have known quiet Rose Valland to have such a spine of steel? Bohn looked utterly abashed, and Sophie could see his actions for what they were: pageantry, an attempt at feigning a forcefulness he didn't truly possess. Threatening his staff, vandalizing the contents of the Room of Martyrs—all of it was a show, and Rose had obliterated the façade, exposing him for the weak and ineffectual man he was.

But as Sophie basked in amazement, Bohn squared his shoulders and turned around to face the staff once more.

Sophie's heart dropped.

Rose hadn't chastened him. She'd goaded him to fury.

He turned and nodded at the soldier holding the canister, who unscrewed the top and began to drench the artwork from the Room of Martyrs with gasoline. The acrid smell of petrol rose in the air, and Sophie thought of all the paint she'd created out of the very substance that was now being used to destroy.

Standing to one side of the pile, Richter watched as the soldier pulled a matchbox from his pocket, his features carefully trained into an impassive mask. Bohn didn't care about the artwork under his purview—he'd never cared, never bothered, in his three long years at the Jeu de Paume, to learn. But how could Richter stand by and watch the destruction of artwork that he'd claimed, like Sophie, to love?

Casually, as though lighting a cigarette in a cabaret, the soldier struck a match against touch paper and flicked the tiny flame onto the pile.

The paintings went up immediately, petrol and solvents and oil acting together to create a sudden, furious inferno.

Entartete Kunst, Sophie thought, allowing smoke-grimed tears to run down her cheeks. Once again, she felt as though she'd been catapulted back in time, watching a similar fire burn outside the Reichstag. Despite all she'd done to prevent history repeating itself, it had happened nonetheless: inevitable, senseless destruction. From the corner of her eye, she saw several other curators flinch, horrified. Were they, too, experiencing Sophie's ghostly sense of déjà vu?

The sight of the fire seemed to embolden Bohn. He smiled, his eyes shining with terrifying conviction. "To steal from the Reich is to steal from the Führer himself!" he shouted, striving to make himself heard over the conflagration. "Dr. Hausler! Step forward."

Gerhardt tightened his grip on his cane.

"Without the walking stick, if you please."

Gerhardt paused. It was clear he knew what was coming, clear that, unlike Rose Valland, he wouldn't be able to brazen his way out of suspicion. He took a step forward and another, unable to stop himself from wincing with pain at his fresh injury.

Bohn's lips curled into a smile. "Old war wound acting up, is it?"

Richter was watching, but he made no attempt to help as Gerhardt hobbled forward, no attempt to hide the disdain on his face as Gerhardt drew up level to Bohn.

"Quite an *old* wound, to be playing up in such a fashion." Bohn clapped a heavy hand on Gerhardt's shoulder, and Gerhardt stifled a cry of pain. "It almost beggars belief."

In a swift movement, Bohn forcefully turned Gerhardt so that he was facing the line of curators. Behind him, the bonfire raged on, flames licking higher as black smoke billowed into the blue sky.

"Name your accomplices," Bohn hissed, and Gerhardt, looking up at the second story of the museum, shook his head. Bohn pulled the pistol from its holster and struck Gerhardt against the side of his head, and though Gerhardt's neck snapped back with the movement he remained upright, resolute.

"Name them," Bohn repeated, pressing the barrel of the pistol to Gerhardt's temple. "You made a vow of loyalty to the Reich, Hausler. Honor it now, and you will leave here with your life."

Sophie let out a ragged gasp, not caring that the tears streaming down her cheeks might implicate her. She couldn't bear the thought of letting Gerhardt take responsibility for a plot of her own making. Gerhardt met her anguished gaze for an instant before looking back up at the museum's façade, and in that moment she knew that his sacrifice would mean nothing if she stepped forward, that Gerhardt had accepted his fate long ago: on the day he'd signed his oath of allegiance to Hitler; the day he learned of Willi's death.

Gerhardt smiled. "My loyalty was never to the Reich."

Bohn let his head drop and stowed his pistol back in its holster, looking almost disappointed at Gerhardt's refusal to talk. As Bohn turned away, Sophie held her breath: she didn't think Bohn capable of shooting him, point-blank. Gerhardt would be thrown to the *Luftwaffe* now—

Bohn put his hand on Gerhardt's chest, gently, as if to offer him a piece of brotherly advice.

"We'll find them, you know," he said, and with one swift movement he pushed Gerhardt Hausler into the flames.

58

It was a brilliantly beautiful summer's day when Fabienne laid Dietrich to rest in Montparnasse Cemetery, the nightingales in the trees belying, by their joyful song, the horrible, farcical tragedy of the moment. Dietrich hadn't been religious, but Fabienne had paid for a priest to say a few words over the grave, more out of a sense of superstition than any real conviction that he was going to some sunlit afterlife. How could he be, when he was in every cobblestone in the streets of Saint-Germain-des-Prés? How could he be, when he was in the sparkling water of the Seine? If there was such a thing as an afterlife, Fabienne suspected that it looked like Paris: the city that Dietrich had loved as though he'd been born there, the city where he'd seen the life he'd wanted one day in the form of a dark-haired woman painting in the Louvre.

The priest finished speaking, and Sophie, standing opposite Fabienne at the headstone, let out a keening wail. Un-guarded, undignified, it was everything Fabienne wished she could bring herself to do: perhaps she would feel better for it, to release her aching pain in a primal howl, let it drain out of her like a faucet left open. But if she were to let go of her grief, all that she would be left with was guilt—and Fabienne wasn't yet ready to face that.

The priest was gesturing to her, though his voice sounded muffled in her head, as if heard from the opposite end of a well. She nodded and stepped forward, held out her hand to release a handful of dust over the polished lid of Dietrich's coffin. Sophie followed suit, then Louis, then Paul Rosenberg, who'd come to lend his support to Sophie.

It had been men in Dietrich's former regiment in the *Wehr-macht* who'd tracked him down as a deserter. A man named Schmidt had been the ringleader, some brute with whom Die-trich had history, though Fabienne couldn't recall the particu-lars. He'd come to Paris with some friends on leave and had come across one of Fabienne's posters by chance touting an evening with Dietrich Brandt, celebrated Socialist and activ-ist. Fabienne had been foolish enough to think that using Die-trich's false last name would be enough to protect him, even after he'd told his story countless times to countless audiences, to French journalists. She could have laughed at her naïveté, in thinking that French laws would protect him against those who'd already sentenced him under laws of their own or that he would be untouchable, in a city as big, as cosmopolitan, as Paris.

Well, she'd paid for her naïveté now, hadn't she? The men who'd murdered Dietrich had disappeared into the night and no doubt returned to Germany as heroes. Fabienne, mean-while, had been left to shoulder the burden of their actions, as well as her own. The world was being brutally remade by those who refused to follow the rule of law, who believed in mob rule and brute strength and who had been told from childhood that consequences were meaningless, so long as they had the requisite blond hair and blue eyes.

What use was Socialism in the face of an ideology as ruthless as that? What use was hope when fear and anger were so much more powerful?

What good was continuing to fight when evil had already won the day?

She flinched when the gravedigger threw the first shovelful of earth into the grave, and the other mourners began to drift away. She wished she had someone here beside her: Maman, perhaps, but Fabienne hadn't sent word to Château Dolus about what had happened. She looked up at Sophie, standing opposite: tears streamed down her face, and as Paul Rosenberg tactfully wandered off, Fabienne held out her hand.

They were the only two left, now. The only two who'd loved Dietrich and shared in the ideals he'd stood for.

Sophie's mouth dropped open.

"You...you expect me to hold your hand? To comfort you?" She looked up with red-rimmed eyes, her cheeks glistening with tears. "When you're the reason he's dead?"

Fabienne jerked her hand away as though Sophie had burned it.

"You told him to speak, persuaded him that it was his...his destiny, and now look at him." Sophie's wavering voice had gained strength, speed, as she spoke, a train rolling, careering down a hill toward disaster. "Is this hero enough for you, Fabienne? He's a dead martyr to a dead cause." She turned; behind her, Paul Rosenberg was watching from a respectful distance with a troubled look on his face. "You wanted more of him than he could give, but he was always enough for me, just as he was. He was always enough."

59

April 1944

Fabienne and Sébastien walked hand in hand through the vineyard toward the gnarled chestnut tree that Hugo, in his long residency at Château Dolus, had come to think of as his own. Unbeknownst to the little poodle, the tree held a longer history for Fabienne: it was here where she and Sébastien used to hide when they didn't want to do their chores in the vineyard, where Sébastien had taken Fabienne on their first date. Beneath the green canopy of the chestnut tree, Fabienne had kissed Sébastien for the first time—at fourteen years old, she'd grown tired of waiting for him to make the first move—and here, at seventeen, where Sébastien had asked for her hand in marriage.

Hugo ran ahead, his tail wagging furiously as he rooted around near the tree's wide trunk before Fabienne shook out a brown linen tablecloth that once had been green and settled it over the earth. Meanwhile, Sébastien set down an old wicker pannier, its lid half-open to reveal the neck of a bottle and the end of a baguette.

They sat, Fabienne arranging her long skirt artfully over her curled legs as Sébastien poured wine into glasses. "What are we celebrating?"

Sébastien opened the bottle with a flourish. "De Vogüé's done it. He's persuaded Klaebisch to give us a license to operate as an independent champagne house."

Fabienne let out a triumphant cry and held out the glasses for Sébastien to fill. "Thank God!"

"Thank Robert-Jean. Of course, we'll have to sell our entire stock to the Germans when it's sufficiently matured, but still."

"That's assuming the Germans are still here by then." Fabienne smiled, touching her glass to his. As head of *Le Comité interprofessionnel du vin de Champagne*, de Vogüé had done battle on behalf of Champagne's winegrowers throughout the war and had interceded, more than once, to stay Klaebisch's hand when it came to Sébastien's recruitment to the STO. She thought of the bottles of '43 maturing in the cellar, which she and Maman had laid down carefully the year before. "What would have happened if he'd failed?"

Sébastien settled back against the tree trunk. "We'd have given our stock to de Vogüé and let him roll it into Moët et Chandon's shipment to Klaebisch, I suppose. But now we've got a license, it's all settled." He paused as Fabienne leaned back into his chest. "You know what else this means?"

Fabienne smiled, relief washing over her. "You're an essential worker once again."

She could feel Sébastien's chest rise and fall behind her as they stared down at the shadows stretching long over the chateau's turreted roof. She closed her eyes, enjoying the warmth of the late-afternoon sun on her face.

She was so relaxed she almost missed Sébastien's sudden change of conversation.

"Do you resent it? Being back here?"

She didn't reply immediately, not wanting to sound like she was protesting too loudly, too quickly. She'd wrestled with her return to Château Dolus, of course. How could she not? It represented too much of her past, too much of her own selfishness and angst. Those first few weeks she wandered through Dolus's halls, worried each time she picked up a pair of secateurs that she was giving up something of the person she'd become in Paris, that each step into her old life at Dolus was one more away from the life she'd built with Dietrich.

The notion of that had troubled her, and she'd grown sullen, withdrawn—until Sébastien had led her up into the south-facing turret one afternoon, Maman and Papa trailing them through the hall.

"We don't want you to fall behind on your artwork," Sébastien had said as he opened the door to reveal a freshly decorated room: an easel and a stool set before the picture window, and a table filled with brushes and canvases, jars of spirits. Maman had stepped forward to present her with a beautiful new set of oil paints, Sennelier's name gleaming on the tubes. "We don't want you to think you can't have the things here which bring you joy."

She found, too, that she didn't miss Paris as desperately as she thought she would. It felt to Fabienne as if, having lived there, she could always go back; whereas Château Dolus had finally revealed to her its true, magical nature. Somehow, the chateau had made room for the paintings she'd brought from Paris, all one hundred and seven concealed in the vast attic, hidden with Maman and Papa's help in old wardrobes and beneath floorboards.

For too long, she'd dwelled on the painful memories that Château Dolus had held for her. But now she valued the opportunity to create new, beautiful ones.

She twisted to kiss Sébastien, his lips soft and endlessly sweet against her own. "I don't resent being here," she replied. "I don't regret a thing that led me back to you."

They'd nearly finished their bottle of wine when Fabienne heard the mechanical snarl of motors in the distance. She looked up, frowning. "Did you hear—?"

"Yes." Sébastien set down his butter knife, looking grave. A moment later, he whistled for Hugo and collected the little dog in his arms.

Fabienne gripped Sébastien's fingers as a line of three olive-green Volkswagens appeared around the curve of the road, each one emblazoned with an iron cross. They were led by a black Mercedes-Benz, its wheels kicking up dust as it turned down the drive to Château Dolus.

"The paintings!" Fabienne leaped to her feet, but Sébastien pulled her back down so hard he nearly ripped her arm from its socket. In a flash, he forced her down into the dirt, his arm heavy over her shoulder as he shrouded himself, Fabienne and Hugo beneath the picnic blanket.

"They're not here for the paintings," he breathed.

Below, the line of vehicles had come to a stop in Château Dolus's courtyard, and a dozen soldiers emerged carrying rifles and handguns. A bucket-helmeted soldier emerged from the Mercedes and held open the back door, and Fabienne watched one shining boot and then another emerge from the vehicle. They hit the ground, followed by a tall man in a black uniform and brimmed cap, bearing on his armband the red flash of a swastika.

"No," Fabienne snarled, and she struggled to get free, but Sébastien held her close. "We need to get down there—"

"We can't," Sébastien whispered back. Below, the man in the SS uniform directed the foot soldiers into the chateau, then leaned back against the hood of the Mercedes. He lit a cigarette, threw the match to the ground. "It would be suicide to go down—"

"My parents are down there!"

"You think I don't know that? You think I don't care?"

"They wouldn't be in this mess if it weren't for me," Fabienne said, her voice—half whisper, half sob—unrecognizable to her own ears. Sophie must have talked; Gerhardt must have broken. What else could have drawn the Germans there?

Sébastien's grip around her arms was vicelike and tender, all at once. "I told you," he replied miserably, "they're not here for the paintings."

Too soon, the soldiers reemerged from the chateau and Sébastien clapped a hand over Fabienne's mouth to stifle her scream as Maman and Papa, their hands tied behind their backs, stumbled into the courtyard at gunpoint. It was clear that they'd been interrupted at dinner, for her parents had taken advantage of Fabienne and Sébastien's absence to have a romantic evening of their own. Her mother was dressed in a ruby-red evening gown, and her father was in his old tails. They looked elegant, genteel, as the soldiers kicked their legs out from behind them to leave them kneeling in the dirt.

"No," Fabienne moaned, and she could feel Sébastien's tears, hot and wet, on her shoulder. "Please, no—"

The SS officer flicked the butt of his cigarette away and straightened, called out something that Fabienne was too far away to hear properly. Papa shook his head, and Fabienne sobbed, terrified but unable to turn away from the sight of her gentle father at the mercy of a monster. The officer backed away and lifted his arm in a careless sort of signal, and another group of people emerged from the chateau.

Fabienne gasped as a family of four—a mother and a father, a gangly son and a short dark-haired daughter—stumbled out into the yard. She'd never seen them before—had no idea they'd been hidden within the walls of the building, but it didn't matter that they were complete strangers, not when she wanted to scream, to charge down from the vineyard to save them all. The SS officer pulled a pistol from his holster and checked the barrel slowly, carefully. She could hear, across the field, the low timbre of Papa's voice as he spoke, and Fabienne knew that he was trying to reason, to find a way out not only for himself but for all of them, the family he'd concealed so well that Fabienne herself hadn't known of their existence, but the officer pressed the barrel of his gun to Papa's temple and pulled the trigger.

His words dissolved into the air.

Fabienne screamed into Sébastien's hand, and she watched the officer hold the pistol to Maman's head next: Maman, who met her fate with ferocity and dignity, who would never have allowed herself to succumb with anything less, but who deserved so much more. The officer carried on, executing the family one by one, and as the convoy drove away, Fabienne knew that she would have traded every work of art hidden within Château Dolus, every piece of art she'd ever painted, to save one—just one—of the victims below; to see, once more, her parents' smiles.

60

Sophie heard a distant, droning buzz and looked up. There, in the far-off sky on the outskirts of Paris, hung a formation of heavy-bottomed airplanes stamped with the concentric circles of the Royal Air Force.

She resisted the urge to wave. Across the street in the Place de la Concorde, German soldiers muttered to one another as they patrolled around the Luxor Obelisk. Allied airplanes were flying ever closer to Paris these days—never close enough to give Sophie hope, not yet, but certainly cause for satisfaction. Whispers of an Allied invasion had grown stronger. Across the country, Resistance forces cut telephone lines and sabotaged railways, while Allied forces carried bombs ever farther into German- and Italian-held territories. She studied the faces of the Germans who asked for her papers, seeing a new tension in their square jaws, in the set of their shoulders.

The grand gallery was full of shipping crates, and Sophie navigated the resulting maze with some difficulty. She nodded a hello to Rose Valland, who was helping two ERR staff members remove a marble statue from its protective wrappings, and carried on up the stairs.

She reached the second floor and skirted around yet more shipping crates. Unlike the incoming crates downstairs, which contained artwork recently purloined from collectors in Dordogne, these ones were outgoing, marked for transport to Carinhall as part of Göring's ever-growing collection. Standing by a half-filled crate, Konrad Richter looked up at Sophie's arrival; then, reddening, he turned his attention back to his ledger.

In the months following the destruction of the degenerate paintings, Richter, it seemed, had abandoned all attempts at pasting a genteel gloss over the ERR's state-sponsored crimes. Rather than setting up the museum's galleries for champagne-soaked private showings, Richter had become obsessed with expediency, packing up shipments of art for Berlin as quickly as Bohn could bring them in. *Presumably to cheer up his precious* Reichsmarschall, Sophie thought acidly. Recently, the RAF had taken its revenge on Göring's *Luftwaffe* for their *Blitzkrieg* attacks on London, pummeling cities all across Germany into ruins. But although Richter was keen to send regular shipments to Carinhall, he found himself stymied with frustrating regularity. With the Resistance blowing up railway lines around the city, shipment after shipment had been delayed, turning the upstairs galleries into a holding room of sorts for Göring's long-awaited plunder.

To Sophie, the issue of the railway lines presented something of a conundrum. On the one hand, blowing up the railways was a blessing, as it kept French-owned artwork within French borders. But the disruption to the railway lines had implications beyond the art alone. Severe food shortages had reached Paris, more dire than the already punitive rationing system. How much longer could the city's residents hold out against hunger, without regular shipments of grain from the ravaged countryside?

Out of the corner of her eye, Sophie watched Richter tuck the ledger under his arm and make his way toward her.

He circled around a stack of shipping crates. "Sophie," he said. "How are you?"

She carried on through the gallery without stopping. "I'm fine."

He waved his hand as they entered another gallery, a half smile on his face. "It's a mess in here, isn't it? I come back from a trip to Poland, and it's chaos. Seems like whenever I'm out of town all order goes out the window. And with the Neumann Collection set to arrive tomorrow, we'll really be in trouble." He paused, craning his long neck in an attempt to catch Sophie's eye. "I could really use someone with your organizational skills to help me process it."

"I'm afraid I'm too busy, Doctor," Sophie replied. She fitted her key into the door of the restoration lab and made to turn it, but Richter put his hand over hers, pinning her palm gently to the knob.

"How long are you going to push me away?" He wrapped his free hand around her waist. "I told you how sorry I was about what happened to the degenerates, but I did what I had to do."

Sophie stepped out of his grasp, and Richter had the good sense not to push his luck. Over the past year, her grief had hardened into fury, but she kept her temper in check, swallowing the words that were clanging around in her head: *What about Gerhardt?*

"Stop punishing me, Sophie. I miss you."

What point was there in putting herself back in Richter's orbit now that the Room of Martyrs was nearly empty? Now that Fabienne was safeguarding what they'd managed to save at Château Dolus?

Self-preservation, she thought grimly. Richter was still in charge of the Jeu de Paume, and Bohn was still hunting for Gerhardt's accomplices. *Information*. She glanced back at the gallery, where stacked crates sat waiting for transport into Berlin. She knew she wouldn't be able to stop the Germans from sending it all into the Reich, but if she worked alongside Richter she might be able to help recover it, one day.

She held out her hand with a grudging smile. "Give me the ledger, Konrad," she said, and Richter brightened.

61

The attic, like the rest of Château Dolus, had been ransacked, its contents tossed aside by the Germans with careless abandon, but mercifully they'd not looked too closely at the many canvases they'd unearthed from within wardrobes and trunks. As Sébastien had told Fabienne only forty minutes earlier, art had not been their quarry.

Wordlessly, he led her through the wreckage toward a dark cavity in the far wall behind a shattered bookcase, and she recalled her first visit up here, wondering at the absence of a half-moon window she'd seen from the outside.

"It was your mother's idea," Sébastien muttered. "The Cohens. You wouldn't have known them. They moved to the village after you left, but Annette met them during the harvest. She and Camille, in particular, they'd become quite friendly…"

Fabienne stared into the cavity, thinking of the young mother whose body now lay in the courtyard, beneath the tablecloth she and Sébastien had brought down from the chestnut tree. Camille Cohen. She'd not looked much older than Fabienne, her sandy blond hair tucked beneath a kerchief; likewise her husband, Ossip, pale and thin. What had Maman seen in Camille Cohen that had caused her to make such a dangerous offer?

Sébastien ducked into the Cohens' hideout with a torch in hand, and Fabienne followed. It was a dark, cramped corridor, long but only four feet wide, which ran the length of the attic. Bedrolls and crumpled blankets lined the floor, books tucked into the space between the rafters that met the floorboards on a steep angle. Paper cranes hung from fishing wire, beautiful and serene, too many to count. Sébastien shifted the torchlight, and Fabienne could see puzzles and toys, long forgotten from her own childhood, brought up by Maman, no doubt, to help the children while away the long hours.

"The day France fell, Annette brought them home. She made *coq au vin* for dinner, set the dining room table… They went down into the cellar after and stayed there until Maurice and I built the hideout, up here. Their son, Georges, had a condition of the lungs, and Camille and Annette felt he would do better up here, in the dry."

She was ashamed at how astonished she felt to learn that Maman had been so devoted to keeping a family safe. Why was it a surprise to learn that her dignified mother had such a sense of duty and compassion? She'd known so little about Maman, and now that Maman was gone, Fabienne regretted all the questions she'd never asked.

He crouched on a mattress in the farthest corner of the hideout and pushed aside several pillows and a stuffed animal which indicated the sleeping space had been used by one of the Cohen children. Georges, or his sister, Hannah? This far in the sloping rafters, the wall was merely a foot tall, and Sébastien ran his hand along it, until he found a catch. Grimly, he tugged the wall aside to reveal another, minuscule sleeping space.

"We kept the other hideout, in the cellar, where the family stayed when they first came to Dolus," Sébastien explained, as he reached carefully into the hole. "We've been using it as a way station for people getting out of France. Downed airmen, Jews, Allied operatives... We are—were—a safe house, part of a network that got people to Switzerland. But given Georges's condition, it would have been too much for him to make the journey. Camille and Ossip refused to split up the family. They didn't...didn't want..." He broke off as he straightened with a bundle in his arms.

Fabienne knew what he held before he turned around, and her breath caught in her aching throat as she followed Sébastien and the sleeping infant out of the hideout. Camille must have pushed the child into the wall cavity when she heard the Germans. It was a space too small to save her other children, but she must have known, at the very end, that Sébastien would know where to find her last, remaining child.

"His...his name is Isaac," Sébastien whispered, his voice breaking as he drew back the blanket. It was a miracle he'd not cried out during the raid. Had his mother given him something to help him sleep undisturbed? She studied his soft features, the dark wisps of hair that covered the crown of his head like feather down. He couldn't have been older than four months. Camille must have given birth up here, assisted, no doubt, by Fabienne's mother.

She stretched out her arms, tears streaming down her face as she collected Isaac close. She pressed the child's cheek to hers, breathing in his baby sweetness, seeking to give him the comfort she so desperately wanted to soothe her own grief.

The sheer scale of what Sébastien and her parents had accomplished, while all the while she was flitting in and out of Château Dolus with paintings under her arm… How frivolous, how futile, her own actions seemed by comparison.

"Last week we gave refuge to an American pilot who'd bailed out over Épernay. He was the last to use our network. I don't know whether he…whether he was captured, or whether he was a double agent for the Germans, but I can't think it a coincidence." Sébastien ran his hand over his red-rimmed eyes. "He didn't know about the Cohens, but as a safe house for the Resistance, we were target enough. I doubt we were the only ones within the network to have been visited by the Nazis today."

It was a sobering, ghastly thing, to realize that someone, through fear or malice, had been willing to put so many innocent people in peril. But wars were built on fear; they thrived on malice. Hadn't Dietrich taught her that?

Isaac stirred, screwing his pink face into a frown as he let out a soft whimper, and Fabienne ran a finger lightly across his brow, lulling the boy back to sleep. Behind her, Sébastien rested his hands on her shoulders, his breath warm against her skin as he stared down at the baby.

"I can't stay, Fabienne," he whispered. "It was only by chance that I wasn't caught up in today's raid. If the American talked, they'll know I was involved in the network too."

"Where will you go?"

"The Resistance has a cell in the woods to the north of here. I can join them tonight. I'll help you…help you bury the—your parents, the Cohens, before I…before I go."

Fabienne swayed gently from side to side with the baby in her arms, willing herself not to turn, not to beg Sébastien to stay.

Though she thought she'd cried herself dry, Fabienne could feel her eyes well with fresh tears. She'd already lost so much today. How could she bear losing Sébastien too? But just as she knew that he needed to leave, she felt certain that he wouldn't go unless he thought she could withstand the pain of being left behind.

"I can't go with you, Sébastien. I made a promise to Sophie, to protect the art... I can't turn my back on that promise. I just can't." She looked down at Isaac, letting her tears fall unhindered. "And the Resistance is no place for a child."

Sébastien let out a breath. "I know," he said quietly. "What will you do if Klaebisch comes back?"

"I didn't have anything to do with the Cohens, or with the Resistance. With luck, I'll be able to talk my way out of any accusations. But leave me with your pistol."

Sébastien clasped the back of her neck and leaned forward, resting one hand gently on the crown of Isaac's head as he pressed his lips to Fabienne's forehead.

"Isaac needs you. The art needs you," he said softly. "But I'll come back, that I promise."

62

May 1944

Konrad Richter's apartment was in an elegant building on Avenue Matignon, half a block away from the bustle of the Champs-Élysées.

"I'm so pleased you finally took me up on my offer to visit," he said, holding open the front door. Sophie stepped in, her hands clasped over the strap of a small handbag as she eyed the slender tapestry hung in the vestibule. *French. Sixteenth-century.*

She allowed Richter to kiss her cheek. "Well, you've told me about your private collection so many times," she replied, following him down a narrow hallway that opened into a wide sitting room. "I thought it was about time to see it in person. What a lovely flat."

Richter's polished shoes sank into the plush of a white carpet. "Isn't it just?" The room was bright and generously proportioned, decorated entirely in shades of cream and ivory, with white curtains framing a set of open-paned doors that coaxed in the breeze from Marigny Square.

He stopped in front of a bar cart, replete with crystal decanters that glimmered in the afternoon sunlight. "I can't take credit for the decor, I'm afraid. A friend of mine helped me pull it all together."

A friend with very particular tastes, Sophie thought, eyeing her pristine surroundings. Bohn's raiding teams confiscated furniture as well as artwork. Had all this beautiful furniture been pulled, wholesale, from a Jewish family's living room? Or did Richter have a mistress with a good sense of style?

Of course, the two possibilities were not mutually exclusive. She pictured Richter arm in arm with a faceless woman, pointing out furniture in one of the ERR's countless warehouses with a manicured nail.

He plucked the lid off a sweating bucket of ice. "I know it's early, but I feel this visit warrants a drink, don't you?"

"Oh, why not?" She smiled as she took in the apartment and its luxurious contents, its tapestries and statuary, paintings hung with care, gallerylike, on the white walls. *Toulouse-Lautrec, near the open door to the bedroom; Frans Hals, by the balcony.*

He drew close and handed her a heavy glass tumbler filled with whiskey. "I watered yours down. I hope you don't mind," he said. "I know the *Reichsmarschall* enjoys his champagne, but I've always preferred something a little smoother." He sat down on an immense cream-colored couch and crossed one leg over the other, stretching his arm long in an unmistakable invitation.

If Richter did in fact have a mistress, Sophie might have had reason to thank her. It would explain why he had been content to pursue Sophie at such a leisurely pace. She took a small sip and turned her attention to a small portrait hung over the bar cart: a young man wearing a black biretta, painted in profile on a wooden panel.

Renaissance, she noted steadily. *Dossi.*

"Remarkable, isn't it?" Though her back was turned, she could hear the puff of pride in Richter's voice. "One of my newer pieces. Dosso Dossi, though I'm sure you recognize his style. I acquired it from a Dutch collector."

She nodded. Holland was one of the ERR's other hunting grounds. How easy had it been for Richter to seize this work of art? "What happened to him? The collector?"

She heard the tinkle of glass against crystal. "Guttman? Who knows. He was a banker, I think."

Was. Sophie traced her finger along the grooves in her whiskey glass, sending up a prayer of safekeeping for Guttman, whoever he was. *Guttman*, she repeated to herself, committing the name to memory. *Holland. Dosso Dossi.*

"And that one behind you," Richter said, clearly enjoying the opportunity to show off his treasures, "is a Rembrandt. The *Reichsmarschall* gave it to me personally, as a thank-you for securing that Titian from Gustav Rochlitz. You remember?"

"How could I forget?" Sophie replied. "Eleven paintings, wasn't it, from the degenerate collection? For the Titian and the...the Weenix?"

Richter chuckled. "I still regret giving him that Picasso," he said. "But we do what we must, don't we?"

She paused in front of a Cubist collage hung on an expanse of wall. "You gave up that Picasso, but you managed to find yourself another one, I see."

Richter got to his feet. "Rather decent, wouldn't you say?" He drew up behind her and placed a hand on her stomach to coax her gently closer to him.

Steady. She breathed in the scent of his aftershave as he

pressed his lips to her neck, resisting the urge to run. She'd worked alongside Richter the past few weeks, taking careful notes about every work of art that he'd boxed up for transport into Berlin: Renaissance portraiture and Greek antiquities, Dutch masters and Persian tapestries. Slowly, painstakingly, she'd copied out the entirety of Richter's extensive ledger, transporting each sheet of paper home in the lining of her trench coat, using Richter's natural tendency toward condescension to draw out information: where the crates were headed, when they expected the railway to be repaired. She'd recorded all that she could in the hopes that her notes might one day prove useful—but there was one more repository of stolen paintings she needed to delve into.

Gerhardt Hausler had begun identifying works of art that Richter had taken for himself from the Room of Martyrs, but he'd not been privy to whatever Richter had taken from the Jeu de Paume at large, stolen artwork that the ERR had deemed ideologically pure. She owed it to Gerhardt to finish what he'd started, identifying whatever Richter had pilfered for himself for his Parisian apartment—and she would withstand Richter's advances, if necessary, to do it.

She gripped his roving hand and shifted slowly past the window. Richter followed, mirroring her movements as though they were dancing. She turned her attention to the next work of art: an ornate tapestry of Artemis killing a stag. *Seventeenth-century*, she thought evenly.

Portrait, Dutch school, sixteenth-century. Biblical scene, Italian Renaissance. Renoir, two girls by a lake. Kirchner, portrait of a young man named Willi, a war hero, laughing alongside the love of his life…

She paused, studying a small smudge in the corner of the Kirchner that looked like a set of initials.

Richter ran his hand along her waist, and Sophie tightened her grip on the whiskey glass, cold crystal cutting into the soft flesh of her fingers. "You've so many works of art here from the degenerate collection... Tell me, Konrad. What makes them so different from the works you let Bohn throw onto a bonfire?"

Konrad paused. "I thought we were past all that."

Though she knew how dangerous it was to challenge Richter in his own home, Sophie couldn't help asking the question. Each night, she returned in her dreams to the bonfire outside the Jeu de Paume, to Gerhardt Hausler's final moments. "Can one really get past the destruction of art?"

Richter looked at Sophie with something resembling concern. "You're such a sensitive sort," he said. "I know how much you cared about the degenerate collection. So did I, truthfully. To think what we could have done with it all, had that criminal Hausler not spoiled it."

"What I don't understand is why you went after Dr. Hausler," she said. "How did you know it was him?"

Richter sighed. "I looked into his personnel file," he said flatly, as though the subject was very much beneath him. "Bohn was horrified to find out that he had a homosexual working on his staff. Who else but a degenerate would commit such a crime?"

A cold fury built within her. "You knew nothing about him. Nothing. He was my friend. He didn't deserve that."

Richter sighed. "It just goes to show, I suppose. And you oughtn't to feel embarrassed. Anyone could have been taken in by a man like that. But there's really no need to dwell on it all." He pulled her closer. "Clearly, I'm the better judge of character."

Sophie smiled. "Clearly," she said, allowing his lips to graze against her neck.

"You know, that first day I came to the museum, there was so much to be excited about," he murmured, stroking her stomach, her hips. "Working with the *Reichsmarschall* so closely…acquiring a Vermeer in the flesh. But the best part of that day, the most unforgettable, was seeing you. Standing there in the courtyard looking so…so proper. So unattainable." She stared at the Picasso, frozen, as he trailed a long finger down her cheek. "I knew then that I would be the one to break through that armor you wear so diligently, find the woman beneath all that poise…"

The Picasso was a portrait of Dora Maar: a woman split, in the artist's gaze, into her component body parts. Hip, arm, breast.

"I knew I'd be the one to break through," he repeated. He bunched up the fabric of her skirt, searching for the clasp of her garter strap. "That armor of tweed and indignation. Perfect, abject propriety…"

She had planned to do whatever it took to catalog the works of art in Richter's apartment, but here, now, the very thought of his hands on her was unbearable, abhorrent, and her cold fury built into a raging fire.

To Richter, she was just another work of art to add to his collection.

She'd put up with him for long enough, and she knew she would be damned before he *acquired* her too.

"I suppose, then, it would come as a surprise to learn how spectacularly you failed. In that, and so much else."

Richter's amorous tone faded. He drew back, frowning. "I–I'm not sure I follow," he replied. "Why don't we sit down? It's been a long day—"

"Actually, it's been a long four years, Konrad," she shot back, switching from French to perfect German. "A long four years playing nice with you while you and your friends plunder and destroy. But I've been watching, Konrad, watching as you dressed up your crimes in civility, watching as you shifted stolen art out of the museum, and you know what? I made some changes to the collection myself."

Richter stepped back as shock, hurt, rippled across his handsome features.

"Your Kirchner, for instance. Do you know the first thing about it? Clearly not, or you would have realized it's a fake. The Renoir too. And that Picasso? I hate to tell you, Konrad, but it's a fraud. Just like you."

Richter went pale, and Sophie knew that she was swimming in dangerous waters, but she simply couldn't stand it any longer: the playing nice, the pretense.

"Hard for you to hear, I'm sure. They're all forgeries. Most of the pieces you liked so much in the degenerate collection—the ones you sold, the ones you destroyed— forgeries. You thought the heist was the worst of your problems?" She laughed, and the sound was shrill and searing, perfect, in its derision.

Richter was silent for a moment, his bloodless face flushing suddenly, violently crimson. "I trusted you," he muttered. This, to him, was the worst, most unforgivable of her crimes: to spurn his advances, to so completely humiliate him in a world he thought he controlled. "I trusted you! With all of it! I-I protected you, loved you. You were *mine*, and this is how you repay me?"

He lunged, and Sophie darted away, but not quickly enough. His long fingers wrapped around her throat, squeezing tight.

"I won't be made a fool of," he growled.

She could feel her life draining away as her vision dimmed, pinpricks of stars bursting in the darkness. *I'm going to die*, she thought with remarkable clarity, and to her surprise she wasn't scared to go. *I'm going to die—*

A voice cut through her mind, clear and forceful as a

bell. *No, you're not*, it said, and in her fading consciousness it sounded like Dietrich.

With what little strength that remained to her, Sophie lifted her whiskey glass and cracked it over Richter's head, hard. His grip slackened, just enough, and she slipped out of his grasp.

Her vision crystallized, and she saw him hunched over, his hands over his face as he roared in pain. She stepped forward, adrenaline surging through her as she lifted the glass once again—

Richter went down hard, his long limbs splayed on the floor as he fell, unconscious, on the white carpet.

She coughed and drew in a ragged breath through her ravaged throat. She was trembling, but not with fear, and she straightened, planting a hand on the wall to steady herself.

"I was...never yours," she wheezed, before standing upright.

She looked down at Richter's inert body until her hands stopped shaking, and then, satisfied that he wasn't going to wake anytime soon, she worked her way through the apartment, quickly and quietly, taking note of each and every painting he possessed.

63

May 1944

The blue half morning had ripened into dawn, and Fabienne watched the plaster cracks in the ceiling as sunlight crept its way into her bedroom through curtains she'd failed to close the night before. At the end of her bed, a housefly buzzed lazily over Hugo's dozing form. It alighted on the little dog's nose, and he shifted, startling the fly back into flight. Hugo turned over onto his back, paws raised askew as he closed his eyes, and Fabienne watched, wishing she could share in his easy return to sleep.

A cry split through the peaceful morning, and Fabienne held back her own tears as she padded, barefoot, across the floor to Isaac's makeshift bassinet—a drawer she'd pulled from Maman and Papa's wardrobe and lined with blankets. She lifted the baby out, and he quietened, nestling into her chest as she rocked him back to sleep. All he ever seemed to want was to be held, and it broke Fabienne's heart to know that hers were not the arms he sought.

Still, she could provide comfort. She took Isaac downstairs, Hugo threading two steps ahead to the kitchen.

She rummaged through the icebox, scowling at the dearth of milk in the bottle as she pulled it out. She would have to milk the goat today, little though she relished the job. She didn't know what exactly to feed a baby, but she knew that milk was a good start. She dipped a clean dish towel in the milk and held it between Isaac's lips, letting out a sigh of relief when he began to drink.

She sank into a chair and soaked the rag once more, pressing her lips together to stop herself from tearing up at the prospect of the day ahead. All she wanted to do was crawl back into bed and sob into Hugo's fur uninterrupted, but how could she, when she had Isaac to take care of? Hugo needed feeding, and the vines needed lifting, the oxcart's wheel needed mending, while the chateau, still in shambles after the raid, needed putting to rights. The prospect of it all was overwhelming, now that she was the only adult within Château Dolus's walls.

It had been two weeks since she and Sébastien had laid her parents and the Cohens to rest beneath the chestnut tree; two weeks since Sébastien had left, slipping into the woods behind the estate in the middle of the night with a duffel bag slung over his shoulder. His departure felt as final, in its own way, as Dietrich's, and Fabienne had stood on the back patio long after he'd disappeared, watching the black trees.

But at least there had been time for a proper good-bye. At least they'd left nothing unsaid between them.

She pressed a kiss to Isaac's forehead, allowing herself one more moment of self-pity before getting up to clear the dishes.

Fabienne had begun to straighten out the sitting room, Isaac fussing in his drawer on the floor, when she heard the sound of wheels in the drive. She looked up as Hugo lurched to his feet and sprinted to the front door, letting out a volley of barks—hastily, she tucked Sébastien's pistol, never far from reach, in the back of the trousers she'd borrowed from Maman's closet.

She knew who the caller would be, and she let out a breath as she studied him for a moment through the panes of the front door. He was tall and immensely broad, with a straight nose and slicked-back hair. To her relief, he was wearing a dark suit as opposed to a uniform, and although he technically wasn't a Nazi, Fabienne found the weight of the pistol at her back reassuring nonetheless.

She opened the door. "Otto Klaebisch, I presume?"

The *Weinführer* greeted her with a self-satisfied smile. "And you, I believe, are the prodigal daughter. I'd heard you'd returned home for good. May I come in?"

Fabienne led him through to the sitting room, watching as Klaebisch took in the ruined space with a measured expression: the feathers from split pillows, piled in drifts in the corners; the broken armoire. For a moment, she was pleased she'd not done much in the way of clearing up what the Germans had destroyed. If Klaebisch had any intention of billeting soldiers, perhaps her lack of housekeeping would make him reconsider.

He crossed toward the fireplace to peer at Isaac, his hands clasped around the brim of his hat.

"Can I offer you anything?" Fabienne asked, and Klaebisch looked up.

"No, no. It's only a flying visit, I'm afraid, and it's too early for wine, more's the pity." He lowered himself onto the love seat, letting up a puff of feathers from the ripped fabric. "That's your child, I presume?"

Fear gripped Fabienne's heart, but she nodded. "Yes. What can I do for you, Herr Klaebisch?"

He settled back on the seat, his hands clasped above his stomach. "Where to begin... It concerns promises made by your parents, *mademoiselle*—your late parents, of course."

"Herr Klaebisch, you must understand—"

"Mademoiselle." Klaebisch held up a hand, and Fabienne's protestations faded from her lips. "I don't care to discuss the particulars of what happened to them. I'm not some fanatic like so many of my countrymen. I had nothing to do with the whole sorry business, and it is entirely beyond my purview. What matters to me is the wine."

Fabienne hesitated. "The wine."

"The wine, my dear woman." Klaebisch's smile broadened. "I am the *Weinführer*, am I not? I've made promises to my superiors, and I intend to see them fulfilled."

Fabienne sat on the corner of a chair and watched as he took a pipe from within the expanse of his overcoat and packed it with tobacco. "Shouldn't Monsieur de Vogüé be here? He's your liaison with the champagne houses, is he not?"

"De Vogüé has been arrested." Klaebisch put the pipe to his lips and lit it, puffing once, twice. "He was found to have been in contact with Resistance forces. He left me with quite the task, I can tell you." Through the smoke, Klaebisch leveled a stern look at Fabienne. "I trust I can count on you to make better choices than your predecessors."

Her heart lurched once again, but Fabienne was careful not to let her feelings show. De Vogüé arrested?

"De Vogüé seemed to be under the impression that Château Dolus would be able to provide its own vintages to help fulfill orders for the German army. Your circumstances being what they are—" Klaebisch glanced meaningfully at the condition of the sitting room "—it's quite clear that you will not be able to fulfill those orders. So I intend to requisition Château Dolus and remand it to the authority of the German military."

From the makeshift bassinet, Isaac let out a cry and Fabienne got up to settle him, using the distraction to cover her sudden dismay.

She bounced Isaac in her arms as Klaebisch attended to his pipe. Alone, she would be incapable of evacuating the artwork from the chateau. Should she throw herself on his mercy, beg him to reconsider? No—this was a man who wouldn't succumb to pleading or pity. He lived in a world of glamour and parties, sophistication and excess. She'd met his type in the lonely, hardscrabble days at the start of the occupation, in hotel bars and at restaurants, looking for the pleasure of a smiling woman's company. She'd learned how to get her way with a man who felt himself above everyone else.

"You'll have to find alternative lodging," he was saying, "perhaps in the village—"

"No."

Klaebisch looked up. "I beg your pardon?"

Fabienne shot him a dazzling smile, wishing she had a swipe of red lipstick to complete the effect she'd honed so many years ago. "That won't be necessary, my dear Herr Klaebisch. I've got the vineyard entirely under control."

He smirked. "Forgive me, *mademoiselle*, but I find that quite impossible to believe."

She perched Isaac on her hip and met the man's gaze. "Believe what you like, but it's true. The '43 is maturing in my cellars, and given the modest acreage of the estate, I should be able to bring in this year's harvest myself."

"Yourself," Klaebisch repeated dubiously.

"That's right."

Klaebisch gaped for a moment, then took his pipe from his lips and let out a booming peal of laughter. "I must say, my dear, I do love a woman with a sense of humor."

"How about a woman with something to prove?" Fabienne's heart was beating wildly, but she stepped closer. "Let me show you, Herr Klaebisch. September is only four months away. Give me until the end of the harvest."

"My dear woman, it's lunacy. You know how much work it takes to bring in a successful harvest. Even a vineyard as modest as yours requires the utmost attention. Given your... other priorities, I just don't think it's possible." He lifted his chin, his smirk broadening.

"I disagree. If the harvest fails, I'll... I'll give you Château Dolus." Irresistibly, she thought of her great-grandfather, staking a hand of cards against a sneering nobleman. "The land, the deed, the keys. All of it. If I win—"

"You'll continue supplying your estate's champagne to the German army." Klaebisch replaced his pipe, looking thoughtful.

It was a bluff, on Fabienne's part. She knew it, and she suspected Klaebisch did too. But he hadn't rejected her offer outright, so she still had cause for hope.

Klaebisch hefted himself to his feet. "All right, then. Until harvest," he said and held out his hand.

Breathless, Fabienne took it. "Until harvest."

Moments later, she watched Klaebisch drive off in a cloud of dust. It was a cruel joke, she knew, to the *Weinführer*—an opportunity to get a family foothold of his own in Champagne, to bully and bribe his way into purchasing back the vast vineyard around the little chateau. But to Fabienne, it was a reprieve—a reprieve and a hope. There was every reason to think that by September the tide might have turned in the war, that Klaebisch and his ilk would be long gone—or, if she was wrong, to make further plans to evacuate the artwork from the Room of Martyrs.

There was every reason to hope that, with hard work, she might just succeed.

Her family's claim to Château Dolus had come with such a bluff, and though Sébastien might think her mad to take such a risk, Fabienne knew that Chateau Deceit would, this time, work in her favor.

She turned away from the building and looked toward the chestnut tree where she and Sébastien had buried her parents and the Cohens. She'd gone up there only yesterday to pay her respects, had trailed her fingers along the vines, which had just begun to flower.

Papa's voice echoed in her mind: *War brings bad harvests.*

She thought of the flowering vines: hard buds, hanging sweetly, perfectly, amid the leaves.

She had nothing to fear because she knew already what this year's harvest would be.

War brings a bad harvest, she thought, *and a fine one to herald its end.*

64

May 1944

Sophie listened through the half-open window to the sounds of Saint-Germain-des-Prés slowly waking up in the street below. Over the rattle of wheels across the cobblestones, she could hear Fabienne's shrill-voiced neighbor berating her meek husband, the snap of wet laundry hung on a wire. She longed to go out into the sunshine and enjoy the day, but she didn't dare leave, not when to do so in broad daylight risked alerting Fabienne's neighbors to the stranger in their midst.

Sophie had taken refuge in Fabienne's apartment three weeks ago, and they had been the longest three weeks of her life, with uncertainty, fear and anger commingling in a nauseating loop that made it impossible to sleep. She knew she hadn't killed Konrad Richter, but she was haunted by the thought that it would have been easier for her if she had. She had humiliated him, humiliated and emasculated him, and he would never forgive her for it. Had he already directed Bohn's men to her apartment, stripped it bare looking for proof of her crimes? If so, he wouldn't find any. She'd gone home immediately after leaving Richter's apartment, taken her records from the Jeu de Paume and her address book, along with every scrap of food in her larder.

In an attempt to take her mind off her troubles, Sophie had done what she could to keep busy. She'd copied out her notes from the Jeu de Paume in triplicate, along with anything else she could remember from her conversations with Richter about art exchanges and shipments into Germany.

Once she'd finished copying out her notes Sophie turned her attention to Fabienne's apartment: the grimy sink and dirty dishes; the dust, caked deep into every surface. Fabienne had never been domestically inclined. Sophie suspected Dietrich had been the one to keep the house clean. She'd pulled out Fabienne's bottle of bleach and scrubbed the apartment till it shone, emptying the claw-foot tub of dirty laundry and scouring the porcelain, washing Fabienne's blouses and hanging them, carefully, to dry over the ceiling rafters.

She tackled Fabienne's studio last, opening the door with the kind of reverence Sophie herself would have hoped for from anyone entering her laboratory. Within, a paint-splattered easel displayed a half-finished portrait, the subject's eyes painted a startling cerulean. On the back of the door hung a man's smoking jacket, and Sophie picked it up to add it to her laundry pile—then she paused, catching in its fabric a whiff of Dietrich's cologne, and set it reverently back on its hook.

She carried on, dusting the canvases that lined the room and cleaning old brushes, scraping hardened paint from the ends of palette knives that sat atop a battered old desk. On the corner of the desk, a photograph stood in a tarnished silver frame, and Sophie picked it up. It showed Dietrich and

Fabienne on their wedding day, Fabienne's burgundy dress muted to a soft gray, Dietrich in his best suit. Sophie recalled ironing the crease into the front of his trousers; how nervous he'd been, yet confident, as he said his vows.

Sophie, too, was in the photograph, standing behind the couple on the steps of the small church. She was holding Fabienne's bouquet, and she remembered the heady smell of the peonies.

Sophie had shared a lifetime with her brother, but Fabienne had only gotten three years of happiness. She ought to have had so many more. But Sophie knew that the best three years of his too-short life had been those he'd spent with Fabienne.

Grief had clouded Sophie's mind for too long, grief and blame over Dietrich's death. In those long months following Dietrich's funeral, Sophie could only see in Fabienne her inadequacies, her weaknesses. But working with her over the past four years—longer than she'd known her when Dietrich was alive, even—Sophie had been reminded of the woman Dietrich had fallen in love with: fierce and smart, creative and audacious.

Qualities that Sophie had come to admire in herself, as well.

She set down the photograph and carried on dusting.

65

June 1944

The heavy curtains in the entrance hall screeched along iron rods, berating Fabienne as clearly as Maman would have done for allowing sunlight to fall onto the fading Victorian wallpaper. *But Maman's not here, is she?* Fabienne thought grimly as she muscled the ancient window open. Flies traced drunken circles along the molded plaster ceiling, and spiders created cathedrals out of silk in the empty space between the staircase spindles, and there was something beautiful, to her mind, about allowing nature to encroach on the crumbling chateau, for what else could she do, when there were so many other jobs that required her attention?

She strapped Isaac to her back with a length of bedsheet, thinking of her unused studio. She'd not had either the time nor the inclination to paint, not while her bet with Klaebisch still rang in her ears. Instead, she spent her days in the vineyard, weeding and tending to the small green flowers on the vines.

She trudged up into the vineyard with secateurs in hand and began where she'd left off yesterday, pruning back the green growth. In the distance, thunder rumbled in the overcast sky, promising a summer storm, and though she welcomed the thought of rain, Hugo seemed unsettled as he circled through the furrows.

"Once upon a time," she said, as Isaac burbled happily over her shoulder, "there was a princess who lived in a tower." She glanced at Hugo and smiled. "She was guarded by a ferocious, Nazi-eating dragon and a handsome young prince named—"

Isaac cut her off with a sudden, earsplitting wail, and she dropped her secateurs and loosened the strap to swing him into her arms.

"All right, then," she said, rocking him back and forth as he screeched with indignation. "You tell the story, if you can do it so much better."

To her surprise, Isaac and Hugo had turned out to be the best possible company a girl could ask for—a pair of knights-errant who'd come to Fabienne in her hour of need. On mornings when she despaired at the thought of even getting out of bed, Hugo was there to lick her face, chivvying her out of bed with the determination of a sheepdog rather than a poodle, and on evenings when she would rather drop with exhaustion than head down to the cellars to tend to the matured bottles of '43, Isaac would reach his pudgy arms out to remind her what she was fighting for.

She offered Isaac her finger, and he began to suck on it, contented. His constant moods amazed her, with his easy shifts from happy to furious and back again. Her stomach lurched at the thought of losing him—but she would lose him, one day, God willing. Once the war ended, she would search for Isaac's relatives, in Paris and farther afield, and return him to his family. It would break her heart to do so. Would Isaac remember her at all, the strange woman he lived with for a short time?

She pressed a kiss to his forehead, putting such thoughts aside. She hoped to reunite him with his family one day, just as she hoped to return Hugo to Lev and Sylvie Lowenstein. She'd saved their lives, she supposed, boy and dog both.

But they'd saved her too.

In the barn, she could hear Otto the ox bellowing in his stall. Had he kicked over his water trough? Cursing, she snugged Isaac close and descended into the courtyard where chickens scratched in the damp dust, listening to the distant thunder.

She reached the barn and found Otto standing in a puddle of mud near his overturned trough. Sighing, she extricated herself from Isaac's blankets and set him down in the back of Sébastien's lorry, swaddled and too far from the edge to get into trouble. She hefted the trough upright and began the long task of hauling buckets of fresh water from the nearby well.

Once the water trough was full, she emerged from the barn, wiping a damp hand across her sweating brow. She collected Isaac and turned back to the chateau, where Hugo had stationed himself on the terrace for a snooze. She half expected to see Maman behind him, sweeping the terrace clean of the sudden flurry of damp leaves that had fallen around the little dog like snow.

She drew closer, frowning at the gust of yellowed leaflets that swirled through the courtyard.

She picked one up, and it showed a map of Europe, Germany's conquered territory hemmed in by heavy black lines. She'd grown used to seeing the borders of the ever-growing Reich in Vichy-controlled newspapers, but the leaflet—dropped by the British? The Americans?—showed a different story. Germany's territory in Russia was almost nonexistent. In the west, it showed a new conflict breaking out all along the French coast and beyond: Allied forces, advancing on Europe from across an unbreakable, endless front.

From far in the distance, thunder rumbled again. Could it be true? Had the Allies finally landed in France?

She went back inside, feeling newly awake as Hugo trotted along at her heels. In the kitchen, Papa's wireless radio sat collecting dust in the closet, and Fabienne pulled it out, twisting the dial in search of the ever-shifting signal of the BBC.

A broadcaster broke through the static, announcing that Allied troops had landed in Normandy nearly a week ago, that they had pushed back the Germans from the beaches, established a front all along northern France.

That paratroopers had landed all along the coast, were fighting in villages and cities within France itself.

That they were close to securing the city of Caen.

She turned up the volume dial, snugging Isaac close. Could it be true? She looked at Hugo, her heart lifting for the first time in weeks as the broadcast fell silent, then crackled again to life with the tinny voice of Charles de Gaulle.

It is quite true that we were and are still overwhelmed by mechanized forces... But has the last word been said? Must we abandon all hope? Is our defeat final and irremediable?

Fabienne's eyes filled with tears as she listened to the leader of the Free French, resistant and defiant. She pictured the beaches of Normandy, overcome with soldiers, landing crafts and airplanes.

For, remember this, France does not stand alone. She is not isolated.

Nor was Fabienne, here with her two knights-errant. Sophie and Gerhardt were fighting to save France's culture. Sébastien was with the Resistance, still finding reason to carry on.

The war is not limited to our unfortunate country. The outcome of the struggle has not been decided by the Battle of France... We can look to a future in which even greater mechanized force will bring us victory.

Victory.

The battle had been lost to Fabienne—lost over and over again. But didn't she owe it to those she'd lost—and to those she'd found—to continue fighting?

Whatever happens, the flame of French resistance must not and shall not die.

De Gaulle's voice crackled into silence, and Fabienne turned off the wireless.

Allied forces in northern France.

Germany hemmed in on multiple fronts.

Her fingers itched for want of a paintbrush, and she thought of her turreted studio and an immense, crumbling canvas.

The battle had ended for the inhabitants of Château Dolus... but the war still raged on.

66

Sophie stared up at the ceiling in Fabienne's apartment, watching the cracks between the rafters above the bed swirl, as she tried, unsuccessfully, to think about anything other than food. She closed her eyes, picturing plates piled high with buttered seafood and oysters on the half-shell, and fresh-baked rolls, pillowy soft and steaming. She dreamed of drifting to the table, sitting down to crisp white linens and sparkling champagne, shining strawberries in a silver cup—

Her stomach let out a growl of protest, jarring her back to the inescapable present. Still living in Fabienne's attic apartment, Sophie had managed to slip out into the streets of Paris a handful of times to buy what provisions she could on the black market, but she'd long since spent the last of her francs. Aside from the few jars of preserves in the back of Fabienne's cupboard and a handful of carrots she'd pilfered from the courtyard vegetable plot, Sophie was nearly out of food. She'd listened to the wireless for weeks, taking heart from news of the Allied *débarquement* at Normandy, but in recent weeks the momentum of the Allied advance seemed to have stalled. The tide of the war had turned, Sophie was certain, but would she survive to see it?

Hold on, Sophette.

She sat up, listening to the echo of Dietrich's voice in her ears. Had he come to bring her home?

A shot rang out in the street, and then another.

She gripped the iron footboard and rose, steadying herself as the world swirled around her. She approached the window, hands trembling as she opened the shutters.

Below, two men with machine guns flew through the street, pursued by a pack of German soldiers. She opened the shutter a crack wider and watched as they dove into an alley across the street. From somewhere not too far in the distance she heard a rallying cry—*"Vive la France!"*—and a staccato spray of gunfire.

It looked to Sophie as though the German soldiers had been suddenly lifted aloft, the force of the bullets pinning them, midair, for a split second before they arced backward into a spray of their own blood.

They hit the cobbled street, and an answering cry rang up from the shuttered windows of the 6th arrondissement: *Vive la France! Vive de Gaulle!*

She backed away from the window. Resistance fighters in the streets of Paris?

She dressed quickly and made her way to the kitchenette, then swept all but one jar of her remaining preserves into a string bag. She opened the final jar—oh dear, pickled turnips—and forced down a mouthful.

If the Battle of Paris had begun, there was only one place in the city that Sophie could be.

She hammered on the door to the Jeu de Paume, gripping the frame as she attempted to peer through the keyhole. She'd made it to the Jardin des Tuileries with little difficulty—the fighting, it seemed, was mainly on the outskirts of the city, though the sound of conflict grew louder by the hour. Gunfire echoed in the distance, the sound a terrifying reminder of the night of the Schloss exhibition, and she glanced behind her, picturing Gerhardt, Fabienne and Sébastien careering out of the city in a stolen truck.

She pounded on the door and it opened, Rose Valland's face emerging from the gloom. "Inside," she hissed, grabbing Sophie's elbow.

She shut the door and locked it as Sophie's eyes adjusted to the darkened vestibule. "Where are the guards?"

"Gone," said Rose, tucking the butt of a pistol in her waistband. "They left days ago, along with whatever they could carry. One more shipment of art for Carinhall, unless the Resistance acts quickly. But I suppose it's out of my hands either way. At least they sandbagged the windows before they went." Her eyes were hard behind the glint of her spectacles. "What were you thinking, coming back here? If Richter knew where you were…"

"You heard about that?" Sophie lowered herself to the steps of the grand gallery, feeling as though her legs might give way if she continued standing. "I thought he might try to pretend he'd fallen down the stairs or something."

"I wouldn't say he's made it common knowledge," Rose replied. "But a working understanding of German has come in handy time and again, these past few years."

Sophie thought back to the ERR's arrival at the Jeu de

Paume, Rose's casual denial of knowing the language and her subtle warning to Sophie to do the same. "So you've been...?"

"Keeping the museum under surveillance, yes," Rose finished. "On behalf of the Resistance network operating out of the Louvre. I've been passing information about the ERR's activities for years. I'm here on their orders, to protect the remaining art until Paris is liberated." She paused as a crack of gunfire, closer now than Sophie had ever heard it, rattled the windowpanes. "Bohn cut the power as they went. I'd hoped to recruit you into our cell, but when you cozied up to Hausler and Richter, we weren't sure where your loyalties lay. However, given the events of last summer... What are you doing here, Sophie?"

Sophie looked up. Steady, determined Rose, a member of the Resistance? "What we might have accomplished if we'd worked together," she said finally, hoping that the Louvre's Resistance network had thought to equip Rose with a hamper for her long vigil. "Sit down, Rose. I'll tell you everything."

Sophie awoke to the sound of a hammer echoing, persistent and harsh, through the museum. Disoriented, she fumbled in the dark until her hand brushed against the metal body of a torch. She turned it on to reveal the long basement of the Jeu de Paume.

She rubbed sleep from her eyes as the beam of her torch caught on a painting by Fernand Léger, its dizzying, Cubistlike composition as familiar as an old friend. It was part of the Jeu de Paume's permanent collection—a collection overlooked, it seemed, by the ERR in their hurry to leave. Over the past few days, Sophie and Rose had worked together to bring every work of art—contemporary and traditional, privately owned or part of the museum's collection—down to the basement in the hopes that they might remain there, hidden, until the war ended. These works of art had survived the ERR, survived even the purge of the Room of Martyrs—but with the fighting intensifying in Paris, would they survive the final battle?

She made her way out of the basement, following the relentless tapping of hammer against wood through to the grand gallery. Even if the Germans lost Paris, it didn't necessarily follow that the artwork at the Jeu de Paume would remain safe. There was no guarantee that the advancing Allied forces would be any more scrupulous toward the contents of the museum than the Germans. Looting, after all, was a well-known repercussion of war no matter which side won.

Rose stood at the top of the central staircase, illuminated by thin light spilling through the sandbagged windows. As the hammering continued overhead, she stared up at dust falling, in thin rivulets, from the ceiling.

"What time is it? What's happening?" Sophie asked.

Without turning her attention away from the ceiling, Rose pulled a rock-hard bread roll from her pocket and tossed it to Sophie. "The Allies have taken the Latin Quarter, and the Germans are preparing the roof of the museum to use it as a watchtower. No doubt they plan to defend the Rue de Rivoli." She rested her hand on the butt of her pistol. "They wanted to use the museum itself as a mustering point, but I told them to go to hell."

Sophie tucked the torch beneath her arm to wrestle the bread roll open. As amusing as it was to think of Rose berating a battalion of *Wehrmacht* infantrymen, it did nothing to diminish the very real danger that they were facing. If the *Wehrmacht* were using the Jeu de Paume's roof as a watchtower, the museum itself was now a target for the Allies—and given the number of German officers who lived in the hotels along the Rue de Rivoli, it was inevitable that the Jeu de Paume would be caught between the two opposing forces.

The museum—and Sophie herself.

Rose lowered her gaze. "If you want to leave, now's the time," she said evenly. "I won't fault you for it."

Sophie swallowed the last of the roll. "You'd best go downstairs to get some rest," she replied. She held out her hand for the pistol. "I'll keep an eye on things up here."

Rose's eyes welled with tears, but she blinked them back with a brisk shake of her head. "I doubt I'll be able to sleep," she said. "But thank you."

A crack of gunfire erupted overhead, and Sophie flinched. Suddenly, the museum felt as flimsy as a house of cards, mere inches of brick and glass, a few bags of sand holding back the rattling windows. She listened to an answering volley of machine-gun fire, and pictured her beloved Jardin des Tuileries turned to rubble, the City of Lights plunged into darkness.

Rose held out her hand and gripped Sophie's fingers as the Jeu de Paume trembled in the wake of an endless round of gunfire.

"I mean it," Rose said as the silence of the museum shattered around them. "Thank you."

67

September 1944

Château Dolus stood quiet as the sun crept over the far-off hills of Champagne. After gilding the edges of the clouds, its rays hit the eaves of the chateau, waking the swallows that nested beneath the fantastical forms of twisted gargoyles. The light spread farther, glinting off the half-moon window in the attic before shining through rickety windowpanes to illuminate the hidden Picasso in Maman and Papa's bedroom.

The light crept lower still, brightening Château Dolus's crumbling foundations as it flooded the entrance hall. Within, a woman in rubber boots descended a staircase hung with paper cranes, their folded wings dancing gracefully in the air. She reached the bottom of the stairs and paused, admiring the newfound brightness of the room. Sunlight showed it to its best possible advantage, she decided, gratified to see her work brought to glorious fruition.

After hearing Charles de Gaulle's rousing wireless address, Fabienne had spent every moment she could creating a masterful mural that encompassed the entirety of the entrance hall: a swirling, abstract rendition of Eugène Delacroix's *Liberty Leading the People*, the figure of Liberty draped in blue curtains that Fabienne had pinned to the wall in graceful drapes and folds. Liberty held the banned *tricolore* aloft, and with her auburn hair and round face, she bore an unmistakable resemblance to Sophie Brandt.

Behind Liberty, defiant figures stood in poised solidarity, one with Sébastien's dark hair and stubble, another with Dietrich's blue eyes. Fabienne had carried the composition throughout the space, wrapping the entirety of the entrance hall in figures. On the wall beside the door, Gerhardt Hausler stood with his hand wrapped around the head of a cane. Opposite Liberty, Maman and Papa were arm in arm with Lev and Sylvie Lowenstein. She'd painted Camille, Ossip, Hannah and Georges Cohen by the staircase, Isaac smiling contentedly in his parents' embrace. Myriam and Dufy and Louis. Swirls of indigo danced up the high walls, culminating in a ceiling that resembled the starry night sky.

It was abstract and colorful, encompassing countless artistic styles from artists whose work Fabienne had copied over the years: Picasso's harlequin diamonds and Braque's refracted shapes; van Gogh's swirling skies and Cézanne's delicate brushstrokes; Kirchner's wild colors and Dalí's fantastical creatures.

It was defiance and grief and joy. Degeneracy at its finest.

She stepped out into the courtyard, Isaac strapped to her chest as Hugo trotted at her heels. It had been weeks since she'd heard from anyone beyond the walls of Château Dolus, and given the infrequent broadcasts on the wireless, she wasn't sure whether the war was going poorly or well. Since the *débarquement* at Normandy, Fabienne knew that Allied forces were fighting their way toward Paris, but she hadn't heard yet whether the city had been liberated or whether it still labored under German occupation.

The one sign of hope that she clung to was the sight of Allied airplanes flying in formation towards Germany, white parachutes blooming as they drifted to earth.

Was Sophie safe? Was Gerhardt? Louis?

Sébastien?

She'd resigned herself to the likelihood that he'd been killed. The Resistance was simply too active, and the Germans too brutal, for her to hope in Sébastien's survival. Much as it broke her heart, there was comfort of a sort in the thought that Sébastien had died for what he believed in, like Dietrich before him.

She cupped Isaac's little head for a moment, picturing Sébastien's easy smile, then she tucked her secateurs in her pocket and hitched Otto to the yoke of the chateau's cart, already piled high with *mannequins*.

No matter what had happened farther afield, there was work to be done at Château Dolus. The harvest season had begun, and Fabienne intended to bring in her family's last, finest crop.

As she led Otto out of the courtyard, Hugo let out a piercing bark, and she stopped, listening to the sound of wheels on the dusty drive. Germans? She dropped Otto's lead and wrapped her fingers around her secateurs.

She rounded the side of the chateau and peered out from behind the bulk of one of its turrets to see six vehicles trundling up the drive, open-topped light trucks carrying soldiers clad in green rather than *Wehrmacht* gray. As the first few vehicles swung broadside to the house, she saw white stars emblazoned on the sides of the doors: *Americans*.

She inched forward but didn't release her grip on the secateurs. What guarantee did she have of good behavior?

The foremost vehicle came to a stop in front of the double staircase, and a passenger wearing a round helmet stood and shook loose her auburn curls.

"Sophie?"

Fabienne dropped the secateurs and sprinted forward to launch herself into Sophie's arms.

She could feel Sophie's tears flooding onto her shoulder as they hugged for what felt like an eternity. Finally, Fabienne pulled back. "I don't understand," she said. "How did you know—?"

"Where to find Château Dolus?" Sophie grinned and glanced over her shoulder. "I had help from a local guide."

Fabienne followed her gaze: there, stepping out of the second light truck, looking dusty and thin but very much alive, was Sébastien, smiling at Fabienne as he greeted an ecstatic Hugo.

She felt as though her legs would give way from beneath her.

She took a step forward, and then another.

"Tell me I'm not dreaming," she whispered as Sébastien pressed his lips to hers.

"If it is a dream," he replied, "then, I never want to wake up."

There would be time for explanations, for everything to be made clear, for champagne and late nights and tears and laughter, all the things which made victory both bitter and sweet in equal measure. But for now, Fabienne turned back to Sophie, who was standing shoulder to shoulder with a man wearing fatigues and several days' worth of stubble.

"Fabienne, I'd like to introduce you to Officer James Rorimer, with the Monuments, Fine Arts and Archives Program," Sophie said. "They're otherwise known as the Monuments Men. Officer Rorimer and his division are part of an Allied effort to return stolen artwork to its rightful owners."

Rorimer held out his hand, and Fabienne took it. "I understand you've quite a remarkable collection of artwork here," he said, the corners of his eyes crinkling as he smiled, "and that you and your sister-in-law have a rather unique set of skills. I wonder, *madame*, whether you might be interested in a job."

Fabienne smiled and tossed back her hair. *"Chérie,"* she replied, feeling some of her old bravado return. "Who says you can afford my salary?"

EPILOGUE

May 1949

Traffic snarled in the crosshatched streets of New York City, where long lines of motorcars inched forward at a snail's pace that Fabienne, consulting her wristwatch with ill-concealed impatience, found excruciating. She craned her neck as the taxicab slid past Lexington Avenue, staring up at the endless height of the city's skyscrapers: forty, fifty stories of apartments and offices, all efficiency and shine, which made Paris's Hausmann buildings look almost quaint by comparison.

Sitting beside her, Sébastien took her hand in his and squeezed it as the taxicab finally pulled to the curb outside a generously proportioned brownstone. "Are you ready?"

She read the name above the door, written out in tasteful gold lettering, *Paul Rosenberg & Co.*, and saw, standing on an easel by the open front door, a placard bearing her name.

Fabienne Brandt: The Art of Deception.

She'd been here before, thousands of miles away, thousands of years ago, waiting outside one of Paul Rosenberg's galleries with anxiety fizzing through her veins. Through the open front doors, she could see a crowd of people. From here, at least, the exhibition looked like it was already a success, though she couldn't know for certain. But Fabienne knew that her success wouldn't be measured by the critics scribbling down their thoughts about her work in shorthand. No, Fabienne's success had been determined years ago, when the canvases that now hung on the walls of Paul Rosenberg's New York gallery had sat in a Parisian museum, fooling the Third Reich's most discerning cognoscenti.

Sébastien cleared his throat. "You know, we're paying this driver by the minute," he muttered. "Maybe you could ruminate on the sidewalk instead?"

"Oh—of course," Fabienne replied, and she gathered the ends of her glittering shawl and slid out while Sébastien settled the fare. Though he'd not said a word about it, Fabienne knew he'd not taken to New York. The tall buildings and claustrophobic quarters, the newness and bustle, were far from ideal for a man who spent his days tromping through the expanded grounds of the Château Dolus Champagne House. But to Fabienne, New York felt like a city alive—as vibrant in its own way as Paris, but somehow more innocent: untouched, it seemed, by the unfurling of swastikas in the street and a population haunted by the memories of what they'd done during the dark days of the occupation.

She brushed a cropped lock of hair from her face, letting her fingers drift, for a moment, to the Bakelite earrings she'd worn in honor of Lev and Sylvie Lowenstein. How she longed for them to be here, sharing in her happiness, but despite her best efforts Fabienne hadn't found out what had happened to them. She knew the most likely explanation for their prolonged absence, but refused, still, to voice it out loud. Instead, she continued to scour newspaper articles and army lists for their names, returning to her old apartment building in Paris with Hugo in tow in the hopes that, one day, they might find Lev waiting on the steps for his beloved dog.

Thankfully, Fabienne had been able to return Isaac to his family. Through Sébastien, she'd been able to make contact with Camille Cohen's sister and brother-in-law, who'd escaped to England in 1941.

As difficult as it had been for Fabienne to say good-bye to Isaac, she hoped the boy would bring them solace for their grief and hope for their future.

Sébastien extricated himself from the car, smoothing down the burgundy tie he'd bought for the occasion. It was almost amusing to Fabienne to watch him fuss with the lapels of his jacket. She'd never seen him dressed in a suit, preferring instead the comfortable linen shirts and worn trousers he sported while tending to his beloved vines.

"You don't have to wear it, you know," she said, watching Sébastien loosen the knot of his tie.

"I'm here to support you, and I want to look the part," he replied. "Besides, all these Americans…they'll expect a certain degree of sophistication from us."

"How gallant of you," she replied, her old engagement ring catching in the light as she took his arm to cross the busy street.

"I aim to please. Just don't expect me to wear it at the wedding. I'll have enough trouble getting my vows out without being choked half to death in the process."

They reached the steps of the brownstone and Sébastien squeezed Fabienne's hand as they plunged inside.

Within, the gallery was full of patrons and critics, and she enjoyed a split second of anonymity before Paul Rosenberg, beaming, caught sight of her and broke into applause. As the rest of the assembled crowd followed suit, Fabienne thought of Paul's gallery on Rue La Boétie. He'd not returned to Paris since the start of the war, nor was he likely to. Though his son Alexandre had managed to recover some of the works of art stolen from him by the Nazis, Fabienne suspected that Paul would spend the rest of his life working to track down his glittering collection, much of which, no doubt, lay in safety deposit boxes belonging to former members of the Nazi top brass.

Paul would spend his life fighting to reclaim his legacy in France, Fabienne knew, but it was heartening to see that he'd built something new, alongside it. Something for the future.

Paul kissed Fabienne on either cheek and led her through the gallery, Sébastien trailing behind them. It amazed her to see how many of her forgeries had been recovered from Germany. She'd assumed that most had been destroyed in the fire outside the Jeu de Paume in 1943, but dozens of her paintings were here—her Dalí, her van Gogh—along with a handful of original works she'd painted in her turret at Château Dolus.

"I wonder whether you might say a few words about the collection," Paul whispered as they made their way past a large black-and-white reproduction of Fabienne's mural in the entrance hall at Château Dolus. "I would be happy to translate."

"If you like," she replied.

Sophie was waiting at the back of the gallery with a glass of champagne in hand. Smiling, she passed it to Fabienne.

"Château Dolus?" Fabienne asked.

Sophie's smile broadened. *"Mais oui."*

Fabienne had argued by letter for weeks to have Sophie's name included in the exhibition, but Sophie, with typical obstinacy, had staunchly refused to accept any credit for her part in the collection. It was Sophie, after all, who'd commissioned Fabienne to create the forgeries and who'd found them in the years following the war. Though Fabienne had turned down the job offered to her by the Monuments Men in order to care for Isaac, Sophie had taken it—and alongside her former supervisor at the Jeu de Paume, Rose Valland, she'd traveled the breadth of war-torn Europe searching for works of art to return to their rightful owners. The job agreed with her, Fabienne could see. Sophie looked happier, healthier, than she'd ever seen her.

Fabienne clinked her glass to Sophie's. "This is your opening too. You're sure you don't want credit for it?"

Sophie shook her head. "This is your moment," she replied, as Fabienne knew she would. Sophie preferred her work to be invisible: masterful, by its very absence.

Fabienne winked, then turned to face the assembled crowd, and as Paul Rosenberg introduced her she looked up and over the faces of the assembled crowd, to the black-and-white photograph of the mural: at Dietrich; Maman and Papa; Gerhardt Hausler. The Lowensteins and the Cohens.

Focus, she told herself.

The crowd erupted in applause, and Fabienne turned her attention to the room with a winning, crimson-lipped smile.

"Well, now," she said, holding her champagne flute aloft. "Where to begin?"

★ ★ ★ ★ ★

AUTHOR NOTE

The Musée Jeu de Paume was liberated, along with the rest of Paris, in August 1944. During its four-year tenure as an ERR repository, an estimated 22,000 stolen works of art passed through the museum, where they were either transferred into the Reich, exchanged with other dealers or destroyed. Following this dark chapter in its history, the museum housed the Louvre's collection of Impressionist paintings before a renovation in 1989. Today, it is home to France's first national gallery of contemporary art. In 2005, the Musée Jeu de Paume formally recognized the wartime heroism of Rose Valland by installing a plaque on the side of the building which chronicles her time with the French Resistance.

Historical fiction lives along something of a spectrum, with novels falling somewhere on the long thread between historical fact and creative fiction. This book, with its fictional main characters, tells the story of the all-too-real impact of the Second World War on the art world, and I'd like to elaborate on that history here.

Throughout the course of the war, Germany plundered hundreds of thousands of works of art—an estimated 20 percent of all artworks in Europe—from those opposed to Nazi ideology: Jewish families, Communists and Freemasons. The sheer scale of their theft was overwhelming and included not only works of art but books, furniture, jewelry and religious artifacts. Hermann Göring's collection alone—much of which was housed at Carinhall, his country estate—contained over 2,000 works of art, at least half of which were plundered from enemies of the Reich.

Today, there is still an ongoing effort by the families of the victims to recover masterpieces stolen from them, not only from private collections but from public institutions which, knowingly or unknowingly, acquired artwork of dubious provenance. Many organizations, including the World Jewish Restitution Organization, the Jewish Digital Cultural Recovery Project, the ERR Project, the United States Holocaust Memorial Museum, the Claims Conference on Jewish Material Claims Against Germany, and the Monuments Men and Women Foundation, work tirelessly to identify stolen artworks and return them to their rightful owners.

The notion of *Entartete Kunst*—"Degenerate Art"—was developed in the 1920s by the Nazi party as a response to the perceived decadence and experimentalism that flourished throughout Germany during the Weimar Republic. Upon gaining power in 1933, the Nazis, led by Joseph Goebbels and Hitler (himself a failed artist), vowed to supposedly cleanse Germany of degenerate art.

In 1937, they seized over 5,000 works of so-called degenerate art from public institutions across Germany and displayed them in a deliberately obtuse and hateful exhibition that traveled across Germany and Austria, attracting over two million visitors. In March 1939, following an auction of the most prominent works of art within the exhibition in Lucerne, the Berlin fire department burned over 4,000 paintings, sculptures, drawings and books outside the Reichstag—a shocking act of vandalism that was repeated outside the Jeu de Paume on the night of July 27, 1942.

Rose Valland worked at the Musée Jeu de Paume under the direction of Jacques Jaujard, director of the Musées Nationaux de France, and Resistance operative dedicated to safeguarding France's cultural heritage. Despite the constant threat of being discovered, Valland secretly recorded every movement of the ERR within the Jeu de Paume, concealing her ability to speak German in order to monitor and pass information about the ERR's looting on to the Resistance. Rose witnessed the burning of the degenerate art in the Jeu de Paume's courtyard in July 1942, and thereafter referred to the storeroom at the back of the gallery as the *Room of Martyrs*—a sobriquet Sophie uses in *The Paris Deception*. Following the war, Valland worked with the Monuments Men, sharing her records about the ERR's looting with James Rorimer to help locate and return stolen art and artifacts to their rightful owners.

Rose Valland received the *Légion d'honneur*, was appointed a *Commandeur* of the *Ordre des Arts et des Lettres*, and was awarded France's *Médaille de la Résistance*, along with the United States's Medal of Freedom, for her bravery. She died in 1980 and was buried alongside the love of her life, Joyce Helen Heer.

Sophie, Dietrich, Fabienne and Gerhardt Hausler are all fictional creations, as is their mission in *The Paris Deception*. However, there was a real-life forger who sold a fake Vermeer to Hermann Göring during the Second World War: Han van Meegeren, a Dutch painter who, depending on your point of view, was either a hero, a reprobate, a criminal or a war profiteer. Understanding the all-too-real complications of forging oil paintings, van Meegeren mixed his paints with Bakelite and baked his canvases to harden the paint—none of which, ironically, even remotely resembled Vermeer's masterful work, but Göring nevertheless traded 137 looted paintings for van Meegeren's *Woman Taken in Adultery*, which he believed to be a lost Vermeer.

The challenge of forging oil paintings is a problem van Meegeren overcame by baking Bakelite into paint; however, such a solution would have overaged the more modern paintings that Sophie and Fabienne were committed to saving. As a result, I bumped up the development of acrylic paint by a few years. Acrylic resin was first developed in 1934 by German chemist Otto Röhm, who used it to create synthetic paint for industrial uses—the painting of houses and airplanes, for instance. Thanks to its versatility and ability to mimic the qualities of oil or watercolor paints, artists began to use acrylic paint for artistic purposes in the late 1940s, most notably in South America. Diego Rivera, for instance, was an early adopter of the medium. In 1947, a mineral spirit–based (that is, acrylic) paint, Magna Plastic Colors, was developed by Bocour Artist Colors; a similar formulation, MSA Conservation Color, was developed by Golden Artist Colors and is used by painting conservators today. These formulations were the inspiration for Sophie's petroleum-based acrylics in *The Paris Deception*.

I'm very much indebted to the many scholars who have focused their research on Nazi looting, occupied Paris, art forgery and wine-making. Some particularly salient titles I relied on while researching *The Paris Deception* are *Göring's Man in Paris: The Story of a Nazi Art Plunderer and His World* by Jonathan Petropoulos; *Rose Valland: Resistance at the Museum* by Corinne Bouchoux; *The Rape of Europa: The Fate of Europe's Treasures in the Third Reich and the Second World War* by Lynn

H. Nicholas; *Wine and War: The French, the Nazis and the Battle for France's Greatest Treasure* by Donald and Petie Kladstrup; *Les Parisiennes: How the Women of Paris Lived, Loved, and Died under Nazi Occupation* by Anne Sebba; *The Last Vermeer: Unvarnishing the Legend of Master Forger Han van Meegeren* by Jonathan Lopez; *The Art Forger's Handbook* by Eric Hebborn; and *The Art of Forgery: The Minds, Motives and Methods of Master Forgers* by Noah Charney.

To this day, the fate of an estimated 100,000 works of art looted by the Nazis from Jewish families remains unknown.

ACKNOWLEDGMENTS

This book began with a dare from my brother, Alec, to best his favorite movie—*The Thomas Crown Affair*. Given that I've never actually watched the movie, Alec will have to be the final arbiter on my success in that regard, but I thank him for setting me the challenge and dedicate *The Paris Deception*, such as it is, to him.

I'd also like to extend my thanks to the National Archives Catalog, LootedArt.com, the United States Holocaust Memorial Museum, the Mémorial de la Shoah, the Monuments Men and Women Foundation, and Dr. Enrique Mallen from the On-Line Picasso Project.

I also extend my thanks especially to the ERR Project, which contains an active database of the more than forty thousand works of art plundered by the *Einsatzstab Reichsleiter Rosenberg* in France and Belgium.

As always, I send my endless gratitude to my editor, April Osborn, without whose guidance and input this book simply would not be what it is. I'm also grateful to my tireless agent, Kevan Lyon, for her unwavering support, and to Priyal Agrawal for introducing this book to new audiences. My thanks as well to Josh Nehme, Vanessa Wells, Evan Yeong, Ashley MacDonald, Leah Morse, Puja Lad and Sean Kapitain.

My thanks as well to my community of authors. I'm very much in awe of your talent and sisterhood, and every note, every post, every text of support means the world.

Though Sophie refers to herself as a "restorer" of artwork throughout this novel, today the term for the preservation of artwork is called "conservation." I am highly indebted to several present-day conservators who were kind enough to share their laboratories, expertise and insights about the ethics of art conservation, as well as give me a close-up glimpse of some spectacular works of art under their care (including a particularly spectacular van Gogh I couldn't resist sneaking into the Louvre): Kostas Xenarios from XC Art Restoration; Katharine Fugett and Michaela Paulson from the American Museum of Natural History; Emily Frank and Joy Bloser from the Museum of Modern Art; Chantal Stein from the Metropolitan Museum of Art; and Stefanie Killen and Patricia Smithen from Queen's University. Thank you all for your remarkable generosity.

I would also like to extend my special thanks to someone who will remain nameless for his insights into the intricacies of forging works of art.

It is said that great artists steal, and I confess to stealing the idea of concealing paintings within the lining of a raincoat from a professor of mine, Valentin Boss at McGill University, who years ago shared his preferred method for smuggling banned literature into Soviet Russia. I'd also like to thank the University of St. Andrews, the University of Toronto, Toronto Metropolitan University and McGill University.

In terms of Château Dolus, I would like to thank Breck O'Neill and Kriss Speegel for providing their insights on the wine-making process…as well as on the complete futility of hiding master artworks in wine caves. I would also like to thank Mirte Keulen for accompanying me through Reims's sun-soaked valleys and Champagne Taittinger's caves during one diligent long weekend of *la recherche*.

Thank you to Vicki Carruthers, my extraordinarily talented aunt, for inviting me to her studio and letting me make an absolute mess of her acrylics.

My thanks as well to John Lennard for our many conversations about art, German Expressionism, music and, of course, Paris.

Thank you to my friends and family. You know who you are and, I hope, what you mean to me. I am so very grateful that you put up with my flights of unbridled imagination.

Alec, Coretta, Hayley, Logan, Rose. What a privilege to have you all in my life.

Finally, thank you to my parents, as always. Everything I write is for you.

THE
PARIS
DECEPTION

BRYN TURNBULL

Reader's Guide

1. The notion of ideological degeneracy is a running theme throughout this book. How do the characters in *The Paris Deception* reflect elements of what the Nazi party deemed "degenerate"?

2. How does Sophie and Fabienne's relationship mature throughout the course of the novel?

3. Fabienne grapples with the notion of cowardice throughout the novel, and when we meet her, she is in a dark and desperate place. How does Fabienne take accountability for her actions—and for her perceived cowardice—as the novel progresses?

4. Sophie considers herself to be at her professional best when her work is invisible. Does Sophie remain invisible throughout *The Paris Deception*?

5. Nazi Germany considered the destruction of Degenerate Art to be a vital part of preserving their culture. Is this mentality ironic or logical (or both)?

6. Do you think that Sophie and Fabienne place too much importance on physical art, given everything else that is occurring in France? Why or why not?

7. Richter considers himself a man of refined tastes whose views can diverge from those of his party and its actions. How is he able to reconcile the two?

8. Perspectives on the possibility of the war ending vary widely among the characters in the novel, from Lev Lowenstein's stubborn optimism to Sophie's father's resigned acceptance. In a similar situation, which might you find yourself adopting?

9. Both Sophie and Fabienne must contend with their parents' dreams for their respective lives. How do they differ in their approaches to breaking from those expectations?

10. Sophie spends most of the novel having to hide her identity: as a German, as a Resistance sympathizer and as a woman who is attracted to other women. Do you think it was more difficult masking one part of her identity than any other, and why?